Mar 2022

WILD

AND

WICKED

THINGS

WILD
AND
WICKED
THINGS

FRANCESCA MAY

REDHOOK

Redhook Books/Orbit
Hachette Book Group
1290 Avenue of the Americas
New York, NY 10104
hachettebookgroup.com

First Edition: March 2022
Simultaneously published in Great Britain by Orbit

Redhook is an imprint of Orbit, a division of Hachette Book Group. The Redhook name and logo are trademarks of Hachette Book Group, Inc.

The publisher is not responsible for websites (or their content) that are not owned by the publisher.

The Hachette Speakers Bureau provides a wide range of authors for speaking events. To find out more, go to www.hachettespeakersbureau.com or call (866) 376-6591.

Library of Congress Cataloging-in-Publication Data
Names: May, Francesca, author.
Title: Wild and wicked things / Francesca May.
Description: First edition. | New York, NY : Redhook, 2022.
Identifiers: LCCN 2021033928 | ISBN 9780316287159 (hardcover) |
ISBN 9780316292290
Subjects: LCGFT: Novels.
Classification: LCC PR6104.O766 W55 2022 | DDC 823/.92—dc23
LC record available at https://lccn.loc.gov/2021033928

ISBNs: 9780316287159 (hardcover), 9780316287395 (ebook)

Printed in the United States of America

LSC-C

Printing 1, 2022

*For anyone who ever searched deep inside themselves and
found a darkness that scared them.
And especially for Callie, who made this book whole.*

WILD
AND
WICKED
THINGS

One for malice
Two for mirth
Three for a death
Four for a birth
Five for silver
Six for gold
Seven for a secret never to be told
Eight for heaven
Nine for hell
Ten to the devil wherever she may dwell

Blessed are the dead that the rain falls on.

—F. Scott Fitzgerald, *The Great Gatsby*

OCEAN
SALT
AND
GRAVE
DIRT

Welcoming the Dark

R. Crowther

Mabon—Autumn Equinox

*T*here is a new witch at Cross House.

Perhaps it is the girl I have seen at the last few gatherings, silently lingering at Priscilla's feet like a ghost, her dark eyes watchful and her angular face solemn, but I cannot be sure. I don't trust my judgement after what I have seen tonight.

I suppose I don't have the taste for any of this anymore. Since the fighting began Priscilla's nocturnal soirees have grown vicious and wild; I should have known better than to be tempted to attend another, but I have always been weak when it comes to wanting to be around my own kind. Still, I couldn't stomach the debauchery for long, all that cowardice in one room, and I fled onto the beach beyond the house, where the sand was pale under the prickle of autumn starlight.

I wandered along the cove until I grew tired. And there—a young woman, I think, but with no childish softness or feminine curves, only sharp edges and long limbs, dressed in a boy's shorts and a man's shirt rolled at the elbows.

She picked herself up off the sand, where rocks grow out of the ocean all jagged and slippery with dark sea moss, and limped a step backwards.

I only noticed because I felt it. It was like a blade scraping against the back of my teeth, its edge skimming my tongue. I could taste it, like nothing I have tasted before. Earth, salt, and an iron tang, bright and startling. And strong, so strong. It flooded me and I froze, letting the darkness smother me with her cloak.

The girl did not see me. She inspected her palm, holding it up to the silver moon like an offering. Blood trickled, dark against the rocks. The magic I could taste was untamed—fierce and angry. She lifted her hand to her mouth, tongue hungry, and when she pulled it away her lips were smeared bloody red.

My own blood sang in response. I coveted that power, wanted it so desperately that I almost went to her. Almost begged on my knees for a sliver of that dark gift. Yet as the moment stretched, the singing in my blood morphed into a scream, a primal urge. Stem it, wrap the wound, stop the spill. *The girl only bared her teeth at the moon.*

I did not care if she watched me flee. I could not stay, could not allow myself to become captivated. There is so much to be done and so many more men will fall for peace. I have vowed to help them. I cannot be like the others, cannot squabble for that taste of power. Oh Goddess, how I nearly forgot the way true power tastes.

Tonight, truly, I am glad I came here. With the scent of the witch's blood still lingering on my tongue, I am relieved I left before I could hurt them. They will not share this fate.

Priscilla is the strongest witch on Crow Island. Until tonight I thought she needed no guidance from the likes of me—and certainly she would not take it. Now I am afraid for her.

This girl... Whoever she is, she has a darkness inside her and it glitters like broken glass.

Chapter One

Annie

Rumour had it that Crow Island was haunted by witches.

As I saw it for the first time, I understood why. People said the witches who had first discovered the island lived on in the bodies of the crows that flocked on every street corner and bare-branched tree. They flew high above as the boat drew closer to the shore, a constellation of black stars against the bright summer sky.

Tucked away beyond the murky water off the east coast, the island's crescent-moon shape gave it the appearance of a curved spine, a body curled secretively away from the mainland. Yet up close the properties, built to resemble American plantation houses and crumbling Georgian manors, dispelled this illusion of secrecy. They loomed large, like spectral grey sentries guarding their land.

On Crow Island, people had whispered to me back home, real magic lurked just below the surface. Wealth seeped from the place like honey. They said that it had a reputation, that here the law looked the other way.

My mother hadn't wanted me to come, but I had pleaded, surprising both of us. It was my father's final request, which felt vital somehow, and I was compelled in a way I never had been before. He had wanted me to do this, to travel to a place I had never been, to sort through and sell his belongings, although I had hardly known him. And I had thought I could do it. I thought, at least, I should try.

I was no longer sure. I had never been away from home, had never slept anywhere but the squat back bedroom in the little stone terrace house I shared with my mother. The thought was both light and sharp. I inhaled a lungful of the salty ocean air, which tasted different here than it did back home, and reassured myself that I could be brave. Crow Island might be haunted, but it couldn't be much different than the rest of England had been since the war, life trudging on despite the ghosts. I would be fine.

In the harbour the final traces of Whitby drained away: here was no Mam to guide me; there were no familiar street corners to remind me of sunny afternoons with Sam and Bea; there was not even to be the routine of the shop, of cosy evenings by the fire or Sunday afternoons visiting the gallery in town. It was an unwritten story. I had never had so much freedom, or felt so timid.

There was a car waiting for me by the harbour office, a swanky hayburner unlike anything I'd ever dreamed of driving, with a paper slip bearing my name tied to the steering wheel. I approached hesitantly, placing my palm flat against the sun-warmed metal. It felt, for a second, like I could feel the heartbeat of the island, the same thundering under my skin I sometimes swore I could feel when I scavenged shiny polished stones on the beach back home. I pulled my sweating palm back and glanced around nervously.

The harbour had long since emptied and I couldn't see another soul. The office loomed ahead, its windows mirrored by the sun. In the letter I had received before leaving I'd been told I would have to go inside to collect the key for my father's car, but some force held me locked in place. It wasn't the office itself that scared me, more the idea that once I had the key—what then?

I stood for a minute watching the occasional cloud scud across the dark glass of the office windows. Two minutes. Five. My thoughts trickled towards my father. I should be more upset by his death, but I was almost indifferent. Perhaps I was being harsh, perhaps he *had* loved Mam once, but she had never said. She had shed his surname as if even the suggestion of his love was painful for her. I almost preferred to think that he had never loved her. After all, what kind of man would abandon his wife and newborn daughter for an *island*? Still, this was my inheritance—money that could mean everything for Mam and me.

The sun beat down on my shoulders and I was hot and impatient with myself. Sam would have thought I was silly. Bea would laugh if she saw me. But Sam wasn't here and Bea was probably still angry with me. My irritation grew. A roaring sound began inside my ears, the same sound I always heard when a panic came on—like ocean waves. Like drowning. I closed my eyes, squeezing them tight, blocking out the sensation of swirling water that clogged my mind.

"Are you...well, miss? Do you need a doctor? Papa says it looks like you might faint."

A girl of no more than ten had appeared, red-haired and freckled, wearing a grey smock. Concern etched her forehead. I must have been standing here for longer than I'd thought.

"I'm—a little lost," I said, fumbling for an excuse. "I think this is my car but I don't have the key...?"

The girl's face sagged in relief and she snatched at the handwritten slip tied to the wheel plus the paper I handed her, my own messy scrawl in the margins of the note my father's lawyer had sent me. When she returned them, it was with a small key ring, which she thrust at me.

"Thank you," I managed, finally able to breathe.

The girl disappeared as quickly as she'd come. I gazed at the car for a moment more, remembering the illicit runabouts in Sam's dad's jalopy. I'd hated them at the time but was glad now, although I was worried that it would be harder here than roaring along the winding, empty country roads at home.

I didn't want to think of Sam, or of home, and that spurred me into action. I threw my meagre belongings into the car, and once I was on the road it came back to me little by little. It was easier than I remembered, or perhaps the car was simply better. The air tasted of tree sap, the future shimmering ahead like a mirage in the heat.

The reality of Crow Island stretched and grew around me as I drove, lavish houses making way for smaller dwellings as I headed away from the harbour, and quiet, crooked streets peeling off the main road through the town known as Crow Trap. I took in the freshly whitewashed shops and the bright, shiny windows. I hadn't seen such a lush air of festivity since the parties we'd thrown after the armistice. The bunting was fresh and neat, fluttering between lampposts, and the children who ran in circles outside the small bakery wore clean aprons and shoes.

It was beautiful, and yet I couldn't help the nervous way my palms itched at the sight of the wooden boards outside shops peddling *Genuine Palm Readings* and *Holidaymakers' Charms for Good Fortune*, and at the windows that offered a glimpse of trailing greenery, framing small signs that proclaimed the vendors' license to advertise faux magic.

It had been this way since the prohibition began after the war. Licenses, posters, and provisos, silly games that danced on a knife-edge as far as the law was concerned. Back home I hardly thought about magic except to avoid the advertisements at the back of the newspaper where faux mediums passed public messages to the great beyond. In Whitby there wasn't much cause for meddling with magic, real or otherwise; most people barely had enough money to put food in their bellies, never mind extra to waste on trifles.

And it wasn't worth the risk.

Mam always said that real magic was cunning and it was best to steer clear. Fake magic was a joke, a party trick for rich people who had nothing better to do, so it was best to steer clear of that too. Her most well-worn bedtime caution over the last two and a half years was the story of a girl in York, Bessie Higgins, who'd been hanged for selling poppets that turned out to have dried monkshood in them, although she'd sworn she had simply picked the weeds near the river.

There must be more to Bessie's story, but talking about magic had always made Bea act foolish, so we never did.

Magic seemed different here. The licenses and advertisements were light, funny. These signs offered a glimpse into the future instead of the past. Perhaps the rich could better enjoy the soft scares of make-believe fortune-telling, since they hadn't lost as much as the rest of us.

I counted seven of the island's famous crows as I headed back towards the coast. They were perched on rooftops and in trees, one more on the pinnacle of a lamppost, her beady eyes and sharp little beak shining in the May morning sun. I acknowledged each one under my breath like a prayer, the hazy words of a half-remembered poem in the back of my mind.

> *One for malice,*
> *Two for mirth . . .*

The stretch of coastline where I'd rented a house for the summer was a jungle of grand houses and sprawling estates, the odd cottage like mine annexed from wealthy land a long time ago. I drove down roads shaded by hedgerows growing verdant and wild and speckled with dark thorns. It was a relief to easily find the cottage, nestled less than five minutes' slow drive away.

It sat atop a sloping lawn, surrounded on three sides by so many trees you could hardly see the sky, or the ocean, or anything but tangles of green. At the back of the cottage the lawn dipped until it fell away into a sandy stretch looking out to the North Sea. I'd used some of my new inheritance for the privilege of being able to see water. That was why outsiders came to Crow Island after all, wasn't it?

There was a man waiting for me outside the cottage when I arrived. He was tall and broad shouldered with greying rust-coloured hair and a cheerful, ruddy face. He smoothed the jacket of his immaculate herringbone suit and smiled.

"You must be Miss Mason," he said, shaking my hand warmly as I climbed out of the car. "Your father spoke very highly of you. My name is Jonas Anderson—it's a pleasure to finally meet you. I'm very sorry about your father. Such a shame to have lost him so unexpectedly."

This was my father's lawyer. The man he'd left in charge of his estate. He was the one who had written after my father's heart attack and begged me to come. *It's what your father wanted. The only thing he asked for.* He was the one who had given me an advance on my father's money—for the cottage. I hadn't expected him to be here, and his presence made my muscles bunch nervously.

"Mr. Anderson," I said, smoothing my hair flat under its scarf. I didn't like the idea that my father had spoken about me at all when it hardly seemed like he'd remembered I existed, but I tried to keep that from my voice. "How nice to see you in person—but I'm here so early. I thought we weren't scheduled to meet until next week."

"No, but I wanted to, ah, welcome you to the island," he said, still smiling. "I wanted, really, to make sure you found the car without trouble, and the cottage…" He pointed vaguely. "I was surprised you chose one over here, but I can understand why. It's lovely, isn't it? Anyway, I know it can be daunting to find your feet in a new place. Especially one like this." He gestured at a single crow that had perched itself comfortably on the bonnet of my car. "So, if you need anything, you mustn't hesitate to let me know. Particularly if it's about your father or his things. We were good friends, you see. I'm sure you must have questions, though I understand if you're too overwhelmed today. I thought perhaps that was why you came early. I can try to speed through the necessary paperwork, but I'm more than happy to give you this week to get settled if that's preferable."

I blinked away the unexpected tightness in my throat at his kindness and nodded as he talked, allowing myself to settle into this new world and agreeing gratefully to keep in touch. Once he was gone I slipped into the cottage, shutting out the sunny warmth to set about unpacking my few belongings.

Now that I was alone, the cottage seemed big and rambling. Frivolous. It wasn't like it was even my money I was spending yet. It was strangely quiet too, the sound of my footsteps muffled by the distant rush of the ocean and the caw of a crow. And there was a different quality to the quiet; it felt like the blackest part of a shadow, coiled and waiting.

I had never been alone like this before. I had spent all my early years with a gaggle of other neighbourhood children, Sam and Bea and a snotty girl called Margot at my heels as we ran and played in the streets behind my mother's chocolate shop. Later, when Sam was gone, I had Mam and Bea, and then Mam. What would I do with all this space? I could walk from one side of the cottage to the other without tripping over Mam's knitting basket or having to slow for Tabs and her kittens. I could swing my arms and not hit a single thing if I wanted to. I didn't want to.

I wasn't sure I wanted to be here.

Until Sam was deployed I'd never thought about leaving Whitby. After he left I thought about it constantly. I was still trying to convince my mother to let me sign up to nurse when we found out he'd died. Just—died. Gone.

It felt like a warning. *This is what happens when you dream.* This is what happens when you get ahead of yourself. For two years Bea and I hardly spoke of him, and when we did we pretended that he was still away, travelling the world and collecting experiences he would bring home to share with us. He never came home. And when Bea had left last spring—when she'd come to this very island—without saying goodbye to me, it felt like I was doomed to lose everything, each part of me slowly chipped away until there was nothing left.

I stayed with Mam, pretending I was content. I did what it felt like I should do, going through the motions like no war had ever happened. How was my loss any different from anybody else's? My life became a pattern of dance halls on the weekends, more out of obligation than anything else, and the shop during the week. Trips to the gallery and the dull excitement of a new sewing pattern. Mam never said so, but eventually she expected me to marry. It had been four years since Sam died, and my inevitable future grew closer every month. I couldn't put it off much longer.

And then...?

That was the part that scared me. The picture of a life already lived, so predictable I could write it point by point in my journal and tick it off. Marriage, babies, hard work, and never enough money to stretch ... The problem was, as much as my father's death felt almost like a windfall, coming to the island scared me too.

Standing here, in this cottage that wasn't mine, I told myself it didn't—*couldn't*—matter that I was afraid. This felt like my last chance to change my path; I needed to grasp it with both hands, pull the opportunity up at the roots, and carry it with me, ready to plant, or else the life back home was all that waited for me.

It seemed like fate that Bea was here. I'd been thinking of her a lot since I set out on the ferry, wondering if she'd truly missed me like her letters said. Whether she was still angry with me. The hole she'd left in my chest ached. If only we could be friends again—true friends—maybe I wouldn't feel so lonely.

Bea and I had been so close, once. Both of us had grown up without fathers, although hers had died when she was just a baby, and we often joked that we were fierce enough not to need them. It felt strange, after all our jokes, all the secret longing we'd hidden behind our bluster, that I was here today because of my father.

Perhaps he had hoped coming to the island would be good for me. Perhaps he had hoped that the island would jostle my soul and wake me from a slumber he recognised—that it would cut this stunted part of me free. Perhaps he hadn't thought of how it would affect me at all. I wasn't sure which possibility I liked the least.

The late-afternoon air in the cottage was loaded with my questions. I wanted to know about his life, about his friends, his work, and his hobbies. I wanted to know why this place had captivated him so much that he had left us without a second thought. And most of all, I couldn't stop the small voice in my head that asked the same thing I'd been returning to for weeks—at home, on the boat, seeing that shiny car for the first time ...

Why now? Why had my father only wanted me to come to Crow Island once he was dead?

Chapter Two

Annie

The moon rose whole and bright like a shiny coin. I made a pot of honey tea and carried a cup out onto the shining blue lawn. The sound of the ocean was loud in my ears. I would never be able to sleep, missing the snuffling sounds of Tabs and the kittens at the side of my bed, the distant rhythm of my mother's snores. Instead I stood and inhaled the new, fresh scents of the wild garden, knowing Mam would love them. She'd always wanted a big garden where she could grow roses, magnolias, geraniums...a dream I hoped my newfound money could soon accomplish.

From my spot on the lawn I could see the ocean spread so far ahead it became the sky. The noises were of nature, rustling leaves, flashes of white that were rabbits darting between the trees near the cottage. Back home I couldn't remember the last time I had been outside alone at night, felt the silver light of the moon on my shoulders and the crown of my head.

I sipped from my cup and allowed my thoughts to drift, dwelling on the stronger teas and tinctures we'd had when I was young. Blackcurrant and licorice tea for vivid dreams, gingerroot and angelica for luck and protection. I recalled the pink, foamy tea Bea's mam had served us once—rose hip and cardamom laced with the barest whisper of hemlock. We'd lain together under a canopy made of old bedsheets and told each other stories for hours, not growing tired until the sun was almost cresting through Bea's window.

It unnerved me how easily we had been led back then, how cushioned we had felt, lulled by the tea's charm. Magic had once felt like fun, before we understood what else it could do. It unnerved me more how I still missed the teas and the exotic chocolates that could make your heart race with joy, the subtle spice in a freshly baked carrot cake; I knew what they did and a deep part of me still longed for them, or for how it had been before everything changed. These days you were lucky to even find fresh lavender, never mind anything dried or sweetened. Ever since the prohibition it had been harder and harder to find things to calm your nerves, anything to alter your mental state at all.

I didn't mean to wander from the lawn. At home I would never have allowed myself to leave the safety of the house this late without a friend. I left the back door open as I carried my cup down the slope until my feet were buried in the cold sand of the beach. I just wanted to escape the thoughts that had followed me from the boat to the harbour and the house. Thoughts of what I'd have to go back to once the summer was over, ghosts that stalked me everywhere I went.

I cradled the steaming cup in both hands. The ocean was black and so still it was like a dark pane of glass reflecting the moon. It reminded me of the stories of the witch's black mirror, of how heathens had once used a surface like this to see the future. The thought made the hairs rise on my arms and I shoved it away. *Real* magic like that, the kind of magic that made witches different from regular people, was the reason we had the prohibition—not because of fancy teas and fortune-tellers but because of the abuse of raw power that had turned boy soldiers into killing machines.

I walked along the beach, blindly drawn onwards by the whisper of the tide. Another crow flew overhead—no, it was a group of them, five or six flocking to the trees around my neighbour's house, their wings beating in time with my heart. I closed my eyes, drawing the sound into myself, and felt an old familiar tumbling deep in my belly, like the flash of fear when you miss a step and your death hovers.

I paused, waiting for it to pass. It happened sometimes, often when I was by the ocean, a dizziness that I usually put down to the cold. Only this night was balmy, the wind faint, and when I opened my eyes the feeling hadn't entirely vanished.

I heard laughter. Music. I turned, straining my ears away from the ocean. The sound of the party grew louder. The noise I had mistaken for belonging to Crow Trap was coming from only a little way along the beach, on the left in the direction the crows had flown.

I heard the sultry swing of jazz, string music and brass and singing too. There was the chink of glasses, a lone voice followed by a chorus of laughter. I clutched the lukewarm cup and followed the sounds along the beach, where I passed a little dock, sand glittering at the edge of my neighbour's lawn. The house caught my gaze and I was drawn like a moth.

It was a beautiful cacophony of grey stone, silver in the moonlight, the many windows twinkling with hundreds of electric lights. The house was bordered at the back by swaying pine trees, and I thought I could make out an old oak with low branches, a swing dancing in the faint wind.

It was already late but it sounded like the party was still young, the noise only growing as I stood, my feet ensconced in cool sand. I listened to the music swell as the laughter took on a wild edge. I could just make out the distant hum of an engine and then louder, raucous shouts of welcome from closer to the house. A tugging sensation began in my chest, the kind of longing I hadn't felt in years.

This house, unlike my little cottage, did not simply allow its lawn to become beach to become sea. Instead, there were elegant steps that shone white leading up to a beautiful fountain, bubbling away beneath statues of women with dark feathered wings—like the island's crows.

I followed the sound of the trickling water, careful to stay on the sand, where I was sure I wouldn't be seen, hidden by a stone wall and the trees between the beach and the lawn. I perched by the wall for a moment, not brave enough to get any closer.

Through the gaps in the trees to the left of the house I could make out the smudged shapes of people, the noise growing as more guests arrived. The women wore sleek, stylish dresses in gold and pink, white and royal sapphire blue; some were dressed in jewel shades that seemed to blend into the dark so all I could make out was the way the moonlight glinted off flutes filled with what looked like champagne, their costume jewellery glittering as they danced and sang. Their laughter was raw, yet somehow honeyed, tinged with abandon. One of the women wore a stylish beaded turban around her hair, and she and a man in a black suit rushed for the swing attached to the oak tree, flinging themselves into its seat. The woman screeched as the man pushed the swing higher and higher, the branch groaning while somebody else clapped.

I ducked farther down behind the stone wall, inching my way along towards the steps at the back of the house. My heart hammered in my chest, stomach churning with a mixture of fear and— want. I knew what kinds of people these were.

They were *rich*. The kind of Crow Islanders I'd heard rumours of, who didn't care if they got caught "promoting witchcraft" and slapped with a hefty fine. I doubted they noticed the cost, which made me think of my mother again, and how she'd almost lost the chocolate shop that had been in our family for six generations when the law changed and she could no longer include the K-class magical herbs in her prized jasmine-lemon white chocolate truffles. There was anger beneath my fear, but I didn't leave.

I reached the pillar at the bottom of the stairs, where I was safely hidden from sight, keeping most of the guests behind me. I placed my cup of cold tea on the closest step, my hands shaking with sudden nerves. I wasn't sure why I was hiding, except for the single irrational fear that if somebody saw me they might ask me to join them. They might think I was one of them. And I wasn't.

Deep down I was also afraid that I would want to say yes.

I turned, about to leave when I caught sight of a partygoer exiting the back of the house, where a porch jutted over the grass. They stepped from darkness into glittering night, just a shadow at first, which made me think of the crows that had flown overhead, and the dizziness returned. I squinted, peering through the darkness to make out the ghostly arms of the house fading off to the left and right. On the porch there was a flickering electric lamp that shed an eerie purple glow.

My eyes were drawn to the light—and to the figure as they came to rest just beneath it. They were tall, lithe, with the easy movements of the rich. Despite my reservations I couldn't help myself, creeping farther up the steps to be able to see better. They had an air of boredom, but they stared out to the ocean in a way that almost seemed hopeful, body alert, searching the black water for an answer.

There was a flicker of light and smoke as a cigarette flared to life, briefly illuminating the figure's face. Narrow chin, sharp cheekbones. Wicked eyes that sparkled like dark gems. Lips...lips curved like a Cupid's bow.

The woman wore a man's white suit, crisply tailored to her slight curves. I blinked, but I couldn't erase her face from my mind. A trembling started in my chest—coming from my fluttering heart.

The woman shifted, taking a long drag on her cigarette. The purple light overhead wavered and the shadows lengthened, catching in the slickness of her dark braid, making her suit stand stark against her olive skin. She was magnetic.

An unravelling started inside me—no, an uncoiling. A buzz of panic whipped through my limbs. My pulse began to thunder; it was as if the longing that had pulled me here was tangible, a pin right through the centre of my heart. It was somehow both pain and pleasure. I backed away, grateful for the silent sand, and hoping for the party behind me and the waves lapping on the shore to drown out the fear that rinsed through me.

I wondered if the woman was my neighbour, or just a guest. I wondered if the purple light had some sort of significance, or whether it was a trick of tired eyes. I wondered if she always wore such masculine clothes. My cheeks burned and I pressed my icy hands against them, ready to laugh, ready to forget the whole thing had ever happened.

Chapter Three

Emmeline

Over the last few years I had learned that the best time to practise magic was not at midnight like my aunt had always said; the true witching hour was the morning after a party, any time after the last straggler passed out in the fountain and before eight o'clock.

I had taken to setting up my altar in the attic long before the others were awake because it was easier when I didn't have to answer questions. In the beginning I'd shared every story with them, lingering on the details I'd gleaned while Nathan made tea or breakfast. If an appointment had been resolved in one sitting, as they so often were, I'd enjoy explaining the clients' faces when I'd told them to swallow a spoonful of honeyed wine spiced with verveine for peace or wild garlic for protection. I asked Isobel to help me find the best herbs for my spells, because she always seemed to know not only which worked best, but how to combine and mix for a better result. I always allowed them to examine my recipes, making suggestions or jokes, although I often ignored them.

These days things were different. Two drops of blood and a concoction I could fit into a vial smaller than my thumb or I wouldn't take it on.

I *couldn't.*

Nathan and Isobel could never know how bad it had become, how the blood in my veins was growing thick and tired, how my magic sometimes felt cracked and dry like a cursed riverbed. I flexed my hands instinctively, drawing the nails into my palms and measuring the weak throb of my pulse.

For my final of last night's clients I used an old recipe of my aunt's, bastardised by years of Cilla's tutelage. I measured out eight drops of lavender oil, a thimbleful of dried ground yarrow, two big sprigs of fresh rosemary, and wax from a red candle, which I mixed with a single drop of blood pricked from the end of my finger, two pinches of grave dirt, and a healthy sprinkle of salt. The herbs made a faint hissing sound as I stoppered the vial and sealed it with more red wax.

Two drops of blood would have been more effective, three better still, but one would have to do. My aunt would have been disappointed if she could see me relying on such a base kind of magic—but she wasn't here.

The pull of the magic as the blood dried on my fingertip was familiar. The pain that roared up my arm and into my chest was new. It faded fast so I ignored it, tidying up the last of the cuttings and the fresh herbs.

The sun had already been up for a couple of hours and the sky through the attic window was clear and startlingly blue. At the peaked window I peered out to where the gardens joined the ocean. Beyond, on days like today, you could see the northern point of the island, a hump of houses that sometimes flickered white as the sun caught their bright stone facades.

Not for the first time I allowed my thoughts to stray to the light on our porch, purple and distinctive. I wondered if *she* might be out there on the northern point, if my imagination had not run wild with the scant details she had left me. If she might be able to see the light and know I was still looking for her.

My gaze moved to the back lawn, shaded but gold dipped at the edges, where three—no, four—guests were draped under a big old oak whose cover had protected them from the worst of the damp night.

There were three women and a man—I recognised none of them—curled together against the dawn chill, sleeping deeply. They were all young, beautiful strangers dressed in bright party garb, their headdresses sparkling, their peacock and dove feathers wilted and crumpled. One wore a gown crafted from gold scales, shining even in the shade of the tree, and another was barefoot, no shoes in sight. It might be hours before they woke, yet. The kazam had run dry at just gone three, but Isobel's latest mixture was certainly potent.

I pushed away from the window, rolled up the sleeves of my shirt, and set to my other work. Downstairs, glasses filled with colourful dregs littered every surface, new rings staining Cilla's antique wooden sideboards, which I marked with indifference. Cigarette ashes overflowed the gilded porcelain trays, and I was certain I'd find spilled tobacco in the creases of the upholstery. I started with the glassware, my thoughts turning to last night, to another success.

Echoes of laughter had filled the hallways, the ballroom, the fullness replaced by a ringing emptiness in the light of day. It had been a party that rivalled all others. There had been a cacophony of noise, the heat of bodies crushed against one another, the light of a thousand twinkling electric stars. The house had flamed; the liquor had flowed: kazam and kyraz; gin and amber whisky; pink champagne with bubbles so soft they were like a thousand tiny kisses on a welcoming tongue. The whole of Crow Island had known about the party.

I hadn't invited them, but it seemed like the whole of Crow Island had come.

Except for her.

I forced the thoughts away as my mood darkened and scrubbed the bar in the parlour harder. I was still there when Nathan stumbled down the last flight of stairs and through the grand archway, his brown hair mussed and his sleepy face drawn. His presence was like a blanket and my resolve threatened to unravel. I wanted to tell him everything.

"Oh good," I said before he could speak. My voice was tight but I didn't care. Nathan would understand if he knew. He would comfort me. I couldn't face it. "Now that you're awake you can go and get rid of those stragglers on the lawn. And when Isobel gets up, tell her she needs to go lighter on the poppy petals next time."

I could smell Nathan's particular coffee-and-cinnamon scent as he wandered slowly through the parlour, picking up two glasses I'd missed on the mantel and returning them to the bar.

"You're lucky she brews it for you at all," he said. His tone was light but I knew an admonishment when I heard one. "You know how she feels about all of this. I'm sure she'd much rather us drink the lot."

I threw down the cloth and marched over to the large bay window that looked out over the front lawn sloping towards our gravel drive. The sun was bright and hot and I leaned against the sill for a moment, my blood settling slowly like silt on the bottom of a river. Just that small morning magic had left me drained.

"You're right, love. I didn't mean anything by it."

"Of course you didn't. I know you're always beastly after a party, so I won't hold it against you." Nathan grinned, clinking the two glasses together, miming celebration, but the sound was empty. Then he sighed, suddenly serious. "Look at us, darling, we're working ourselves to the bone. We should get more help than just the waiters. Or maybe we should take Isobel's advice and reconsider the parties altog—"

"We've had this conversation, Nathan," I said, not turning from the window. "Isobel has her clients and I have mine. If I choose to charge them, and how I choose to invite them to the house in the first place, is up to me. Besides, it's not as if the parties are just for attention."

Nathan laughed incredulously. "Aren't they entirely about attention?"

I gripped the sill, forcing my knuckles to whiten, watching the blood drain from them and thinking of last night, of all those people, all that magic in this house. A success. And yet still, a failure. "You know it's not that simple. We don't want the attention of everybody. We want—*her*."

Nathan said nothing to that. He was partly to blame. If he'd kept an eye on her—if he'd only done as I'd asked—we wouldn't be in this position. Never mind if *I* hadn't done the unthinkable in the first place.

The sound of a door slamming somewhere outside startled me. Nathan heard it too, abandoning the dirty glasses to come and see. The trees between our house and the annexed cottage next door were thin and spindly and we peered for a better view.

"That cottage has been empty for months. I wonder which misguided soul has taken it on this time. Haven't they heard about the raging heathens who live here?" Nathan smirked. "I hope they like noise."

A woman left the cottage and walked towards a cream-coloured motorcar. She was young and fine boned, her golden hair wrapped up in a loose knot. She moved cautiously, with a measured kind of grace, like a cat weighing her surroundings.

Nathan kept speaking, but I couldn't hear him over the sudden, foreign roaring sound in my ears and a wrenching feeling deep in my chest. I recalled a similar moment last night, when I'd been standing on the porch and watching for signs of life in the grand houses on the northern point. It had felt, for a moment, like being stung by a bee. Sharp, painful. After a moment it grew dull, the ache moving towards my heart, the faint sound of the ocean ringing in my head. I'd assumed it was the debt, and ignored it.

I clenched my fingers tight as a new sensation washed over me; it was akin to being swept by a wild gust of ocean wind, bitter and raw. It was fear mingled with a strange kind of longing. When I blinked I saw darkness and ruby flowers, three pairs of crows' wings, flapping madly, damp earth under my fingernails, my veins tinged black by the sluggish slip of my blood.

Without thinking I bit down hard on my tongue and threw up my mental barriers, grabbing the slippery feeling and hauling it down into the recesses of my chest, where it hid, cowed by the iron tang of my blood. Distantly I recognised the normal sounds of life as Nathan spoke again about the cottage, the woman, about the guests still sleeping on our back lawn, and eventually another voice joined his, thick with sleep.

"Here you two are." Isobel, her dark ringlets still bundled in an old silk scarf of Cilla's, headed for the window. She wore a pair of shorts under a nightshirt, the collar slipping off one shoulder. In her hands she held two steaming cups of coffee, one of which she immediately thrust at Nathan. I forced myself to look away as the blond woman next door climbed into the cream car. "What are you two gawking at this time of day? Did somebody do something foolish on the lawn last night? Is it a big horrible mess? If it is, I absolutely will say I told you so."

I took my coffee from Isobel, grateful I didn't have to reply. It was weaker than the kind Nathan made, which was always dosed with cinnamon and strong enough to stand a stick up in. As the car pulled away the feeling in my chest dulled, a faint roar of surf in my ears as my heartbeat returned to normal.

"Em's mooning over the new neighbour." Nathan sipped his coffee, his face the picture of innocence. "Probably about time she got a new hobby."

I didn't say anything.

"Who?" Isobel asked, craning her neck.

"Gone now, darling. You slept too late and missed all the fun. She's some pretty young thing."

"It's a pity it's not some strapping man for me to flirt with," Isobel teased. Nathan's cheeks coloured and he slapped away the long finger Isobel wagged as she continued. "An extra pair of strong, sturdy hands certainly wouldn't go amiss around here."

"I wish you two would make yourselves useful instead of teasing each other," I said churlishly. "Or teasing me. I'm too tired for this." I turned fully away from the window, planting my feet firmly. "You"—I pointed at Nathan—"need to get those hangers-on off the back lawn or so help me I'll lock the greenhouse and overwater all your plants. And you"—I turned to Isobel, who raised an eyebrow in challenge—"what on earth did you put poppy petals in the kazam for?"

Isobel looked surprised, letting out a bark of laughter. "You mean why did *you* use the syrup I specifically told you not to use, which was labelled *For Isobel*, when you made the wine? The wine I told you not to brew yourself? I told you that syrup was for my work, not yours. Serves you right for thinking the world revolves around you. And now you owe me, dearest, because that batch took me two weeks to make. So I suppose I shall have to ask you kindly to spend some time helping me brew another one."

I rolled my eyes at her smile, but I was glad for Isobel, who always felt like a tall tree to shelter beside—even when she was bawling me out. Perhaps especially when she was bawling me out. I was always grateful for Nathan's gentle warmth, but Isobel's love felt like a firm pair of guiding hands. I wondered, just for a second, whether they would simply be grateful when I was gone.

I followed Nathan and Isobel farther into the house as they carried on bickering, about the booze, about the parties, about me and my clients. I followed them away from the cottage and the woman.

Away, too, from that tugging feeling, still there, deep down inside me, which felt like a warning.

Chapter Four

Annie

Crow Island was shaped like a waning sickle moon, its points angled towards the north and the east. As I'd had my morning cup of tea on the lawn, I'd perched on a well-worn deck chair the previous inhabitants had left behind. From there I could make out the northern tip of the island across the bay, where the houses looked huge, towering over the trees nearby.

Bea had written in a couple of her letters that she was living somewhere to the north of Crow Trap with her very rich husband, but I knew little else of her new life, her notes full of details I could never hope to understand. After she left home with barely a word, our contact had been limited, but ever since I found out this was where my father had also come to live, I had a renewed urge to see her and make sure she was doing as well as her letters suggested.

I hadn't told her I was coming because I was afraid that she was still angry with me, although she had said she wasn't. I worried that the silent way she had left, and the hurt that had blossomed between us in her absence, would hang there forever, unspoken but not invisible, but this morning I had woken up with a burning desire to at least find out for sure. After seeing those partygoers on my neighbour's lawn I was...if not brave, then at least determined.

If I was being honest, I had not told her I was coming because I wanted to force myself to do this without her help. If I didn't try, how would I ever be able to rule my own life? When we were growing up, Bea had always been the one who plotted and schemed, and I was her shadow. Sam and I followed her because she had the best ideas, knew the best places to play and the way to score leftover honey cakes from the baker whose daughter had died of flu. It was only after the war, after Sam died—after Bea lost her brother too— that things changed. *She'd* changed. She wanted booze and boys, long nights on the pier that I couldn't bring myself to enjoy.

Sam had tempered Bea, and without him she was never the same. The three of us had been so close that losing him was like losing a limb. My future had ended then, but Bea's was only just beginning.

Whatever my plans had been, I couldn't come here and not see her.

I found my way to her address with a wildness inside my chest, some hint of rebellious spirit finally growing there. The isolation I had felt last night gave way to a little excitement, which made me drive faster than the day before, revelling in the wind blowing in my hair, the sun's warmth kissing my bare arms.

In her driveway, perfectly bordered by conifers and bluebells and pretty little common dog violets, my joy dimmed. I sat in the car for a moment, gripping the steering wheel tight. I hadn't seen Bea in more than a year. What if she had changed again? What if I *hadn't*? Was there anything worse than me being the same boring, meek Annie she had been so tired of she'd left her behind?

In the end it wasn't bravery that drove me to Bea's door; it was embarrassment that somebody might see me, sitting alone in my dead father's car, too nervous to go inside, and they might think I was strange.

The doorbell jangled like a handful of silver coins. I was ushered into a foyer by a maid not much younger than me, where moments later Bea appeared in a flowing green dress and an elegant string of pearls, her red curls artfully coiled and her lips soft and stained rose pink. She looked exactly as she always did, bright and shiny and gorgeously, perfectly full of life.

She was surprised, silent for a moment that seemed to stretch for an eternity. I started to speak, to apologise, to beg forgiveness, but when I opened my mouth I thought I might cry. I hadn't known how much I'd truly missed her until right this second.

And then she grinned and all my awkwardness fell away.

"Hullo, Bea."

"Annie, darling!" She swept me into an enthusiastic hug, enveloping me in her new rosewater-and-gin scent. Briefly I thought of the way she had used to smell—a little spicy like the speciality teas her mother had once brewed, a little sweet like the sugared scones we used to steal—but I blinked and the memory was gone, swept away by Bea's new life. "I can't believe it's been a whole year since I last saw you. You look—just the same! How come you're here? Why didn't you tell me you were coming?"

I hugged her back tight, swallowing the lump in my throat.

"My father died," I said quickly. "Apparently he lived here. I'm sorting through his things. Your mam will be so happy when I tell her I've seen you."

"Oh, my *mother*," Bea said. She'd gone to great lengths to drop some of her strongest northern twang but it was still there, just under the surface. A shadow passed over her face. "How is she?"

"She asked after you when she found out we'd been writing." I took a second to examine the hallway, which was filled with mirrors. I caught my face staring back at me and I was momentarily stunned by the pink in my cheeks, my ruffled hair, no hat in sight. "She said you don't."

"She's always been overly sentimental, a bit like you."

"I hope you don't mind me dropping by," I added quickly to hide the hurt. Old questions rose, about why Bea had left so quickly, about why she had never said goodbye, but I swallowed them. This wasn't the time. "I should have called. I won't trouble you—"

"Don't be silly, darling." Bea looped her arm through mine and began to draw me towards the back of the house. "Now that you're here you must meet Arthur—he's going to be *thrilled*. He says I never talk about my old friends."

Bea had never called me *darling* before. Had never called me an *old friend.* It was as if she'd become somebody else while I was grow-ing more like the old Annie I'd always been. A sharp pang of loss cut through me.

Last spring, in those months before she left, was this who she had become? Had I been too focused on my own fear of the inevita-ble to notice? Perhaps she had been a little quiet, but Bea always was prone to sad spells, so I hadn't thought anything of it. Our days con-tinued as normal: work and play; long walks in the evenings full of Bea's scheming for the future; new boys, and the same boys; a drink or two at the Crown…

One day she was simply gone.

She'd turned up here months later, engaged. *Be happy for me, Ann,* she'd written finally. *I'm free.* That was Bea all over. Unpredict-able, wild. Wilder than me.

Bea guided me to a large sunroom that looked out over the ocean. On a sideboard there were a few photographs and paintings. There was one of a young boy who I thought must have been Arthur, a painting in full colour that showed bright blue eyes and golden locks of hair. Everything in this room was lush and expensive in shades of gold and cream and a soft pastel pink that made me feel very small and grubby and out of place.

It wasn't just the furniture, though. Plants grew on every avail-able surface. Roses, marigolds, all sorts of out-of-season things. I spied a fresh lavender plant, worth more than my mother made in weeks, more if you considered how much money you'd be fined for owning it. And there it was, just sitting in the windowsill, stems wilting in the heat. My nerves started again, my muscles as tense as they might be if I was getting ready to run away. It was so close to real magic that a warning bell began in the back of my mind.

If Bea noticed me flinch, she didn't say anything. One fresh lav-ender plant—the scent to dull the nerves—clearly wasn't out of place in her new life. Did she remember all the summers we had spent as children scouting for new herbs and flowers for my mother's choco-late or her mother's teas? How we'd gathered them and dried them and pickled them in jars? That was a world away.

"Arthur's out on the decking," Bea said over her shoulder. "You'll like him. He's so strong and funny—and very clever. He's a lot like how I imagine Eddie might have turned out." Bea's brother had been so different from her, with his sandy hair and freckles, and the gentle way he had punched me on the shoulder and called me *little chicken*. When he died fighting, Bea had cried every day for a month. Afterwards she was brighter, harder, brittle, all her tears cried out, her sadness replaced with glass.

Bea wandered over to a large bar with an array of shining liquids, crystal goblets glittering invitingly from behind their polished glass cabinet. Some of the bottles looked strange and squat, their contents a deeper shade of red, a honeyed shade of brown.

Bea had always been a rule breaker, but kazamed booze was another thing, even out here on the island, wasn't it? Magic and alcohol were a dangerous mix, but I didn't want to destroy this strange new truce so quickly by getting upset.

"I'd like to meet your husband," I prompted.

She caught my wary gaze and let out a laugh that sounded full of the old Bea. *Silly Annie, she's always so nervous.* I bristled, although she was right.

"Oh, goodness, Ann, don't be such a bore. It's just plain old booze. Whisky, gin, some ginger wine too, I think. No kazam. Arthur really is a stickler about that. He only lets me have the lavender to help with my monthlies. Do you want a drink, though? I've got some gin. You always liked that, didn't you?"

She didn't wait for me to answer and soon presented me with gin in a large bowl-shaped glass filled to the brim with ice cubes. She took a sip of her own and sighed.

"Come on, Ann," Bea reprimanded when I didn't try any of the drink. "You can trust me. I know you're angry with me, but I'm still the same old me. I'm hardly going to poison my best friend. Let's head outside and you can tell me everything I've missed. Tell me about your life. I think of you so very often. I want to know about your father. Did you say he lived here? Is that how you ended up in paradise?"

I let her lead me out into the blazing sunlight, for the first time truly regretting my decision to visit her at all. I had never felt like I fitted in at home, but it was no different here. I was still nervous, meek little Annie, desperate to be coddled. And the way Bea said *paradise* made my skin prickle.

Chapter Five

Annie

Bea's husband was older than I thought he'd be, nearer thirty than twenty. He was one of those handsome men I'd been frightened of when we were in school—tall, naturally tanned, and athletic, with lean limbs and golden curls like a crown. He had kind eyes set deep in a broad face, sharp cheekbones, and a wide, passionate mouth, which morphed into a confused smile when he saw us.

"I wondered where you'd wandered off to," he said.

"Annie, this is Arthur. Arthur honey, look who's come to see us. Annie and I knew each other as children, isn't that grand? We were inseparable for *years*."

Arthur smiled, and it was so much like the sun coming out, blinding, that I felt blessed. I stumbled my way through an introduction, my gaze snagging on the beauty of the scene in front of me. Arthur lazing on a wicker sofa padded with plush, impractical white pillows; a delicious spread of bite-size sandwiches and little cakes laid before him on a low table. The decking at the back of the house was like a raised porch, and beyond there were rolling gardens in full bloom right down to the ocean.

"So, are you here for the summer?" Arthur asked as I sank onto one of the cushioned chairs. When he looked at me the world dropped away, his gaze intense and genuinely interested.

"That's the idea," I said, explaining about my father's death. "I'm here to sell his things."

Bea gathered me a plate filled with little sandwiches and pressed it into my free hand.

"Eat!" she exclaimed. "We have far too much food."

"You said this is your first time here?" Arthur appraised me, taking in my windswept hair and my dress, which I'd made from an old pattern of my mother's, and I shifted uncomfortably. But if he found me lacking in any way, he kept it to himself. "How are you liking it so far?"

"It's certainly special," I said earnestly. "I found myself a lovely little cottage. It sure is livelier than home."

Arthur laughed. "I've had a home here since I was a child," he said. "My parents liked to summer here. I know Beatrice's did too, didn't they, love? All rather exclusive, of course."

I raised an eyebrow and glanced at Bea. Her mam was not *exclusive*. Nor had she ever summered anywhere but Whitby. Bea's mother still lived in a little two-up two-down like the one I shared with Mam.

Bea's eyes widened in alarm. Possibly it hadn't occurred to her to worry that I knew too much—of her old life, of the mistruths she had obviously told. I was sad that she thought I would ruin it for her, but I was here to prove myself, wasn't I?

I said quickly, "Yes, of course. Bea's always had the nicest things." Bea's face softened, her green eyes sparkling with relief. "I've never been here before, but my father had a house on Woodcote."

Arthur raised his beer bottle and took a long swig before he spoke. He was considering me differently, now that he knew where my father had lived.

"I'm sure the property will raise some interest. The houses on Woodcote always sell quickly. Lots of class up there, councillors and lawyers and the like. Where did you say you're staying?"

I glanced at Bea and she nodded encouragingly. This was Crow Island, a place of fortune; I could blend in here, just like her. It was all about wealth, having so much money that magic was just a game, and my father had not been a poor man. This wasn't the real world.

"It's a cottage on the east point," I said, giving Arthur a bright smile. "It's only small but it suits me. There's the most gorgeous house next door. I don't know who lives there, but if last night is anything to go by, they throw the most exciting parties."

I expected Bea to grin at the mention of the party, like she would have back home. Instead she stopped faffing with the sandwiches and sank down next to me, an expression I couldn't read flitting across her beautiful face. She watched Arthur as his whole body tensed, though neither of them moved.

"There's a house around there that has a reputation," Arthur warned. "Cross House. You'd better avoid it. The whole island is enamoured—well, the people without sense are anyway—"

"Oh, darling, they're just parties," Bea said weakly.

"Have you ever been to one?" I asked.

"We wouldn't put ourselves at risk like that." Arthur gripped his beer bottle tightly.

"No, no," Bea added. "We haven't been to the parties. Arthur doesn't like them."

"Why?" I asked. I thought of the people I'd seen last night on my neighbour's lawn, laughter and dancing, champagne under the stars. It had seemed harmless enough. "Parties are meant to be fun. So they get a little wild... What's so bad about that?"

"They're illegal gatherings," Arthur said roughly. "I've warned Bea and I'll warn you as well: you shouldn't get involved with them. Those people are courting trouble, and you'll be likely to take the fall."

"For a party?" I sipped at my gin, holding the sharp taste on my tongue.

"For *magic*," Arthur corrected. "Those concoctions they offer seem harmless enough, but they're always dosed, kazamed up to the gills. They'll tell you it's all fake—that's what the island is known for, right? Faux magic as much as the crows?" He snorted. "It's not fake, not at that place. It sets a bad example. Did you hear about the arrest last month? I've heard sometimes we make the mainland papers."

I shook my head. Bea avoided my gaze, embarrassment pinking her cheeks.

"There was a party that got broken up," she said quietly. "Just a normal party. Only a few of us, some people I didn't know too well. We—I—didn't think anything of it, because Rosalind was my friend. I thought—"

"There was magic," Arthur cut in. "Real stuff. *Strong* stuff. Ended up with somebody jumping off a roof thinking he could fly."

Suddenly Bea's embarrassment made sense. She had been there. She must have known that people were drinking things other than regular booze. The law was explicit: the consumption of real magic, in any form, but especially mixed with other state-altering substances, was strictly prohibited.

"Rosalind—I don't think it was anything to do with her, but she's in so much trouble," Bea went on. "They've had to hire a mainland lawyer to defend her case."

"Somebody mentioned hanging," Arthur added grimly. "Because the man who jumped died."

"And Cross House?" I prompted.

"How it's not been shut down is beyond me. People flock to that house every weekend to get absolutely zozzled. There used to be *flyers* promoting the parties, if you can believe that. They're obviously using magic to get away with it. I bet it's bribery, spells and potions to keep themselves out of jail. There are all sorts of rumours. People say the woman who owns the house turns into a crow at night and that's why they can never catch her. I think the whole lot of them are being set up for a big fall.

"In any case, I'd make sure you're not around when it happens. The owner of Cross House is a witch, and you don't want to mess with magic, no matter what the tourists would have you think."

I thought of the woman I'd seen on the porch last night, the purple light shining on her face. Was that what a witch looked like? That tugging sensation deep inside me, was that how witches made you feel? Was that how they lured you in? I shivered.

Arthur grew restless, the conversation unnerving him as much as it did me. He glanced down at his wrist. Annoyance morphed his face and Bea tensed.

"Did you move my watch this morning?" he asked.

"No, darling. I think you had it on when you left for the club last night, but I've not seen it since."

Arthur grabbed another sweating beer and drained it nearly halfway before stalking away from the table, his expression thoughtful.

Bea pushed another miniature sandwich onto my full plate.

"Sorry," she murmured. "He really thinks he's being helpful. He doesn't know you like I do."

———)●(———

After lunch we took Bea's car into town. She drove carelessly, laughing as she barrelled round corners and poking me in the arm when I flinched.

"I'm not drunk," she reassured me. "Anyway, people will get out of the way."

We roared along a coastal road, narrow but empty. I could see the curve of the island, the way the eastern point jutted out into the ocean like a promenade. I could see the faint cluster of houses along its edge and wondered if we might see mine, or my neighbour's. I thought of what Arthur had said. I could be living next door to a witch. I pictured the stones I collected at home, the way their polished surfaces felt between my fingers; I had always assumed magic would feel a little like that. Stolen. Natural, like the rocks worn smooth by ocean salt, but not truly mine any more than the pebbles were.

"Do you think my neighbour really can turn into a crow?" I asked.

Bea didn't take her eyes from the road. "No," she said quickly. "Or—I don't know. Maybe if she really wanted to."

I chewed on the thought. Too soon we pulled back from the ocean, cutting through towards the wider road I recognised, houses on both sides growing smaller, less tidy, but nothing like the ramshackle, winding streets back home. These houses were short, squat things, bordered by bushy flowering hedges. Bea paid no notice, not when the road grew busy and not when she had to brake hard twice to avoid a collision.

By the time we made it to Crow Trap I was breathless and *alive* the way only Bea could ever manage. We tumbled out of her shiny new auto still laughing.

"C'mon," Bea urged. "You'll love it here. Let me show you around. Arthur really can be a bore about the fake magic. It's harmless—everybody says so."

We wandered down the street arm in arm, just like we had as children, and for a second I forgot that everything had changed. It was a shock to see so many people out on the streets—and so many men. Since the war I'd gotten used to streets full of women, and that hadn't really changed over the last few years. Here it was almost like the world had been before that dark time; there were couples, families with young children between them, an air of holiday and frivolity.

Bea and I both squealed when a young child came rushing up to hide behind Bea's skirts, and she pointed out two young men on the other side of the street who were staring at me as we collapsed into unladylike giggles. I blushed awkwardly and nudged her onwards. Bea only laughed harder.

She was more herself here, away from her husband and the gilded trappings of her new life. There was more of the Bea I had known since childhood, the girl who delighted in simple joys, who laughed freely and spoke without restraint. Although she was not entirely the same.

"So tell me about Arthur," I said as we dodged another family with two young children, one a babe in arms. "Where did you meet him?"

"Oh, just around town. There are a few places I'll show you. There's a dance hall I simply *adore*. It was love at first sight with Art. That is, I saw him and I had to have him, for better or worse." She laughed, but the sound was brittle.

"What?" I asked. "Aren't you happy?"

"Yes," Bea said earnestly. "I am. Only I'm sorry about today. He got a bit spirited, didn't he? He's not normally like that, especially when we have company."

I shrugged. "He's just being protective."

Bea said nothing for a moment, and then more quietly, "The war was hard on him, I think. He doesn't talk about it, but I know he has nightmares. The things he saw. Sometimes he wakes up thinking he's back there. I keep hoping it will get better, but he only seems to be getting worse. Especially with all the magic laws. It's changing here, Ann—they're getting stricter. There are more severe penalties for crimes of magic committed on the island than there were only six months ago. More cases like—Rosalind. It's bringing up a lot of memories for him."

Bea stopped walking, pulling me underneath an awning that hung over the cobbled pavement. Behind us a small poster advertised *Fully Licensed Faux Palm Readings*. I leaned in for a closer look, but my skin prickled.

The wind dipped behind me and my discomfort intensified. It was like eyes on my back. I turned, expecting to see the boys from earlier, or somebody else flirting with Bea—but there was nobody there.

"We'll never know what it was like for the men," I said uncertainly. "The important thing is that you're happy here—"

"I *love* it here, Ann," Bea said earnestly. She started walking again and I hurried to catch up. "When I first got here I was lonely, sure. I missed you so much. Don't look at me like that—it's true. Art works a lot, and it's not like home where neighbours are neighbours, but I've made friends now. I've made a life—better than I ever dreamed. And...this place." She gestured aimlessly, unable to find the words.

I understood what she meant. Crow Island wasn't anything like the home we had left behind. It glowed, somehow. The air smelled better here, fresh bread mingled with the tang of the ocean, sweetness and a freshness that cleansed everything it touched. Bea wasn't staying just for Arthur. It was for all of this. The whole shining total of her new life. It felt like a world the war hadn't tainted, like a world where things had begun to blossom again with new life.

Understanding that didn't mean I didn't notice the unease that threaded between us when we talked about Arthur, though; how he seemed to be here with us as we walked, a part of the old Bea hidden in deference to him. I wondered if this was what a happy marriage looked like.

A crow swooped overhead and we both charted it as it disappeared between two buildings.

"It was killing me, Ann. That place was killing me. I know you couldn't see it because you've always been so good at being content with your lot. After Sam and Eddie . . . I had to get out. There had to be more to life than that."

"You didn't say goodbye." I forced myself to say the thought that had been circling in my head for more than a year. "I was convinced you hated me. *Do* you hate me?"

"I couldn't tell you I was going because I knew if I did, I would never leave." Bea blinked and I swore there were tears in her eyes.

"I would have come with you, if you'd told me."

"No," she said softly. "You wouldn't."

Her words were like a punch to my gut, leaving me breathless. She was right. I wasn't here because I was truly brave. I was here because of the promise of my father's money. I was here because fate had twisted my wrist and forced my hand.

"Am I selfish for wanting to change?" Bea asked.

I got the sense that there was more she wanted to say but couldn't. I didn't press her. Old habits taught me she wouldn't say any more today, and there would be time for more this summer—we would make time.

We passed a window dressed in silver foil stars, the glass dark against the sun. Bea stopped to peer inside, and I stumbled a second behind her.

A dark blur caught my eye. It was another crow taking flight. My eyes followed its reflection in the glass, a dark smudge against the sun. There was something else there too—I couldn't make it out at first. The darkness seemed to ripple like an ocean. It reminded me of the first night terror I'd had as a girl. My mother had found me on the beach two miles from our house—half-frozen, my limbs locked, sick with dizziness. It felt like that now, like I was fighting off a panic I couldn't pinpoint. My heart raced and my palms grew slick, the same faintness building behind my eyes, an image just out of focus. I closed them.

It took me a moment to understand that what I had been looking at in the glass had only been the shape of a man, dressed in a dark suit, his face a wavering mirage. I opened my eyes and looked again, but the glass was merely sun dark, not ocean-like at all. And the man had gone.

"*Annie?* Are you all right?"

"Oh, sorry." I peered down the street both ways, but there was nobody around. "I just went a bit dizzy—it's the sun. What did you say?"

"I'm inviting you to a gathering, darling," Bea said. "At my house this week. Just a small one. Very exclusive. It would be a great opportunity for you to meet some people, make some friends. I know you'll need some encouragement, but I won't take no for an answer. What do you say?"

I shook off the sense of foreboding, telling myself to stop being silly. Sam would never have let Bea get away with being this pushy, but he wasn't here. And, besides, Sam would have gone to her damn party.

"I guess I have no choice," I said. Bea grinned.

Chapter Six

Annie

My first days on Crow Island were exhausting. The freedom, which had seemed so captivating when I was constantly falling over my mother, soon chafed. It wasn't just the emptiness of the cottage—it was also the lack of routine, how daunting it felt to wake up every day with no plan. And, too, it was the sense that any moment somebody would realise I wasn't meant to be here. That this place, these people, were not meant for me. I hated the thought of being sent home almost as much as I hated the thought of staying here by myself all summer.

I had arrived on the island more than a week before my original schedule, mostly thanks to my own anxiousness, so I had nowhere to be until my appointment with Mr. Anderson to collect the keys for my father's house next week. It didn't feel right to interrupt Bea again until her "gathering," and I had no other friends here, so I filled my time with all the things I never had the pleasure of back home. There had to be something to enjoy.

On the first day I walked out of my house and onto the beach, turning right in the direction where the island reached its easternmost point, and walked until I grew tired and hungry. In the afternoon I drove into town and hunted amongst the shops and stalls until I found an artist's gallery and admired the paintings through the window. The next day I walked to the left of the beach, past my neighbour's imposing house—silent, as it had been since that first night—until I grew bored. Then into town again to find a shop where I might buy clothing patterns, fabric, anything to keep my hands busy into the evening.

I awoke after several days of this to the numb realisation that I was doing exactly the same as I had always done back home. Yes, the setting was different, but the activities I chose were safe, dull. Sam would have said they were *Annie choices*. I had dreamed of Sam in the night, of his warmth, but when I climbed out of bed it was with a sense of shame nudging at me, my hope fractured by the idea that I might never be able to change.

Bea had come to this island and she had become somebody new. Had that been because of Arthur? He was so much like the imaginary man Bea had always dreamed she would marry. He was handsome and wealthy; he had class and, if their house was anything to go by, taste. Was she happy, though? As much as Bea had promised me she was, had shown me hints of her old carefree self, I couldn't tell anymore.

I wondered as I brewed my tea and bathed and dressed whether a similar change would have happened to me too, if I'd married Sam. Would I have become a different version of myself, all the undesirable pieces hidden away?

No, it wouldn't have been like that. Sam had been my best friend, almost like a brother. He was another part of me and had always been willing to overlook my flaws. My mother had pushed us to marry, to take over the shop. And we would have, although we always said we didn't want to. It felt inevitable to me—until the war. I remembered the three of us, Bea and Sam and me, sitting in Sam's garden the afternoon he'd told us he'd signed up to fight.

"I've got to help them," he'd said, his freckled face so open and earnest. We'd all heard about what was happening over there. The violence. The magic that was turning normal soldiers on foreign shores into weapons, and the call for strong, eager men to fight them. Sam looked almost excited.

"I don't want you to go," I'd said softly. Bea just shook her head. Eddie was signing up too, but she took it all in her stride. I had a horrible taste in my mouth, bitter like Mam's unsweetened cocoa, and looking at him made me dizzy with loss, all his lines blurred inside my mind. I'd awoken on the beach again the night before, cold and sobbing, a dark tide of emotion washing over me, rinsing me out.

"I know," Sam said. "I can help, though, so I should. They need all the men they can get. They said with our help it'll be over in no time. It will be fine. I have a good feeling."

Sam had reached out and held my fingers in the warmth of his palm. He was so comfortable, so safe. I had hoped that he was right.

I thought of Sam again as I finished dressing, but he was distanced by the gentle lap of waves, by the sound of the crows cawing overhead as I walked out to the car. My car. The air was soft with the sense of impending rain, but the sky was still vibrant.

As I climbed into the car I glanced over at my neighbour's house, playing over what Arthur had said. Was it really magic that had people rushing to this house in droves, or was it some other thing? I could almost believe I felt the physical pull myself—but that was silly.

Sam had hated magic from the day his mother died. He never spoke of what happened, but Bea and I gleaned over many years that her death had been at her own hand. She'd purchased some herbs and made a poison that killed her in minutes. Sam had been with us that day, and I don't think he ever got over that. We hardly talked about any of it, and I wondered what he would make of this place, of Bea here. Of me here.

The thought that my neighbour might be responsible for allowing others a gateway to magic like Sam's mother, a path to breaking the law and to punishment as well as the dangers that real magic posed...it made my skin crawl. And yet, buried deep, there was a part of me that wanted to know why people enjoyed it, wanted to know what it was like to feel magic inside you, to make things happen instead of simply wishing.

I pulled the car onto the road. Today I had determined I was going to be a different Annie, the kind of Annie who tried new things. Maybe I could be a daring Annie. It felt like a good day to try.

I headed directly into Crow Trap to pick up the supplies I would need for packing up my father's house. I wasn't sure exactly what it would entail, but I drove to the middle of town and found a grocer's I had seen on my walk with Bea. The sun was warm on my back as I entered, a small bell above the door letting out an eerie jangle.

"Three."

I paused, glancing over to the counter where a middle-aged man stood holding a pair of gloves and some pruning shears. A plant I didn't recognise sat on the counter beside him.

"I'm sorry?"

"Three crows." The man gestured out the window. I turned, spotting the birds he was referring to perched on the back of my car. Their feathers were glossy and blue-black like oil.

"Oh," I murmured. "Yes, I see them."

The man went back to his pruning, nipping sturdy-looking stalks and gathering them into a pile. I browsed the front of the store, running my fingers over several small stuffed crows for sale. I flinched, pulling my fingers back. For a second I'd sworn I could feel an echo beneath their soft embroidered wings—like the nip of strong wind, except it was under my fingers, pushing them back.

"Excuse me," I said to the grocer. He glanced up indifferently, so I continued. "Isn't there a poem about crows?"

"Normally magpies, yes. Round here it's crows. One for malice, two for mirth. Three for a—"

"Death," I said, the word coming out of my mouth unbidden. I clamped my lips shut, horrified. The man nodded.

"Guess we'd better keep counting," he said, unfazed.

I stumbled backwards, pushing farther into the shop, finding relief in the dusty shelves as I slowed my breathing. It wasn't magic, I reassured myself. Only superstition, which was different.

I closed my eyes but my thoughts swirled like water. They felt like a hand around my ankle, trying to pull me under. I breathed and breathed, sucking in the dusty air until I could laugh about it. Sam would have laughed.

Finally I was calm enough to browse properly again, the fear settling a little. I scanned my list, walking farther back, scanning rows of stock for twine or brown paper. I came to a stop when I saw it: adorning the back wall was the taxidermic head of a Highland stag, a huge thing with antlers longer than my arms. Its glazed eyes stared at me hollowly. My skin crawled as I stepped quickly back behind the row of shelves, but I couldn't shake the feeling that its gaze was following me.

Dizziness threatened to overwhelm me again. Mam would tell me to close my eyes, to stand very still until the attack passed. Instead I grabbed a bundle of what might have been brown string and rushed back to the counter, trying not to look like I might cry. Everything felt like it was too much: too much noise, too much sun, too much magic.

"What's with the deer?" I bit out as I handed over my purchase, ignoring the way the hairs on the back of my neck stood on end, refusing to acknowledge the way my vision threatened to blank. I was determined not to run away until I was finished.

"That's old Mal." The shopkeeper gave me a grin that was full of humour. "Got him shipped over from the mainland. He wards off real magic. Said he can spot a witch from ten feet."

I couldn't get my thoughts in order to respond. I paid for my things as quickly as I could and backed out of the shop, Mal's eyes on me every step of the way.

—◦•◦—

As I stumbled out into the morning sun I found myself face-to-face with my father's lawyer. His expression morphed from surprise to pleasure as he let out a cheery greeting.

"Finding your way around all right, I see?"

I shuffled my bag from the grocer's to my other arm so I could shake his extended hand. His palm was warm and very dry. We stepped to the side of the shop underneath one of the many colourful awnings, an array of brightly striped sugar rock and fudge flavours displayed in the window next door. I nodded.

"I'm managing okay," I said. The dizziness had eased but I was still a little off-kilter. Maybe I was hungry. "It's a lot to take in, but the island is lovely. I'm just starting to figure out where everything is, but I'm afraid I haven't really explored town as much as I'd like yet."

Mr. Anderson smiled sympathetically. "It's certainly very eclectic, lots to see. Perhaps you might join me for tea and I can give you some hints. There's a museum I think you'd like, for instance. Your father was one of the benefactors, you know."

At home I would never have said yes, but I was worried that if I didn't sit down soon I might fall over and embarrass myself again, so when Mr. Anderson began to walk, I followed him readily enough. Mam would probably have a fit, but this man had been my father's friend and I liked his warmth. I wondered if my father had been like that too. I remembered him as large and imposing, but it had been seven years since I'd seen him. The memory might not be very accurate.

We walked a short way down a path between two shops and came to a small square courtyard outside a quaint café decorated in pinks and whites that made me think of candy floss. Inside, Mr. Anderson ordered us a pot of tea and a plate of rich, currant-speckled tea cakes that came with a pat of creamy salted butter.

"You said my father was a benefactor," I said, settling into the familiar rhythms of pouring and sweetening tea, sharing fresh milk from a little jug. Anderson helped himself to one of the piping-hot tea cakes. "Was he very interested in the arts, in culture?"

"He loved it all," Anderson said, dabbing at his copper moustache with a napkin. "He was fond of traditional art, painting and sculptures and the like, but really his passion was just collecting knowledge. He was very learned."

This sat well with the little I knew of my father. My mother had told me when I was young that they'd met when he was studying art and history in London and she was visiting an elderly aunt. Before his death, I had only met my father three times. The first time he took me to an art gallery. It wasn't a place suitable for a five-year-old and yet I remember being utterly enthralled by the stormy gothic paintings, the slashing strokes of black and gold. He asked me about my life, whether I could read or grow things in the garden, if I believed in ghosts or faeries, and I'd laughed and said obviously I did. I didn't see him again for another five years.

"Do you know what sort of things he liked to learn about?" I asked. If it felt like begging for scraps, I didn't care. This was my only chance to learn about the man whose blood I shared. "Did he have many friends on the island?"

Anderson let out a little cough, thoughtful for a second. "Not many," he said. "Colleagues mostly. He was, ah, very fond of his privacy. I know he liked architecture, and he had a very green thumb. His gardens are lovely—you'll see—and he planted most of them himself."

This was unusual. Since the prohibition, most folks seemed to have become wary of their gardens, scared of growing the wrong kinds of weeds. They'd rather hire somebody else to make sure any green spaces they did have were clean and safe—and legal.

Absurdly, this made me think of my new neighbour's gardens, how beautiful they seemed from a distance, how wild yet controlled. I wondered if she designed them herself too. It seemed like something somebody who hosted those kinds of parties would do.

"Mr. Anderson," I said hesitantly. "Do you—have you heard anything about the house next door to mine?"

Anderson raised his eyebrows, considering how to answer. "I was a little surprised when you told me which property you had selected," he admitted. "Cross House does have rather a reputation, ah... The parties, you see."

"Yes, I've heard about those."

"Not the sort of gatherings a nice girl like yourself would want to get involved in, I'm sure."

My cheeks burned and I shook my head, almost nudging my

cup out of its saucer. "No, sir," I said. "I didn't realise, before. I just wondered if you knew—anything else. Somebody told me there are rumours about...somebody turning into a crow?"

Anderson relaxed at my answer, visibly relieved at my naïveté. He let out a little chortle. "Yes, there are lots of stories about crows around here. You might have noticed." He gestured aimlessly outside, to where at least nine or ten of the island's crows currently pecked around for scraps. "Nothing to the stories, but Cross House is certainly worthy of its reputation."

"I—"

"I must warn you, Miss Mason," Anderson interrupted apologetically. "I'm sorry, but it must be said. There are things on this island that a Yorkshire girl like yourself might be new to. The island is, ah, *fonder* of these things than where you're from. You must resist the temptation to stray."

"I wouldn't—"

"I don't say this to lecture you," he went on. "I just know that your father would want me to look out for you. He was very respectable and wouldn't have wanted you getting into any kind of trouble. I suggest if you feel...concerned about it, worried at all, that you might come to me for advice—as you have done today. I'd be more than happy to provide guidance on the matter."

I closed my mouth with a click of teeth, realising it would be futile to explain to this man that I was the least likely person to get involved with magic. For starters, I would never be *invited* to join anybody in making or consuming the stuff, never mind have the gumption to accept. So I simply nodded, allowing a small bloom of sadness to grow in my chest as I wondered if my own father would have cared enough to warn me.

Chapter Seven

Annie

I awoke with a start. I had been dreaming, a dark murky dream full of flapping wings and roaring waves, of dirt piled on top of a wooden box and worms in the wet earth. The buttery morning light was a balm to my hammering heart.

The knocking happened again.

I dragged myself out of bed, groggily pulling on the terry-cloth robe I had brought from home and slipping my feet into my shoes. I hovered uncertainly for a moment in the bedroom doorway, the temptation to remain hidden so strong my limbs were like stone.

I recalled the reflection of the man I had seen in the window in Crow Trap with Bea; it felt like an omen, a premonition that hadn't abated. The knocking came a little louder, right from my front door. At home I would have ignored it. I would have waited for my mother.

Here, I was on my own; there was nobody to hide behind. So I squared my shoulders, forced my limbs to move, and opened it.

On the threshold there was a man, maybe a few years older than me, dressed in a dark suit that was tailored to his narrow shoulders and lanky frame. His hair was long and tied loosely at the nape of his neck.

I stepped back nervously, but this man was too young to have been the blurred figure I thought I saw in the window in town. He gave me a smooth, practised bow and brandished a cup. When he pressed it into my hand, my fingers were stiff, slow to react.

A jolt of recognition shot through me as I held the china, delicate and wrapped in a pattern of golden blooms. It was one from the cottage, the same cup I had carried out on my first night here. I must have left it there after the party, next to the steps, before I fled. My cheeks flamed as I cradled it to my chest.

"Yours, I believe?" the man said. His voice was soft at the edges, but his eyes, intense and brown, felt like they would bore into my soul if I let them. "Or perhaps you intended for it to no longer belong to anybody at all. Though I can't say it's so ugly I'd encourage throwing it away." He smiled.

"I'm sorry," I blurted. "I didn't mean to leave it. I don't know anybody around here and I heard people outside—"

"I'm only teasing, darling," he said. "Please don't apologise. We were getting ourselves ready for this weekend and I found it on the beach. I have a rather ulterior motive by bringing it back today, actually. We'll be having another little party tomorrow, so I wanted to stop by and apologise in advance. Things might get a little noisy. It's a hazard of the cottage, I'm afraid. It's been so long since anybody lived here that we're not used to taming the guests."

"Oh," I said, incredibly aware that I was hardly dressed, that I probably looked afraid—which I was. My cheeks continued to flame. I swallowed. "Erm, thank you for bringing this back. I won't trouble you again."

"It's no trouble," he said. "I just wanted to make sure you didn't feel scared off, is all."

The man's smile shifted. It was apologetic, yes, but tinged with playfulness. A suggestion, perhaps. An opening. I baulked.

"Please enjoy your weekend," he said.

He left silently, slipping away into the shadowy ferns outside my front door while I remained, frozen.

Another party... Arthur had said that the owner of Cross House was a witch. I still wasn't sure if the witch was the woman I had seen on the porch, her face glowing under that eerie purple light, but if not, perhaps another party meant she would be there again. A shiver needled my spine. If it was fear that held me in place—and it must be fear because that was the only logical emotion—then why did it feel so much like excitement?

————)•(————

That evening I climbed out of my car just as the sun was beginning to set. Bea and Arthur's house looked different in the twilight, its blinding white stones tinted with pastel pinks and oranges and blues as the sun dipped lower. Paper lanterns decorated the drive, where several other cars were already parked, their shiny exteriors coated in a fine layer of dust from the white gravel.

This was more cars than I'd expected. More guests. Bea had said *exclusive*, and I had thought she meant four or five people. There must have been at least five times that.

I considered turning around, driving away. I wasn't good in crowds, wasn't good at making small talk. Bea had always excelled at that, and when I was by her side new territory had never seemed as frightening. That was when the territory was new to both of us; this felt like walking into a patch of exquisitely lit woodland without a map or a compass.

I steeled myself at the door, smoothing down the blue dress I'd made only a few months ago, tucking away a stray blond curl that had escaped its knot. I tried to ignore the way my muscles bunched nervously as I reached up to ring the doorbell.

"Annie, you came!" Bea was delighted when the maid deposited me in a room I hadn't seen on my last visit, also at the back of the house, with an endless view of the ocean. The air was heavy with floral perfume and the sharper scent of alcohol; people mingled all around the room, gathered in clusters by the two damask sofas and the grand fireplace.

Bea wore a dress of a deep emerald green, setting off the sparkle of her eyes. I could tell just by looking at her that she'd already had more than her fair share of gin, so I wasn't surprised when she wrapped her arms around me and hugged me tight.

"You didn't exactly give me much choice," I joked when she let me go. She grabbed me by the arm and began to drag me towards the back of the room, where a polished cherrywood liquor cabinet stood with its doors opened invitingly.

"Help yourself," she urged, "and then come and meet some people. We don't stand on ceremony—no service tonight; I'm sending the maid away. It's more fun this way!" She laughed, the sound high and tight.

I made myself a weak gin cocktail and turned my back on the cabinet. I spotted Arthur by the open set of doors that led onto the same decking where we'd had lunch at the beginning of the week. He spoke to a woman who wore a flowing white dress and a golden band around her arm. She was tall and athletic, with long tanned limbs. She wore her dark hair in a bob and her eyes were dramatically darkened with kohl. When she saw me looking she gave me a little wink. I averted my gaze, my cheeks flushing absurdly.

Two other women stood by the fireplace laughing loudly over the music that spilled from a hidden gramophone. Their dresses were long and hand beaded with thousands of tiny, sparkling stones, and their hair was the same silver blond, worn in finger waves, which suited their matching features.

Bea pulled me over to a small group of women in more fine dresses, introducing them so quickly that I immediately forgot their names, urging me too quickly towards another group and another. I sipped at my drink each time we moved, until my glass was empty. I glanced around. Bea had disappeared.

I made myself another drink and stood by the cabinet nursing it, taking in the opulence around me. Bea's mam wouldn't know what to do in a house this size. Neither would mine. It was so open and bright, everything polished and edged with gold and shining white marble. Even the wood gleamed—a far cry from the dingy, well-worn little houses we'd both grown up in.

Somebody let out a shriek. The woman with the dark hair had spilled her drink and the glass lay shattered on the bare floor. Instead of being upset, or even apologising, she broke into riotous laughter, and Arthur soon joined her.

He was more relaxed tonight than he had been when I saw him last. There was a softness in his gaze, and the colour in his cheeks suited him. He held a drink in one hand but sipped slowly, his interest trained on his guests instead. Perhaps that was what Bea had skirted around when we spoke; perhaps her husband was too fond of drink. I watched him closely, but he only sipped and talked, and when he retreated from his spot by the doors I didn't follow him.

It was too loud. There were too many people in this room, no matter how light and airy it was. I carried my drink away, wandering back the way I had come, into the hall. There were fewer people here, but those I found were roaring drunk. The gathering had probably begun soon after lunch, knowing Bea—or before, if she felt daring. I was several hours behind everybody else, though; that much was clear.

In another room I found a bathroom, empty of people but so clean and shining it felt like heaven. A huge gilt-edge mirror hung on one wall, and there was a basket filled with neatly pressed linens for drying your hands. I walked until I found the kitchen, a wooden block table piled with fresh fruit, and a machine for juicing oranges with a fancy little spout on the side. At home if we wanted orange juice we generally had to make do with wanting.

By the time Bea came to my rescue, a kind of hysteria had built inside me. Her hair was wild, as if she'd been running her hands through it, and her expression was harried. She guided me back into the main gathering like she might do a child.

"Should have known you'd end up in the kitchen," she said. "A lot of your mother in you."

I glared. She said it so lightly, like it didn't matter. Perhaps by being here she had simply forgotten what it was like to have the weight of expectation on your shoulders.

She searched behind me, half her attention trained across the room where her husband stood amongst his friends. No, I was wrong. Bea hadn't forgotten those expectations—she had simply traded one set for another.

"Come on, darling." She pouted. "Have a little fun. Please. I so want you to have a good time."

"Bea, I don't belong here."

"What? Why?"

"Look at me." I gestured at my dress, which was smart but plain. My face was bare of makeup and I wore no jewellery. I was nothing like these shining, careless people. "I don't fit in. You don't need me here."

"Of course I do!"

I pulled her back to a quieter corner, watching as the dark-haired woman who had been talking to Arthur made a move towards the twins, leaving Bea's husband with a tall, red-haired man in a pastel shirt I'd met earlier. Arthur's gaze settled on us and he frowned.

"I don't feel comfortable," I said, my voice low.

"You never felt comfortable back there, either," Bea said, oblivious. She took a long swig from her drink to illustrate the point, but I noticed the way she avoided saying *back home*. Whitby wasn't home anymore. I suppose it never had been for her. She was right about me, though.

"Everybody here is so stylish and so chic—"

"Well, of course they are, darling." Bea laughed. "That's because they have money—and you'll have money soon too. You'll have pretty dresses and nice things, and you'll fit right in. I'm glad you're here. I think...I think Sam would have been pleased to see us together again."

Hearing Bea say his name always pinched the air from my lungs, she said it so rarely. It sounded worse here—as if he didn't belong here any more than I did. I clenched my fists.

"Come on, Bea. That's not fair. You only ever bring him up when I disappoint you. But it's not just the clothes. It's all of it. The posture, the accent, the attitude. Like—her—" I gestured at the dark-haired woman, who had her back to me. The way she dressed, the way she stood, made a strange warmth coil in my belly—embarrassment, probably. I wanted to be brave enough just to *want* to be like her, that was all.

"Joey?" Bea rolled her eyes. "Oh, don't compare yourself to her. She's wild. Her money's so old her family can't remember where they got it."

"Well, exactly!" I swallowed another mouthful of gin. It was stronger than I'd thought beneath the shockingly sweet ice cubes and I could feel my limbs growing loose and heavy. "I'll never be like her."

"You don't have to be like her," Bea said earnestly. "You just have to be here."

I finished my drink and Bea paused the conversation to make us each another. I started to relax. It was just a party. Nobody knew who I was. I could be anybody at all.

"Why *here*?" I asked suddenly.

"The party…?"

"No, why did you come here? Last year. You left without a word, you never told me why, and you've hardly written to me since, just silly little notes as if nothing happened."

Bea wobbled, putting an arm out against the wall. "I don't really want to talk about it," she said, too brightly. A hint of that brittle Bea I recognised from the war was there, just under the surface. She glittered dangerously.

"There had to be a reason," I pushed. "You could have gone anywhere. Why did you choose this place?" The place where magic lived and breathed, where it butted up against the law and people couldn't quite bring themselves to care.

"I said enough, Ann." Bea shot me a look so cold it shocked me into silence. "Drink up and come dance."

She excused herself and disappeared into the throng that had grown. I'd lost sight of the dark-haired woman and the twins. More people must have arrived. I drank my gin and made another, letting myself settle into the golden limbo I was familiar with from the nights on the pier, booze flowing and Bea chasing boys. Time seemed to slow down. Laughter floated around me. The shining chandelier overhead swayed, or maybe that was more to do with me.

Somewhere outside somebody began to shout. It was a man's voice, forceful. A woman raised her voice back. For a second the party noise dipped as everybody quietened down to listen.

"I don't care!" roared the man. It sounded like Arthur. I listened carefully. "It's not up for discussion, so just stop talking about it."

There was a crash, the telltale tinkle of smashing glass, and then one of the twins began to cheer from her new spot by the door. Somebody else joined in until there was a chorus of noise. Bea stepped back inside, her cheeks pink.

I stayed where I was, my heart thudding and my legs going like jelly. I searched Bea's face for a hint of what had happened, but her expression was shuttered. A hiss of old, protective anger rose in me, followed swiftly by a cooler confusion. It was likely that Bea had provoked him the way she had provoked me not long ago—right? I almost wanted to believe that she had been spoiling for a fight, because if she had instigated an argument with Arthur, then our harsh words meant less.

I did not have time to give voice to the more insistent part of me, the one that recalled the way he had looked at her when we had stood together, the disappointed gleam in his eyes, because before I could move, Bea was gone, swallowed into the throng of guests once more.

It seemed very dark in here, the air heavy. The candles and electric lights did nothing to illuminate the room. Darkness flashed in front of my eyes and I squeezed them shut tight. It was too loud again. I needed to move. I left my last drink half-finished on a polished side table and staggered out into the hallway, fumbling until I found the bathroom again.

I located the sink and thrust my hands under the cold water, splashing it onto my face until the darkness receded and I could see normally again. When I rose, panting, I noticed I was not alone.

The dark-haired woman, Joey, stood with one hand pressed against the wall, her other on the second blond twin's waist. She half turned, smiling wickedly before she pulled away. The blond woman wiped her mouth, which bore traces of a darker lipstick.

"I…"

Joey sauntered over to the mirror and leaned against the edge of the sink, right next to me.

"You're Bea's friend," she said, "from the mainland."

I nodded numbly.

She was very close to me. I could smell cigarettes and an undercurrent of unripe fruit, bitter and sweet and dark on her breath. She leaned towards me and I inched backwards, my heart pounding, but she only reached down beneath the sink and pulled out a small silver flask. She shook it a little, giving the blond woman another wicked grin when it sloshed. They both laughed.

Joey unscrewed the top of the flask, her eyes on me as she took a sip and then passed it to her friend.

"Want some?" she asked me. "It's a beautiful bootleg, brewed right here on the island."

It wasn't booze, not gin or some kind of sloe syrup. I could smell it, an acrid hint of herbs buried deep between layers of clove and spice. I backed up, right the way until my elbow hit the bathroom door. Joey took another swallow of the liquid, her eyes going glazed.

I fled.

Chapter Eight

Emmeline

Tonight's party was in full swing by the time I packed up the konjure set, slotting the worn cards into their protective sleeve and smoothing out the grave dirt so that it sat flat in the bottom of the teak box.

Nathan and Isobel were downstairs managing the guests, guiding Ruth and the rest of the staff, hopefully putting money into Sergeant Perry's pockets and kazam into his hands, and otherwise generally making themselves useful. It was handy to have a councilman with a vested interest—especially one with a modicum of humanity who kept the rest of them off our backs.

Isobel normally helped with the preparations and disappeared for the events themselves, but when I'd asked her what time she was slipping off tonight she'd only said, "Nate asked me to help."

I didn't need help. I had it down to a fine art after years of practice with Cilla. But I didn't argue. If Nathan was worried about me, that was all the more reason to act like everything was fine.

I slid the box containing the konjure set under the loose floorboard, resting the piece of wood back in place and pulling the rug over the top. Nathan always joked that if my customers saw this battered old set they'd probably abandon me for greener pastures, maybe a faux seer with a shiny pack full of cards with pictures of naked ancient Greeks on them, but these cards weren't for anybody's eyes except mine.

The top floor of the house was off-limits to the guests, and thanks to one of Isobel's wards it stayed that way. She told me it was because she'd caught some middle-aged banker pawing through her extensive underwear collection once, but it was because none of us could bear the thought of anybody else being up here. Isobel hated being able to hear the full noise—it brought back a lot of memories for her—so the wards were useful for that too.

Besides, this was our space. Ours, and Cilla's.

I stepped out into the dim coolness of the hall, shaken from my reading. The cards had been getting progressively worse over the last few months; ocean waves and black crows, all seen through a strange foggy patina I'd never encountered before. Today was the worst it had been.

I'd seen nothing but darkness and black water, or maybe blood. I told myself that sometimes the cards were like that. Unspecific. They warned and coaxed. Over the years I'd learned not to fight them, but tonight's reading left me with a sour taste in my mouth that was like rot.

Through the wards I could hear the faint sounds of the party below. The music was lively, twanging strings and the off-kilter tinkling of the old piano that Cilla had always hated. It sounded, if you half listened, through the creaks and groans of the old house settling, a bit like the clink of money.

I used the back stairs, fighting against the ache in my body that was worse than yesterday. There was a second kitchen at the back of the house, just in front of the porch, that was used for clients and grabbing a moment of quiet. I found Nathan lingering over the small stove, his jacket draped carelessly over the back of one of the wooden chairs.

He didn't turn around as I entered, but he grabbed a second cup from the collection that lived next to the stove. "Tea?"

I shook my head. Nathan always made the best charmed tea, using fresh ingredients he grew himself in the greenhouse. Sadly, I needed to keep a clear head tonight.

"Isobel's out the front. She said she's got a client to go and see tomorrow, so try to go light on the lovage. We're getting low and she needs some for the next batch of kazam."

"I'm sure she can use any other manner of things instead," I muttered. My clients paid for their magic; Isobel's didn't—apart from the kazam, which *I* sold for her—yet she always ended up with the choicest ingredients.

"She's helping people, Em," Nathan chided. "Don't act spoiled. That's my job."

"Don't give me that. I'm helping people too. They just pay me. And you're the least spoiled person I know, anyhow."

I used the leftover water to make myself a cup of coffee, and we sat on the rickety old chairs together. Nathan leaned his arms on the table and nursed his tea, resolutely avoiding my gaze, a small smile playing on his lips.

"Have you seen her tonight?" I changed the subject. Whatever else he was going to say, I wasn't in the mood for it.

Nathan's smile dimmed as he shook his head. "Not yet."

He didn't say the rest. *Not ever.* He didn't want to upset me. Not when I had guests in the house who would soon be begging for a charm. Not when I was getting weaker every day that she didn't come to me. Nathan knew me better than anybody, and even he couldn't tell how bad it was.

He sipped his tea. The cinnamon scent was strong. Nothing was strange except the feeling inside me—foreboding. I thought of the konjure cards upstairs and my concern grew.

"Nathan," I said. "Did you do something you shouldn't have?"

He finally looked up and grinned again, the playfulness back.

"Maybe, darling. I do a lot of things I'm not supposed to. Who can say what I've done this time?"

"Nathan," I warned.

He leaned back and stretched his arms over his head with the satisfaction of a cat. "All right, all right, I gave your new neighbour her cup back."

"You what? Nathan, I told you I'd send it back myself when the timing was better."

He rolled his eyes.

"Don't worry, I told her not to come to the party."

"Oh, Nathan, I wish you'd asked first. We don't know anything about her. She looks like a mainlander. I haven't got the energy tonight to be worrying about some nervous, old-fashioned girl."

Nathan folded his arms, nonplussed at my moaning. "Haven't you seen her car, darling? She's hardly old-fashioned. She's got cash to burn and the face of an angel. I bet you any money she'll have her glad rags on and be out in five, tops. You're always saying I should be more useful."

"What makes you think she'll come? You *said* you told her not to."

"Well, I did. Although she might...get the wrong idea and come anyway...?"

Frustration burbled inside me. I pushed my coffee away and reached up to my hair, tucking the loose dark strands into the tight plait that kept it off my face. I was sick of fussing with it but hadn't had the nerve to cut it yet. Nathan's face clouded over as he watched my expression, the cheekiness leeching away.

I wasn't sure whether I was more unnerved or angry. He was right, of course. Normally this wouldn't be a big deal. But I couldn't explain about the konjure cards, the swirling darkness of my visions, without worrying him, so I leaned into my annoyance instead.

"Why did you do it *now*?" I demanded. "Why not wait a week like I asked? You never bloody listen to me."

"Would next week truly have been better? You're the one who insists on these hideous parties. I was just trying to give us a bit of fun. And I figured it was a bonus if she turned out to be a paying customer later on. I'm sorry that it didn't fit in with your secret plans."

I scowled at Nathan's back as he stalked out. He knew better than to make a move like this without consulting me first, even if he was right. Even if it was meant to be a bit of fun, some extra cash. The rich ones always made the easiest marks. They wanted things only *real* magic could buy: love, happiness. They had all their money, but they didn't have it all.

It wasn't the money I was thinking of tonight, though. It was the way I'd felt when I saw the neighbour girl, that sensation in my chest, in my belly, in the very deepest parts of me that I still couldn't pinpoint, although I was starting to suspect. I would need to be careful.

"Don't be too hard on him." I heard Isobel's warm voice before I saw her, her hair tamed by a beaded headband and a dress that Cilla would have adored, red silk like roses. She slipped into the light of the kitchen with a smile on her lips, but sadness there too. "He's just trying to look out for you. For us. We both are. You make it very hard for us sometimes."

"I know that, Is," I muttered, fighting the urge to turn away. "I just wish he would talk to me instead of playing tricks. We both know he only invited her because he's hoping I'll fall madly in love and stop pining. He doesn't understand."

Isobel regarded me silently, and I couldn't tell what she was thinking. Where Nathan had become the voice of my conscience over the years, Isobel had tried to morph into my keeper, always trying to mother me where Cilla had failed. Always trying to nurse, to help, to heal. As far as she was concerned, my way of keeping us happy and healthy, well fed and housed long into the future, was the wrong use of our collective gifts.

If she knew how badly I'd fucked it all up, she would be so disappointed.

"You can't control the world, dearest," she said. "You can't think for us, and communication is a two-way street. I know we don't always agree, but that's what it's like, to have a family. We understand each other even when we don't." Her eyes darkened.

"I know," I said. She was wrong, though. I had to control the world, because if I didn't... It didn't bear thinking about.

"Suit yourself," she said. "Just don't get angry at Nate for not being able to read your mind when you're determined to keep us out. Anyway, I'll let you get on with..." She wafted her hands at me, towards the back door, the pillar candles and incense waiting for clients. Then she swiped a stale biscuit from the plate beside the stove and gave me a stern look before finally heading back to the party.

Craving the darkness and the moonlight and the breeze from the ocean, I marched to the door, trying to ignore the magic in my chest that guided me, encouraged me with whisper-soft words, to a conclusion.

Isobel was wrong. I wasn't being unfair. Nathan had made a mistake.

Chapter Nine

Annie

By the next afternoon I could stand my silent cottage no longer, but outside I was little better. As I walked I only turned over again and again that moment in the bathroom: Joey and her companion wrapped together against the wall; Joey's smile as she swallowed whatever concoction waited in that silver flask.

Last night I had been so desperate to get away that I had barely said goodbye to Bea. The shock of seeing such a brazen display of affection, much less one between women, was like a fire that burned deep inside me. Joey's expression as the kazam hit her had consumed my thoughts all night, and the feeling had not abated with the dawn. It had been pure pleasure.

My whole life I had been told that magic was dangerous. It altered your consciousness; it made you act *unnaturally*. Last night, overwhelmed by my fear at the sight of two women together, a further curious tingling brewing inside me, I was terrified that was true.

This morning, though, I wasn't sure. The Joey I had seen in the bathroom, her lips pressed to another woman's neck, had seemed the same as the one I had seen laughing over broken glass. Impetuous, but not unnatural. She had looked confident. Satisfied. What was so dangerous about that?

If Joey had strayed in the bathroom, who was to say that it wasn't simply the booze making her bold? People were more relaxed here when it came to magic, so maybe it was the same with relationships of the same sex. Bea had said Joey was wild, after all.

Surely, I reasoned, the fault lay in the person, not the magic. Bea might grow more chaotic, but she was already fraying; Joey had merely seemed braver in her recklessness. What about me? If I consumed magic, would I become meeker? More of a mouse? Or would I become—bearably closer to being the lion I wished?

The question circled in my head as I walked. Just one taste of kazam—it wouldn't be enough to harm me, to drive me to Joey's wildness, but could it free me of my nerves? What about the self I wished so badly to slough off like a dried-out second skin?

By the time I made it home I was exhausted, my skin sticky with dust from the road and my hair snarled. I made it past the car and onto my lawn before I felt it, the tugging sensation like a fishhook in my chest, sharp and demanding. I peered over my shoulder, my gaze drawn to my neighbour's house.

And there she was. It was the same woman from the porch. The front lawn was peppered with new furniture, crisp white fabric deck chairs and a roughly hewn picnic table decorated with virgin pillar candles for their party tonight. My neighbour stood easily with the man who had brought my errant cup back. She wore a pair of dark men's trousers, loose and belted at the waist, and a white shirt. She had rolled the sleeves up in the heat of the day and pointed to some unseen thing, shading her face with a strong, capable hand.

The tugging in my chest grew, solidified into a cord I sensed rather than saw, bright like polished silver in my mind's eye and running from my heart towards the unknown. My pulse hammered in my ears and I stood, entranced. Her face was hidden by her hand, but I caught the sharp curve of her jaw, the bob of her throat as she laughed. My stomach dipped nervously and the cord in my chest was so strange, so tempting, that with a great effort I tore myself away, stumbling into the cottage and slamming the door behind me.

I remained there in the dim hallway, panting, for a long minute, my pulse slowly returning to normal. I tried to remind myself of Anderson's warning, of the rumours Arthur had mentioned about crows and the police setting her up to fall—but all I could see was her.

———◦•◦———

As night fell the entire front portion of my neighbour's house became illuminated with a million tiny lights, some glowing with electric embers and some of them open flames in small jars. Colourful streamers hung from the trees on the lawn that joined our properties, and people stood and danced underneath them, glasses of fizzing liquor in their hands.

I tugged at the hem of my dress, trying to get it to sit above my ankles as I walked up the long drive. The other guests wore dresses of silk and chiffon in dulcet shades of sapphire and emerald, scandalously short.

I hadn't intended to come. Until half an hour ago I had done my best to think of anything but her, the party, the magic. Yet the alternative thoughts were just as unlike my own, of Joey in the bathroom, dark lipstick on her companion's mouth, her neck. I should stay home and curl up, hide behind my sewing patterns and the book I'd bought with reproductions of famous paintings. But...

But what? It felt foolish to admit that the house had been calling my name since I first saw its weathered grey stone and glittering windows. Since I had heard that first peal of glorious laughter, had seen my neighbour, dressed in men's clothes lounging on her porch. A tiny thought at the back of my mind whispered that when I looked at this place I could almost *taste* magic on my tongue, could feel its promise of transformation humming in my veins. There was just enough of it in the air to make me feel brave.

The party was bold and fearless. Scores of people were packed onto the lawn outside, some lazing in the deck chairs and against the picnic table, the pillar candles lit and their flames flickering so that everything seemed to wink and winnow. Music poured out into the dark night, and somewhere I could hear singing, the voice female but deep and raw.

These guests—they couldn't possibly all be invited, could they? How did my neighbour know so many people? I half expected to be turned away, tossed back to my cottage like a stray cat, but instead I was swept into the melee. A woman wearing an elegant gown the colour of molten silver reached for my hair. "It's so beautiful," she cooed, "like spun gold!" Another seized my shoulder and drew me farther into the throng, thrusting a glass into my hand. It was filled with a ruby liquid, thicker than wine but with that same fruity scent, a tang of anise or cinnamon. It reminded me of my mother's chocolates—or what they had tasted like, a long time ago.

Panic began deep in my chest, in my limbs, but it was a dull ache not unlike a tiredness. The party was so alive, so pulsing with energy, that even as I tried to give the drink back, as I was forced across the lawn and into the house by welcoming arms, urged on by that whispering silver cord inside my chest, I soon forgot to be afraid.

I peered around the first room I came to, a big reception space, with furniture pushed against the walls, where men and women danced, spinning and swirling and jumping to the music that spilled through from the next room.

The glass was still in my hand, held tightly between surprisingly steady fingers. It was just a drink, although it might be laced with more. Could it really be so much worse than Bea's gin cocktails? I thought of Bea, how she'd called me a bore, how she'd begged me to have fun. I thought of Joey, the pleasure on her face. I thought of how I'd turned tail and run away, forever a coward.

Living with my mother, losing Sam: both had made me small-minded, turned me into a mouse, quiet and obedient and lonely and sad, when all I wanted was to be *more*. I wanted to be adventurous. I wanted to be bold. And my father had asked for me to come here, so maybe he had known I needed help. The thought consumed me.

I drank.

An explosion of flavour made me shiver with delight; it was rich wine spiced with cinnamon and clove and an earthy deepness; it was so much more than all of that. I curled my toes as the tension drained from my muscles.

I let the music charm me farther into the room, my cares dropping away with every sip until the drink was gone and the glass had disappeared. What did it matter if I didn't know my father? What did it matter that he was dead and I never would? What did it matter that without Sam I was adrift, used up before I'd begun, and I hadn't loved him right anyway? I was here and the party was good, anonymous and intimate in a way only big parties could be.

The crowd swept me through a ballroom decorated in shades of navy and gold, the grand floor-length windows open to the night. People surrounded me, more people than I'd ever seen, more gold and pearls, jewelled throats and glinting rings, than I'd ever dreamed of. That strange feeling in my chest was growing brighter, sharper in my mind. I noticed it slowly, with a growing awareness that it, not the crowd, was drawing me through the house and out into the gardens, where the party continued, a quieter stretch of lounging couples, blankets laid under the stars.

My feet wandered of their own accord, limbs bewitched until I came to the fountain with its crow-maiden statues I had spied from the beach. I'd seen it when I first saw *her*. I turned, my pulse thrumming, my palms itching, not with fear but with excitement.

And there was the porch. The purple light.

She sauntered into my mind unbidden. Her olive skin, her smooth hair brushed and oiled like a man's. My heartbeat thundered; the roar of the ocean seemed impossibly loud in my ears. I wasn't sure why I was here, why I could think of nothing else but her. This was what I had been warned about, only now I hardly cared.

I climbed the porch steps. There was a breeze, fragrant with an earthy, metallic tang. Like blood and dirt. It sent my carefully coiffed hair back to the wildness it loved best.

My fingers grazed the wooden door. It swung open, smoky darkness greeting me.

And a voice said, "Well, here you are."

———(•)———

The room beyond the door was cast in ghostly relief, shadows stretching as candles guttered. There was a table dressed in a black velvet cloth that sparkled like the night sky, and I could smell the same earthy scent as before. My knees buckled.

It was *her*.

My instinct was to apologise for disturbing her, for coming to the party uninvited. I didn't. I was brave. Powerful and in control as much as my mind and heart were untamed by her presence, like a spell had been cast over me.

"If you're going to stare, at least do it inside," she said. Her voice was gravelly deep.

She moved back towards the table, where she stood with her cigarette dangling from her lips. The fog in my mind began to clear a little, the hammering of my heart slowed, as if her physical presence had made it worse.

As she shifted, my gaze was drawn to the slight swell of her chest under her waistcoat and the strength in her folded arms.

"Do you want to sit?"

I obeyed without thinking, knees folding.

"What's your name?"

My lips were dry and my tongue heavy. I swallowed hard. Seconds later there were two small champagne flutes on the table filled with a pearly liquid that smelled like a fresh summer wind.

"Drink," she said. "It won't hurt you. It's kyraz."

I'd never heard of it, but the wine from earlier had dulled the warning in my brain. The glass was pressed to my lips before I had a chance to consider if this was a mistake, but it tasted even better than it smelled, like a summer meadow on my tongue, fresh like a cold brook and bright like sunlight.

"I'm Annie," I said, a surprising fire in my voice. I belonged here. "Annie Mason. I live next door."

"Hello, Annie Mason," she said, her tongue rolling languidly over the syllables. She drew the second chair from under the table and sat down. The pulling sensation started in my chest again and I tried to fight it back, failing as she pursed her lips thoughtfully. "You're not from around here."

It wasn't a question, and yet an answer tumbled out. "Yorkshire," I blurted. "I'm from Whitby. I'm here for the summer."

There was a magnetism about this woman that made me want to

speak, to tell her everything. I wanted her to know me. I wanted to know her. I wanted her to *want* to know me. She could have asked me to get undressed right there in front of her and I might actually have done it.

The thought sobered me and I unconsciously scooted my chair back, pulling away from her until I could breathe freely again. She smiled, exposing two sharp canines.

"Who are you?" I asked.

She raised an eyebrow and cast her gaze over me appraisingly.

"I'm Emmeline Delacroix. This is my house."

"Is it true?" I asked urgently. "That you can turn into a crow at night? People say you can."

"I don't know," she answered. Then she paused, almost as if she was surprised by her own honesty. Her eyes twinkled with it. "I've never tried."

She watched me for a moment. I was sure she could see every inch of me. Every fear, every wish—the dark parts shone as much as the light.

"It's not a joke," I said. "People say awful things about you. What do you really do here? I've seen the parties. You brew kazam, don't you? It's *illegal*."

"Technically I don't brew it. I just…embellish."

"What if you get into trouble?"

Emmeline threw her head back and laughed, exposing her throat in the same way I'd seen this afternoon. It felt careless.

"I don't get into trouble," she said. "I maybe *make* a little of it, but it's only what people expect. They come to me for desires. That's why you're here, isn't it? Even though you know you shouldn't be?" A sudden coldness swept through me. "What is *your* greatest desire, Annie?"

My skin was flushed. I couldn't wrestle my thoughts. Things about Sam, about my father, Bea, they all tangled inside me.

Adventure, I thought. *I want to be brave like Bea.*

Emmeline smiled, surprise tinging the edges. Almost as if she could see it all on my face.

I couldn't tear my gaze from her lips, from her gem-like eyes, from the sharpness of her cheekbones. I shook my head, pushing the chair farther away, thinking if I could just get some distance I might be able to think clearly again.

"I don't know what you're doing, but I don't like it," I lied. "You're manipulating me. You put magic in my drink to make me feel odd."

"I don't need to manipulate you with kaz—"

Before Emmeline could finish, the door behind her swung wide. The intruder was a young woman wearing an evening dress the colour of rubies. Her black hair was curly, tamed only with a thin beaded headdress, her golden eyes fashionably smudged.

She didn't apologise, just gestured out into the corridor behind her, where sounds of the party were audible. I became aware how quiet it had been in here. How isolated.

How dangerous.

I was the one who had been careless.

"She's here," the woman said urgently. "We only just spotted her. She's totally smoked."

Chapter Ten

Annie

Emmeline stubbed her cigarette out on one of the candles and a plume of sweet-smelling vapour rose to obscure her as she rushed from the room. It was hollow without her, as if she had taken the magic with her. The walls looked dingy and I could make out a stove and other mundane things I hadn't noticed before.

I teetered on the chair, the unsteadiness still within me but fading fast. She had bewitched me. She must have. Whatever intoxication had drawn me here, it had clouded my senses so I could see nothing but her, think of nothing but her. I had almost lost control of everything. I had liked it.

I should leave. I should escape out the back door and along the beach to the safety of my little cottage. Who knew what magic Emmeline had wrought to make me so dazzled by her? Leaving was the sensible thing to do.

It was what Annie Mason from Whitby would do.

I didn't want to leave, though. The longer I sat here, the better I felt. If I ran, I would be the old me. I didn't have to be that woman anymore. There was no Mam here. No Sam. And I had so many questions still to ask, so much more I wanted to know. There was anger in me, and fear, but this curiosity was like a shock of freezing water down my back. I made it into the hallway and paused. I wasn't sure which way Emmeline and the other woman had gone, or whether it was safe to follow them.

I caught a whiff of freshly turned dirt and I followed it without thinking, the *thing* in my chest singing. Distantly—impossibly—if I closed my eyes, if I concentrated, I knew I would be able to pluck it by thought alone. I didn't dare rest on what it was, whether Emmeline felt it too, whether she had made me feel this way. So I followed my heart.

The cord led me back to the ballroom, to a door that opened just beneath a balcony where countless guests drank and danced and glittered under the electric lights in their ornate chandelier.

I paused again. There was a reason Emmeline had rushed off—and it had nothing to do with me. And yet...My eyes searched the crowd; I didn't have to look long or hard before I saw her.

I watched as, on the other side of the room, she darted from the throng of dancers below the balcony stairs, stopping only when she was pulled back by the woman in red. Emmeline cut a stunning figure, her sleeves rolled and her dark hair slicked away from her face. If you didn't know better, you might mistake her for a man. A rich man who owned everything in this place.

She seemed different out here, away from me. Was her behaviour around me meant to tease? Was it a game? I knew what people like Arthur and Anderson would say, that she was trying to trick me, to hurt me, but that wasn't how it felt. She had seemed as surprised at her own openness as I was.

I ducked back beneath the curve of the stairs as Emmeline's dark gaze shot past me. I wasn't sure what it was that made me stay and watch, but as I stood there my vision began to blur. My heart thundered and I clenched my fists.

Mam had always called moments like these my *panics*, said they were a kind of hysteria because I was so anxious all the time. She said they were a hangover from nearly drowning when I was too young to remember it—the same thing that drew me to the ocean at night sometimes when I dreamed. I couldn't explain the roaring sound, the waves and the darkness inside my head, any other way. I'd become so skilled at pushing the dizziness down, forcing it away until there was nothing left, that I no longer wondered what caused it.

On the island it was different. It came with a flapping of wings, impossible to ignore, and I knew in my bones that Mam was wrong. I did not feel hysterical. This time, instead of pushing it away I breathed slowly, keeping my eyes open wide.

I scanned the crowd on the balcony that had drawn Emmeline's eye. Several young women had taken their shoes off and were dancing with their skirts hitched up around their thighs. A musician cradled a broken violin, laughing with a kind of mania that could only be kazam induced. And there, amidst the chaos, was Bea.

I hardly recognised her.

My oldest friend wore a dress of midnight blue that was barely long enough to be decent. She had piled her red curls up on top of her head, and they swayed as she lolled against a man who absolutely, definitely wasn't her husband.

Her skin was flushed, her eyes so glassy they might as well have belonged to a puppet. Everything about her was wrong. This was kazam, but it was more too. The roaring in my ears grew.

She told me she hadn't been to any of Emmeline's parties. Had she lied? After her gathering, seeing Joey in the bathroom with a hidden flask of bootleg kazam, hearing the story of her friend who had been arrested for the same, I no longer knew Bea well enough to say.

She stumbled against the weedy man. Her knees buckled and the glass of purple-stained liquid in her hand hit the floor and smashed.

It was like the world jumped into motion. Emmeline yanked her arm free of the woman in red and launched herself towards the stairs, loping up them two at a time. She reached Bea in seconds. It was clear from Emmeline's face that this wasn't just worry about her public image, some drunk girl dancing with a stranger; they knew each other. More than that.

Bea reached blindly for somebody, groping until she found

Emmeline. There was a moment of recognition in Bea's eyes as the older woman grabbed her arm, seconds of warmth followed by a glimmer of fear. She struggled to her feet, knees skating on the broken glass as she tried to stumble away.

"You can't!" she yelped. I heard it over the music, clear as a bell. "I need you to help—"

Emmeline didn't let go of Bea's arm.

"*I didn't think you*—"

Emmeline's voice was raw. The pain on her face was unmissable. Bea closed her eyes, shutting it all out. I started to move, a desire to protect Bea, to stop Emmeline, or maybe to help her, driving me on. I made it to the third step before I shrank back.

Because there, without warning, was Arthur. He was on the stairs Emmeline had just left, moving for the balcony, his golden hair shining and his snarl like a wolf's, so different from the charming man I had met.

I stumbled backwards, fear taking hold. I wanted to run, to flee like I had last night. But I couldn't leave without being sure Bea was all right.

Arthur reached Bea's side. He shoved Emmeline away. She resisted but the force was enough to throw her off-balance. She let go of Bea's arm.

"Don't you *dare* touch…" Arthur said, the rest of his words engulfed by the music, which was untamed by the confrontation, the sounds of the party rolling on more raucous than before.

Bea's face paled as Arthur's hands landed on her shoulders. She tried to run for the stairs, but he held on to her with ease. Her hand was a fist at her side.

"…you not to come here." He gazed at his wife, sadness quenching his anger for a moment before it morphed into disgust. She flinched, pulling her face away from his.

"You can't control her." Emmeline's voice rang over the din. She squared herself up to him, shoulders back, and she was every bit the man he was. *Danger*, my body whispered. "Get out of my house."

"Why, so you can disgrace her further?…is *disgusting*. I know what you are. What you do to girls like her…" Arthur's words were swallowed.

Emmeline laughed. I noticed that she did not expose her throat to him. She flicked her attention to Bea, who shied away, and her expression hardened.

"Bea," she said. The word was brimming with power. "You are brave. Don't let him scare you. I need you to do it, now—"

"Don't be a fool," Arthur snapped, recovering himself long enough to yank Bea towards him again. "Don't let her corrupt you."

Bea swayed between the two of them, her skin taking on a green tint. She looked like she wasn't sure whether she wanted to cry or vomit. Then she turned towards her husband.

It unfolded before me in slow motion, Bea's hand flowering, a shard of broken glass from her spilled kazam glinting wickedly in her palm as she lifted it up. Up, towards her husband's arm. Her face was slack; she hardly knew what she was doing.

The glass was jagged. I wanted to run to them, to shout, but it wouldn't help.

Bea lashed out, the glass slicing clean through Arthur's shirt. He jumped back, surprise and anger blossoming on his face as a faint red line appeared across his pristine sleeve. Emmeline inhaled sharply.

"Beatrice," Arthur said, and it was a warning. The music, the party, melted away. "Put that down and come with me. *Now.*"

He raised his fist. Just enough to be deliberate. Bea baulked, her whole body going rigid as she glanced between Emmeline and Arthur.

The spell broke.

Bea turned back to her husband, her whole body limp and docile. The piece of glass in her hand fell to the floor. Without another word Arthur led her away, down the stairs, holding her hand as you would a child's. I followed Bea through the oblivious crowd with my gaze. I wanted to go after her, but embarrassment held me fast. My own, and hers. It wasn't my place. And I doubted she would want to talk while she was in this state.

When she was gone I looked back. Emmeline remained rooted to the same spot—but she was looking right at me.

I stumbled away, through the ballroom and the puzzling maze of the house I no longer wanted to solve. I didn't stop until I reached my cool kitchen, where I leaned over the sink panting. I guzzled two glasses of clear, cold water, but I could still taste the earthy, bloody scent of Emmeline's kitchen. I drank more, until I was sober and myself again.

Here, finally, was the wash of fear I should have felt earlier, tight and cold in my bones. Whatever had happened tonight between Bea and Arthur, it had been big. I had never seen Bea act like that before. The way she had lashed out with the broken glass scared me almost as much as the way his face had changed, morphed so easily into rage. I returned to my earlier questions about Arthur and Bea, about their marriage. It seemed like I had been right to wonder.

My neighbour was involved in this somehow—and I was almost certain it was because of magic. I thought of Mam's warnings during the war; there had been stories of spells to guide bullets, a blight on the crops on the French border, and darker tales of a malice that left our men, at least those who survived, hollow-eyed at magic's mere mention. It wasn't just a party favour.

I had been foolish, so eager to be like Bea and her friends that I'd forgotten every rule, every cautionary tale my mother had ever told me. Yet I couldn't pretend I had not seen what had occurred tonight. Bea was my best friend in all the world, and I had already failed her once, so wrapped up in myself that I'd let her go. I wasn't about to let it happen again.

I crossed to the kitchen door, looking out over the black ocean and the sweeping expanse of dark sky. But the way I felt wasn't just about Bea. I was bewitched, too, by the memory of Emmeline's throat as she threw her head back and laughed, of that tugging sensation deep inside my chest that had drawn me to her. What kind of magic could do that? I had felt the thread form, shining and silver, before I'd touched a drop of Emmeline's concoctions.

I watched a crow fly across the waning moon, felt the cold air raise gooseflesh on my bare skin. Tonight should have scared me, and I'd be lying if I said it hadn't, but in the dark stillness of the night I could admit something else: despite everything, the magic and the danger all tangled together, a part buried way down inside me liked the way Emmeline made me feel.

Chapter Eleven

Emmeline

Dawn was just dusting the sky pink as I crawled out the window to sit on the roof outside my bedroom. Idly I wondered how many more sunrises I'd see. I pulled my knees to my chest and counted as seven crows fluttered to land on the lawn, picking worms in the grass. There was one in particular that was larger than the others. I had seen her before. Normally she was alone. I had considered often whether she was like me—better off when she couldn't hurt anybody else.

"I thought I'd find you counting the crows again."

Isobel's head popped through the open window behind me. She no longer wore her party dress and looked like she'd slept a little too. It was unusual to see her before noon since she usually slept late after the parties, plagued—I suspected, though she never said—by bad dreams. Last night it had been me lying awake until the sun rose, thoughts spinning, skin marble cold as my blood turned to dirt in my veins. I wondered if seeing her had made it worse, or whether it was simply being one day closer to the end.

I couldn't say any of that to Isobel, so I gave her a small smile. "You're up early," I said.

"I was worried about you, dearest." Isobel's golden eyes caught the dim light as the sun began to crest on the horizon. She waited for me to tell her to go back to bed, and when I didn't she clambered out onto the narrow roof to join me, an unspoken promise between us not to nitpick before breakfast. "And I promised I would go and visit Hilda early—her daughter is unwell again. I said I'd take the same broth as last time, with the milk thistle and thyme."

Isobel settled onto the roof beside me, dangling her long legs over the edge. Not for the first time I wondered what she would do when I was gone, whether she would stay here and keep nursing in this same small way, or whether she would leave and discover she had wings.

"I know last night didn't go how you intended it to," she said, turning towards me. "Is it really so bloody awful, though? You look...defeated."

I fought the urge to laugh. If only she knew how urgent it was. I thought about the way Bea had slashed at her husband with that piece of glass. She had really intended to hurt him. The way my magic had coiled, viperous and eager, as I recalled the bloom of his blood. We were running out of time.

"It's over, love," I said. "Last night was a mistake. I don't think she'll come back." Nathan had been on the other side of the property when she left. So, once again, we had no idea where she'd gone after she fled Cross House. We could find her, I was sure, but the goal was the same as always. This had to be on her terms, and I was fast running out of options.

Bea wasn't the only thing on my mind this morning. There was also the question of my new neighbour. Who was she, really? I considered the way it had seemed, in the smoky dimness of my kitchen, as if some lightness in her had seen—truly *seen*—the darkness in me. And she hadn't been afraid.

I also thought of the sensation that had piled into me when she was close. At first, it had seemed a fluke, a strange trick of my senses as my magic drained away. Seeing her last night, watching as she reacted to my proximity and I was swept up in hers, I was convinced she felt it too, an intoxicating thing. A dangerous thing.

"The blond girl," I said to Isobel eventually. "Do you know what happened to her after the party?"

"The one you were with? No. She left after your scene with Bea. I think we frightened her off."

"Good," I said, rubbing my hands over my face. Relief washed through me, chased by unexpected sadness. "She wasn't supposed to be here. She's—the new neighbour."

"Ohh," Isobel teased. "Are you saving her for later? Nate said you were mooning—"

"No." I shook my head firmly, picking at the corner of a loose tile by my knee. "She shouldn't come back here. She's not like the other clients. She's..." I didn't know how to explain the feeling I'd had from the moment I saw her—of connection, yes, but also of unease. There was a word for it, but I couldn't find it. "She's innocent."

"That won't last long," Isobel said grimly. "The island will get her eventually. All that money, the kazam...People can't resist it, can they? It's like the crows call to them. There must be more witches on this island than anywhere else in Europe—Cilla was right about that. If the girl's got any magic in her blood, she'll be back."

"That's the point, Is," I muttered. "I don't care what Cilla said; I don't want that innocent girl in this house. She'd be better off forgetting all about us like the rest of the witches who walked these halls. If she comes back I'll only end up being responsible for ruining her too."

My finger slipped, the soft skin slicing open on the corner of the jagged tile. Blood welled. A surge of pain flared through me, my magic twisting, vying for release. I clenched my teeth against the tang of spilled blood, a rumbling echo somewhere beneath me as the tiles underneath us began to tremble. Tiny sharp chips of mortar rained to the ground far below.

Isobel gripped the roof.

I thrust my finger into my mouth, sucking it dry. I held it there until the twisting under my skin stopped, the need to maim, to destroy. Until the bitter anger faded and the world settled.

Isobel's eyes were wide, a little of that old childhood fear of blood magic in her expression. Her parents had taught her what mine had not. As far as Isobel was concerned, it was an accident that was still waiting to happen. I turned away until all I could see was trees and ocean and sky.

"We don't take in strays anymore, right?" I said calmly, holding in the wave of hopelessness that threatened to drown me. "Those were your words. The girl doesn't belong here." It felt like a lie, even as Isobel nodded cautiously, even as I added, "Magic could be dangerous for her."

"Magic is dangerous for all of us," Isobel murmured. "It's saved us, though. Sometimes."

I glanced over. A fresh shadow passed over her face, and I knew she was thinking about her parents. They'd been dead over eight years, and yet their memory hounded her. Just like Cilla's did. I would plague her one day too, and the thought made me cold. All the more reason to keep it to myself, at least until I couldn't hide it any longer. I wanted to give her time to build a life, so maybe when I was gone it wouldn't shatter again.

"It wasn't magic that saved us," I said quietly. It hadn't saved Isobel's mother and father on the moors, hadn't saved my aunt. It hadn't saved Cilla, only ruled her until it had drained her dry. And it hadn't saved us when we were children. It had always meant for us to save ourselves.

Isobel lapsed into silence, and my thoughts strayed back to the neighbour girl. To *Annie*. Her presence had sparked a fire in me, and as much as what I'd said to Isobel was true, I wanted to experience it again—if only to be sure. But it couldn't be...I had to be wrong.

By the time Nathan turned up the day was bright. He came bearing coffee, one dosed with cinnamon. He passed the other two cups out to us and stood in the window.

"Mucked last night up, didn't we, darlings?"

"The cards were an omen," I muttered darkly. After all these months, more than a year of waiting and scrying, I'd had Bea and her husband right in my goddamn house and I had ruined it. "I don't know why I didn't listen to them. And, for the record, Nathan, I knew I wasn't being spoiled when I told you off."

I wriggled my fingers experimentally, but everything hurt as much as it had earlier this morning. The Giving was getting closer every hour. I could put it off for a day, maybe more, but it would cost me.

"Honestly, Em, I still don't understand why you didn't force her to hear you out," Isobel said tiredly. "Instead of all of this pining. You don't need much from her, right? Just enough to balance the spell. A drop or two to smooth things out. She owes us that much after everything we gave her."

I didn't answer, afraid to speak in case she could hear the lie. It was so much worse than she knew. Nathan, I suspected, had a better idea, but he was being remarkably quiet this morning.

"Wait," I said. "Why do you look like you've got a secret? Did you sense Bea? Nathan, I swear, if you're playing another trick on me..."

Nathan just rocked back on his heels, ever the tease. If he wasn't my brother in all but blood—and if he wasn't so damn cheeky—I'd have lost my temper with him a long time ago.

"Oh, for goodness' sake, Nate," Isobel grumbled good-naturedly. "*Spill*, will you? I'm already sick of looking at your smug face, and Em's brassed off enough as it is without you driving her to slap you."

Nathan puckered his lip, pretending to be hurt. Isobel reached through the window with the speed of a cobra and smacked him lightly on the chest. He chuckled. She was the only person who could get away with touching him like that. Others were too much for him, just the mere suggestion of another human making contact with his skin could make him flinch, but he once told me that Isobel was different. "I can't explain it," he'd said. "Except that she's gentle. She feels like warm rain."

"Nathan," I pressed, "*did* you sense anything about Bea?"

Nathan could blend into the world like a shadow, a combination of magic and instinct that he'd spent a lifetime honing; he might have made a perfect spy if not for his remarkably robust conscience. He, or his magic, saw things in people—things they thought they could hide if they didn't say them aloud. He knew how to listen.

"No, but I've not been entirely useless," he said finally, smiling triumphantly. "That darling neighbour girl? The one *you* didn't want here."

I tensed. "What about her?"

"She saw what happened, didn't she?"

"Yes," I snapped impatiently. "So what? Half the room watched Bea cause a scene."

"I followed her afterwards. I figured the aim was getting Bea back here—organically. And I could sense it on the neighbour girl without getting close. It was all over her, the panic—the worry."

"Nathan, get to the point."

"That is the point. She *cared*, darling." He leaned out the window, his hands pressed against the frame and his biceps flexing for Isobel's benefit. "She saw what happened and she cared about it."

"I thought you said she didn't know anybody here," Isobel pointed out. "That's why you—uh, didn't officially invite her to the party."

"That's what she said," Nathan agreed, "and she's obviously a long way from home. But, Em, she knows *them*. She must be close to one of them. Maybe she can get Bea to come back."

The new cut on my finger was already gummy, and I resisted the urge to pick at it. If I could just talk to Bea for long enough to convince her to pay what she owed, there was a chance it wasn't over for me yet.

If I could get Annie to help me.

What if she wouldn't? Without Annie's help, after last night there was no way Bea would give me the time to explain. She didn't know how bad it was, had no idea how desperate I was—but maybe Annie could change that.

What if Annie needed persuading? Normally it wouldn't bother me. I'd give her a dose of camphor and dragon's blood resin, just a gentle nudge to lubricate her will, and think little of it. Except… there was an edge to her that made me stop and think.

I wondered, just for a second, if I could use this thing between us that heightened every sensation in me when she was close. I wondered if I could let it run wild so that she would feel compelled to help me—if I *should*, but also if I wanted to.

Well, either way, I could be persuasive.

The Fool

Emmeline

Last spring

I wasn't expecting an early client today. I'd been up late, exhausted myself trying to help a man who had fallen in love with his best friend's wife. He had come to me for a love-renewal potion towards his own wife, which he was sure would set him back on his life's true path.

"She's all I can think about," he'd begged. "I don't want this. I don't want her. Please, I need to stop thinking of her. I just want my wife—only my wife."

I had brewed my magic for him on the spot—three bright drops of blood in the mixture—and sent him off to his home when the night was at her thickest. I assumed I might be able to sleep late into the morning, but dark thoughts kept me awake until well after dawn, when I finally gave up on sleep and dragged myself into the kitchen.

The drop-ins nearly always came under cover of night, as they had for Cilla. They waited patiently for us to light the purple lamp, the rumours of our practice having long spread beyond the island. This morning's client had either not heard of the lamp—or she didn't want to wait.

The knock was hesitant.

Nathan had been reading the morning paper and smoking a skinny cigarette he'd made with some fragrant thyme. At the sound of the door he gathered his things and left me alone in the little kitchen.

I rolled up the sleeves of my shirt, smoothed back my hair, and opened the door, catching a rush of spring-smelling air. The wet-grass smell melded perfectly with the bright green of her eyes, which were dry but red-rimmed. She had a swathe of hair, knotted from its pins by the island wind, and wore a grey dress and straw hat that made her look very young.

Her gaze, however, was world-weary. I guessed she was around twenty, maybe a little older, possibly from one of the small fishing villages on the mainland.

"You'd better come in."

I settled her at the kitchen table with the cloth Isobel had made for Cilla. It was designed to look like a night sky, complete with constellations that Isobel had seen on the long nights aboard her ship from Spain as a child. The young woman splayed a hand over the tablecloth in awe.

A knot formed in the pit of my stomach. This was the cry for help that I'd learned to feel the echo of in my bones. I watched her as I poured another cup of coffee for myself and one for her. She was cautious but curious too, her eyes wide, drinking in the watery March light.

"Is it true what they say about you?" she asked.

"What do they say?"

"That you can fix things." Her eyes ran the length of me, taking in my shirt, my trousers, Nathan's old things that Isobel had helped me take in. They made me feel powerful. A lot of people didn't like that I wore them, but I had stopped caring. Soon I was going to buy new ones, made especially for me. The girl only flicked her gaze back to my face. "That you're not like other women."

I sipped my coffee, purposefully taking my time in answering so she knew that I meant what I said.

"I'm exactly like other women," I said. "That is why they're afraid of me."

The girl hid a smile behind calloused fingers. She didn't come from money, not with that accent, but the calluses looked new.

"What about fixing things?" she asked. "Are they wrong about that too?"

This time I mimicked her smile.

"It depends what kind of things."

Her own smile faltered and the ghost of sadness returned. She wrapped her hands around the cup of coffee and leaned into the table as though she wanted to tell me—was dying to—but she shivered and sat back again.

"I can't."

If it had been anybody else I would have tossed them out onto the doorstep. We didn't have time. If we weren't with clients, Nathan and Isobel and I spent our time concocting. Isobel was a dab hand with the brews, but most kazam took a long time to produce if you did it properly. This was our world, not Cilla's, and we weren't done building it yet. The foundations were there but they had to be strong; I needed to build them—us—a future.

Still, this girl held my interest.

"Don't talk about that," I said. "Tell me about yourself instead."

The girl shook her head.

"Not even your name?"

Her mouth rounded into a little O shape.

"Sorry. I'm Beatrice," she said. "Bea."

"Where are you from, Bea?"

"I…"

I rested my hands in my lap, waiting. Cilla had taught me that silence could be a useful tactic.

"Yorkshire," Bea said eventually. "My mother owns a tea shop. I've never been here before. I heard about you and I thought…" She glanced around my kitchen, rubbing at her face. "I thought it would be different."

"Crow Island is a summer haunt. The islanders are a quieter bunch."

Quieter, but no less troubled. The problems were subtly different since the war, but they had the same flavour. Charms for lost love, a concoction for a little boy who refused to talk since his daddy died. Yesterday I had seen a girl who reminded me of Isobel, young and bright and fierce at heart, who wanted a spell to make her less tired so she could help her husband, who'd lost both legs and one arm in France. I did what I could.

"I can't help you if you don't talk to me," I said.

"I know."

She glanced out the window over the lawn. You could just see the corner of the fountain and through the trees the gentle blue of the sky where it met the ocean.

"Do you need somewhere to stay?"

It would break every rule we had. Isobel would be furious with my hypocrisy, especially after I'd told her that her nursing was better done out of the house. Yet I couldn't turn her away; it was like fate, somehow. Isobel always said it felt good when she helped people for free.

Bea's face crumpled with relief and a little dry sob broke out of her, startling me.

Perhaps this was to be my retribution for what I had done. For Cilla.

———( ) ● ( )———

The second week in April there was a heat wave. The island was flocked by newcomers, the beaches packed with filthy-rich families who had nothing better to spend their money on than enchanted bathtub gin and ice cream.

Customer after customer waited in the darkness for the purple light. I slept little and ate less, my blood singing with the charms I crafted late into the night. Love, loss, betrayal; the island bred them all, and it was my job to fix them. There were only two rules: if anybody official asked, the magic wasn't real; and if the spell didn't work, if the unfaithful lover grew too attentive, too possessive of a client after they applied my charm, or if their newfound wealth seemed to cause them nothing but strife, they could not say I hadn't warned them.

Isobel said it was reckless, that people weren't prepared for the results, but the money was good, and after Cilla...

At least I gave people fair warning.

Sunday came and it was the hottest day. That evening there was to be a pop-up fair on the beach on the backbone, carousels and circus acts, candy floss and toffee apples.

"You need a night off," Bea said over breakfast.

She still hadn't told me why she was here. She was an expert liar, mostly by omission. Nathan couldn't get a read on her at all. He sensed loss, but neither of us thought it was a love spell she'd come for. Her predicament had the sense of an unwanted beginning, not an ending.

I had slept maybe two hours last night and they could all tell. I started to roll my eyes, but Isobel nodded in agreement. Bea and Isobel rarely agreed.

"God forbid, dearest, but I think that's a swell idea. There will be plenty of trouble to fix tomorrow night. Why don't we go to the fair?"

Nathan stood in the doorway smirking. "I thought you hated clowns, darling."

Isobel fought a grimace. "I'd kill for a toffee apple, and you know how much I love candy floss and bright lights and watching silly sods like you trying to win the ring toss."

There was a lightness in the house with Bea here, although Nathan and Isobel pretended they didn't notice. Her quiet softness had beguiled them as much as it had me. We spoke more, laughed more. We were like a proper family.

"I haven't been to a fair since the armistice," Bea said. She was deep in thought, tugged by some memory, and her smile faltered.

"I haven't either," Nathan said, "so I for one am in favour of going, just so we can see what Isobel does with a clown chasing her across the Spine."

As the day stretched into evening we packed up a basket filled with bread and cheese and three stoppered carafes of Isobel's latest kyraz experiment—strong and fruity with a velvety chocolate bite—that we'd bottled that morning, and set out in Cilla's old yellow car, Nathan doing a fine job of keeping it on the road.

The Spine was a long stretch of beach that ran right from the northern point to the southern part of the crescent, walled away from the rest of the island by low hills. Visitors often claimed that the faux magic gave the island a brightness that the mainland didn't have, and they were right. Of course, there wasn't anything *faux* about some of the magic. Cilla told me once that the soil, the island itself, was prehistoric. It was full of old energy, and that was why witches had always felt at home here.

At the fairground children ran in the sand in their Sunday best; girls in white dresses wore ribbons on their beautiful hats. I thought of Cilla's crowded great room during the war, wondered how many of these young men were here today because their fathers had paid for their futures in blood.

It was strange to see Bea out of Cross House. She was different here than she ever was in our dark hallways. She rejoiced at the sand in her shoes and her hems, and she sloughed off that final bewildered, sad part of herself. Her face was open—more beautiful, if possible, than before—as if by being here, by pretending to be happy for this one day, she finally could be. As we walked I noticed other things, things I had ignored in the safety of my home: the way she held her shoulders back as she moved; the graceful, pale curve of her neck; how her lips looked, soft and rose-pink, when she murmured my name.

Seeing her like this, the joy it gave me, made my heart tumble as I understood that what I wanted from Bea was not just friendship. Despite her sadness she had brought fun to our family, joy we hadn't known we could have. When she saw the Ferris wheel on the pier she grabbed hold of my hand in excitement. The warm calloused pressure made my heart tremble.

Nathan and Isobel ran ahead, whooping like children. Nobody stared at me as we passed. I had opted for a white summer suit, my first not to belong to Nathan before me, and an open-necked shirt. My hair was oiled and plaited, a hat on my head keeping the sun off my face. I kept my chin level, my free hand in my pocket, maintaining a leisurely pace as Bea pulled me towards the pier. I could have been anybody, any rich man or woman, quietly powerful and invisible in plain sight. When I was with her, her beauty was all people saw, and nobody looked at me twice.

Nathan and Isobel waited with whipped ice creams enough for all of us, and tickets for the wheel. Then they slipped away, presumably to find those clowns that didn't scare Isobel. When Bea and I were alone, she grew pensive as we waited for our turn. I had become used to her shifts in mood, so I remained quiet. Already the sadness had seeped back in, bled around the edges of her excitement, until I could hardly breathe, waiting for what was to come.

We were settled in our seats, the wheel moving glacially and lifting us up into the balmy summerlike air. The chair was a tight fit, and Bea's thigh was right against the length of mine. She stared out over the grey-blue ocean, her red hair floating loose from its knot under her hat. Her teeth worried at her lip.

"Em…"

"It's all right, Bea." I didn't know exactly what she was going to say, but I didn't want to hear it. Just the way she said my name was full of sadness, and I wanted to think of her happy again. Then she sighed again and leaned against me.

"I have to tell somebody. I can't keep it in anymore."

I took a breath of salt-and-sugar-scented air.

"I can fix it," I said. "If that's what you want. There are risks, but…"

"I want to be free."

I'd only known this girl for a month, knew little about her life except that she had a trick for falling for the wrong men. But I could help her—and Cilla never would have.

That was all I needed to know.

———⟨●⟩———

On the night everything ended, only a week after the sun had scorched us on the beach, there was a storm. The snow fell and the four of us huddled together in the great room.

Isobel and Nathan favoured this room because they had never been in here with Cilla. They'd never had to sit and rub her feet or watch as she held court with her clients, the men she seduced into believing magic could solve everything.

I never told the others that this was where some of the worst nights of my life had been spent, fire burning and wax scalding and blood twisting as she taught me how to make people want—no, *need*—you forever.

Bea had grown more withdrawn since the fair. Isobel didn't notice, and Nathan pretended not to, but the change fractured us all the same.

The storm howled outside. The smoke from the fire was fragrant and hot. We hadn't cleaned the chimneys since Cilla, had actually been afraid to invite people in to figure out how. The house had held power with her here. Now it was just a house.

"I'm already sick of the cold." Isobel stretched her arms above her head and yawned. "I'm going to bed. Maybe I'll dream up a way to con the weather into giving us a break before Nathan cries over his garden again."

It was a bad joke—entirely unfunny because she'd done it once before.

We never spoke of it directly, but a long time ago Cilla had brought Isobel to the house in chains. She had come from the moors, where she'd been living off berries and rabbits she caught with her hands, her magic wound tight inside her like a snake. Cilla had said Isobel could not come inside until she was clean and obedient. She meant for the girl to wash using the bucket and soap provided. Instead, Isobel had hunkered down in the mud, closed her eyes, and began to carve intricate patterns in the dirt with her nails. The heavens had opened in a burst of hot summer rain that washed the muck from her face and flattened her beautiful black hair to her skull. Later, she had confessed that she didn't know how she had done it.

"I just wanted it," she said. "The runes were a channel, I think. My parents... Anyway, I've tried again, and—nothing."

No matter how hard Cilla tried, Isobel wouldn't—couldn't—do it again.

"I won't use blood," she said. "Not unless it's life or death. It's too easy to do it wrong."

Isobel never talked about her parents. Sometimes, if you pushed her too hard, she would disappear for days and return wild. Once, Cilla whipped her when she found her in the pantry with her mouth around a skinned baby rabbit, lips bloody and dress ruined.

The moors were haunted, and we learned not to ask.

Isobel and Nathan went to bed, and Bea sighed, her hands clutched in her lap. Just her and me, and the wind howling outside.

"You know once we do this there's no going back."

Bea narrowed her eyes. "Yes," she said. "You've told me. I know it's dangerous. But *you* know what you're doing. I just want this over—before…" She didn't finish the thought. We'd brewed the mixture already so she didn't have to labour the point.

"You can't tell anybody about it," I reminded her. "If you tell anybody—it's my life that's at stake. This sort of magic…"

Crow Island was more accepting of magic than the rest of the world, but this was beyond love charms and posies; this wasn't enchanted booze or the promise of a good time. Spells like this were how witches ended up dead at the end of a rope.

I thought of my aunt, flashes of our last minutes together coming unbidden. Cold floorboards underfoot in the middle of the night, torches and baying dogs in the distance; Rachel's capable hands shoving me out the door and her hoarse, urgent voice as she whispered, *They cannot have you, love. You must run.*

If anybody found out about this…But no, Bea wasn't like those women, the ones my aunt had helped. The ones who had betrayed her.

Bea shrugged. "Who would I tell?"

I retrieved the solution from the kitchen. It was a murky brown and smelled like rotting leaves; like death, ripe and heavy. For the first time fear really hit me. I remembered the ingredients that Aunt Rachel had used—or, I thought I did. I had had to make a couple of substitutions. Was it right?

"Is it ready?"

Bea sat on the overstuffed damask sofa by the fire. She'd changed into a nightdress that Isobel had given her. It had belonged to Angelica once and it was too long. Bea almost looked like a ghost. I blinked the image away.

"Almost, I think."

I carried the glass to the fire and sat on my haunches while I drew out a small knife. I'd carved the candles already with the few runes my aunt had taught me. Protection, healing, balance. I lifted the knife to the fleshy part of my thumb, felt the familiar bite as the blood began to well.

My magic unfurled from its secret place. Bea's face paled as she watched me squeeze a drop of blood into the mixture. Slowly it changed colour, not to red but to a dark grey-black. I hadn't expected this, but I reined in my nerves. It would be fine.

"It's the only way I know how to do it," I explained. My aunt had died before she had been able to teach me the correct incantations, and Cilla hadn't believed in them. My blood was strong enough. "You have to understand that I don't know if it will work. I've never done this before."

"I need it to be over," she said.

Bravely Bea offered me her hand, and I used the knife to slice the tip of her index finger too. Her blood was bright, and she added a single drop to the mixture.

She reached for the glass.

The snow had stopped falling. Wind gusted through the cracks in the walls, sucking the curtains so the brocade danced like dark spirits.

A wave of intuition made me snatch at the glass. My blood throbbed in my palm, the magic curdling in a way I'd never felt before.

"Wait—"

Too late. Bea had already swallowed the mixture down.

Chapter Twelve

Annie

Monday morning I forced down a breakfast of milky tea with a sprinkle of sugar, though I hardly felt like it, and headed out to my father's house on the northern point of the island. I'd almost forgotten about my meeting with Mr. Anderson, had woken instead with a pit of dark worry over Bea in my belly that consumed all other thoughts. I hoped she had made it home safely, that Arthur was not too angry with her. I debated, again, if it would be my place to telephone and see how she was. She might not want to talk to me, and I didn't want to upset her. She might not even remember it, and that was a small mercy I would not deprive her of if it was true.

I did not allow myself to dwell on the darkest of my worries. I ignored the quiet yet insistent voice that reminded me of Arthur's expression, which had been beyond anger. I told myself that if Bea needed me urgently she knew where I was, and for now I would give her some space. It had probably been a blip. Just a lapse in judgement. Bea always had lived on the edge of temptation.

Once I was out in the greyness of the day, I was glad for the distraction from my circling thoughts. The streets near my father's house were exactly as I expected. The houses were huge, with grand columns like Bea's or built in the Victorian style with extravagant front porches and long, elegant windows.

Although I was half an hour early, Mr. Anderson was already waiting for me outside my father's house. He wore another well-tailored suit and grasped my hands warmly in his. I managed only a wan smile, though I was glad to see him.

"Good morning, Miss Mason," he enthused. "It's nice to see you again. Did you manage to make it to the museum yet? You've probably been having far too much fun."

"Oh," I said. "No, I haven't had time. I, uh, have been getting reacquainted with an old friend." It wasn't a lie, and yet this half-truth seemed to twist on my tongue. Would a true friend have stood idly by last night?

"Ah, lovely. Well, here we are. I haven't been inside since the funeral, as per your father's requests. Are you sure you're ready?"

He waited for me to nod before beckoning for me to follow him up the front steps, which were crafted from a chalky stone that Anderson explained was native to the island.

"It's perhaps the thing it's known best for, ah, aside from the crows, that is." It didn't escape my notice how Anderson skirted around the island's reputation when it came to magic. He certainly hadn't shown the same reserve about Cross House.

"What keeps the crows here?" I asked. "Don't they move on in the winter?"

"No, no. They're as much a part of the island as the stone." Anderson pulled a bundle of keys from his jacket pocket and began to sort through them. The jangling startled one of the nearby crows and it set off with a flap of feathers that made me jump. "The scientific theory is that there's a specific kind of invertebrate that lives on the island that they love, perhaps to do with the stone. Of course the folktales are a little stranger."

"Oh?" I took the shiny silver key that Anderson offered me, holding on to it for a second, the metal warm in my palm. I tried to imagine my father, unlocking this door after a day of work, striding inside to his empty hearth. Would it always have been empty? I didn't know. "What kind of folktales?"

"I'm sure you don't want me to bore you," Anderson said.

"Please? I'd like to hear."

"Well, ah . . . the most common one is that the witch who founded the island was cursed." Anderson scratched at his beard thoughtfully, obviously a little uncomfortable. "The story goes that there was a witch who sold her soul to the devil for the gift of darkness, hoping to rival the night. She hungered for power and desperately wanted to harness the magic that was more potent before the light of dawn. So she carried a sacrifice into the heart of the woods, a crow that she had caught in a wooden trap, and cut out its heart in offering. The devil took the offering gladly, the heart and the blood and the feathers all.

"He didn't stop there. He dragged the witch down into the depths of hell and showed her true darkness, the kind that suffocated and tortured. He expected the witch to react as a mortal, to be fearful and awed by its monstrous power. She was not. So he held her in the darkness for three days and three nights with not a drop of water or a morsel of food. The witch would not be broken, for she had seen this darkness and she craved it as she had before. She drank her own blood before succumbing to her thirst.

"Seeing he'd met his match in her, the devil gave the witch her gifts. He gave her darkness, which could be summoned with the sacrifice of blood. He warned her that the power was not unlimited, but he knew she would not listen.

"As she rose from hell, the witch came to a black ocean. In the sky hung a shining crescent moon, and its light burned her eyes after the depths of the devil's caverns. So she called upon her darkness, pulling the moon from the sky until its shadow crashed into the ocean, leaving the night sky empty and still. An island formed in the water before the witch's feet, a whisper of the moon's old shape in the sky, and as the witch stepped onto the virgin earth she could feel her own dark magic calling to her from within.

"And that night she reigned from her island throne, twisting the land to her will, creating a queendom for herself and her kind. She slept only as dawn approached, hidden amongst the fronds and trees, sound in the knowledge that she ruled all. As the moon rose the next night, the witch tried to cast the same magic again, to banish the light from the sky. She was tired, though, from her night of revelry, and she did not heed the devil's warning. Worst of all, she had forgotten to give a sacrifice of blood.

"So instead of bending to her will, her magic, pulled from the depths of hell, transformed her into the shape of a crow, a form that would forever contort her on nights when the moon's silver light shone. Over the years other witches attempted the same bargain with the devil, hungering for power and corrupted by its promise, and they flocked to the island because they felt an echo of themselves there, long after they were cursed never to leave."

Anderson finally paused. My pulse pounded in my throat and my mouth was dry. I swallowed with an effort, still clutching the silver key to my father's door. The lawyer's cheeks grew pink with embarrassment and he let out a small cough.

"Ah, sorry," he said. "Your father told me that story once. He was much better at that sort of thing. Of course, nobody believes a word of it. Witches don't turn into crows and a bit of money and power never hurt anybody. Why don't you open up that door and I'll give you a hand getting to know the place."

———)●(———

My father's house was tastefully decorated, dust collecting on white sheets draped over furniture, the walls reflecting the buttery daylight. The furniture was gorgeous and very expensive, but the walls were unadorned and the library was nearly empty. All the bedrooms were uniform, one identified as belonging to my father only by a pair of slippers and a monogrammed dressing gown.

I'd always assumed my father would be a collector. Somebody who enjoyed standing before his fireplace with a glass of rare scotch and a cigar. Instead this was the house of a man who valued peace and quiet. He didn't even have a gramophone.

"I thought you said you hadn't removed any of his things," I said.

"We haven't touched anything." Anderson shook his head. "Your father valued his space. On the day of the funeral I, ah, took the liberty of cataloguing a few of his more expensive books, just so we had a record, but this is what we have to work with."

I glanced around. For all his wealth, his wish that I should come and sort through his things, it felt insubstantial. What things were there to sort? "And there's nothing else?" I asked.

"Only this." Anderson retrieved another small bronze key from the key ring. There was a brown paper tag attached with a piece of twine. It simply said *Crowther*.

"What does it open?"

The key was about half the size of the one that opened the front door, an old-fashioned ornate little thing. I took it from Anderson and a jolt went through my palm, almost like a recognition. The familiar roaring started in my ears and I clenched my fist around the key, trying to hold it at bay—for just a little longer. Not while I was here, not while I wasn't alone. I gritted my teeth, and as quick as the dizziness had come, it was gone.

"I have no idea," Anderson said, oblivious. "There's no documentation with it, but I'd be happy to help you look?"

We set about searching the house together, though I suspected that we wouldn't stumble upon the answer by accident. We tried the locks on each of the bedrooms, a cupboard, a trunk with my father's embossed initials monogrammed on the side; we tried two windows, and outside we tried the gardener's shed that stood beyond the expertly cultivated rose garden.

"Bad luck," Anderson said as he made to leave. "I'm sure whatever it opens will turn up eventually. Do let me know when you figure it out, won't you? I'm very invested." He chuckled and left me with the details of our next appointment to go over some more paperwork from my father's estate.

Once he was gone I wandered until I landed on the top floor of the barren house, questioning why my father had wanted me here at all. What could he possibly gain? There was nothing here, just clothes and books. I didn't know what I had expected, but it was at least a few pricey pieces of art, artefacts that would require a little care.

Yet, there was the key. Cautiously I opened my fingers, turning it towards the light. It was barely bigger than my little finger. I reached up with my index finger, tracing the swirls and scrolls on the head. The metal was impossibly warm under my touch, like it had been baking in the hot sun for hours.

The room that was closest was one we had passed earlier in our hunt, but I hadn't paid much attention to it. It was unfurnished, except for a bare desk, a wardrobe, and three unfinished oil paintings leaning against the wall. I entered again, looking with new eyes.

I peered closer at the wardrobe. Unlike the ones in the other bedrooms it didn't stand alone or lean away from the wall. It was made of dark wood, its handles dulled with use, and it fit perfectly into the alcove. I inched closer, catching a familiar scent. The ocean was as comfortable to me as my blood and I would recognise that salt-brine smell anywhere.

I pushed the doors open. Inside the wardrobe was a doorway, dark and salty and cool, leading up a set of wooden stairs.

I climbed the stairs two at a time. I wasn't sure if the feeling inside me was dread or excitement, or both—whether it was residual from last night, fuelled by worry or the "panic" I'd averted earlier, but I drank it in.

At the top of the stairs was another wooden door. The handle was made of brass, the same colour as the key, and my nerves surged. I could still smell the sea, as though it had seeped through the doorway, around the wood, and into the very veins of the staircase. My breath coming short, I pushed the key into the lock and turned it.

Suddenly it all made sense.

Why my father had never told Anderson what the key opened, why his house was so sparse, so characterless. Why he didn't trust anybody else to do this job.

I'd found what he was hiding.

Chapter Thirteen

Annie

I stepped hesitantly into my father's attic room. Its sloping ceiling, whitewashed walls, and exposed beams gave it a fresh, open atmosphere. Ahead there was a small, round window, its pane cracked, which explained the sea-salt breeze. It wasn't a big room, maybe two or three yards wide in both directions, a tiny little box at the top of the house with a view of the ocean; it was a solace, a safe place.

Except...

Unlike downstairs, this room was ornately decorated. There was a chaise longue with a sapphire-blue velveteen cover, cushions scattered across it adorned with unfamiliar gold-stitched symbols that made my hackles rise, years of rules and laws and warnings tearing through my brain. There was a desk beneath the window made from wood that was so dark it reflected the sun off the sea, its surface cluttered with papers, ink, a blotter, a large shining crystal in a stand...

There were cream-brown shapes amongst my father's things, and I shuddered. One was the skull of a creature that might have been a fox or a small dog; the other was birdlike and frail, one end pointed like a beak.

My heart thundered as I spun, taking in the bookshelves that lined the bottom half of the walls, filled to bursting with leather-bound tomes that were worn and well loved. The floor was carpeted with a plush patterned rug, more of the same sapphire blue with gold thread.

Everywhere I looked another vicious detail caught me by the throat. Herbs hung from beams overhead, crumbling slowly to dust in the salted air. More herbs, already dried and poured into little glass vials, were painstakingly labelled in an unfamiliar cursive, the ink fading brown.

I held my arms by my sides, afraid that if I moved them I might knock things, touch them, somehow incriminate myself. This was illegal. Against all laws—of God and man. It wasn't just party favours and frippery. It wasn't whatever Emmeline did, crass magic that had made her wealthy and famous. This was real, secret, *treacherous* magic. It was sharp and intoxicating. I could actually taste it, the sharpness sitting on my tongue as I breathed.

I expected the panic to engulf me, that old roaring fear, but instead numbness seeped into every part of me. If anybody found out—this wouldn't just be a slap on the wrist, a fine I could pay off and pretend afterwards to forget. This was worse than what had happened to Bessie Higgins, who had hanged for those poppets, dead for the sake of dried-out old weeds. This room... It contained enough to have me punished a thousand times over, all perfectly preserved and laid out ready for a trial.

And yet, a part of me, a part so deep inside me that I hardly recognised it, was not cowed. That part wanted to touch everything; I wanted to run my hands over the glossy surface of the crystal ball, which reminded me of ice on a river; I longed to thumb through my father's books, to draw them to my chest and smell their warm leather scent.

This, almost as much as the room itself, terrified me. It was enough to nearly bring me crashing to my knees, and only the idea of losing myself here, of not being ready to run when I needed to, kept me upright. My logical thoughts were those of warning. *This is temptation, Annie. You must flee. This is how magic snares you.* But the heat in my cheeks, the excitement in my belly—it was already familiar to me. It was how I had felt at the party with kazam thrumming in my veins; how I'd felt sitting in Emmeline's smoky kitchen. It felt full of possibility.

It must be a lie. A spell. These feelings weren't—couldn't be—truly mine. And yet, I swore they were. The way this place soothed me despite my fear; the way the scent of herbs tickled some distant memory inside me... This room felt like *home*.

For the first time in years I allowed myself to think of the last time I had seen my father. Seven years ago, during the war. When he sent a letter asking to see me, I'd asked Mam if I should go. "No," she'd said. "I know you will, though, because despite everything you want to please him." She was right.

Mam hadn't mentioned why he might not be fighting like so many other men we knew, and at fifteen I assumed there must be a reason. Maybe he suffered from the same "panics" as me—they certainly weren't from my mother, who always seemed afraid when they happened.

It was the third time in my life that I'd met him, and it was the worst.

We met in Whitby, on the pier where families walked together enjoying the summer day. He gave me a bouquet of baby's breath and I held on to it with confusion, a strange cool, watery sensation in my fingers. I had thought perhaps I was allergic to it, except that it wasn't unpleasant.

"It's for luck," he said, as though that explained everything.

We wandered without touching, not even once when I stumbled in the street. I could see the remains of the ruined abbey up on the East Cliff, its skeletal shape looming like a slumbering beast.

Eventually he led me to a museum tucked away in a corner off a crooked, winding street I had never known existed. I would have been scared except that—somehow—I was excited instead. The museum was nothing like the gallery he had taken me to as a child.

It was a museum of curios. Morbid things. Jars filled with jelly and bones, a dusty altar that had been reconstructed from the house of an accused witch—a real blood witch, not just any regular person who meddled with kazam—and a carved bone athame sitting jagged in a polished display case, its vicious blade pointing right at my heart. This was three years before the war ended and the prohibition on magic came into effect, but I already knew that this was wrong.

"We shouldn't be here," I said.

I wanted to leave. All my learning, everything my mother had taught me, told me I should run away, run until I made it out into the safety of the open air, where nothing could trick me or lure me into the wrong kind of devotion. A dark, rebellious part of me wanted to stay.

My father was a tall man, imposing with his swath of dark hair, yet he had the ability to blend with his surroundings, and standing in the dimness of the museum—empty except for us and a little old man, too old to fight, who had paid the entrance fee in handmade fudge—my father somehow merged with the walls until I could hardly see him.

"I am taking a risk bringing you here," he agreed, his voice terse, "but I think it's important for you to understand."

He led me deeper into the museum, where there were fewer glass cases and more items on display within touching distance. My blood hummed at the presence of some of them and a responding prickle of fear raised the hairs on the back of my neck.

"I don't need you to teach me anything," I said. "Mam teaches me plenty. Magic is for people who need more than they're brave enough to take themselves. Magic isn't for people like us, and it's dangerous to let yourself be tempted. You didn't need to bring me here to scare me. I'm not stupid."

"Child, I never said you were stupid."

My father came to an abrupt stop. I almost walked right into him. That felt like a betrayal of some kind, to touch him, so I stumbled back, clutching my baby's breath and curling my fingers amongst the stems. We were so deep in this crooked place with its dusty, brutal relics; it was dark and true fear that hummed in me.

"Antonia, one day you will understand the decisions I have made.

I only ever wanted to keep you safe. Magic is not something to marvel at, to make fun of—to treat as play. Real magic, the kind that flows in the veins of a select few, is dangerous and unpredictable. It's not like a pinch of Saint-John's-wort, a drop of feverfew tonic. It does not, by its nature, heal or cure. It's...in the blood. It might manifest in skill, yes, in luck. More often it is like a curse. It's a beautiful, *monstrous* thing, and you must never meddle in it. You must resist its siren call, because it will destroy everything it touches. Do you understand?"

I glanced around the dingy room full of relics and I nodded. What use did I have for ceremonial knives or crystals or dirty old bones? What use did I have for magic? I would be like Sam; I would train to nurse using proper medicine and see the world, and I would never need its bewitching touch.

I'd told my father I understood, that I would follow his rules. And then there was the prohibition, and if I ever felt a little strange, if ever I woke on the beach in the dead of night and felt the singing of the ocean in my bones, I buried it beneath meekness and obedience where it might be overlooked.

I inched towards my father's desk. The wishes of my fifteen-year-old self felt foolish, ill-conceived and ridiculous. At fifteen the whole world had been ripe for the picking. Now it was wide and empty and so damn lonely.

I should leave. I should run away as I always did. That was the safe thing, the *right* thing, to do. Instead, I thought of Bea. Something had driven her to Emmeline's house last night. Was it the temptation my mother always spoke of, honey-gilded magic with hidden claws that made good girls stray, or was it more complicated than that?

Before I knew what was happening, my hands were on a leatherbound journal and it was warm to the touch. I lifted it to my chest, let the scent of paper and ink tickle my nose. With a deep breath I opened it, the pages spilling open in a flutter. Unfamiliar handwriting, dates that meant nothing, names and locations and more. *Mabon, Cross House, Priscilla...*

And as I read, words jumping eagerly into my brain, I began to understand. *Equinox*, *blood*, *hunger*...I'd thought my father had wanted to scare me that day. I'd thought he had seen the threat of new, dark wartime magic on the horizon and that he was afraid. Years later I thought that maybe, just maybe, Mam had asked him to show me that horrible, alluring place, so that I would understand why I had to ignore the strangeness inside myself.

The sand was pale under the prickle of autumn starlight, the strongest witch on Crow Island...

I was wrong. My father wasn't *afraid* of magic.

She has a darkness inside her...

He was a witch.

PROMISES

AND

LIES

The Bone Queen

Lilith

S he was half-dead when they found her. She'd been sleeping rough for months, in doorways and alleys, the January nights long and cold. She only had so much blood magic to keep her warm, and though it made her sick to keep using it, she didn't know any other way.

The dark lady who rescued her was the most arresting woman Lilith had ever seen, with her thick hair like electric midnight and her sleek, shiny auto. Lil knew, instinctively, that she was rich. Richer than rich. She could smell it in the musky notes at her pulse points, could feel it in the way the woman held her, unaccustomed to the weight of a child. The woman wrapped her arms around Lil, and it felt so good, so safe, that Lil wanted to cry, but she didn't have the strength.

She'd made it as far as the harbour. She'd been too unwell to board the boat she'd bargained passage on, but too stubborn to die. The black-haired woman and the little blond girl she was with fed her perfect cucumber triangle sandwiches, spooned her good, hot tea. She hadn't eaten in so long that she was sick minutes later, but it tasted all right coming back up too.

The woman wrapped Lilith in blankets and lifted her easily, although Lil was gangly at fourteen, murmuring words under her breath that wrapped Lil in a comforting cocoon. It reminded her of her aunt, the woman who had raised her since she was a baby and who had taught her the little she knew about her magic. The same magic that made her cling to her aunt's battered old konjure set although she could have sold it. It was the cards that led the lady right to her.

They sat inside the warm, plush car as the boat carried them across the stretch of ocean and into the waiting arms of the island beyond. Lil had heard it looked like a moon, its back turned towards the tight lips and rules of the mainland, but to her, in that moment, it just looked like everything she had waited for since her aunt shooed her off into the night when the men came for her. It looked like home.

———)●(———

The woman's name was Cilla. Lil wasn't the only child Cilla had found on the mainland, starving but with that magical fire in their blood that marked them as worth saving. She *collected* children; her eyes and ears were always open for more. More than just that, she was their mother, their father, their teacher. She taught them to hone their gifts, and she took her payment in kind.

The day Cilla found Lilith she'd also found the blond girl, Angelica, whose father had thrown her out two weeks before. She'd been robbing gentlemen in Brighton, using her magic to make them believe she was the devil while she had her hands in their pockets.

Cilla put them to work right away. She ran Cross House like a battleship. Delacroix, she explained, meant "of the cross." She said she was doing the work of the church and the council—at least, the work they refused to do any longer. The ten or twelve youngsters who lived there were her pets, handpicked and primped. They ran errands, satisfied her every whim, and in return they got a warm bed, free food, and the chance to learn about the magic that ran in their blood from Crow Island's infamous witch. They got to feel safe, and if Cilla sometimes asked of them more than they could give? It was worth it.

They all had one thing in common, which Lil didn't realise until she'd been living with Cilla for two or three months: all the children had come into their magic on the streets. They came of age with nobody to guide them; they learned bad habits, and Cilla said it was her job to fix them.

Lil loved her, but she never did like the way Cilla said *fix*.

———⊰•⊱———

Lilith had been in the house six weeks when she was woken one night by the sound of laughter. The cigars smelled like the ones her aunt had favoured. She could smell them from her bedroom. She clambered out of her bed and wandered down, down, until she came to Cilla's favourite room. It was decorated in reds and golds and contained statues and trinkets that were worth more than her aunt's whole house had been.

Lil followed her nose to the crack in the door and inhaled… And she listened. There were men in the room that night. So many men. Councilmen. A whole group of them, sharp suits and waxed moustaches, rings on their fingers and cigar smoke hanging lazily in the air.

Lilith knew about money. It bought the wrong people the right things. She'd heard men begging her aunt, back then, back in the old days, for things they shouldn't want. Things they didn't need. Her aunt said no. Always *no*.

Lil watched Cilla and her men for hours, frozen in the cold hallway with one eye pressed to the crack in the door and one hand pressed to her aching heart. She couldn't force herself to leave. She thought of her aunt, of the black night when they had been driven out of their beds by men *just like these*. The girl to the open arms of darkness—the midwife to a rope.

She thought of how the terror had wrapped her lungs in ice and forced her out into the cold September night, the sickle moon waxing and silver overhead. The coins had jangled in her socks; her hair was still wet from her bath. She remembered the pain in Aunt Rachel's face as she waited for Lil to run before she went to the door. Because she knew what would happen—what always happened when a woman said no.

Cilla sat in her damask throne with a veil over her face and blood on her tongue—the mother none of them had, the teacher all of them wanted. And when the men in the throne room asked for her help, Cilla always said yes.

Chapter One

Annie

I locked the attic room with my father's book still clutched in my arms. I shut the wardrobe up tight and stumbled to my car as my head rang. I drove without thinking, my father's book stowed under my seat, where it tormented me. I wanted to speak to Mam. Had she known about my father? About what he was?

I couldn't do it. My mother hated magic. If she hadn't known about my father, telling her would kill her. After all, what did this mean for me? So many questions swirled in my head. Could magic be inherited, like blue eyes or a strong jaw? Was it magic in my blood that sang when Emmeline was near?

Perhaps Anderson could help. He had said I should talk to him... Only I was sure this wasn't what he had meant. He had warned me away from Emmeline and Cross House. What would he say if I told him about my father? What might it mean for me if he shared my secret with anyone?

When I came to my senses I was outside Bea's house, the splendour no less dazzling than it had been the other night. I sat in the car until my hands stopped trembling, and then I rang the doorbell. Bea answered the door herself, dressed in a fashionable cream dress, a small velvet purse in her hands.

"Oh, Bea," I said. "I'm so glad I caught you."

"I was just stepping out. Are you headed into town?" Bea glanced behind me, towards my car, which was still running. Confusion creased her brow. "Annie darling, is everything all right? You rushed off so quickly the other night I wasn't sure we'd see you again."

Bea's gathering seemed like a million years ago. I wanted to tell her about my father, wanted to tell her I'd been at Emmeline's party, that I'd seen her. I couldn't say any of that. I trusted Bea not to go to the police about my father, but Arthur...? What would he say if she told him? And after the party, how could she not?

"I've just come from my father's house," I explained. "It was— upsetting. Do you have time for me?"

We drove to Crow Trap in almost perfect silence. I focused on the road ahead, on the light rain that fell, anywhere but the journal under my seat. Its presence felt like a brand, burning itself into my consciousness. I wanted to ask Bea about Emmeline's party, about her connection to that house, to those people and their magic, but she wouldn't answer me if I mentioned it directly.

Crow Trap was busy despite the turning weather, people strolling with umbrellas and small children. I parked under a leafy tree and we walked together, conversation slowly growing, the distance from my car giving us space to be free.

Bea led us to a café with a display of cakes, the sugary scent guiding us to a table not far from the window. A young girl took our order and scurried away. I gazed across at the cut glass decorating the cake displays, rose-tinted and meant to look like real crystals, at the twisting ivy vines winding from the top of the window right the way down to our little table.

Out of the corner of my eye I caught sight of another one of those *Licensed Faux Magic Vendor* signs propped in the window, and my pulse fluttered. My father...All these years I thought he'd avoided me because he didn't care about us.

Was it possible he was trying to protect us? And what of the journal, what would he think if he knew I had it? That I had read it? His attic was so different from Emmeline's kitchen, a practical workspace that seemed much more threatening than the weaving of visual tricks, strong alcohol masking a way to make quick money. He wasn't some eccentric, bright young thing. He wasn't peddling spiked liquor and dreams. He was a middle-aged man with a secret attic. If anybody had known about his collection he would have been hanged.

Instead, he'd had a heart attack—if that was what really had happened. I had no proof of that. I wanted to ask Anderson about the circumstances of his death, but the thought filled me with roiling dread. It would be so easy to say something incriminating. And what then? This unlawful collection was mine. It was my responsibility. My stomach heaved and I swallowed bile.

"Annie," Bea said gently. I started.

"Sorry. I'm..." I tucked my hands under the table and raised my face to Bea's, noticing how tired she looked, how pale. I'd done it again—so focused on myself that I hadn't checked whether she was okay after last night. "I'm just worried about you," I said.

"Why?"

I stared at her. How could she act like nothing was wrong? After all the years Bea and I had been as good as sisters, couldn't she trust me? The last year stretched between us, a chasm that was impossible to bridge.

"I just want you to know that I'm here," I said.

Bea appraised me evenly, then smiled, and there was the dazzling Bea who had always made me forget I was only seeing half the picture. "You too," she replied.

—)●(—

By the time I got home I was exhausted; my bones felt moth-eaten with worry. I should have pushed Bea harder. I wanted so badly to understand. If she was in any trouble, with Emmeline or with Arthur...But pushing Bea had never ended well; I was just as likely to drive her away as get a straight answer.

I inhaled the cool evening air, counting the crows as I sat in my car. I saw nine, one after another, and tried to remember what nine crows meant.

I was out of the car before I noticed it. That faint, glittering pressure inside my chest. The little hairs on my arms prickled. I glanced back and forth amongst the twilight shadows, the salt-tinged dimness gilded by the sinking sun and the rising moon.

I slammed my car door hard and feigned disinterest, all the while fighting to control my breathing and my hammering heart. She wasn't visible right away. It was only when I saw the glow of her cigarette that I noticed how close she was to my front door.

Why did that woman make me feel this way? Was it magic that made her proximity so precious to me, that made my mind so wild and bold and unlike my own? It must be. I thought of my father's journal, the pages I had skimmed. *She has a darkness inside her...* Why did that line make me think of her?

I shivered.

Emmeline stepped away from the shadow of my house and stubbed her cigarette out in the dirt.

"I'm sorry if I startled you." Her voice was husky, genuine. We could have been old friends.

I should be afraid. The distant thought of the journal, still under the seat in my car, circled in my head. Yet, like last night, again her presence made me feel brave, not scared. Unmasked.

I had blamed the kazam then, or the frenetic energy of the party at least. I had been lulled, tempted. I hadn't been myself. But this time there was no such cause, nobody to blame but me—and her. I wasn't sure whether that made it better or worse.

It should have mattered that the closer I got to her, the closer I wanted to be. No—it *did* matter. I stopped at the edge of the path, my pulse skipping.

"You didn't scare me," I said. "I knew you were here."

Emmeline's mouth quirked in surprise.

"I wanted to apologise for last night," she said. "I'm sorry I left you so abruptly. It was rather rude."

"Oh, no—"

"And I'm sorry if you saw anything that you might have found distressing."

She wasn't going to deny it, then. I could still feel an echo of the fear and longing that had hummed between her and Bea, that moment of horror when my best friend had hurt her husband and flinched away from his retaliation. And now Bea was pretending it had never happened.

"I won't tell anybody," I blurted.

"I'm not worried about that." So why was she here? "The parties are always chaos. Somebody usually gets hurt. It wasn't polite of me to abandon you."

I had shifted away from her, but at this I stopped. Was it possible that what I had seen was nothing more than too much kazam? Emmeline's tone suggested this was the sort of thing that happened on the island all the time and I was only naïve.

"Even though I shouldn't have been there in the first place?" I murmured, meeting her gaze.

Emmeline's smile was feline. Knowing. "Even then. Can I make it up to you?"

I took an involuntary step closer, and it was like the pull of Emmeline's magicked wine, deep and irresistible. This wasn't how I was meant to feel about a woman, let alone one like Emmeline. She had bewitched me by some magic, some witchcraft; I hadn't been myself since I'd met her.

No, my brain whispered. *Before you were only a mouse. Now you are growing fangs.*

I stepped back again, fumbling for my keys, afraid of my thoughts. Afraid of how easily I had dismissed my concerns about Bea. I didn't know what to think. My brain felt like it was full of Emmeline's cigarette smoke, hazy and hot.

"It's fine," I stammered. "I don't need anything—"

"I thought maybe you might join me for dinner tomorrow night—not quite a party. Say, seven o'clock? You could, perhaps, bring our mutual friend."

I could smell the smoke from Emmeline's lips, the blood-and-dirt scent that seemed to follow her. I tried to tear my gaze away from the man's shirt she wore and the cut of her waistcoat. I could see every slight curve and plane of her.

I had enough to worry about with Bea and my father without adding Emmeline to the mix. I should say *no.*

"Yes," I blurted.

Emmeline smiled again, wider this time, a genuine grin that exposed her canines.

"Good," she said. "Very good."

I waited until she was gone before I grabbed the journal from the car and hurried into the darkness of my cottage, my heart still pounding. I put the kettle on to boil and leaned over the sink, noticing faintly how the tugging sensation of a silver thread tied around my heart calmed with every moment I was away from Emmeline, how my thoughts settled until I could think clearly again.

It must be magic—there was no other explanation. Why else would I be so lost in her presence while feeling so whole? I came back to the surprise in Emmeline's expression whenever we spoke, how she seemed as shocked by this connection as I was. That didn't feel false. It could be a ruse, a trick...but I didn't think so. It had seemed so real.

The shadows pulled and stretched around me as I waited. The kettle began to whistle. I was halfway across the kitchen to lift it off when I heard another sound. Distant, like the rumble of a car engine outside. Then silence.

I removed the kettle, paused, listening.

Another sound. This time it wasn't like a roar, more like a rustle. Boots on gravel. I headed for the front door, nerves creeping under my skin. I flung it wide. My eyes fought against the fading light.

"Is anybody there?" I called.

Nothing. Just eerie silence.

"Emmeline?"

Ahead, briefly, I thought I caught sight of a shadow near my car—but when I looked harder it was gone. Had somebody been lurking out there? I shut the door fast, glad I'd emptied the car of its secrets when I had.

At the table I slumped over my tea, spent. My thoughts swirled. I had been wrong, outside, to believe Emmeline's flippancy. Whatever had happened between her and Bea must have been bad, for Bea and Arthur to both behave as they had. For Bea to keep it a secret from me today. It was more than drunken chaos, of that I was again sure. It would be reckless to do as Emmeline had asked and extend the invitation.

And yet…how could I not? Ignoring what had happened wouldn't make it go away, and Bea fully intended to ignore it. Not long ago I would have ignored it too, but this felt vital somehow. Somebody had to be brave—and for once it could be me.

And I could be selfish too. With Bea there I might be able to talk to Emmeline without this strange madness taking hold of me; I might be able to ask for her help with my father's things, or at least get an idea of what to do next. I didn't know who else I could turn to.

In the end, it took me only the length of a cup of tea, about until my hands stopped shaking, before I found the shiny, perfect cottage telephone and called Bea. In the end, it took only six words to convince her to say yes: *I saw you at Emmeline's party.*

Afterwards I stood cradling my elbows, back against the wall. It was fear that held me there, long after the sun had gone down, although it had nothing to do with Bea. It had only a little to do with my father and the journal hidden deep under my mattress.

Mostly it was the realisation that if she got close enough, apparently I'd do anything Emmeline Delacroix asked of me.

Chapter Two

Emmeline

I need the house tonight."

Nathan and Isobel looked up from the concoction between them on the stove. I caught a whiff of rose hip and garlic and resisted the urge to grimace. Isobel's clients swore by her balms, but they absolutely reeked.

"Why?" Isobel turned, one hand on her hip. I almost laughed. She was always trying to mother me though it should have been the other way around. I had been here first.

I *didn't* laugh. It was unfair to tease her for a wholesomeness I could only dream of, even after everything that had happened. Losing Angelica had been the hardest for her, and if this was how she dealt with it after all these years, throwing herself into healing and mixing, I should let her. The debt was making me beyond irritable.

"I just need the house."

"It's to do with her, isn't it," Nathan said. "Bea."

I didn't respond, but that was answer enough.

"Em, darling," he said. His brown eyes were soft but his voice was tinged with his trademark sass. It was his armour and he was rarely without it. "Why won't you talk to us? You know we're both smarter than you."

"Don't bother." Isobel rolled her eyes. "I've already tried. She's hopeless."

"What use is there in talking?" I sighed. The pressure grew in my veins, blood tossing at the mere mention of Bea, at the hope this meeting held. If I could only convince her to pay what she owed... All Isobel's nagging could stop. Nathan could stop worrying.

When all this was over I could admit to them—and to myself—how stupid I had truly been. I would be able to confess everything, to weather their disappointment. Only then would I be able to accept how close I had brought our family to ruin—how close I had come to becoming just like Cilla.

"Talking helps, Em." Nathan shrugged and continued stirring the pot. "It means we can look out for each other. You don't always have to be the strong one. Especially since you're so goddamn terrible at looking out for yourself. You're like a cat."

"I'm *fine*," I said. "Whatever it was that Is made last week really helped. I just need to refine my plan."

Isobel's concoction hadn't helped. It'd tasted like pomade and had a similar consistency. My gorge rose at the thought. Isobel was the strongest natural witch I'd ever met, but she was also the most cautious, which meant that most of her magic ended up on the weak side, which was fine for her clients. Not that it would matter for me. This wasn't the sort of problem Isobel could ever fix.

"Emmeline Delacroix, you are a bloody awful liar," Isobel said. "Stir faster, Nate."

I shrugged.

"We're just saying we can't help you if we don't know where to start, darling," Nathan continued. "I know you modern women love your independence, but don't you think you're taking it a bit far?"

"Be careful, Nate, you're starting to sound like an old codger—I said *stir faster*." Isobel shook her head.

Nathan had stopped stirring altogether, and he stared at me, suddenly intent. I recognised that look.

"For God's sake, Nathan, stop looking at me like I've grown horns."

"I'm not doing anything." His expression flickered, shadowy concern etched in the planes of his face. Then the moment passed. Nathan's grin grew again and he shook off whatever he had seen in my head like a bad spell. "Honestly," he joked lightly, "read a girl's mind once and she'll never let you live it down."

"Stop it," I snapped tiredly. "My mind isn't a book. You won't find anything you don't already know." The stuff in the pan on the stove started to bubble, and I wrinkled my nose at the acrid aroma. "I think that's burning—anyway, I need the house tonight. Just for a couple of hours."

Isobel swooped in and lifted the pan off the heat, clucking as Nathan held his hands up. The burner was finicky as hell, but Isobel could usually temper it. I don't know why she insisted on trying to train Nathan to do it too.

"Hell's bells, Nate," Isobel muttered. "You had one bloody job. How on earth did you manage to make this kind of a mess?"

"The whole house?" Nathan asked me, ignoring her.

"The whole damn house. Frankly, I'm not asking you. I'm telling you. Why don't you go with Isobel. You could both check in on Hilda and her daughter. It would do you good to get out of the house."

"Pot, meet kettle," Nathan said. "When was the last time you left?"

"That is hardly the point."

Isobel slid the pot back onto the stove and sighed at the congealing mass in the bottom.

"Honestly, I don't know why I bother trying to teach you anything," she said, not unkindly.

"Because I'm very charming and you enjoy my company?" Nathan winked, his concern well hidden now. "Besides, I'm a damn sight better than Em and you know it."

"Oh hush," Isobel said, wafting her hands at Nathan. She turned to me. "Anyway, say we leave you be tonight...What's in it for us, dearest? Say, if Hilda wasn't home. Say, if I don't want Nathan tagging along?"

I raised an eyebrow.

"If we agree to get out of your hair," she went on, "can you promise the house will still be standing later? Every time we leave you to your own devices you get us into some trouble or other."

"That's hardly fair," I said, though it was true. "If you're very worried, I've invited the new neighbour too, so it won't only be the two of us."

"Oh, the so-called innocent one?" Isobel smirked. "The one you didn't want back here?"

"Yes." *The innocent one.* Maybe not so true, after all. Standing outside her house in the dark last night she'd seemed timid, yes, yet somehow fierce. A spark had grown inside her already, one that reflected back like sunshine. Before long the island would have its claws in her, like it did all of us. "I need the house," I said firmly, flexing my hand behind my back. The blood was more sluggish than ever. There wasn't much time left. "Give me until midnight."

———⟨ ● ⟩———

This time Bea didn't flinch when she saw me. Sober she seemed to remember what we had almost meant to each other. The things we had both sacrificed, the promise she had made. I put my hands in my pockets as she breezed in like she had only been gone five minutes, only the faint downward curve of her lips betraying the truth.

"I thought you wouldn't come." Suspicion scratched my throat with claws made of relief.

Bea was ravishing as always, her red hair swept off her neck with a clip of stones that shone like moonlight and pearls around her neck. The tea dress she wore was a pale green that matched her eyes.

"I almost didn't," she said. "Arthur..." His name hung between us like a ghost. "Annie called. She told me to go and fetch her but I didn't. I wanted to ask first...Does she know? About us? About...it?"

"No. I just didn't think you'd return without her."

Bea's face said it all. She regretted coming already. The house around us was silent, not even a clock ticking to mark the moment.

"Will Annie still come?" I asked. Bea's expression closed at the mention of her, as though Bea didn't actually want her here.

I ignored my disappointment, like the flutter of a moth's wings, light but persistent. I knew it was just because of the thing, that vital magical *thing* forming between us—the thing I refused to name, that I desperately needed to prevent—and yet.

"I don't know," Bea said coolly. "If you're such good friends, why don't you ask her? We're not joined at the hip. Perhaps she decided not to come after the scene you caused at the party. She told me she was there."

I let out an acidic laugh. "The scene *I* caused? Beatrice, you're the one who turned up drunk as hell with your dumb rich husband acting like I was trying to curse you."

"Well, he's right to worry!" Bea exclaimed. "Isn't he? For God's sake, Em, this is all your fault."

"My fault." The words sat heavy on my tongue. "Bea, you haven't even considered—"

"Oh, don't you blame me! You're always trying to make me feel foolish. It's not my fault that you got us into this. You didn't *warn* me this would happen, that everything would fall apart. Look!"

Bea gestured at her shoulder. There was a handprint seared into her flesh, purple and green and wretched. It hurt to look at.

So that was why she was here. Not because of me. Because of him.

Anger swelled under my skin, magic biting for release. I curled my fingers tight into my palms. How dare he.

"Bea, that's... That's not the only thing—"

"*This* is what's happening," Bea snapped, covering her shoulder again. "I came to ask for help, which I know is a foreign concept to you. Did you do this on purpose? To make me come here? You need to fix it. The magic is wearing off and he's going to k—"

The doorbell sliced between us, driving us both into shocked silence.

I gave my arms a quick shake, trying to gather all the broken pieces of myself. Bea made it to the door first. She opened it like she owned the place, her assured mask firmly back in place.

It was Annie, her golden hair damp with rain. The magic between us flared, but this time I was ready, my mental walls going up, my body straining as blood leaked under my tongue. She wore an old dress, wrung thin in the wash, and she buried her hands in its pockets.

"How long have you been standing out there?" My words came out harsh as I tried to balance the shield. Annie shook her head.

"Not long. I'm sorry I'm late." This was pointed. Directed not at me but at Bea, who looked away. "Bea said she'd come and get me and when she didn't I thought she'd decided not to come. I only just saw her car."

Bea brushed at her fine dress.

"I'm sorry," she said quietly. "I meant to—"

"I'm not dressed for dinner, but do you mind if I still join you?" Annie interrupted, speaking directly to me.

The second Bea had turned up without Annie, I had made a plan. If Annie came, I would send her home. It was the best thing for everybody involved. I had half hoped she would not come at all, because then I wouldn't have to be cruel.

She had turned up, though, and now I had a decision to make, I found that I couldn't bring myself to turn her away. *Go on*, I thought. *Be the witch she thinks you are. If you embarrass her she'll never come back—and isn't that exactly what you wanted?* But I couldn't do it.

Was it the magic, seeping through my barrier already? Or was it simply that I was too cowardly to deal with Bea alone?

Despite my best efforts, Annie's presence felt like a balm. I smiled for the first time, my face stretching with it. The conversation with Bea would still have to happen tonight.

"Of course I don't mind," I said. "It's a pleasure to have you here."

I couldn't ignore what needed to happen—but first we needed wine. And if I was to hold a mental barrier all through dinner, I'd need quite a lot of it.

I led them through into the dining room. Annie marvelled at the emptiness of the house. I purposefully took the route that meandered through several reception rooms, the ones with dark polished wood and expensive instruments—a harp and a piano that had both belonged to Cilla—and through the parlour with the bar, empty this evening but still tempting with the promise of kazam-laced liquor. As much as I shouldn't want to, I longed to impress her. I wanted to share Cross House's beauty with her and watch her fresh face light up.

Our dining room was long and thin, decorated in brown and gold tonight, the shimmering chandelier lit and tall candles surrounding the large fireplace too. I'd chosen the fine white china with gold rims, polished the silverware bright, and laid the table for three. The spread I'd catered was fine, cold turkey and salad, small sausages and pork pies topped with cheese and chutney, and a carafe of wine the colour of liquid gold. Annie gawked at it all and I swelled with pride.

We settled at the table, the silence overpowering. Bea fiddled with her cutlery awkwardly, and I did my best to seem unaffected. I poured each of us a glass of the wine, which Bea immediately drained and refilled. Annie glanced between Bea and me, her gaze unconsciously assessing.

"Your house really is beautiful," she said eventually. "It puts my little cottage to shame. I always dreamed of houses like this, but I never thought I'd get to see one."

I felt a surge of warmth towards Annie, grateful for her conversation when Bea had barely said a word. It was clear that my barriers, dulling that thread between us to a faint throb, were helping her to feel more comfortable, but I had to admit I missed the way she looked when she was bewitched by me. I missed the way I felt too, the sharp brightness that crackled under my skin when she was near, but I didn't want to think about that.

I wondered if she knew what it was, this thread that grew—but she would surely run if she did. Maybe I was glad for her innocence.

"Cross House is a relic," I said. "It hasn't had a lick of paint in years."

"It's a museum," Bea muttered darkly. She drained her glass again, refusing to even pretend politeness. Already her eyes had taken on a glossy shine. I moved the carafe to top up my full glass, placing it pointedly out of Bea's reach. She only glared.

"Well, I should love if it was a museum," Annie said, "so that I could visit whenever I wanted." Her cheeks coloured but she kept her chin raised, daring. I saw a flash of excitement in her eyes—at her own bravery—and I rewarded her with another laugh.

"I would have to charge admission," I mused. "Though there is nothing I want more than the company of friends."

Annie's blush deepened but Bea remained maddeningly silent, rolling the stem of her glass between her fingers. I wanted her to look at me. To acknowledge this mess we had made.

"Friends are a good enough currency," Annie added, relaxing into her joke. "But I'm not sure it's very sustainable. Bea's always hated museums and is liable to pitch a tantrum, so we'd have to throw her out, and then where would we be?"

I laughed again, and Annie joined me, her expression suggesting that she was shocked by herself, her boldness at Bea's expense. She looked at me, a question in her gaze, and I didn't look away. This, I wanted to reassure her, was nothing to do with me.

No, this fire was all her own.

Chapter Three

Annie

The tension was so thick when I stepped into Cross House that I knew I'd interrupted them. Bea's face had been flushed, a lock of Emmeline's carefully slicked hair out of place. I could have left them to whatever argument was unfolding, yet I didn't want to. Worry for both of them gnawed at me; they were in trouble, and somehow in watching whatever it was that had matured, wild and thorny between them, I'd allowed myself to become ensnared.

The conversation at the table turned to the strange normalcy of small things, the weather and the food. Sitting like this it was easy to forget Emmeline's reputation, to forget how dangerous it felt when we were alone together. Emmeline met my gaze as she topped our glasses up again—Bea's by a cautious half—and I saw my thoughts mirrored in their intensity.

The wine was, thankfully, just wine, and I sipped it gratefully and looked away, peering around the grand room. I'd been awed by the sight of it, but the most breathtaking thing of all was the flowers. White lilacs bloomed on every surface, on the floor and the mantel and strung around the windows, their petals like confetti. The scent was overpowering, seeping into the room and filling the air. Bea had sucked in a breath when we entered, but Emmeline had only waved her hand.

"What made you choose lilacs?" I asked.

"They're Bea's favourites," Emmeline replied simply. Bea let out a startled trill of laughter.

I saw the room with new eyes. This another detail I had never known about Bea. What else had I never noticed? A lot, it seemed.

Well, if Bea wouldn't talk to me, maybe Emmeline would.

"How do you two know each other?" I asked. It was a question with an edge, loaded with suggestion of commissioned magic, of kazam, of arguments that struck with a bloom of blood. It was not an impolite topic in normal circumstances—would not, in those circumstances, question the legality of their connection—but these weren't normal circumstances.

Emmeline flashed Bea a smile that was all teeth, and my body vibrated in response. There was a brief blaze of silver in my chest, like the sun between clouds. Only for a second. Emmeline's dark gaze fell on me, cutting. I blushed and averted my eyes.

"Bea came to me for a little help last year," Emmeline said, uncertain at first. I wondered if I'd distracted her. Or if this was a story she didn't want to tell. Yet something made her speak, her voice deep. "That's what I do. I provide services that help people, usually in exchange for payment. I'm not a charity."

Bea shifted uncomfortably.

"You sell desires." I wanted to ask if this was normal—for people like her. Did my father do this too? I wanted to see how much she would tell me. I needed to know whether I could trust her.

"Desires, yes. And futures. I unbraid the past."

"You admit you are a witch, then?" I demanded.

My body trembled with the word. Bea gasped. Thoughts of my father were close in my mind, but there was worry about Bea too. What had Bea desired so badly it had driven her here?

"I have never claimed otherwise," Emmeline said.

I turned to my best friend. "You let me think she was a stranger. I think I have a right to ask, since apparently you won't talk to me."

Emmeline raised an eyebrow at my frankness but said nothing more.

"It's complicated," Bea fumbled. Her breath came faster and she gripped the nearly empty glass in front of her, her fingers turning white on the stem. "Emmeline helped me last year, that's true. I need her to fix it again. I can't...I can't do this. I thought I could, but I can't pretend I'm not repulsed by the sight of this place."

She jumped to her feet, flinging the glass over in her haste. It fell to the table with a thud, dregs of gold liquid staining the pristine ivory cloth.

"*Bea.*" Emmeline's warning came out as a growl.

"No, you don't get to do this," she blurted. "I shouldn't have come. He'll find out and it will all be for nothing. I thought I could talk to you like a human, but I *can't*. You're not human. I can't believe I let myself think that you ever cared about what happens to me. You don't get to act like I owe you—"

"Bea," I tried. "Calm down. Let me help."

"You *do* owe me." Emmeline spoke over me, icy calm on her face but a storm raging behind her eyes. "You promised."

Whether it was the wine or what Emmeline had said I couldn't tell, but Bea was balled up. Completely untamed. She backed away like we were a pack of feral dogs. Emmeline didn't move, so I did. I stretched out, reaching for Bea, but she slapped my hands away.

"No! If you won't help me, I need to go home. You saw him—I can't give it to you. It'll kill me."

She turned and ran. I rounded on Emmeline, ready to demand answers, but the look on her face stopped me.

She sat completely still, one hand holding her full wineglass. Her dark eyes were filled with unshed tears.

"What did you do to her?" I breathed.

She looked at me, sadness etched into every pore.

"I gave her what she wanted."

———|) ● ( )|———

I wasted no time hurrying after Bea. She was already in her car, bent double over the steering wheel as tears streamed down her face.

"Bea," I said. "*Bea.*"

"Go away, Annie," she cried.

"Why won't you talk to me?" I begged, pushing myself right up against her car. It was raining but I didn't care. "Bea, what's going on between you two? Maybe I can help."

"You wouldn't understand."

"I think I'd understand plenty."

Bea swiped a hand angrily across her face, which was blotchy and red. Her hair had come undone from its clasp, but she made no effort to fix it. She stared up at me like we hadn't known each other our whole lives.

"It's impossible," she said sadly. "You only ever see what people want you to see."

"Bea," I repeated. "Did Arthur hurt you? Was it because of the party?"

She laughed, a hoarse, broken sound. "Something like that. You can't fix this, Annie."

"I can't help you if you won't talk to me—"

"You never helped me when I did talk to you," she retorted. "Sam was the only one who cared, and even he loved you more than he loved me."

The words hung between us, heavy in the dim evening air. It was like it had been last spring, a gaping maw of emotion grown so large between us that there was no way to pass, years of resentment and grief all mingled together. Sam's ghost was a barrier we could never break.

"You're wrong," I whispered. "He loved us both the same."

I wanted, more than anything, to wrap my arms around her, to comfort her. To apologise—because she was right. Sam had loved me more, and I had never deserved it. Bea would have made a better wife than I ever would have—and she had loved him exactly as she should have. Exactly as I couldn't. But those were words I could never bring myself to say aloud, for they meant too much.

Before I could move she began to reverse the car, careless of my feet.

"This isn't about *us*, Ann," she said darkly. "It's better if you don't get involved. Don't play with this stuff—you'll only get burned. I learned that the hard way."

"We will talk about this," I called. "Sooner or later. You can't ignore me forever."

After she left, I was adrift. I didn't go home, couldn't bear being hemmed in on all sides, no air to breathe. Instead I wandered the long way through the grass and towards the beach, where the sand stung my legs and the vicious, salty wind made tears track down my cheeks.

Bea hadn't answered my questions about Arthur. Had he found out about Bea's use of Emmeline's magic? How badly might he hurt her if he found out where she had been tonight? It couldn't be so bad, surely, if Bea was willing to go home. And Emmeline...I couldn't stop picturing her at the empty dining table, defeated. Why had she looked so broken after Bea fled?

I was involved in all of this, even if I didn't know what *this* was. And it was clear that Bea would never tell me what had happened last year, so it must have been awful. I stood and let the rain rinse my thoughts, until I could be brave again without the wine.

I turned back towards Emmeline Delacroix's house. That silver thread was still there in my chest, anchored around my heart. It grew in strength the closer I got. I inspected it, felt its strength— it was only barely tangible. Concern rang inside me, my mother's old warnings tolling. Was it the sort of magic my father might have wanted to protect me from? Had Emmeline used it to manipulate me? I couldn't work out why it had been weaker tonight, like a candle burning low.

I planted my feet firmly on the beach, allowing my body to settle into the wind and the rain, the shocking cold numbing my skin as I reached into myself. I closed my eyes, locating the silver thread again and homing in. I pictured it in the dark, a thin stream of flowing energy—that's what it felt like—leading away from my body, to hers. I reached out with my mind, imagined strumming it gently. A whisper. A greeting.

For a second it thrummed like the string of the harp in Emmeline's house. It was good. It was like a song. And then, abruptly, the thread pulled again, this time sharp and alarmed. I hadn't done it. A very real pang of fear shot through my chest.

Emmeline.

Chapter Four

Annie

My fingers were numb with cold as the thread pulsed and tightened, driving me back to Cross House. *Danger. Danger.*

For half a second I considered fighting against it. Emmeline scared me.

The thought of Emmeline in trouble scared me more.

I hurried through the garden from the beach. The pale crow maidens were frozen in their dance around the fountain. Tonight there was no purple light above Emmeline's porch, and the path ahead was black as tar.

The house was dark. Wind battered at my back as I leaned in to knock, and the sound was ripped away. I waited, closed my eyes and listened, trying to separate the sounds of the storm and the surf from the house before me. The noise was deceptive, blanketing the world in a haze of radio static.

Beyond it, there was nothing. Not even the glowing silver thread in my chest. It was abruptly, terrifyingly slack.

Panic ripped through me.

"Emmeline?"

The kitchen was cast in shadows. I smelled a burning, only the smoke wasn't warm like woodsmoke; it was acrid. Like herbs.

Like magic.

I ran through the kitchen and out into the dark hallway.

"Emmeline?" I called again, louder this time. "It's Annie. Are you all right?"

The tether twisted, white-hot and ugly, panic feeding it. It tugged my body forwards almost by its own force alone. I stumbled into the hallway, dripping rainwater all over the polished floors. I followed my instincts blindly, up stairs and through a long narrow hallway that looked like it should lead to servants' quarters.

The house seemed to be holding its breath. I bit back a startled cry as a face loomed out of the wall ahead, an older lady with black hair and piercing eyes like shards of ice. The painting made me shiver in a way that wasn't from the cold.

I ran on until I lurched into a room at the end of a totally unfamiliar hallway. It was cloaked in dim orange light from a fire that burned despite the season in a large grate.

On the floor there was a shadowy shape before a threadbare sofa that had once been plush. A ball of black clothing and a shock of dark hair.

Emmeline lay prone, one arm outstretched and the other tucked beneath her, her face pressed into the carpet. I caught that herbal smell again, cloying at the back of my throat. Emmeline's face was away from me, towards the fire, and when I reached over her I saw that it was slick with sweat.

"*Emmeline.*"

She didn't move. I dragged my arms under her torso, lifting her from the floor. Blood streaked her skin, pooled beneath her. Two candles almost down to stubs sat on either side of a bowl that was filled with more. It seemed to be smoking.

I hauled Emmeline farther over. The arm that had been beneath her was sticky. There was a long cut down her wrist and onto her hand. I repeated her name, forcing my panic aside as I tried to figure out whether she was still breathing.

Her chest hitched, eyelids twitching. She let out a moan that was low and guttural. What should I do? What would my mother do?

I propped her up against the threadbare sofa, ripping at the edges of my dress for a loose thread that might mean I could tear it up for bandages. I couldn't manage it. My fingers were too numb. I glanced around wildly for whatever Emmeline might have used to draw her own blood, but I found nothing that looked remotely sharp.

Letting out a frustrated yell, I ran out of the dim room and into the hallway. I searched the length of it until I found a bathroom complete with a box full of medicines and pastes. I dumped it all across the tiled floor. There was a strip of too-short bandage, which I grabbed, realising too late I'd smeared it with blood in great swipes.

When I got back to Emmeline she was still upright. Barely. I skidded on my knees across the carpet, smearing them with more wet blood. I pressed my thumb to Emmeline's neck, searching for her pulse. Some part of me stirred, the cord between us pulling tighter.

"Can you tell me what happened?" I asked urgently.

I needed to bandage the arm and get her help. I didn't know the island enough. I couldn't take her to Bea because of Arthur; Anderson was the only other person I could think of, but I couldn't take her to him either. Not in this state.

I wiped at her arm, revealing a line of strange glyphs carved into her skin. Fresh blood welled up again instantly, dark and so thick it was like tar. Emmeline mumbled, her fingers clawing inwards, nails scratching. I pulled her hand away but wasn't fast enough. There was a rumble. The floorboards creaked and groaned, the whole house trembling as I was thrown backwards, pushed by invisible hands.

I landed hard, my head slamming against the wooden arm of a chair. Stars burst across my vision and something hot and wet dripped down the back of my neck. I staggered to my feet, unsteady but driven.

Emmeline was still clawing at her arm, opening the wounds further. I battled her fingers away, using all my strength to hold her arm steady while I wrestled her out of her waistcoat and her shirt, using one of the sleeves to hold her still.

The fight went out of her all at once. She slumped back, a

deadweight, into the growing pool of blood. Her breathing was shallow, so shallow. She would die if I didn't do something.

I stared at the supplies I'd found in front of me, still dazed, my head aching. I let out a frustrated cry that hurt so badly tears sprang to my eyes. What good was all of this if I didn't know how to use it?

There was a noise behind me.

Footsteps that had been obscured by the weather were instantly loud. I jumped back as the door rocked on its hinges. My hands and dress were caked in Emmeline's drying blood.

A man and a woman stood in the doorway. I didn't recognise them at first, dressed in casual clothes instead of party garb. The woman had worn the red dress. I rushed over.

"Please!"

"Are you alone?" the woman demanded. "Who knows you are here?"

"It's just me," I sobbed. "I won't tell anybody about it—just please, *help her.*"

I stood in a daze while the man and woman worked together to gather Emmeline into their arms and move her into the bathroom. The woman filled the giant claw-foot tub with blankets and together they hoisted her in, propping her legs over one end of the tub and hooking her injured arm up against the side.

I followed them on numb feet, my vision threatening to blank as the roaring started in my ears. The silver cord in my chest jangled, its presence a shivering weakness. Or perhaps that was the cold that seeped into my bones and raised goose bumps on my arms from my sodden clothes.

The woman I had seen at the party disappeared and returned quickly with a selection of candles and pots and herbs. With a practised ease she lit the candles at the foot of the tub, crushed some fragrant petals into a copper dish, and added in a dash of water, and then, with a pause, she bit her finger so hard that blood leaked down and into the bowl with a faint sizzle. She stirred the mixture into a thick paste.

"What are you doing?" I asked. I sounded pitiful. "Will that help her?"

"Nathan," the woman growled. "Get her out of here—"

"Sorry!" I yelped, stumbling away. "I won't get in the way…"

Nathan barely looked at me; his forehead was beaded with sweat.

"I told you it was worse than she said," he hissed. "I told you I could sense it. You're using blood; that means it's serious."

"All right, Nate," the woman snapped. "*Later.*"

"What was she doing?" Nathan turned to me finally. "When you found her?"

"She was lying on the floor in there, unconscious. There was blood everywhere…She tried to make it worse, open the wound more. She hurt me." Unconsciously I reached up to my neck, the base of my skull, and when I pulled my fingers away they were stained with fresh red blood. I felt faint at the sight.

The mixture in the bowl began to froth. I could make out a lavender-coloured foam at the edges, tinged with a reddish brown, and I reached up to cover my mouth as the woman applied a thick handful of the paste to Emmeline's bare arm. There was a hiss from her skin and a foul red-stained smoke rose. She exhaled heavily as the salve smoothed over her skin.

The smell in the air was strange, iron like blood, only different. I glanced down at the stains on my dress. They were darker than they should be. Almost black. Like dirt.

"Do you think she Gave too much by accident?" Nathan asked. "I don't understand why she didn't tell us."

"She's a damn fool, that's why," the woman said coarsely, but her expression softened as she dipped her hand into the salve again and brushed more of the frothing paste onto Emmeline's arm. Already the sheen on her face was receding, her skin growing less waxen.

"It was my fault," I said quietly. "At dinner she wanted to talk to Bea, but I was there. I was in the way. I'm sure I ruined it. Bea left and Emmeline was upset. I didn't realise she would try to kill herself."

They both turned to me as I stood in the doorway, my hands and arms coated with Emmeline's black blood, my head pounding.

"Don't you get it, darling?" Nathan asked. "She wasn't trying to die."

"This sort of magic..." The woman set aside the bowl and perched on the edge of the tub tiredly. "She was trying to *live*."

———◦•◦———

Slowly the colour started to return to Emmeline's face. Nathan and the woman, Isobel, wouldn't let me into the room, but neither of them would leave Emmeline's side to throw me out either.

Eventually Emmeline began to move. She pulled her legs down into the tub, followed by her freshly bandaged arm. I was trembling with the cold, and something like relief, as the thread in my chest gave a sturdy, thrumming tug. Emmeline's dark eyes fluttered open. She took in Nathan, Isobel, and finally me.

"You absolute angels," she said.

"I'm going to pretend I'm not fuming, Em," Isobel muttered. "Why didn't you tell us it was this bad? Why didn't you wait until we were home, at least?"

"I needed to assuage the debt," she croaked. "Didn't want you to see me like this. Thought I could handle it...I've been putting off Giving for three days. Waited too long though. Gave too much."

"Well, better too much blood this time and you keep your sanity than not Giving enough and going mad." Nathan swiped his hand through his dark hair. "It is just this time, isn't it?"

Emmeline didn't answer. Isobel let out a curse and kicked angrily at the pot that had held the healing mixture. It clanged across the bathroom.

"What do you mean?" I asked, cupping the back of my head tenderly. "Giving? What debt? I don't understand. What's going on?"

"I'm sorry you got hurt, but that's what happens when you get involved in other people's business," Isobel said coldly. "This isn't anything to do with you."

"In case you haven't noticed, it's got a whole lot to do with me," I retorted. "Bea's my best friend. Is this going to happen to her too? Has it got anything to do with Arthur? And the..." And the silver thread.

I was about to say it, but Nathan and Isobel's presence stopped me. I looked at Emmeline, the darkness of her gaze. She felt it too. She had to. And from the fear there, I could tell that whatever this connection was, however it had come to pass, Emmeline had not caused it any more than I had.

Nobody answered me.

"Well?" I demanded.

The silence grew. Anger wasn't familiar to me; the emotion sat high in my throat and I ignored their glares as I stepped into the room. I strode towards the tub. Emmeline didn't move and yet somehow she still looked powerful, even with her pallor, her hair wild and knotted in its braid, her stained white vest and ruined tailored trousers.

"Emmeline," I said. "I'm worried about Bea. Is all of this because of something she did? What does she owe you? Is it money? Because if it is, we can pay it."

Emmeline sighed through her nose. Isobel started to speak but Emmeline cut her off.

"Bea owes me blood," she said frankly. "Her husband's blood. A good deal of it."

I had never been taught this, but I was sure there were only a few things that might require that kind of sacrifice. Life, death, or... love. And Bea had bought at least one of them from Emmeline.

"You cast magic to give her what she wanted, and you've been using your own blood to pay this debt?"

It made sense. The way Bea had refused to talk to me. The way she had acted tonight, almost like when I had caught her lying about how much she was drinking back home—only so much worse. I could have kicked myself. All the signs had been there and I had refused to admit what they meant, to believe how much trouble Bea might truly be in.

"It doesn't pay the debt. It *delays* it," Emmeline corrected. She tried to move but struggled, her body trembling. "I can't pay it all without bleeding too much, but I can loan some of myself. Not for this long—it never should have been for this long. I've been trying to get Bea back here for a year, but she just disappeared until... the party. I won't be able to keep this up if I have to keep Giving. And I have to. If you don't Give enough it makes you…unstable. It fucks you up, makes your magic—lethal."

"If magic is so dangerous, if you knew this would happen, why did you do it? Why did you agree?"

"I thought it was the right thing to do. I was wrong."

"And Bea knows all this?" I asked. What did this mean for Bea? And if Emmeline died…would she be responsible? I couldn't believe that Bea, knowing the bargain she had entered into, could just ignore Emmeline's plight.

Yet I saw the sadness in Emmeline's expression. The anger. And beneath it all, the resignation as she said, "Yes. She knows. The magic is unravelling—that's why she came tonight. And she ran because she can't face it. She'd rather let me die."

The Devil

Emmeline

Last summer

Where's Bea?"

Nathan was in the greenhouse, his fingers grubby with fresh dirt and his shirt rumpled in the heat. The air smelled like his trademark cinnamon scent, another pot of tea endlessly brewing on the little stove he kept at the back.

"How should I know?" He rolled his shoulders and glanced up from his work planting some fennel bulbs, leafy fronds splayed in his palm. "I may be very smart, but I'm not her keeper, darling."

"She left hours ago."

Nathan laid down the plant and came to join me at the door. He glanced at the sky with a hand shading his face, judging the sun. It was early evening and Bea had been gone since dawn.

She had hardly spoken to me since it had happened, since I'd bathed her gently and put her back to bed that morning as her fever broke, so much festering between us.

"You said you knew what you were doing," Bea had whispered.

"You might still be able to conceive in the future..."

I was probably wrong. I had laid my hands on her. I had felt the tight emptiness within her belly, felt my magic stretch for it, urgent to fill the gaps that we had made. Not just an absence but a shadow.

I should have known better than to give more than I had to spare. I should have said no.

I'd hardly seen her since, only caught her in the kitchen or the corridor outside her room and received stony glances for the trouble.

"She's probably in town," Nathan said. "She was there yesterday too. There's a speakeasy popped up behind that billboard—the old factory."

"What in the hell does she think she's doing?"

Nathan narrowed his eyes, doing a remarkable impression of Isobel. "What do you think, darling? She's making friends. She isn't one of us, Em. You can't keep her cooped up here like a rare bird."

"She should leave if she hates it so much."

Nathan sighed. He wiped his hands on a cloth he kept in his back pocket and reached out to squeeze my shoulder. It was a gesture I should have been thankful for, so rarely did he touch anybody at all, but it only stoked my anger.

"You messed up," he said softly. "She's found what she wants somewhere else. A smart lady knows where her bread is buttered, darling. She's been here two months without paying any rent or lifting a finger to help. Wouldn't you want to stay?"

"It's not like that," I said. "*She's* not like that. We're . . . She's . . ."

My excuses were empty.

"She got what she came for," Nathan said. When I looked at him his face wasn't unkind, his dark eyes warm, but anger rose in my fingers, the magic pushing and flexing, begging me to let it loose.

"That's not true," I growled.

"We warned you, but you were too besotted to see it."

"Don't you dare."

"She'll be gone soon and you'll just be a distant memory of a time when she made a mistake and somebody magicked it away. Whatever you felt for her, Em, she didn't feel the same. You feel bloody awful because you hurt her and she can twist the knife. She *will* because it's easy to lay the blame elsewhere.

"You'll do whatever she wants."

I couldn't take it anymore. I slapped him. Nathan let out a grunt and staggered, startled, but he didn't fight back. Cilla had hit him in the old days, touched him because he couldn't bear it.

I had just done the same.

"Nathan," I blurted. "I'm so sorry, love—"

"Go and calm down, Emmeline." Isobel squared off on the flat patch of grass behind the greenhouse, her arms folded and her eyes like thunder. She was ready to fight me to protect him. "I don't care how you feel. You never, *ever* lay your hands on him."

"I didn't mean to. I lost control..."

My very marrow writhed with disgust at what I had done, at who I had allowed myself to be. I watched as Isobel crossed to Nathan, lifting a tender hand to his cheek to check the thin line of blood I had drawn with my ring. She didn't let their skin touch until he nodded gently.

I wasn't like them. I didn't have a warm heart, a good soul.

I was, and always would be, too much like Cilla.

———— ( ) ● ( ) ————

It was after midnight. The air was hot and we'd opened all the windows. I heard Bea arrive home, a chorus of giggles. They'd come along the beach path. She was drunk.

There was a man with her. Blond crown. Skin like burnished gold. They reached the house still laughing. The sound of Bea's voice was like a purse of jingling coins.

I leaned out the window. The air kissed my fiery skin, soothing my ragged magic as it threatened to spill outwards, wound up with love and hate and everything in between.

I saw Bea's copper curls dance as she shook her head. She tilted her head up, angled her lips so they fell against his. He laughed a throaty sound, drunk on her. Bea looked at the house. She saw me and locked her eyes on mine.

She kissed him harder.

———— ( ) ● ( ) ————

I made the trip to the graveyard with my aunt's konjure set tucked underneath my arm. The air was filled with the scent of night-blooming flowers, and when I returned to the house under cover of darkness, the box freshly filled and the cards ready to spill their secrets, I could smell the moonflowers Nathan had imported and planted all along the walkway. Their white blooms shone in the moonlight.

When I opened the front door I was confronted by Beatrice. She sat at the bottom of the grand staircase in the foyer, her hands clasped in her lap. There was a ceremonial knife glinting across her knees and a small canvas bag at her feet.

For a second, unease feathered my spine—but she didn't intend to hurt me. There had been days where she would come back to the house every night with a different man, just to rile me, but over the last month or so we had moved into an almost peaceful cohabitation.

"I'm not taking anything that isn't mine," she said, gesturing at the bag. "I mean, the things you've given me."

I stayed silent because I didn't know what to say. My eyes wandered to the knife. It was one of Isobel's, a beautiful thing with runes carved into the handle. Isobel said it had been her mother's, but this was a lie. The day Isobel arrived she came with nothing but the bloodstains on her skin and a string of dirty glass beads. We all created fantasies to get us through what Cilla had made us do. Isobel made herself strong; she gave herself a backstory of a family who had loved her more than the magic that destroyed them, a future where she might mother her new family and nurse those who needed her. Nathan made himself funny and soft; gentleness was Cilla's greatest hatred and he embodied it almost to spite her. Myself, I wasn't sure what was fantasy and what was reality. The clothes, the house, the clients, the mystery and intrigue and fear...I needed it all.

"I've outstayed my welcome," Bea said.

Her green eyes glittered like malachite.

"I don't know what you want from me," I said quietly. Something inside my chest began to cleave. Perhaps it was my heart. "I've done everything I could for you."

"You ruined me." Bea gripped the handle of the knife harder. "Before I met you . . ."

"Before you met me, what?"

"I . . ." She spidered her fingers to the end of the knife, the point catching under her fingernail. "Goddamn it, Emmeline," she swore. "I'm not who you want me to be. This was meant to be easy."

"It was never going to be easy."

"It was meant to be business, then. I'm sorry if I made you think I felt that way about you. You weren't supposed to love me. I thought we were *friends*."

"We are friends."

"No," she said quickly. "We're not. I don't mean to be horrible. I just need you to understand. When I came here I was lost and afraid. I needed help. Emmeline, you made me trust you. I never should have trusted your magic. And now . . . Well, it's over."

"So why are you waiting here?" My voice grew stiff with hurt. I clutched my konjure set to my chest. The presence of the cards inside was cushioned by the fresh grave dirt; I could feel them whispering to me the way they had done ever since I was a little girl in my aunt's parlour. "Why didn't you just leave?"

"Because I need this from you first." Bea climbed to her feet, the knife still balanced in her grip. She walked towards me, holding it out like an offering.

"I don't . . ."

"I can't leave without some kind of hope of a future. I won't go back to that place, to that life. My mother just wants me to be like her, to marry some fisherman and work my whole life. God, Emmeline, that's not *me*."

"I can give you money—"

"It's not just money I want," she cut me off. "I found a man who I really like. Love. He likes me well enough, but it's all a lie. Everything he knows about me is a fiction."

"You want me to tell him the truth?" I asked.

"Don't be dim. I want you to make it all true."

"Bea, I can't create something out of nothing. I've told you that's not how it works."

Dread curled in my belly. The magic in my blood was stronger than it had ever been, pulsing and pushing inside my veins, wishing to be let out. I hadn't used it in weeks—a month maybe—and it was itching and crawling inside me.

"I won't do it," I swore.

"That isn't fair. You ruined my life when it suited you to do it. What, did you think that once the baby was gone I'd miraculously fall in love with you? That it was the only thing coming between us?"

"I didn't think—"

"No. Exactly. You didn't think."

I knew what I should say. That Bea had just waltzed in here with a problem and expected me to fix it, that she had waited so long to ask for my help that it became dangerous, that she hadn't listened to me. I wanted to call her selfish, bitter, childish... All true. Yet I couldn't say any of it, because I had enabled it. I had loved her—perhaps not even despite these things; perhaps it had been because of them.

"Emmeline, Arthur is a good man. He will make me happy. He has money; he's a war hero. He lives *here* on the island, goes to all these fancy parties. All I'm asking is for you to make him feel about me the way... the way that *you* do."

She lifted the knife, pressed the point into the soft tip of her finger until a bead of blood welled at its tip. Her eyes never left mine.

My magic jumped in my veins, but my head and my heart knew that it wouldn't be that easy. The kinds of tonics I sold to lovesick teenagers and cuckolded husbands weren't going to be powerful enough to create love where only infatuation existed—at least without his blood to tie the spell to.

"Will you do it, Em?" she asked. "Can you?"

She pushed the knife towards me. Her blood stained the blade, shining in the moonlight. I took it reluctantly.

"There's only one way," I said. "It's a blood bargain, Bea. Proper blood magic. It's dangerous. We need blood from him—and from somebody else who loves you. One now, one later."

This was magic I had never seen anybody attempt. I knew what I had to do like a whisper inside my mind, my magic guiding me from inside. Blood. Saliva. Quartz. A debt in exchange for a promise.

"I can do it," I said. "But, Bea, I'll need his blood within the year. To pay the debt that this kind of spell creates. Do you understand? It's…It's sacrifice. I…" *I'll do it for you. Trade my love for his. My blood for his.* "I'll do it, but you have to come back of your own free will. I won't be able to compel you. You must promise."

There were tears on her lashes. She blinked them away.

"Thank you," she said. "I'll tell him once we're married and we can get his blood after. I promise."

Chapter Five

Annie

I wandered down the drive that cut between Emmeline's house and mine. Fear and tiredness twisted together, shadows dancing underfoot as I circled back to Bea's expression at the party. Horror and guilt—and anger too. I considered the way Emmeline had spoken tonight, lying there in that bathtub. Desperation. The scent of her black blood, which made my dress stiff and heavy, still clung to my hands, though I'd washed them twice before leaving.

I stopped at the top edge of my front lawn. My house was quiet. The shadows on the front doorstep pooled, wavering as I stepped closer.

The door was ajar.

For a second, just one single fleeting second, I wished for Sam. He had always been so brave. But Sam wasn't here anymore, and he would never have wanted to be *here*, would never have understood why I was beginning to.

No, it wasn't Sam I wanted as much as his old familiarity, the kind of comfort I'd been hoping to rediscover in Bea.

I banished his ghost as I lifted a trembling hand, pushing the door back and stepping into the warm house. The yellow lights dispelled the shadows, and the sudden tightness in my lungs eased.

Had I left the door open earlier? I must have. My heart thumped and I let out a breathless laugh. It seemed like days ago. All those years living with Mam picking up after me and I'd never learned.

I locked the door firmly behind me.

In the kitchen I stripped out of my dress and threw it straight into the sink. It was ruined. The smell clung to me, dark and earthy. A shiver chased my spine.

I glanced around. Everything looked just the way I had left it. My cup standing empty on the kitchen table, the loaf of bread I'd left uncovered earlier. I stood in my stained slip, in the middle of the kitchen, frozen.

Everything looked right, but something didn't *feel* right. Not just because of Emmeline, because of what I'd seen. This was more like a premonition. A question. *Had* I left the door open earlier?

"Don't be a dummy," I whispered.

I finished undressing, cleaning the blood off every inch of myself, checking the cut at the base of my skull, where the skin throbbed painfully. I ignored every wavering shadow, every dark corner.

There was no reason to panic, though I did calmly walk into my bedroom to check under the mattress for my father's journal. It was still exactly where I had left it. I must be imagining things; hardly anybody even knew who I was, let alone that I was here.

I refused to let the fear grip me, because if I hadn't left the door open—that meant somebody had been inside my house.

—◦●◦—

The doorbell dragged me out of bed before nine. I slept badly and had been awake for hours, nerves jangling at every sound. During what little sleep I had managed I'd dreamed about dusty pages, circles of chalk drawn upon waxy floorboards, black blood and frothing potions, fingers dripping crimson, Emmeline's pointed teeth bared in pain.

Everything seemed softer in the daylight. The cottage was quiet, the air salt scented and gentle. There was no doubt in my mind that I had been imagining things last night. What I'd seen at Emmeline's house had upset me; that was all.

I wrapped my threadbare robe around my shoulders and shuffled to the door. I half expected to see Nathan or Emmeline but instead found a bouquet of freshly picked flowers, still dew damp. The bundle, rich white and ivory, smelled like lilies and was speckled with little green coils.

There was a small note card tucked amidst the blooms that read simply *Thank you*.

I put the flowers into water and ran myself a bath, hoping to soap away the last of my anxious thoughts. My head was still throbbing. Growing up, we hadn't the luxury of a tub with feet or taps, both Mam and I sharing the same tin bath in front of the fire, where the water always seemed a little grey and never hot enough. After the war Mam's shop had not flourished, and the water had only been greyer.

The cottage bath was luxurious. It had taps that ran bubbling, steaming streams of water, and I sank into it gratefully. My mind soon turned to my father's attic again. Not the horror of my dreams but the real thing, warm and bright and *mine*. I'd been told my whole life that magic was dangerous, and looking at Emmeline last night I'd known that to be true. Yet this morning the attic felt to me like an offering.

Emmeline was young. Was it possible she didn't know everything about the magic she used? If the books I'd seen told of a way to pay the blood debt without Arthur, Bea would no longer have to worry. Emmeline could be healthy again.

And, whispered a small voice, *she might help me in return*. She could dispose of my father's things, or hide them—if that was what I wanted.

I shoved the unfinished thoughts away. By the time the bathwater had grown cold, I had made a decision.

———()●()———

My father's house greeted me like an old friend.

I headed straight up to the attic. The staircase still smelled of salt, fresh like the rain in the air, and I sucked it into my lungs as if they were on fire.

Although nobody had been in the house since I had last visited, I still breathed a sigh of relief at finding the room exactly as I had left it. I wandered cautiously, growing slowly braver. I ran my hands gently over the desk, the grooves etched in the wood under the pads of my fingers bearing echoes of my father's pen strokes; I avoided the skulls but held a small crystal the colour of the ocean in my palm, feeling its heavy, oddly comforting weight. I opened a packet of herbs, holding it far away from my body but able to catch the scent on my tongue. I waited. For a telltale sign that I had gone too far, that I'd touched something I shouldn't have.

Nothing bad happened.

The warning inside my head was quieter inside this room, as if the magic itself had insulated me against it. *See?* it whispered. *Let me help you.*

From the bookshelves I pulled out the heaviest tome, letting my body gravitate towards it of its own free will. The leather was cracked and brittle.

My skin tingled with anticipation. I didn't know what I was looking for, but the promise of discovery left me breathless. The book didn't have a title, and the pages seemed older than the leather that contained them. I wondered where my father had found it, what he had sold or bartered to get it here. The price couldn't have been small.

For the first time since arriving here today, a zinging fear flew up my spine as I thought of that cost, and the cost if anybody should find it. If they should find me.

Crow Island wasn't the mainland, but this wasn't licensed faux palmistry, or even a little spiked liquor at a party. This wasn't Joey kissing a girl in the bathroom where anybody could discover them; it couldn't be chalked up to unwise choices. This was more akin to whatever bargain Bea had made with Emmeline. Always, always, I thought of Bessie Higgins, hanged over a poppet of herbs.

I glanced nervously at my father's things, the crystals, the drying herbs and the small animal skulls, and closed my eyes for a moment before turning back to the book. Magic could harm—I knew that already—but it must be capable of good or else Bea wouldn't have asked Emmeline for her help in the first place. I could be careful.

I flipped the book open. To my dismay, much of the text was in what looked like Latin. For some reason it made me think of Mam. She'd never really liked to let me read. Now I wondered if my mother's reluctance wasn't aimed more at my father, at who and what he was. I wondered if, deep down, she had suspected.

My skin crawled as I considered what she would say. What would she think of me? I nearly put the book down, walked away. Only thoughts of Bea, of Emmeline—of my father—held me in place.

I thumbed through more of the book's ancient crumbling pages. I recognised a sentence of English here and there, not that it made sense anyway; mostly I was drawn to the illustrations, captured in sweeping thick strokes of red and grey and black ink.

Some were of nature, stone formations like Stonehenge. The government had only left it standing because of the cost that would be involved in taking it down. If they ever saw this book I was sure they'd tear it down regardless of the hours it took or the war veterans they'd have to pay ridiculous fees to do it.

Later in the book I found strange glyphs, similar to the ones I had seen etched into Emmeline's arm. There were a series of triangles with various lines drawn through them, a circle in the middle of the page. Twelve more symbols below I couldn't begin to decipher.

My mouth was dry and my heart heavy. I was wrong. This wasn't going to help. It wasn't going to do anything except put me at risk and give me more nightmares about my father. He was a witch—and now he was dead. Was there a connection?

Thoughts swirled and dove. I was alternately terrified and excited, and then ashamed and afraid again. I flicked further through the book's illustrations. One depicted two hands tied together with a black ribbon.

At the back of the book there was a double-page spread, the ink faded. Here the text was in English, but the font was so looped and ornate that I struggled to read it. I held it towards the light, making out only a few words.

Witch
Initiation
Blood

The illustration showed a woman standing in a circle with her arms outstretched. Overhead hung a swollen silver-grey moon and the skeletal frames of leafless trees. She wore nothing but the skin she was born in, her stance proud, her body angular in a way that reminded me of Emmeline. From her outstretched finger drips of pink-red blood flowed down into the earth.

A surge of panic washed through me. I couldn't explain it but it felt like I was peering over somebody's shoulder while they asked for privacy—it wasn't for my eyes. And yet a spark deep inside me made me not want to look away.

It reminded me of the journal entry I'd seen in my father's book, the snippets of what I had read stitching together in my mind over hours and days. A girl on the beach years ago. Blood on her hands. *She has a darkness inside her.* I'd been rolling over the stolen phrase in my mind ever since I'd read it, and now I was sure. It had been Emmeline my father had seen near the ocean that night seven years ago. It had to be.

He'd been afraid of her. And with the danger Emmeline was in, Bea tangled up in it as well, I understood why. I was afraid of the darkness inside her, as I had always been taught to be—but mostly I was afraid of the way it called to me too. It scared me how easily I had come to the attic today, how quickly I had abandoned a lifetime of caution.

I couldn't look away from the image of the woman, the way the waves crashed at her back. A moment ago I had thought there were only trees, but now the ocean rose behind her, vast and dark. As I watched, the full moon grew sharp edges, wasting to a sickle point. I leaned in, eyes glazing as the image seemed to move before me. The woman morphed, her skin shifting, the creaking of bones echoing inside me as she became somebody else. Pale skin, red hair—Bea.

The figure no longer faced me. Instead she stared at the darkness to her right, where through the leafy fronds of trees there was a window housing a single shining candle. I was filled with dread. I stared harder, trying to unpick what I saw, but that made it worse, the image blurring and tossing, my gorge rising as I fought back the dizzying sickness that came with my panics. Finally I closed my eyes—and all that was behind them was blood.

I rocked back in my chair, panting until the nausea passed. Sweat beaded on my hairline, on my lip, between my shoulder blades. I pulled my hands into my lap, shaking. Dust motes swirled, the whole room smelling like lavender and salt. The sun had dipped. How long had I been here? It was getting late and I was starving, sick with hunger.

I heard it again. A creaking sound that I had written off as the settling of the house, the twisting of imaginary bones. The book was still, the image back to the one I had seen at first, that swollen silver moon and a witch.

The creaking didn't stop. Footsteps.

I leapt like a startled cat, tumbling out of the attic room and down the stairs so fast I almost tripped over my own feet. I skidded into the hallway, closing the door behind me just as a figure in a dark suit stepped through the door.

"Miss Mason," said Mr. Anderson cheerily. "I saw your car outside. I hope you don't mind that I let myself in—the door was unlocked. I was just stopping by to drop off a book your father lent me. I forgot I had it. I thought you might want to catalogue it." His gaze strayed behind me to the closed door. "My dear, are you all right? You look a little flushed."

"It's fine," I said, fighting back the last of the dizziness. "I'm glad you brought it back, but I'm sure my father wouldn't have minded if you'd kept it. I'm—I'm okay, just a little faint. Hungry, I guess. Will you walk me out...?"

Anderson tossed another curious look at the door but didn't argue. We made it into the street, to my car, before it hit me. I hadn't locked the attic door.

Chapter Six

Emmeline

I woke to the smell of Cross House in early summer. Freesia and jasmine, beeswax polish and rain. My bedroom was dark, the curtains pulled close so I didn't know what time it was. My whole body was heavy like it always was after a Giving—only this was the worst I'd ever felt. Normally there was a sense of relief at the brief reprieve. This time exhaustion was all I had.

"You really scared us, dearest."

Isobel perched in an armchair by the bed, one she must have pulled through from one of the other rooms, because it wasn't mine. Her knees were drawn to her chest, her chin resting on them as she watched me with golden eyes. I shifted, careful not to let on how much my body ached.

"I'm all right, love," I assured her.

"You wouldn't have been if she hadn't found you."

"Who?"

Isobel raised an eyebrow. "Don't you remember? Annie."

"Really?" I tried to move so that I was lying on my side but couldn't manage it. Instead I put my energy into getting more upright, knocking my head against the headboard.

I sifted through my memories of the last hours. I remembered dinner—how good it had felt to have Annie there. How I'd wished it felt any other way. How Bea had left without care. I remembered the Giving, bits and pieces of it at least. I remembered Isobel applying a salve to my arm. I flexed it, the scabbed runes twisting uncomfortably. The last ones had only just healed over.

"I think you really scared her, you know. Knocked her about a bit too, by the sounds of things."

"I didn't…"

I did remember Annie coming to me, later. Her bright, lovely face. Her blue eyes narrowed in concern, in panic, as she leaned over me. And my magic, lashing out like an untamed beast—like a monster.

"Oh," I murmured.

This was why I needed to keep her away.

"Why didn't you tell us how bad it was?" Isobel pressed. "We could have helped. There are still so many things we can try. Salves and mixtures and…"

"Really?" I said wearily. "Isobel, you know as well as I do that only my blood can hold off the debt. Salves and potions won't make it go away as much as you might wish otherwise. Without her husband I'll just have to keep Giving and Giving until there's nothing left."

"You told us it was under control." The way her shoulders hunched, the way her eyes filled and she blinked hard—both made shame slither beneath my skin; it was betrayal, that look. "You said you had a plan."

"I lied, okay? Is that what you want to hear?"

Isobel's silence was worse than another lecture would have been. I had broken her. I had promised her we would find a way to live without Cilla. I had lied about that too.

If I had really understood the risks when I agreed to help Beatrice, would I have still done it? It was a question I had asked myself again and again since. Would I have sacrificed myself—the safety of my family—so easily?

Had Cilla known when she entered into her own bargain? I

always thought she must have, but perhaps that was the arrogance of youth. Perhaps she had no more seen where her magic would lead than I had. It occurred to me that maybe we had, neither of us, *wanted* to see.

"It probably isn't as bad as it looks," I explained tersely. "I've been putting off Giving. I didn't know how much I'd have to Give last night, but I hoped...I hoped she would be more receptive. That maybe I could wait just one more day if she said she could help..."

Isobel snorted mirthlessly, wiping a stray tear from her cheek with mild annoyance. "What, given her past behaviour, gave you that idea?"

I closed my eyes and inhaled the garden smell. A faint breeze wafted the curtains and I pictured Bea's face, how sad she had looked at dinner. How scared. There had always been a part of me that felt like Bea brought out the best in me. She made me softer, kinder, and when she lived here with us the house felt *full*. The truth was that she also brought out the worst in me.

Had I agreed to the bargain out of selfishness? Was it a wish that what I'd done would count less against me if I helped her? I had, desperately, wanted her to stay on the island; I just hadn't thought it would lead to this.

I couldn't blame her. Bea hadn't understood—truly understood— what would happen to me when she asked for this final thing. That was my fault. Maybe she would never have agreed to go ahead with it if she'd known the full cost.

Or maybe she would have done it anyway and I was a fool.

"Did I really hurt Annie?" I asked. "I mean, *really* hurt her?"

Isobel was thoughtful. "She was badly shaken up. I think she'll be fine. Nathan said he left her some flowers."

Annie didn't deserve any of this. It would be best for her—for us both—if I could keep her as far away as possible. And yet...

"I should go and apologise. How long have I been asleep?"

"Not long enough. Nathan made you some of his special tea but you wouldn't drink it."

I started to climb out of the bed, drawing my legs up in slow, painful movements better fitting an elderly woman. Isobel leapt from her chair and waved her arms, always the nurse.

"What on earth do you think you're doing?"

"I'm getting up," I said. "If that's all right with you."

"It's not! You're not well enough. You have to rest—"

"Oh, stop fussing around me like a mother hen," I muttered. "I can't just sit around here all day. I have things I have to do."

"Things?" Isobel demanded. "Like what?"

"Like talk to Annie. Like clients to see. I can't start turning people away. We need the money—"

"It's always about money with you, isn't it." Isobel shook her head. Her curls were glossy this morning, but the dark smudges under her eyes betrayed her worry more than her sharp tongue.

"It's always about money, not just with me," I retorted. "This is who we are. I want a life for us, one that will last longer than next week's party."

The truth was, since the war it had been harder and harder to turn a profit. Cilla had been right about one thing: war made people desperate. Before, they came out of desperation, flocking to Cross House every night; now, most of them came here for weekend fun. One was vital, the other just a symptom.

"You always say that, Em. Maybe this isn't the way to do it anymore," Isobel said. She held up her hands, which were smoother than mine but still bore the signs of the blood magic she'd cast under Cilla.

"It's the only way," I argued. We'd had this argument before. "Magic is all we know."

"Yes, but it's been getting worse, dearest. It's only a matter of time before the wrong person gets hurt at one of your parties, before you skimp on the magic for a brew because you're exhausted and you refuse to ask for my help and it goes wrong again."

"That was an accident and it won't happen again."

"Won't it? You're playing with fire. If people turn on us—did you ever stop and think what would happen? They're picking out example cases. Like that hotshot athlete they arrested yesterday. She's not even one of us. She's just a girl having a good time and getting a little too wild. Who's to say it wasn't the Council, trying to get rid of people who draw the wrong attention to the island? You're putting us in danger, Em."

"It's fine," I reassured her. "The Council only care about themselves. They don't care what we get up to as long as we don't cause any trouble. People have fun here. We've got the police *and* the Council in our pocket—"

"And what about when Sergeant Perry gets bored?" Isobel threw up her hands in exasperation. I hadn't seen her like this before, so stubborn and afraid. "He's our only connection with both. What if he gets tired of our money and my kazam? What then? Do you really want to keep risking it all for *more*? Are you that greedy, Emmeline, that you don't know when to stop? Our life is good—"

"It's good *now*!" I cried. "It's good because I've worked hard. *We* have worked hard. This won't last forever, Is, you know that. What happens when the money runs out?" *What happens when I'm gone?*

"We will figure it out," Isobel snapped. "We can't carry on like this. It's ludicrous. Look at you, Em. This is what comes from meddling in other people's lives. Isn't that exactly what Cilla did? Isn't that what we wanted to stop?"

Isobel didn't see it. If we had money—if *they* had money—I'd know they would always be okay. I did these things because I *didn't* want to be like her.

"Stop acting like you're so high-and-mighty," I said, anger burning to mask the sadness that burrowed deep. "Just because you don't charge people for your services doesn't make them any safer for us. You're putting us just as much at risk by practising magic out there as I am. By brewing your kazam."

"Em, that's not fair. You're the one that sells that stuff. I told you, I just like to make it—"

"And at least *I* have the guts to use my full magic when I'm with clients instead of relying on natural herbs."

Isobel went silent.

Instantly I regretted it. All that she had worked for, all that I had genuinely wanted to encourage... I had just thrown it all back in her face. Like it meant nothing.

She swallowed, fresh tears in her eyes. Another spark of anger flared in me. Good, I thought meanly. This was *good*. If people couldn't trust me, couldn't love me, they might be safe from me.

"Don't pretend I'm your enemy," she said quietly. "None of this is my fault."

She met my gaze and I was reminded of the first time I had ever seen her, cowering in the dirt with her fingernails bloody but the same cold fire burning in her eyes. Isobel's magic wasn't the same as mine. Hers was like water, sometimes still, sometimes soft and healing, but capable of brute force—only Isobel never let it loose. Mine had always been glittering edges, blood drawn by a sharp blade, and whether or not I wanted it to, it always snapped with the jaws of a wolf. I couldn't keep it caged if I tried.

My anger slowly ebbed away, leaving behind only exhaustion.

"I'm trying my best," I said.

"It doesn't matter, Em. Get some rest. I've got some errands in town but I'll be back to change your bandages after dinner."

The room was barren once she'd gone. Slowly I hauled myself out of the narrow bed, dragging my aching body across to the window. I opened the curtains, letting in a slash of yellow-blue early morning light.

Sucking my teeth, I rolled up the sleeve of my nightshirt. The bandages that Isobel had applied were already bloodied. I peeled them back, exposing the black-beaded scars from last night to the sunlight. My aunt had taught me as a child that blood magic was safest when used with direction; runes, words, it didn't matter as long as you used more than just *desire*. The instinct was to prick your finger and wish for things, but that was the worst thing you could do, because without the runes to cling to the magic ran wild.

I just wished she had taught me about the consequences of casting blood magic for other people. How if you weren't careful you could end up as a husk of your former self. You could tie yourself into a bargain that devoured your body and your sanity, one drop at a time. You knew what was happening and were still powerless to stop it.

If I'd known...I thought again of Bea's face, her crooked smile, and how badly I'd wanted her to make me laugh. It wouldn't have mattered. I would have done it anyway.

Footsteps on the stairs, a tread heavier than Isobel's. I turned as Nathan stumbled into the bedroom. His brown eyes were creased at the corners with worry, none of the usual mischief in his face. His shirt was streaked with a stripe of mud from the garden.

"What's the matter?" I asked. My whole body prickled with alarm. I felt it in the cuts on my arm and in the magic that ran through my veins. I was light-headed and I had to grab on to the windowsill for support.

"She's been reported missing."

Chapter Seven

Annie

I rushed straight to Emmeline's house as the sun set. As I got close the tether, which had been small and forgettable while I was away, grew larger in my chest, glowing silver-white as it tugged faintly, then harder, a magnetism that today I didn't want to ignore. I latched on to it, racing to the back of Cross House, praying she could help me, praying she could explain what I'd seen in my mind while I'd sat in my father's attic.

I didn't bother to knock.

Inside, the air smelled like dirt and blood—faintly, as though Emmeline had been in the kitchen not long ago. I found her in a downstairs parlour, dim with the curtains drawn and several candles dotted around. A small table in its centre was laid out with a set of cards unlike any I'd ever seen. They were worn around the edges, their decoration painted in ivory and emerald and black. Emmeline sat at the table, her head in her hands.

She spun when she saw me, but she didn't seem surprised, only relieved.

"It's you," she said.

"I'm sorry to barge in. I wanted to talk to you," I panted. "I was— I saw... I have a horrible f—"

"Bea's missing," Emmeline interrupted. She crossed the room quickly in her comfortable-looking trousers. On one arm I saw a bandage peeking from beneath a rolled-up sleeve.

"Missing?" My stomach lurched.

"Her husband reported her missing this morning," Emmeline said urgently. "He's saying she didn't go home last night, but Nathan—he says she did. He checked. Her car's there."

The floor threatened to crack beneath me. I reached out for something to hold on to, my hand landing on Emmeline's outstretched arm. When our flesh met it was electric, like a jolt right through my skin and into my bones. I yanked my hand back.

"Why would Arthur say that if it wasn't true?"

Emmeline shook her head.

"If he doesn't know where she is... If we can't find her..." I pictured Bea last night, crying in her car. That awful pained expression. The last words we'd spoken had been full of sadness and anger. And the things I'd seen in the attic, blood under a waning moon... What if she'd hurt herself? Panic whipped through me like wildfire. "We have to find her."

"I sent Nathan to the Crow and Sickle. Bea loved it there last year. I don't know where else to try. Isobel is asking her network. They'll—"

"God, I knew it," I cut her off. "I felt...I saw—Emmeline, if you have a vision, is it a sign of the future? Or a warning?"

"A vision?"

"Yes. I don't know how to describe it. Just—does it always come true? Can normal people have visions? I couldn't get it to focus. My eyes...I was so afraid."

Emmeline glanced at the cards on the table. Up close I could see that the emerald patterns on them were more intricate than I'd thought, reminiscent of the glyphs I'd seen carved into her arm, in the book in my father's attic.

"Visions need focus. If you repress them they fracture. It's easier with a tool, like the cards, to direct them."

"Show me how to do it." I didn't know what I was saying, didn't care that Emmeline hardly knew me, that a week ago I'd have rather set myself on fire than touch those cards with my bare skin. Now I only cared that it might help. Bea was in danger. If what I thought I had seen meant something; if she had hurt herself…"Please," I begged.

Emmeline didn't question. She sat down again at the card table, cross-legged on the floor. With nimble fingers she picked up the cards, sweeping them into her hands.

"Sit down," she said.

She shuffled the cards with fluid movements, so fast that her hands were a blur. Her knuckles were slightly swollen already with arthritis, although she was young, and the backs of both hands were marked with scores of tiny white scars. The room smelled like aniseed, the scent thick and cloying—underpinned by Emmeline's dirt-and-blood smell. It had taken a moment but the thread in my chest had settled the way a horse might if it were reined.

"Close your eyes," Emmeline instructed, her voice guiding me. "Think of Bea."

I did as I was told. I tried to imagine her, safe at home with her husband. Instead I couldn't help thinking of her in the car in her dinner dress, her hair coiled at her neck, her sobs breaking my heart. Of the way she'd left Emmeline distraught. Of the things she had said about Sam.

"Not too much emotion," Emmeline warned. "That's it. Open your eyes and cut the deck. Take three cards."

I took a deep breath, forcing the trembling in my limbs to settle. When I touched the cards their surface was smoother than I expected, the noise in my head quietening. I held the deck for a moment, conjuring the image of the Bea I had seen in my father's attic, hazy and unfinished. I let my fingers linger on first one card, a second, a third, choosing ones that seemed right and laying them facedown.

"Turn them over. Tell me what you see."

My movements were jerky with urgency. I flipped the cards over. All three were etched in dark shades; purples and greys, black and white and green. The first showed a skull sat atop a mound of dark grey-brown dirt, the eyes vacant and staring. Beneath the skull sat a child's rattle. The second card was a silver goblet filled with purple wine, the stem flowing into ivy that blistered with poisonous-looking blooms. The third card was a simple crescent moon above a glittering lake, but in the bottom right corner I noticed that the corpse of a bird had been painstakingly captured in the sandy dirt.

I leaned in, focused on the cards like Emmeline told me. My vision wavered. I heard the roaring in my ears, the sound I had always known was mine alone. I could feel Emmeline's eyes on me, studying my face, my hands. I burned under her gaze. The roaring dropped away.

"I can't," I whispered.

"You can. You just need a nudge. Here."

I watched with horrified fascination as Emmeline bit down on her lip, drawing blood. She swiped her finger through it and then dragged it across all three cards, leaving a dark smear. Instantly the air in the room shifted. Emmeline let out a breath, relaxing, and the tether in my chest was writhing and snapping at her presence, tugging with such white-hot, brilliant urgency that I was breathless.

I was powerful.

"Use it," Emmeline hissed.

I sucked in a breath, tasting blood, earth, and my thoughts came unstuck. A crash of images rushed through my mind; there was the ocean black under a sliver of silver moon between clouds; there was Bea's back as she turned away from her house and ran; there she was crumpling onto the sand, her red hair covering her face.

"We need to go to her house," I bleated.

———❪●❫———

Bea's house loomed like a castle, dark and cloaked in the scent of the ocean spray. The sloping path to the beach was treacherous. Emmeline's black coat flapped behind her like wings as we ran.

"This way!" I yelled.

There was a rocky outcrop ahead, beneath another lawn, and a small cove that was not visible from the house. Under the rough, bulky shape of the rocks I could make out a shadowed bundle against the sand, illuminated by the scrap of moon.

We surged forward together, sand scattering like confetti.

"*Bea.*" Her name escaped Emmeline's lips like a curse.

Up close I saw a flash of milky skin, a swath of her glorious red hair, matted and damp with salt and sand. Emmeline fell to her knees, gathering Bea into her lap.

"Annie, help me."

Bea's hair was tangled like seaweed and it made me think of other nights, nights when I had woken on the beach, terrified but *alive*. Magic, haunting me always, pebbles in my pockets and the ocean in my bones. It felt like those nights had led me here.

"*Annie!*"

Emmeline's voice pulled me back, to Bea's face, all bloodied and bruised, and the tentative rise and fall of her chest.

"We have to get her back to the house," I gasped.

Her skin was like ice, pimpled with the cold. Emmeline shrugged out of her coat and bundled it around Bea, who didn't stir when we tried to lift her upright. I wrapped my arms around Bea's legs. Emmeline looped her arms around Bea's waist, and together we half carried, half dragged her towards the house.

We struggled to the back of the house, to the sloping lawn I'd seen at the party, the decking. The doors were open wide, curtains billowing.

"Where's Arthur?" I panted.

Emmeline shook her head.

"Don't care," she snapped. "Blankets. A fire. We need to get her warm."

We managed to get Bea through the doors, into the white room where a table had been set for dinner. Emmeline swept the rows of beautiful china onto the floor with an earsplitting crash and laid Bea down on its surface. I set about building a fire in the cold, black hearth. My hands shook so badly I struggled to light a match.

When I turned back, the fire beginning to lick at paper and coal,

Emmeline was rubbing Bea's hands with her own, whispering in a foreign tongue that sounded harsh and guttural.

Eventually Bea began to stir, the colour slowly seeping back into her limbs. In the glow of the fire I saw that her face was marred by streaks of scarlet blood. One of her eyes was sealed shut and she bled from a cut above her eyebrow. Her cheekbone was swollen and egg-like. More blood trickled from a split in her lip as she moaned.

"Are you hurt anywhere aside from your face?" Emmeline asked. She looked visibly exhausted.

Bea tried to speak. She licked her lip and grimaced.

"Ribs," she croaked. "Think 'e cracked 'em."

"Who did?" My voice surprised me. Cold and clear, not betraying my fear.

"Arthur."

"Bea...He reported you missing. He..." The words fell flat. Horror turned my limbs to lead.

"He knows," she whispered. "About the blood debt. This is what he did."

Emmeline sank against the table.

"Well," she said. "That's it."

My fingernails bit into my palms. "Where's Arthur now?" I demanded.

"I don't know," Bea said quietly, expression showing her jumbled thoughts. "He was—he was like an animal. I've never seen him like that before...He hit me. Beat me and then he was gone. I think people came looking for me but I crawled onto the beach. Didn't know if they were with him...I must have passed out. I didn't know I was in the water."

"Why would he leave y..." I started to ask the question but the answer slammed into my stomach like a punch and forced the air out. *He thought he'd killed her.*

"The debt," Emmeline said. "It's breaking down. My blood isn't enough to stop it."

"We have to go," I blurted. Bea started to argue but I cut her off. "For God's sake, Bea, we can't stay here."

Bea blanched. It occurred to me that she had never seen me angry before. I was always just gentle, stupid Annie. Well, not anymore.

"Annie's right," Emmeline agreed. "It's not safe here."

"Let's go," I said. "I'll put out the fire. You get her to the car."

Emmeline started to move. She hooked her arms under Bea's armpits so they could stand together. They were partway to the door when Bea stopped, going rigid.

"Eddie's ring," Bea said, turning to me, her eyes pleading. "Ann, I can't leave without it."

"Bea," I warned.

"It's all I've got."

"Where is it? You're not wearing it?"

"Arthur won't let me. It's too masculine. I keep it with my underthings. Upstairs, first door on the right."

I swore. Bea had never taken the ring off, not once in all the years since her brother had died. I should have noticed. I should have noticed and I hadn't.

Bea's room was decorated in shades of pink and cream. There was no sign of Arthur, either his person or his things. I wondered if the bargain had been worth this life.

I rooted through several drawers of clothes before I found the right one. I pulled out a nightgown that looked older than the rest. It could have come from home, with its lace neck and ragged hem. I folded that, along with an old jacket and a few pairs of underwear, for Bea. Then I dug deeper in the drawer, looking for somewhere you might keep a ring.

My fingers snagged on cool metal. I brushed aside the underwear and sucked in a breath. Beside a little blue box, which no doubt contained Eddie's ring, there was a gun.

I lifted it out hesitantly, hefting the weight of it in my palm. It was unfamiliar and yet it fit snugly in my hand. I thought it might be loaded. I'd not seen a gun since I was a child, when one of the farmer boys who lived just outside Whitby had brought one to school and paraded it around the yard until a teacher confiscated it.

This was different. Smaller. I thought about what Emmeline had said, about the debt breaking down. If I hadn't come here, would Bea ever have told me how afraid she was? Or would I have had to read about her death in the newspaper? My throat constricted and my eyes began to itch. I refused to cry.

Instead I slid the gun into the pocket of my dress right next to the little velvet ring box.

Chapter Eight

Annie

I just checked and she's still sleeping," Emmeline said.

Hours later and we had ended up on the sloping lawn outside Cross House, barefoot and jacketless in the warm morning, the sunlight gilding the trees. Neither of us had slept. Around dawn Bea had woken, screaming, her legs tangled in her sheets and nails slashing. Isobel had to give her a sleeping draught.

We didn't wander far. The day was quiet yet there was a sense of foreboding hanging over everything, a rush of adrenaline from last night that had never fully dissipated.

Nathan had agreed to head back to Bea's place to wait for Arthur, assuming he eventually went home. Nathan's face had been stormy when we'd brought Bea home, half-frozen, still bleeding, but he hadn't said anything. Isobel was gone too. She'd left to trade for more of the black pepper and sage she said she'd need to make another batch of the sleeping draught if Bea needed one.

The house was too empty without them. Everything echoed. It was why I'd suggested getting some fresh air.

"At least if she's asleep she's not likely to hurt herself," I reminded Emmeline softly. "We can talk to her later, when she's had some time to process what happened. We can decide what to do."

I had no idea what that meant.

We walked a little farther down the lawn, Bea's bedroom window still visible behind us. My skin prickled all over, nerves grating. Emmeline hardly spoke, her face drawn and weary.

She hadn't come near me since we'd left my car. As we walked she didn't look at me. Her body was coiled tight like a spring.

Perhaps almost losing Bea had reminded her of everything I wasn't. Not brave, not adventurous. Perhaps I had done the wrong thing by asking to use her cards. I wondered if she knew about the gun, which still sat nestled in the damp pocket of my dress. I fingered it gently, reassured by its presence.

Emmeline stared ahead. Her jaw was tense, her eyes dark with worry. It hit me like a jolt—a painting appearing in my mind unbidden, formed by a collection of isolated strokes merging into one image: the way Emmeline had looked at Bea over the dinner table the other night, an intimacy hidden behind her disappointment; the fear she had concealed so badly while we read her cards together that went beyond the consequences of her bargain; even the way she stood out here on the lawn, her expression one of loss as well as concern.

This wasn't simply fear of what her magic had wrought. A new, sharp pang of envy forced me to speak.

"You and Bea..." I said, unable to stop myself. The thoughts came into crystal clarity as the words tumbled out of my mouth. "You weren't just friends, were you? You were *in love* with her."

Emmeline turned to me sharply. I froze, but she didn't look offended, only shocked. "What makes you say that?"

I swallowed, trying to dislodge the lump in my throat. "The way you still look at her sometimes," I said tentatively. "Like you've lost something. The way you trusted her. Why else would you bring her here after everything she's done?"

"I'm protecting my investment," she said thickly. "I need her."

There was more to it than that. I could see it in the slope of Emmeline's shoulders, how she stared ahead. It was grief, but it was anger too, faded and cold.

I scrunched my bare toes in the thick, soft lawn. From here I could see the beach, the little tufts of scrubby grass that grew, the brackish colour of the ocean fading as the sun rose higher.

Emmeline let out a sigh. "If Bea is here..." she added more softly. "I don't know. It gives me hope. I suppose it's one less thing to worry about. She scares me."

Finally she looked at me, properly looked at me, as if she was searching my face for a hint of her own truth, and I was dazzled by her. The sun glinted off her sharp jaw, her cheekbones. She stood in that same easy way, one thumb hooked on the pocket of her trousers. Her dark eyes shone and I recalled the first time I'd seen her, how it had felt like I could hardly breathe.

Instinctively I reached for the tether, expecting it to be pulled taut, expecting it to be the source of this fluttering inside me. I expected to feel the accompanying surge of fear, of confusion. Instead it nestled, comfortable and faint, as it had been the whole time we'd been outside.

I blanched, my legs going weak. That meant the emotions—the envy and the fear and that deep, heated *want* inside me—were mine alone...

"It's not just you," I said quickly, turning away so Emmeline couldn't see the way my face burned.

"What?"

"Bea," I said. "The way she makes people feel. It's not just you she scares." I scrubbed a hand over my face. "She always could make me do whatever she wanted when we were kids. She's got this way...a strange sort of non-magic. God, this is all so confusing. I don't know how to feel about any of it. I don't even know who I am anymore."

"Because of the cards?" Emmeline asked. "The things you saw? Is that what you mean?"

"Yes. No—I don't know. I..." My throat was tight. I wanted her to help me; I wanted to tell her about my father and have her offer a solution. I wanted things to be easy, to be told that I had not strayed, had not broken a lifelong promise to my mother, and that I could not be punished—that who my father had been meant nothing—even though it was a lie. And I couldn't find the words for any of it. "My…He…Does it mean I'm…?"

"Annie," Emmeline said calmly, understanding. She reached into her pocket and pulled out a couple of crumpled cigarettes. "The world teaches us that these things are black and white. That magic is wrong and the law is good. I can tell you it's not that simple. What happened yesterday, what you saw in the cards—it doesn't mean anything about who you are. It doesn't have to mean anything at all as far as I am concerned. You and Bea share a connection that goes back a long way. Just because she's been on the island doesn't mean it's gone."

"How do you know?" I demanded. "We don't have much of anything anymore. Bea left me. She thinks I'm weak-minded and boring. She chose this place—she chose you and magic and didn't even tell me." The loneliness in my words sounded stark, echoes of myself I'd hoped I'd left behind. Any other time I would have been embarrassed, but I was too tired, too conflicted, to care.

"She talked about you, you know. When she was here last year."

I was silent.

Emmeline lit one of the cigarettes using a broken match, letting out a puff of fragrant smoke.

"I didn't realise it was *you* at the time," she continued. "I didn't put it together until you both came to dinner. She didn't talk about home much, but she told me about you, and your other—friend—who died during the war."

I flinched. I had hardly thought of him for days, and the mention of him made me baulk. Sam didn't belong here.

"Sorry," Emmeline said. She shaded her face against the sun as she gazed out over the water, once again refusing to look at me. "What I'm trying to say is that I didn't mean to drag you into this. I tried not to. I shouldn't have made you help me last night."

"You didn't make me do anything. I made a decision," I argued. The tether, whatever it was, couldn't have caused the wavering images I'd seen in my father's attic, could it? They felt so different, and the tether had been dormant the whole time. Emmeline hadn't made me go back into that hidden room, hadn't caused the things I'd seen, as much as I wished she had. She *couldn't* have.

"You should go home."

I looked to my right, where I could see the faint outline of my cottage through the trees. Part of me thought Emmeline was right. I *should* go home, try to sort through this mess of emotions. Figure out exactly what had happened yesterday and what it all meant.

Another small part of me, a part I couldn't ignore, warned me not to leave. It said that this wasn't over yet.

Emmeline started walking again, following the line of the lawn. My ears began to hum.

"I mean *home*, Annie," Emmeline said. Her voice was cool. "I don't mean the cottage."

"What?" The sound in my ears grew louder. I could hardly hear over it, the sound of the waves dropping away, replaced by the ones inside my head. Why did this keep happening to me? Why couldn't I just ignore it anymore? "Why?"

A look of panic flashed across Emmeline's face, the tether trembling strangely between us, before she obscured it once more. She dropped her cigarette.

"It's complicated," she said, her voice muffled.

"Do you honestly think that I could leave?" I asked through gritted teeth. We had nearly reached the fountain when I stumbled, my vision going dark.

"Ann—"

"Bea is my friend. I can help," I mumbled, reaching out for the fountain's edge as my balance went, the ground rushing up. "My father..."

"*Annie!*" Emmeline was next to me, her hand around my arm; all I could see was darkness. "Breathe," she barked. "Plant your feet firmly. Keep your eyes open and look around—like you're searching."

I was panting. Her voice was distant, punctuated by roaring waves. I tried to do what she said, my eyes wide. I pretended I was a child again, playing hide-and-seek with Bea in the dark of her mam's cellar.

"Grab hold of my hand," Emmeline said. "Here."

I did. The touch was like a spark. The silver cord that looped between us expanded rapidly, filling me up so that it was everywhere, glowing like moonlight. Unconsciously I reached for it in my mind's eye, holding on tight.

The silver light exposed the scene in front of me until it was clear as water. A rush of pleasure flooded my veins even as I recoiled from the horror ahead. I saw blood. I saw the hem of a white nightgown worn ragged. I saw three silver-limned crows, their beady black eyes searching, their beaks knife sharp.

I knew what it meant.

"Bea."

Chapter Nine

*H*e can't believe it took him this long to think of the house. The house with the witch—the place where everything went wrong. She's still alive—and he was foolish enough to be relieved. But with twelve hours of bourbon running hot in his veins, he's only angry. How dare she run back there?

He's only seen the house at night before and it looks different during the day. No obvious hints of debauchery. No lights burning in windows, no cars out front; no sign of those careless people drowning in champagne and stars. He pushes into the house like a ghost.

He knows he isn't thinking clearly. It's like the other episodes he's been having—increasingly often since he got married. His brain is sluggish and the ideas are slow forming.

What would Violet say?

His wife won't make a fool out of him again. The more time that passes since the wedding, the more he's not sure what's real and what is a dream. He liked her before they married, sure. Did he love her? He can't get his head around it.

He doesn't know why he married her. He can't remember asking. He wouldn't have if he'd been thinking clearly. Not even if she said she was the Queen of Sheba, because he knows she's never been the queen of anything.

He's burning angry again. She mentioned his blood. He'll be damned and slapped in bracelets by a copper if anybody is getting a drop of it. How dare she ask for that?

He's heard the stories; he knows that witches are meant to bathe in the stuff for eternal youth. He saw the things they did during the war. Men with no emotions, no thoughts except the ones they were given. Germans like zombies, like machines, slaughtering Englishmen for sport. What if she wants to make him do things? Things more than leaving Vi and marrying a penniless wretch? He didn't make it home from those bloody, screaming fields for this.

He finds his way up some stairs and through a succession of empty rooms and hallways. He shoves doors open at random, rage driving him on until he finds her.

There she is.

The sight of her standing there in her white nightgown—the one she wore the night after they got married, the only one she had, already lying about who she was—it makes his blood boil. He'd thought it sweet at the time, but he should have known what it meant.

Seeing the way it clings to her curves, too short and too tight, he realises that he knows nothing about her. Has she told him the truth about anything? About who she is or where she's from?

She's swaying slightly in front of the fireplace in the bedroom, staring at it like it's a window and she's sleepwalking. She doesn't turn at the sound of his footsteps, or at the rumble of his breath. His heart beats steady, calling to hers. Traitor heart. Traitor body. Does nothing belong to him anymore?

"What did you do to me?" His voice is thick.

She turns, slowly. She's awake but barely. She doesn't scream and run like he almost hopes she will. Her face is a goddamn mess. Look what she made him do, for Christ's sake. He isn't a violent man.

"I needed you to love me," she answers. It's the closest thing to a truth she's told him yet. He can hear it in the ring of her voice and it makes him sick.

"You used magic."

"You thought I had money. You thought I belonged on Crow Island with the rest of you. I had to make you believe I was the sort of girl you would marry. I couldn't lose you."

"How could you?" he growls.

"I needed you to love me," she says again. "Forever. I knew if you found out who I was, you wouldn't want me anymore. I couldn't let you go, Art. I loved you. Really loved you. Please—if you just pay the debt it'll seal the deal and we can go back to how it was before. You'll feel better—"

"You were never supposed to be my wife!"

He doesn't realise he's shouting until she stumbles back into the cold hearth, her heels knocking against the fireside companion. The poker tumbles to the floor and she bends to grab it, to ward him off. He can't help the laugh that rumbles in his throat.

He doesn't know what he saw in her; she's like a dog that's been kicked a thousand times, still crawling back for the next in the hope of scraps.

"I never wanted you," he says. "I would never have married you."

He doesn't wait for a response. He hurtles towards her, grabbing the poker in one hand and wrenching it away, wrapping his other fist in her curls. They're damp and matted with sweat and sand and dirt. It's disgusting.

He brings his knee up to knock her legs out from under her. They tumble together. She's thrashing like a frightened bird, but it doesn't take much to hold her down. He gets one hand on each of her arms, pinning them to the ground.

"Get your hands off her."

The voice is like a boom of thunder. He spins and sees her. She's everything he hates. It's true what they say about her. She's not just a witch. She's unholy. She wants to be a man. And Bea—he bets she's seduced her. Corruption flows on the surface here.

The witch stands firm, darkness dripping down the inside of her arm, the white sleeve of her shirt stained scarlet.

"You did this." His wife wriggles underneath him and he smashes one of his elbows into her nose with a satisfying crack. She falls still, trembling again.

"Get off her," the witch says.

She's calm. Part of his brain says he should be afraid. He should go home, do it the legal way. There's a coldness, oily and persistent, inside him and he just can't ignore it. Some fear of what will happen to him if he doesn't end this.

"Why should I listen to you?" he spits. "You're unholy. You can't just twist people's lives, make them do things, feel things… There has to be a consequence. You can't get away with this."

The air changes. It has become dangerous. Like the edge on a razor, deceptively mundane but still capable of splitting skin and drawing blood.

"Get. Off. Her," the witch repeats. This time the tremble of her voice in the air is like a hurricane, although she isn't speaking any louder.

He won't let her win. Beatrice doesn't move beneath him. She's holding herself as still as a doll. Slowly he presses his palm to his wife's neck and begins to push. One way or another this will end tonight. He will be free.

It's the wrong move. Within seconds the witch is flying towards him. The blow connects before he sees it, a pressure in his stomach that knocks him clear from his perch. He lets out a surprised bellow.

Somebody else screams but he can't tell where the sound comes from. Sunlight flashes and blood arcs as the witch shakes her arm. He flinches, covers his eyes and his mouth as he scrambles away. He can smell the iron, a smell like damp dirt after a rain.

The witch is chanting unintelligible words, blood smeared across her face like war paint. It's smoking, somehow it's smoking, and his bones hum with it.

He reaches for the knife that's tucked in his pocket. It's cold and firm and reassuring and he brandishes it like it could be a sword. Beatrice shrinks away. The witch doesn't stop and he throws himself at her. She's got magic, but he still has strength on his side. He catches her right knee with a well-aimed kick.

She tumbles to her knees. He advances fast, knife raised. Better to get rid of them both, start fresh, than have this panicked darkness hanging over him forever.

The witch stares at him with ruthless determination, but she doesn't move. Some other thing catches her gaze; she jolts her head and her expression changes to one of warning.

He won't be fooled.

He hooks the tip of the knife to the soft flesh beneath the witch's jaw, lifting it so high it must hurt. Blood trickles, dark like tar. Unnaturally thick. The cut is deep. Bea trembles in the corner, fingers stuffed into her mouth as tears stain her face, and there's blood everywhere. He doesn't remember cutting her. How did he ever think she was beautiful?

"I don't want to do this," he says. He means it, he thinks. He's been driving himself crazy but he knows this is right.

"Then don't do it."

He turns. There is the other girl. His eyes focus on the glinting metal in her hands. It's pointed directly at him.

"You too?" he spits. "Christ, she's got her claws in all of you."

The girl shakes her head, her lip trembling. Her hands aren't steady. She won't shoot him.

"Annie, don't," the witch says.

"Shut up, witch." The knife slides into her skin so easily. She cries out.

What happens next happens fast. There's another zap in the air like lightning. Then a clap of thunder except it's louder, hotter. White hot. It's in his chest, in his lungs. He glances down. Crimson blooms across his shirt.

He stumbles backwards. Somebody screams. He staggers, the knife dropping from his hand. It seems to take forever to hit the ground. He follows it what seems like half an eternity later.

And all he can think is it should hurt more.

Blackness makes his vision fog.

"Annie..."

Voices are distant. Cold. Everything tastes sour.

"You're bleeding. Oh God, it's bad. Put pressure on it. Bea, put pressure on it! I thought you were dead already. I had to do something—why didn't you do something?"

He's cold.

"Annie, what did you do? Arthur. Arthur!" Bea's voice like a sob.

"What about the debt? Emmeline, what happens to Bea? To you? If you—if he... No," Annie murmurs. "No, no... I didn't mean... I wasn't trying to hit him. Please."

He sees her when he closes his eyes. The witch. He hopes he's killed her. He can see the point of her teeth, the sharp jut of her jaw. She's like a gargoyle, a wolf. No, she's a demon. She destroys everything she touches.

She's the end.

BLOOD

AND

WATER

The Drowning Boy & the Healer

Lilith

Ten years ago

Lil was fifteen when Cilla brought the new boy to Cross House.

Cilla had always preferred girls. Girls were easy creatures to love; their blood, which Cilla used for her spells, flowed frequent and free, and they already understood what would happen if they strayed. She taught them to ignore the stories they heard in town: stories about how if a man bedded a Delacroix girl it would cure him of any ills, if he got her in the family way he'd never worry for money again. Cilla said she would protect them.

It wasn't until the boy came to Cross House that Lil understood. Cilla had created the stories herself for the power they gave; she had crafted a reality all her own. The boy was part of a different reality. He was skinny like a broom, not yet beginning to broaden in the face or chest, with a mane of long chestnut hair. Unlike the girls he did not garner attention, and Cilla did not want him to. He was invisible.

The boy noticed things, though. And with the company of his watchful gaze Lilith began to notice things too. Things she had forgotten to find strange. Like the scars, the ones on her hands, on her arms; the rings around her forearm like bracelets, the earliest of which Cilla had begun the first time she caught her watching as she entertained.

To Lil, the scars meant Cilla loved her. Lil needed instructing— they all did. That's why they were living at Cross House. The boy didn't see it that way. He recoiled when anybody came close to touching him, refusing to give blood for Cilla's spells and potions unless he could cut the skin and fill the vial himself. He disappeared like a shadow, lurking in the library or the garden, the only evidence of him the pervading scent of cinnamon.

Lil watched him for a long while before she approached him in the library. He sat with his coffee, sprinkling cinnamon into the cup until the smell was overpowering.

"Why do you do that?" she asked.

He glanced up when she spoke. Cilla had made him wash his hair and braid it, but he hadn't let anybody touch it since because he said it hurt, like a direct injection of emotion into his skin. And it was worse with tools, metal or wood, that carried memories of their own—of fire, of an axe.

"The cinnamon blocks the voices in my head," the boy answered. "I don't like knowing things about people that I shouldn't."

"Oh."

"Cilla will be angry if she finds out."

"So why did you tell me? You shouldn't tell *anybody*." Lil arched an eyebrow and folded her arms across her chest. *Stupid boy.* "How did you know I wouldn't blab? The other girls would."

"I didn't use my magic on you, if that's what you're thinking," the boy said quickly. "To be honest you sort of scare me." He flashed her a crooked smile. "But I had a feeling you'd understand."

Lil had never kept anything from Cilla before, but the boy was right. Lil did understand—and she wouldn't tell.

After that the two of them stole any hour they could together. They made coffee and carried it out to the small vegetable plot where they could sit in peace. Nathan built the garden with his nimble fingers, breathing life into the earth, while Lilith ran the dirt through her fingers and sensed out the little earthworms and bugs that lived beneath the surface, occasionally, *treacherously*, wondering what it might be like to squash them.

There they coughed their way through their first illicit cigarette as Nathan told her how he had come to the island.

"Mum married a bookie. They used to have me sit in on poker games to see who was bluffing." Nathan handed the cigarette to Lil with disdain. "It's harder when there are lots of people, and I'm entirely rubbish if it's cold and everybody's in jumpers."

"Do clothes stop it working?"

Lil noted the way Nathan sat, his legs spread wide, and she wished she could do the same.

"Not usually. I can feel it all the time, but it's stronger if there's nothing in the way. When somebody's skin touches mine, when they're that close..." Nathan's mouth settled in a grim line. "But some people are good at hiding their feelings no matter what. So the gambling didn't last long. Gavin and his brother dragged me down to the docks and smashed up my face because they knew how much I hate to be touched."

Lil sensed there was more to the story. She found out later that his stepfather and uncle had held him underwater for two minutes, their bare hands on his neck. And they left him on the dock to die.

———|) • (|———

Cilla woke Lil an hour before dawn.

"Get up."

She dragged Lil down the stairs, her black housecoat trailing. They came to the lounge that Lil referred to as the Throne Room, her body singing with dread.

"Sit."

Cilla shoved Lil towards the damask-covered throne chair. *Her* chair.

Lil bit back a whimper.

"Go on. If you want so much to be the boss of this house, *take a seat.*"

Lilith couldn't. It was too big, too plush, the wood too dark.

"I thought so." The old witch's eyes got that wicked gleam. Lil had seen it enough times to recognise it. Madness. Every day Cilla couldn't cast magic of her own, every day she Gave her blood to whatever old bargain tormented her, a little more of her slipped away.

Lil would never use her magic like that.

"I think it's time for a firm hand," Cilla said. "So I've taken your cards."

Lilith fought the gut-punching breathlessness that made her light-headed. The konjure cards had been Aunt Rachel's, Lil's mother's before that. They were *hers*.

"And your name. You need something *feminine*." The way Cilla said the word made Lil tremble. "Oh, I can see it, you know. The way you look at the boy. Not like the other girls, fawning. No, you look at him as if you wish you could *be* him."

Lilith blanched. She hadn't thought anybody could see the way she longed to be like Nathan, free from her stupid petticoats and monthly bleeds. The freedom she wanted from the swell in her magic, every new moon bringing her deeper, darker, into some violent delight that she could not control.

"I think we will make it French. Continental."

Lil clenched her teeth as Cilla pulled out her favourite bone athame, carving another smooth, stinging stripe of punishment along Lil's arm, just above the last one.

Blood welled, Lilith's magic thrashing in response. Cilla swiped a finger sharply across the wound, pressing the bright red blood to her mouth. Refilling the maw that her bargain had created where her own magic should be.

"I think," Cilla said, sighing as Lil's magic filled her up, "I will call you Emmeline."

———⊷•⊶———

The last girl came to Cross House two years after Nathan. When Cilla found her she'd been living on the moors for months, her hair matted and her face slick with dirt and coppery blood. She was all nut-brown skin stretched thin over bones that jutted at her hips, shoulder blades like the stubs of severed wings.

Emmeline had never seen magic like hers. They all gathered in the dirt outside the house and watched with fascination bordering on fear as the girl summoned rain clouds from nothing and drenched herself clean.

Emmeline alone had understood the look of raw terror on her face. The hunger. The girl—like Cilla, like Emmeline—had the kind of power that grasped and gnawed, always screaming for more.

Later, they sat together in the girl's bedroom. She spoke little at first, just slippery Spanish that Nathan couldn't understand.

"I think she's saying they...ate her. Her parents? She just keeps talking about madness, maybe? No. *Magic*."

"It's all right, love," Emmeline soothed. "You're with us now."

"Isobel," whispered the girl, massaging her chest. "Isobel."

It was weeks before Isobel was comfortable enough in Cilla's gilded cage to speak again, before she explained in accented English that her parents had died on the moors. They were scientists who came from Spain when the gobierno de España cracked down on their experiments—there was a ritual, and something had gone terribly wrong.

Isobel said nothing more about them, but it reaffirmed what Emmeline already knew: so many of Cilla's girls stayed at Cross House because they were afraid of the world; of their magic; of the things they had already done to survive. More afraid than they were of Cilla.

Once war broke out with Germany, Cilla's lavish, glittering parties grew only larger. People came from all over for her help. Some brought money, but these days Cilla's preference was secrets, and the world was brimming with them. Soon she began to offload her easier clients to Emmeline and, rarely, Angelica, whose gifts for illusion often came in especially useful.

"You're the only one who truly has the gravitas to handle them," Cilla said appraisingly.

Emmeline took the scrap of Cilla's trust like a half-starved dog, grateful while knowing it meant nothing. Cilla knew how to twist their wants, to push them harder than they would ever push themselves.

Isobel understood that better than most. Isobel, whose only acceptance of her own magic was in crafting poultices to soothe the wounds the other girls' magic incurred, who felt Cilla's hand—and her blade—more often than anybody except Emmeline, but who also received the most praise.

"She knows it's better than returning to motherhood herself," Isobel had said once. "Helping our girls is what I was born to do, so she lets me. I think she's hoping one day I'll rediscover whatever magic it was she sensed in me on the moors. Fat chance, I say."

As Cilla's court grew, so did the rumours about the Delacroix girls—about what a man might do if he caught one. The youngest girls were fifteen, sixteen. Isobel tried to mother them all.

"I'm going to teach them some of the things my mama taught me," she told Emmeline and Nathan one night as the three of them sat at Cilla's kitchen table before dawn. "They don't truly understand what those men will take now they are no longer girls."

Isobel stared down at her hands.

"If Cilla catches you," Nathan warned.

"She won't care as long as the men get what they want in the end. Most of the girls will be willing to marry if it gets them out of here, and if Cilla gets paid she's happy."

"And those that don't want to marry?" Emmeline asked darkly.

"Those are the girls who need my help most."

Isobel was right. Many of the Delacroix girls drifted out of Cilla's service as the war went on—though Cilla didn't always set them free. The weaker ones she sacrificed readily, for a scrap more power or influence in town. Not girls like Emmeline, like Isobel.

The day of the autumn equinox party, Angelica—smiling Angelica with her beautiful, ravenous gift—had asked Cilla if she might marry a boy from town. Cilla refused. Cross House still needed her.

That night Angelica went to the party with Isobel; they danced, laughed, enjoyed the attention of Cilla's men. They drank spiked gin and ended up on the beach, where the stars were bright, the sky so peppered with them it felt like eternity. That night, Isobel said, Angelica was chaos in human skin. She unleashed her magic, built a miniature golden palace right there on the sand from nothing but boulders and blood alone, replete with shining towers and waving people no bigger than the size of a thumb. It was an illusion so powerful even Isobel was fooled.

And when she was spent, her magic exhausted and her body close to breaking, Angelica begged to be alone—to mourn for the life Cilla would never let her have.

The following morning Isobel found Angelica, still on the beach in her party dress. Somebody had strangled her.

————) ● (————

The parties took on a manic tilt after that, the world shifting as attitudes towards magic changed. The change wore on Cilla. Every night Emmeline was summoned to the suite of rooms at the front of the house, where she helped Cilla to undress, ignoring the self-inflicted incisions down the length of Cilla's stomach and thighs, often still bloody. One drop of blood at a time. Her body was a patchwork of some darkness Emmeline didn't yet understand.

During the parties she was almost like her old self. She was fire and smoke and ash, ruinous and alluring.

There was a party that December, more raucous than any of the others. The waves that night were jagged tourmaline, thick with foam. The house was full to bursting. They had music and dancing, wine and kyraz and canapés on gold platters. Cilla had made Emmeline and Nathan drag the throne onto the balcony of the ballroom, and she sat watching the festivities as her guests hid behind hideous carved masks.

The veil Cilla favoured didn't seem ridiculous anymore. The war had made the men brave. Conscription had brought newcomers to the island in droves to test Cilla's famous magic, and she watched with gleaming eyes as money and gifts and secrets exchanged hands—always flowing towards her, always into the very deep pockets of Cross House.

Emmeline slipped away from the party, like Isobel often did now Angelica was gone. She disappeared into the quiet hallways, and as she passed one of Cilla's rooms she heard a familiar voice.

She backtracked, her satin slippers silent as she crept closer. There came another low moan and a gentle wail of pain she recognised from those first days when Nathan had arrived.

She burst into the room and unleashed a coil of dark, angry magic. There was a man hunched over Nathan on the sofa. Neither wore any clothes. The man staggered backwards, hands going automatically to his groin as Emmeline's magic nipped at his skin. Nathan's eyes were glassy.

"Lil!"

She saw the money on the table next to the sofa. The man came at Emmeline, his fist raised. He hit her, palm crunching into her nose. Emmeline hardly felt it. Blood poured, her magic flaring.

The man fled.

"How could you?" Emmeline demanded, turning to Nathan.

She wasn't asking if he liked boys as well as girls. They had talked about the fact that he liked both. This wasn't a matter of boys and girls and stolen kisses or *love*.

"I listen," Nathan murmured. "When we're—close. I learn their secrets. Some of them are witches from the Council. They know things—about the war. They don't realise they're paying me to rob them."

Emmeline's blood was fire in her veins.

"Why?" she demanded. She stalked towards Nathan, throwing his shirt and trousers at him. "Why put yourself through so much pain?"

Nathan's expression was one of an animal, whipped beyond sense. Fear. Shame. His eyes filled with tears and he hung his head.

"Because she *makes me*."

Chapter One

Annie

"They can't find out."

Emmeline knelt by Arthur's body, her shirt stained with his red blood and her own, black as tar. Sickness rose. I swallowed it down only by sheer luck as Emmeline let out a broken noise that sounded like a brittle laugh.

"We need to call a doctor," I bleated.

It was no good. There was so much blood—he was so, so pale. Eyes staring. I was still clutching the gun and I threw it down with a bang so loud Bea wailed in surprise.

"Nathan and Isobel," Emmeline repeated. "They can't find out what we've done. They can't. It would break them..."

A surge of anger rocked through me, at Bea, who cowered in the corner, no longer looking at her husband's body. At Emmeline, who just sat there.

"That's what you're worried about?" I cried. "God, Emmeline. He's *dead*, and that's what you care about?"

I couldn't believe it. And yet...Wasn't this a glimpse of the Emmeline I had been warned about? Dangerous. Selfish. Some force had made me take Bea's gun; another had made me use it. It wasn't me; it couldn't be me; I wasn't myself.

Emmeline didn't look at me. Instead she stared at Arthur's body long enough that all emotion drained from her face. Her gaze was assessing. Almost like she was cataloguing how much blood we— I—had spilled. I let out a frustrated growl.

"The police, then," I pushed. "If we can't call a doctor. We need to tell them what happened. We need to explain. Bea, you can tell them about last night, how he beat you..."

Neither of them answered.

"Will somebody say something?"

My voice echoed, my breath coming short and sharp, a balloon of panic about to burst inside me. Bea continued to cry, her nightgown stained crimson, her face pressed to her palms as sobs wracked her body.

"It's no good, Annie," Emmeline said eventually. Calmly. She turned, her knees skidding in blood, and looked up at me. "It's different here, but this is still murder. If they find out, we'll hang."

"No," I said, panicking, "it was self-defence. He attacked Bea. He came back to hurt her again. You were here, you saw him, look what he did to you! He was going to kill us."

"And you honestly think they'll believe us?" Emmeline pulled herself to her feet slowly, achingly, one hand pressed to the wound at her throat. "They will take one look at us—a house full of women—and decide we are no good. They will find the kazam, the herbs, Nathan's greenhouse. It would be our word against Arthur's reputation. They will make their minds up, and they will hang every single one of us."

Emmeline's truth sank inside me like a heavy stone, filling me with such a chill that my teeth began to chatter, my whole body to shake. She approached me, slowly, like I might run.

Her shirt was ripped, streaked with two kinds of blood, her hair wild and face splattered with gore. She was a shadow in a man's suit, her small chest rising and falling as she drew in long, broken breaths. It hit me with a jolt that no matter how I felt about her, no matter what had caused the thing that seemed to tie us together, I did not know Emmeline at all.

Bea's husband lay on the thin carpet, his golden hair so bright it shone like a crown.

"Do you want that?" Emmeline insisted quietly. She grasped for my arm and I felt the blood, slick and cooling on her hands. I could taste it, like iron and glitter, sparking on my tongue. I had done that. Me. Not Emmeline.

I shook my head numbly.

"I'm telling you: for their safety, Nathan and Isobel can't know. They need to be able to deny it. We can't but they can."

"I didn't mean to hurt him. I only wanted to scare him. It was like a hand—guiding. Like..." *Like magic.*

Mam was right. Magic was ruin. It felt good. It felt powerful, *useful,* and it lulled you little by little until you were in so deep you couldn't escape. Magic was a trap and I had let myself be snared.

Emmeline picked the pistol up from the floorboards. She held it in both hands, cradling it like a frail bird, and then she tucked it into the waistband of her trousers. A shadow flickered across her face, the ghost of an expression, a memory of fear that disappeared too fast.

She inhaled. I could smell it too. The smell of blood and death. She glanced at Bea, who stared at her husband's body with a mixture of anger and sadness and disbelief.

I took in the scene with fresh eyes, seeing not the potential to explain to doctors and police, seeing not a way out where we might plead for understanding. Instead I saw all the ways they would find to blame us, as they should: the gun, which I had taken to protect us, would be an indication of premeditation; the second shot, which I'd fired after the first had missed because his knife had been at Emmeline's throat, about to kill her; the stain of Emmeline's black blood, brackish and thick, the clearest evidence of magic I had ever seen. And, quickly, my thoughts turned to my father, to his secret attic—the door I had never locked, which they would find with no problem at all.

We would hang.

So I walled up that grief inside myself, forced down the panic and the guilt that filled my body to the brim until I could let myself feel it. I turned to Emmeline.

"We need to bury him."

———⟨ ● ⟩———

We rolled him in the rug he'd fallen on, but it was too long. Emmeline fetched a pair of jagged, rusting scissors and between us we hacked off the excess material, pulling strips of the expensive old carpet to ribbons. Bea watched us through the slit of her swollen eye.

I'd thought it was the only option. She had been in as much danger as Emmeline had. I had tried to save them both.

Instead I had doomed us all.

Shock muffled everything. I couldn't think beyond the next step, the next lift, the next twist.

"It's broad daylight," I panted. "Anybody could see us."

Emmeline shook her head.

"In these parts anything before midday is practically the middle of the night." She reached for me, her hand finding mine reassuringly. "It isn't ideal but it will be fine. Nate and Isobel will come in the front and nobody bothers with the beach except you. Nobody will see us, I promise."

"Okay," I said. What choice did I have but to trust her?

Together we dragged Arthur's body out onto the landing and down the stairs. We made it out into the back garden, stopping only when we reached the grass, our backs and foreheads damp with sweat.

Outside the air was fresh and smelled floral sweet. The sun was harsh, scrutinising, as if the weather knew what we had done. At least the garden smell finally overwhelmed the stench of blood and death.

The lawn seemed vast, too open, too risky. I twitched at every noise, every slight shift or vagrant crow taking flight. Emmeline barely glanced around her, forging onwards like she did this sort of thing all the time, but I could see the tension in the slope of her neck, her clawlike grip. I fought the urge to glance over my shoulder, ignoring the cold fingers of dread.

The fear made me think of the other night, the stretching shadows outside my cottage, the noises. What if I *hadn't* been imagining that somebody was out there? What if somebody had been watching me then—and what if they were here now? I opened my mouth to speak, but all that came out was a breath, squeezed tight.

Emmeline was right. I was allowing my fear to cloud my judgement. Nobody came. Nobody stopped us. Nobody knew we were here.

Another wave of guilt threatened to drown me. This was my fault. What would Sam say if he could see us? A dull ache in my chest said he would be sick with it, with what I'd done. With this life I was choosing with every breath. And now Bea's life was ruined, and Emmeline... I didn't know what it meant, but I knew it wasn't good.

"There's got to be another way to get us out of this mess," I said quietly.

"There isn't. The bargain still requires a payment of blood and Arthur can no longer give it. The blood starts to cool as soon as the heart stops pumping. You need fresh, hot blood for a Giving, willingly sacrificed. It wouldn't have mattered if I'd acted faster after you shot him; I wouldn't have been fast enough for everything I needed.

"I thought I was doing the right thing by Giving a lot at a time instead of a few drops a day. If you spread it out too much you go mad. It meant Arthur owed me a lot and the debt was getting out of control. I didn't think about that. I didn't think how it would affect anybody else. I just didn't want to be like..." Emmeline's face was mournful.

"I meant now," I snapped, surprising myself with how much anger seeped into my words. I couldn't deal with Bea's shock and useless grief and I definitely couldn't deal with this. Part of me wanted to lash out, to reach for the tether lying strangely quiet in my chest, where it had remained since I'd shoved it back after rushing to Bea. I wanted to give it a sharp tug to remind Emmeline that this affected me too. "This isn't just about you," I said instead. "I meant that we can't just bury him anywhere. We can't just do this and expect Bea to be okay. What does it mean for her?"

Emmeline didn't seem surprised or hurt by my anger; she was only numb. I watched her jaw tense as she fought back an obvious urge to ignore me, and I softened as she said simply, "I don't know."

Emmeline picked up her end of the rug again, and careless of the wobble of my legs, I followed. We dragged him through a copse of trees, past the back door on the porch to where another section of the house sprawled away into a smaller, more private garden.

Here there was a greenhouse like the one my grandmother had had before she died, the small glass building sitting like a haven of life with a plantlike patina to its windows. I could smell the fragrant, forbidden herbs from here.

"We used to grow vegetables," Emmeline said. We reached the back of the greenhouse, where there was a patch of black dirt. No plants grew, but the soil was tended carefully, a bundle of fresh, pale chrysanthemums tied with a ribbon resting to the side.

"You...grew vegetables? Here?"

Despite the circumstances, a shiver of recognition whipped through me. This was an important admission. A clenching in my belly said, *This is for you. This is an offering.* The silver cord that bound us together uncoiled from its prison, stretching as if from a slumber; I didn't know who had disturbed it, whether it was her or me, but I stepped towards her involuntarily.

Her gaze jumped to mine.

I desperately wanted to touch her, to grab her hand, to reassure myself that she was human, that she was as mortal as me. I wondered if she knew how this tether had happened. Only the thought that refusing to name it, to admit this dangerous, treacherous thing, might be the only thing holding us together, stopped me from asking.

"Come on," I said. "Before Nathan and Isobel get back."

Emmeline nodded gratefully, her gaze going distant as she gathered two shovels—one much smaller than the other. Despite every instinct in me telling me to stop, screaming that this was wrong, that it would only make things worse, I helped her bury Arthur's body behind the greenhouse.

Chapter Two

Annie

By the time we were finished, the sun was high in the sky. We washed our hands in a metal trough filled with rainwater and dumped the rest on the turned earth. Emmeline's shirt was pink at the cuffs, and the wound on her neck glittered like a black-beaded choker.

"What about Bea?" I asked. "She's not going to be okay. How could she be? She isn't...she isn't built for secrecy."

I had never thought of Bea like this before, but it was true. I had always thought she was brave, bold, but that same unpredictability in her wouldn't help us now.

"She won't say anything." Emmeline's expression was fixed, cold, as she wiped the remainder of the bloody dirt off her right hand and onto her thigh. "She's not innocent in this, even if she didn't kill him."

"How, exactly, is she involved?" I demanded. "Nobody will tell me anything. For God's sake, Emmeline, I just helped you bury a man in the garden. A man *I* killed while trying to protect us. Don't you think I deserve to know what I'm dealing with?"

Emmeline swallowed hard.

"When Bea first asked for my help—it went wrong. I made a

mistake. So when she asked me for help a second time, I did it. Regardless of the consequences. I forgot everything I ever learned because I wanted her to be happy. I should have known better."

"The blood debt," I pressed, ignoring Emmeline's recklessness. "Was Arthur's blood truly the only way to fulfil it?"

"Yes," she said. "It's the only way to pay back the magic I used. It needed to be his blood in a Giving ceremony. Fresh, willingly given blood. And now he's dead and every Giving I have to make is getting more and more insistent. It'll bleed me dry."

"If he's dead, why doesn't the debt just... stop?" I asked. "There has to be some kind of solution. Can't you just make a new debt?"

"That's not how magic works. It's about balance, like nature. It took a lot to make him love her. The blood I Give back is getting weaker, so I have to Give more and it still requires payment."

"What about Bea? What happens to her?"

"I told you I don't know," Emmeline snapped. She started towards the house.

"This is not over," I said, racing after her. "There's got to be another way. I don't believe there's no answer!"

"There's no use getting angry with me—I just told you the truth."

"I'm not angry with you!" My voice was very loud. Emmeline shot me a warning look, but I couldn't stop. "No, that's not true. I'm fuming, but that won't solve anything. I'm angry at this whole situation. This wasn't supposed to happen!"

"You didn't know it would turn out like this—and stupidly I wanted to believe it wouldn't. Now it's happened we just have to focus on keeping it hidden."

We'd reached the porch. I checked over my shoulder. The lawn beyond remained just as empty as it had been all morning.

"I thought Nathan and Isobel were like your family," I said. "Do you honestly think they won't help you?"

Emmeline frowned.

"They *are* my family," she said emphatically. "And I don't deserve their help. I can't put them in danger."

"But you can risk yourself?"

"I risked myself a long time ago."

Inside, Bea had already cleaned herself up and made a start on the mess we'd made in the bedroom. She wore a pair of Emmeline's trousers, which were too long, and a large shirt. Her expression was hollow, the last remnants of my Bea, the girl from my childhood, scooped up and tossed aside.

"How is your face?" I asked softly. Bea didn't answer, only a shrug. "We'll have to have a story. People will ask. Those bruises are nasty."

"We'll tell the truth," Emmeline said. "That he attacked her and she ran. That he reported her missing to scare her home."

"That's it?" I said. "What if people ask where he is?"

"That's not our problem. He was drunk. He could be in the sea for all we care." Emmeline peeled back her shirtsleeve, peering at the bandage beneath with a grimace.

"Annie, you should go home." Bea stared at me, unblinking. I glanced down at myself, taking in my filthy dress, my hands, which were still creased with her husband's blood.

The Annie Bea had always known would run. She would hide, let her fear consume her. I wasn't sure I could be that girl anymore, even if I wanted to. The thought of my quiet cottage, those echoing walls... If I went home I would be forced to think—would be forced to face what I had done. I couldn't bear it.

"No," I said, my voice surprisingly steady. "We have to act normal. I would be too worried to leave you. You're my best friend."

"Annie's right," Emmeline said. A forbidden thrill whipped through me. I shouldn't care what Emmeline thought, but her praise eclipsed everything. Her presence was like a dulling of my senses, like kazam, even with the tether resting deep. I couldn't make myself step away. "We need to get our stories straight," Emmeline added, her gaze resting on me. "If the police come looking for him, we need to be ready."

—◦•◦—

When Isobel finally returned it was late afternoon. Emmeline had kitted us out in hand-me-down bathing suits, though nobody had any intention of swimming, and sundresses for Bea and me, and forced us to head down onto the beach. She brought a hamper with a glass bottle full of some mint-infused sparkling wine, and sat under an umbrella on a long white towel, scowling at the glittering ocean.

Bea had scrounged up an old pair of sunglasses and a hat with a wide, floppy brim. She sat right by the waterline, refusing to look at us.

I was surprised to find that the sun and the ocean spray and the gentle sound of lapping waves made me tired. The memory of the heft of a shovel and the mint wine left my limbs leaden.

"There you are! I worried when I couldn't find you." Isobel stumbled onto the beach. "Honestly, I spend all morning schlepping around town for black pepper and you're here having a party without me."

"Something like that," Bea said airily, though the relaxed effect was ruined by her split lip. She turned and brought her damp legs up onto drier sand. "I said we should have cocktails to celebrate my miraculous escape, but all Em brought was this shitty mint julep."

"Oh, is that what it is?" I asked.

Emmeline bobbed one shoulder in a careless shrug.

Isobel glanced between Emmeline in her shirt and waistcoat, her sleeves rolled up and her thin feet bare in the sand, and the way I sat perched on a rock six feet away in a dress that wasn't mine, and shrugged back.

"A party suits me fine," she said. "Though I wish you'd cover your shoulders, Bea—you'll burn them sitting there like that. Who's got the booze?"

Emmeline handed her the sweating bottle, and Isobel carried it over to the picnic blanket Bea had spread behind her. She plonked down and took a big swig. She cocked her head, examining each of Bea's injuries and clucking.

"You poor dear. Looks worse than it did this morning. Are you nauseous?"

Bea gave a small shake of her head. It had been one thing to sit on the beach and pretend nothing was wrong when it was just the three of us. It was another entirely to do it when it mattered, the fact of Arthur's death lashing between the three of us like a living thing, coiling and itching to strike.

"Is Nate not back yet, dearest?"

Emmeline was about to answer when Isobel turned, waving. "Speak of the devil."

The rest of us all swivelled in the direction of the house, where Nathan's dark head bobbed into view.

Emmeline's smile was convincing enough, if only from a distance.

"Look at this," Nathan joked. "One witch short of a coven—oh, and Annie and Bea too. You look rough, darlings. How are you holding up?" Bea dipped her head and I caught Nathan's warm gaze, his eyes roving over my clenched fists and my tense back. I tried to find that sleepy stillness again. His face grew serious. "There's no sign of Arthur at your house, Bea. I doubt he'll head back there now. Bet he's run off with his tail between his legs after what he did to you. Are you any better? Do you need anything else? I can show you my version of the tango if you'd like." He made to start dancing, but Bea shook her head.

"I suspect laughing would only hurt. The sun helps, though," she said quietly.

Nathan sank down on the blanket next to Isobel, taking the proffered bottle gratefully. They began talking between themselves, and Bea turned back to the ocean, where I couldn't see her face. I listened to the lapping waves, tasting the salt and the warm grass on Emmeline's lawn behind us.

Every now and then Nathan turned his chin towards me, and his eyes were like a light pressure on my skin.

"You ought to let me have another look at your face," Isobel was saying, Bea half listening just in front. "I know Nate's got some witch hazel around here somewhere, and there's some clove oil in the greenhouse. Actually, Nate, why don't you go and grab—"

Emmeline's face paled under her parasol and she lurched forward at the same moment I blurted, "I'll go and get it. I need to stretch my legs."

Nathan's eyes snapped to my face, and I forced my lips into a small smile.

"I'll come with you." Emmeline climbed to her feet unsteadily, and despite myself, my heart tripped at the prospect of spending more time alone with her.

We brushed sand from our clothes and headed back up the blindingly white steps, past the fountain with the statues, and around the side of the house, where just this morning we had dragged Arthur's body.

I was bitten by a chill, the sun overhead lost behind trees, and I shivered at the memory of the carpet and the blood and the thud of earth from our shovels. Was this what it would be like, forever? Normality—and then *this*?

Emmeline stopped, leaning against a tree. Instinctively I moved closer, breathing in her familiar smell.

"Annie," Emmeline said abruptly. "Go home."

My stomach bottomed out and the ground seemed to shift underneath me.

"I told you I'm not going anywhere. You agreed it was a good idea for me to stay."

"That was before—and I was wrong. Nathan can read you like a book. The more relaxed you get, the better he can see. You need to leave."

I thought of my empty cottage again, the vast quiet I thought I'd craved when I'd been stuck at home with my mam and which now terrified me. "No, listen—"

"I can't have you to think about too. I can't take it."

"I can look after myself!" I exclaimed. "And Bea is my best friend. How can you expect me to leave her?"

"This isn't just about Bea, though!" Emmeline narrowed her gaze; the jut of her chin, the way her stance shifted, was mean. Spoiling for a fight. "Annie, this world wasn't made for you. I should never have got you involved."

"I told you: you didn't make me do anything. It's not like you compelled me to come to your party, or to dinner. I'm perfectly capable of making my own choices."

A beat. Emmeline said nothing, only stared at me as if struck by sudden grief.

"Emmeline," I prompted. "This *is* my choice, isn't it?"

Panic whipped through me. Was everything a lie? I'd known whatever this connection was between us could draw me in—it was intoxicating; it was temptation—but I had always thought the final decision was mine alone.

"Yes, it's your choice," Emmeline said, but it was without conviction. "At least, I think so. I can't be sure."

"What do you mean you can't be sure? What is this thing?" I fought to keep steady, but my lungs felt too big for my chest. I couldn't breathe. I admired Emmeline for her strength, for the way she forged on despite everything. The way she stood so easy in her men's clothes, like the rest of the world didn't matter. I admired how brave she was, how she took charge.

Were any of those feelings mine?

Emmeline ran a hand through her hair, every inch of her body taut. She didn't answer my question. "If I compelled you... God, I didn't mean to. I wanted you away from here. But you kept—you kept coming back." She clenched her fists, as if daring me to ask about the tether again. "What if I did that?"

"And what if you didn't?" I demanded. The panic was frenzy whipped, tasted like anger instead. Was it so hard to believe that I would choose this? *Yes.* I knew that. And yet the first time I had met Emmeline I'd wanted to spill all my secrets, right there in her kitchen. I'd wanted to tell her instantly that I wanted more, more than home could ever give me, that I'd never loved Sam, not the way I was supposed to, because it felt like she alone would understand. I had—and I was as certain as I could be of this—chosen to play my part. "Maybe I'm not what everybody thinks. Maybe I *like* danger, and that's why I'm here." I lifted my chin defiantly, childishly.

It wasn't what I had meant to say. I wanted to tell her about my father, about his secret room and his magic books, to prove that there was more to me than Emmeline thought, but she was so close I couldn't think straight.

"That's what I worried you would say." Emmeline shook her head. "You need to go away, Annie. This is too much. Leave on your own—or I will make you."

"No."

Emmeline's jaw clenched, the tether lashing between us as she set it free. Tears snuck up on me, stinging my eyes, and my breath whooshed from my lungs. It felt like every emotion rushing at me at once; wild, unrestrained joy and a fear so dark, so heavy, it suffocated me. Worst of all was the heat, right in the pit of my belly: it was longing; it was desire; it felt like love. I reached out without thinking, my mind looping around the tether as I snatched it back, shoving it down deep.

I *wasn't* helpless. I had claws and I could learn how to use them too.

"Don't you *dare* push me away because you're scared," I hissed. "Don't pretend you don't understand why I'm here. You asked me at your party what I desired. What if this is what I want, Emmeline?"

What if you are what I want?

The thought hung between us, unspoken but not silent.

"How do you know?" Emmeline said hoarsely. Her eyes glittered and she was more broken and exhausted than ever. "You don't know me. It's not *this* you should want." She waved her hands towards the house, her bandaged arm lifted to the sun. "Please go home, Annie. I don't want you here anymore."

Chapter Three

Emmeline

It was already so much worse.

Since Arthur's death—since we had murdered him—my blood was slower than ever, the pulse a dull, distant thud. It turned to tar inside me and there was nothing I could do. Fear was cloying, swallowing everything.

Until the moment Annie fired the gun I had believed, no matter how faintly, that there was hope. I had been wrong. There was no reasoning with the magic that congealed in my veins, the debt that hung around my neck like a noose.

I didn't sleep. Normally I would wander the house, make preparations for the weekend, but what was the point? Besides, Isobel had spent the night working on a new recipe for an elderflower kazam—a quiet, focused activity she always turned to when she was on edge. She said it was soothing, finding the right formula as taste and magic entwined in a perfect match and knowing those ingredients had never been experienced exactly this way before. Every witch's kazam tasted different, and Isobel's was the best—brewed with love.

If she heard me she would want to talk instead. She would want to make sure I had a plan for how to handle Bea's "disappearance" if the police traced her here; she would want to make sure we were safe from Arthur. The thought chilled me.

I could hear Nathan too, in his bedroom down the hall, the faint thud-thud-thud as he threw a tennis ball against the wall, a nervous habit he'd once used to avoid thinking about the things that Cilla made him do.

My bedroom was too hot, the air too close. I would suffocate if I stayed there any longer. So I did the only other thing I could—I climbed out onto the roof. The air was balmy, forecasting another hot day, but the tiles were damp under my bare legs. I crossed my ankles and sat looking out over the gardens below, panic coming in surges up my throat like brackish water trying to drown me from the inside.

I pulled a cigarette out of the pocket of my shirt and lit it with my last match to occupy my shaking hands. Nathan had got to my stash and replaced it with his herbal kind, and this one should be mint scented, smoke unfurling in a green-tinged plume—but it wasn't right: it tasted like ash on my tongue.

I fumbled for logic, for reason I could latch on to to give me direction. I had a month left before my next planned Giving. I could make it go a little longer, could stretch it for maybe three days if I was lucky. That was enough time to make plans, set things in motion. To make sure Bea was safe, that we handled Arthur's disappearance together.

Afterwards, either the debt would take my body, or it would devour my mind. I could feel myself slipping, day by day. More anger. More numbness. Less control. I could so easily have hurt Isobel on the roof the other day, and it would only become worse, my magic snarling like a cornered wolf, ready to snap at the first hand that offered help. Until one day when maybe it would not come at all.

I feared not only for Isobel and Nathan but also for Bea and Annie. My brother and sister could look after themselves—they understood how magic could be. Bea worried me, though. Annie had been right to ask how the debt, how my death, would affect her, and I hated that I didn't know the answer.

And Annie…

I pictured her sun-speckled face, the soft curve of her lips. How she had squared up to me when I'd told her I didn't want her here, fire burning in those blue eyes. How she had curled her mind around this bond that connected us and yanked it back into submission like she had been born for it. Her closeness had felt like a kiss of magic, except like no magic I had ever felt before. Not of blood, or brittle, old bones. No, it was like ocean air, fresh and clean and new.

This connection terrified me. If Annie was right and I hadn't compelled her, then somehow this magic had come into existence with no intent, birthed with its claws already honed. Worse, I *wanted* it. I craved it. Keeping it subdued when we were together was getting harder, not easier, and I didn't know how much of that was the debt, my exhaustion, and how much was my body rejecting the decision of my mind. The energy that stretched between our chests, glowing and silver and firm like a rope, had a mind of its own.

I pulled my knees to my chest, shivering despite the warmth of the night. The pressure was building right behind my heart, although it had only been days since my last Giving. Fear squirmed in my belly, cold and oily. I had so many questions and nobody to ask.

What would happen to Annie when I died? Would the connection simply shatter, or would the debt steal a part of her too? It was better that she wasn't here—I couldn't bear the thought of her goodness, her light, tainted by my magic—and yet my eyes turned to the lawn behind the house again and again, treacherously scanning for a hint of her warmth.

I shifted, trying to find a comfortable position, but it hurt no matter what. I knew one thing, though: I was glad I hadn't let it go on as long as Cilla had. Her magic had eaten her up and spat her out, a husk of a woman ruled by broken thoughts, wild, instinctual magic, and blood she stole from her daughters.

She had never told me how her own bargain came to be, whether it was that which enabled her to seize a position high in the Council, which had coaxed the island's wealthy witches to her soirees, where they praised her knowledge, her power. These were the same witches who now watched us from afar, claiming old loyalty to Cilla, happy to let us alone with war no longer ravaging their families. As long as Perry fed them a steady diet of reassurance, of promises to keep the parties fun and the tourists happy, they were content. Perhaps Isobel was right and they were simply biding their time, waiting for us to fall so they could cannibalise Cilla's leftovers.

When I came to the island Cilla was already old, had already begun to break under the pressure of her debt. I thought of her smoky eyes, of the mane of hair that was eternally as black as night. Of how she always smelled like red wine and ash. Had I become like her after all?

I was so lost in my thoughts that I didn't hear Bea until she was climbing through my bedroom window. She still wore my old shirt like a nightdress and she clambered through with two cigarettes in her mouth. Her lip had split again despite Isobel's salves and blood trickled onto her ghost-pale skin.

"Take one, darling, will you?" she mouthed around the cigarettes. So I held them both while she settled herself on the roof and pulled out a small bottle that smelled like gin from the breast pocket of the shirt.

"Why didn't you just stick them in there?" I asked. It was easier than asking how she felt knowing her husband—the man she had wanted so badly she'd sold both our souls for it—lay buried in the damp earth just out of sight.

"Bottle leaks," Bea said, her words clunky. "Need to keep the cigs dry."

We lit them the old way, with two drops of my blood. I should save it, should save every last bit, yet I couldn't bring myself to care. Some small part of me still needed to believe that my power gave me hope. Without my magic I had no idea who I was.

We sat smoking in silence for a long while, watching as the sky began to pale into a fuchsia dawn and the stars winked out one by one. Finally Bea turned to me. Her eyes were very green, more so because of the bruises that surrounded them. Her face really was a mess.

"I never wanted any of this, Em."

I didn't trust myself to speak. I stared at my hand, the little scars on my knuckles from years of ritual bloodletting.

"You have to believe I didn't want this. I just thought, if I waited...When it started to break down, when he started to hurt me—I wanted to hurt him too. I didn't realise I was being bewitched."

"I never should have agreed to do it." I took a drag on the cigarette and grimaced at the bitter, ashy taste.

"You can't have tried everything," Bea urged.

I turned to her, trying to control my temper. "What else would you have me do?"

"I don't know!" she cried, throwing her hands up. "This can't be it. He can't have—died for this."

"Did he have any family?" I demanded. "Brothers or sisters, anybody close?"

Bea shook her head. It didn't matter; it probably wouldn't work. Magic was like a well and you couldn't just keep draining it and expect it to keep giving. I could expend the same magic over a month or a single night and the hangover would be the same, and while it might replenish, it would never grow to a point where it might save me.

It would need to be a child of his, and that would only halve the debt, draw it out for longer unless Bea and I could Give enough alongside. I wouldn't last long enough anyway. Soon the debt would be bigger than the blood I could safely Give, and that would be the end.

Cilla spread her payments out over thirty years by offering a single drop of blood every day, casting no other magic of her own. I had done the opposite, determined not to lose my mind.

"I didn't realise this would happen," I said quietly. "I thought—maybe I would suffer, my magic would drain. I didn't think you would just disappear."

Bea took another long swallow of gin and wiped her mouth with the back of her hand. Her expression was mournful, not just for me but for all of it.

"How long do you have?" she asked. She was staring at the tree line, towards the cottage. I wondered if Annie had taken my advice, started packing for home yet. I hoped she had.

I hoped she hadn't.

"A few months, maybe."

"Why did you agree to it?" she demanded, her voice breaking. "You didn't warn me—"

"I warned you, Bea. Just like I've warned Annie. Magic is...a trickster. It draws you in, makes you think you can control it. You get a taste and then you get careless. You can't control it any more than you can the tide or the rise of the moon." I stubbed out my cigarette.

"Annie," said Bea. Just one word, and it summed up everything. Annie's lightness, her hope. I couldn't bear it. The magic stirred in my chest, like the sun warming my aching bones. I didn't have the energy to squash it all the way.

"She can't be ruined by this, Bea," I urged. "We can't let her. She's—*good*. You have to promise you'll stick together, you'll help each other. Please."

My heart thudded painfully.

"Em, of course, but it's not just Annie. There's someth—"

A shout startled both of us.

"Somebody open the door!"

I glanced down, the coil in my chest spinning free before I had the chance to catch it. For a second—just a second—I was glad. There on the sun-warmed grass stood Annie. Her blond hair was wild, blowing free in shining, dishevelled curls, and her borrowed dress—still the same as yesterday, the swimsuit beneath it—was streaked with dust. In her arms she carried a book so big she had to hug it to her chest.

And then I remembered. I had sent her away. She couldn't be here. I didn't want her here.

"It's locked for a reason, Annie," I snapped, my fists clenched so tight against the *want* in my chest that my palms stung, blood drawn. The answering call of my magic followed. What was left of my cigarette went up in flames, a bright flash of fire that burned so quickly it was gone in seconds. Bea flinched, scrambling away.

"I don't care," Annie shouted. Her expression was grim as she hefted the book higher. The warmth in my chest faded, a pair of hands other than my own restraining it, and left behind was a clanging, echoing fear. I faltered. "I need to talk to you—it's about the debt."

Chapter Four

Annie

I don't want you here anymore.

Emmeline's words echoed in my mind. I couldn't shake the way her lip had curled in disgust. She had seen me, seen the real me, and I had failed every test. *You don't know me.* She was right. I didn't know her; I didn't know Bea; I didn't know anything at all.

I couldn't go back to my cottage, where the failure would settle into my bones—where I would be able to think of nothing but the horror of what I had done. Of how badly I had wanted to help and how badly I had fucked things up.

The cottage did not feel safe—had not since the moment my mind had played tricks on me, conjuring the image of cloaked figures in the dark. If I couldn't trust myself, my emotions, how did I know it hadn't been real? How would I know if I was making it up?

I could not spend the evening imagining Arthur, lying there in that scarlet slickness, his blood and Emmeline's future seeping into the carpet. Instead I began to walk. I still wore my borrowed sundress and swimsuit underneath, a pair of Isobel's canvas sandals dusty and rubbing blisters on my feet. I counted crows along the road. One, two, three. No more for a mile as I retraced now-familiar steps into town. Then one, two, three more. *Death. Death.* It followed me.

By the time I made it to Crow Trap my legs were tired, my eyes gritty with dirt from the road and not enough sleep. I wanted to cry, but I didn't have anything left to give. Emmeline's mint julep had left my throat dry and my head aching.

I had come without any money. I paused on the edge of town, where the houses tumbled away in matchstick rows, smaller and cosier than Cross House and too much like home. Anderson had mentioned a museum. The promise of an open, public space, so unlike my lonely cottage, filled me with hope. Galleries and museums were safe places—places I had always felt more myself.

I followed the vague instructions Anderson had given me that day at the café, finding the large brick building festooned with summery bunting. My heart swelled. This was a place for me. I hurried inside, grateful for the cool marble floors and whitewashed walls that drew me in. I wandered through rooms filled with artefacts and paintings, sculpted busts of forgotten women.

Solace. It was peace; it was gentle rain on my soul. I was exhausted, tears welling in my eyes. How had I believed that Emmeline's life was for me? The tether lay in my chest, dim and forgettable. Perhaps she was right. I didn't belong here.

It didn't matter that there were parts of me that didn't fit into my old life, that had never fitted: dark nights wandering between sleep and waking, visions that roared like waves; none of that had to mean anything. Emmeline had said as much. I had lived my whole life knowing if I just ignored those parts of me, if I just found the right dream, just *appearing* to fit in could be enough.

I didn't have to be my father.

I'd come to rest in front of a small, delicate woman cast in alabaster. She was young, beautiful, and perfect—except for two monstrous wings that grew from her back, eclipsing her lovely face. She was sad, so impossibly sad. Yet there was some grit in her that made me think of Emmeline.

I closed my eyes, chasing the shape of her, but it was Arthur I saw. I imagined dark roots creeping out of the black earth where we had buried him, crawling through the windows of the museum, unfurling and slithering around my dusty ankles, a warning, a scream.

I backed away, alarm ringing in my ears like the call of ocean waves. I stumbled into the main foyer, slamming directly into the chest of a man. I staggered back, hand going to my mouth as I mumbled an apology.

"There, lass, there. Slow down," he soothed.

His hands landed on my upper arms, holding me in place. I peered up. He was tall, with a head of oiled dark hair, a moustache obscuring his lips. He was perhaps Anderson's age, no younger, lean but strong. I resisted the urge to baulk, to cry out, panic clogging my throat.

"Sorry, sorry," I said again. "I wasn't looking. Careless."

"Are you okay? Here." He guided me towards the wall, where a carved bench sat under a dimly lit portrait of a man in a doublet and hose. "Sit. You look like you're about to faint."

"No, no, I'm—"

"I insist." The man finally released my arm, but he did not move away. Instead, he cast an appraising eye over me. I shrank back from his shrewd gaze, the cold of the bench biting into my legs, freezing me in place. I was sure it must be written all over my face: I was a magic user, a murderer. My cheeks burned and I felt the sweat trickle down my spine beneath the borrowed sundress. I glanced down, focusing on his tie, on the little golden crow pin he wore there.

"Say," the man said. "Might be a reach, but you look a little like a fellow I knew. Used to come here a lot. I think he was a scholar—no relation of yours, hmm? He had the same eyes. Perhaps a father or an uncle?"

I snapped my attention back to his face. His expression was carefully schooled to neutrality, but I recognised something in it—some hint of real curiosity buried in the blue of his eyes. My blood cooled, a different fear snaking within me. A primal feeling that I couldn't explain. His lips barely moved beneath the moustache, the pin on his tie winking at me.

"I…"

"Because if you knew him, well, that sure would be a boon. I'd wanted to discuss something with him but I heard he passed on. Such a shame. You know, my fellows and I would love to talk—"

"I'm sorry," I blurted again, not waiting to hear what else he had to say, ignoring the layers I was sure his message carried. Not caring if I was rude, I slid off the bench before he could react.

"Wait, miss—"

I ran, my borrowed sandals slapping loudly on marble and then on the dusty stone path outside, until I came to a corner where a small grocery stall spilled its wares into the street. I was panting.

I couldn't live like this—with the guilt. I should go to the police. I should explain to them what I had done, why I had done it. Maybe with my father's money, his resources, I could escape punishment. But what about Bea? And Emmeline? Would they be so lucky?

And the man inside. The way he had grabbed me. I looked over my shoulder, half expecting to see him behind me. There was nobody there. Was the menace in his manner, like the shadows outside my house, all in my imagination? I didn't think so. I didn't understand. Who would care about my father if they didn't know his secret—and if they knew it, why not simply involve the law? It felt like the world was closing in, like I was a rabbit caught in a snare.

I turned in the street, stumbling as my heel caught in the crooked cobbles because my eyes were fixed on this evening's newspaper. The headline.

"Search for Missing Wife Escalates as Husband Evades Police Question."

I'd been wrong. That old life, the old Annie who could live it? She was gone. This was all I had left, the only place that might take me.

———()●()———

At home I didn't pause. I was in the car and on the road again within minutes, driving fast, ripping back through Crow Trap like it might chew me up and spit me out if I gave myself time to breathe. In the moonlight I counted the dark silhouettes of crows in the trees. One for malice. One. One.

My father's house was untouched but it felt like it hadn't been entirely empty since my last visit. I thought with a jolt of Anderson, who had taken advantage of an unlocked front door the last time I had been here. But when I reached the secret room I found everything as I'd left it. Of course it was. I laughed off my foolishness, the sound loud.

Relief bubbled deep inside me anyway—not just for myself in the face of the law, but also for my father's things. *My* things. What truths could I uncover with these objects?

I headed straight for the books tonight, pulse pounding in my throat. The man in the museum had shaken me badly. I had no idea who he was, whether I had been right to run, but I was concerned about the headline too. If the police couldn't find Bea, couldn't find Arthur, how long would it be before somebody learned about Emmeline's party—where they'd had a public fight—and the police search led them to Cross House? Would we be able to hide Bea, to lie convincingly? Emmeline was right: they could easily take one look at the house, the kazam within, and decide we all ought to hang.

And if by some miracle we didn't hang? Bea would be the one they would suspect of Arthur's death, even if I confessed. She was his wife—his penniless wife who had lied about her life before, given up everything for his hand. For this island. For these people. Finding out about her past gave Arthur motive, but didn't it give Bea motive too? And which one of them was dead?

I wiped my slick hands on my dress, which was still dusty from the sand, and grabbed books at random. Words jumped out at me and I wasn't sure whether they were from the page or my mind: *freedom, magic, desire, intent, sacrifice*...I ran my hands over my face.

I worked my way through four volumes. I found everything: love spells; posies for attracting attention or money; brews that could heal a broken limb or stitch torn skin back together; kazam-infused concoctions to help conceive a child, to call forth magic, to bind two witches together in their power. All things that only days ago would have made me sick with worry and now seemed like mere distractions.

A page caught my eye.

The Awakening.

There was a sketch of a man lying supine on a workbench with his eyes closed, ruby spell-work carved into his chest. In one hand he held flowers, half in bloom and the other half decaying in shades of brown.

I closed my eyes, tried to blink away the image, but all I saw was Arthur's body, his crown of blond hair and all that blood...I thought of my father's journal. Of what he had written. *She has a darkness inside her.* Fear gripped me with icy hands.

Yet the man in the illustration looked peaceful, simply sleeping. I wanted to look away. Instead my eyes were drawn to the page, to the dead man waking from his eternal sleep. I should feel revulsed—and some parts of me were. Except...

This magic didn't look any darker than the other things I had seen. The man's body was surrounded by live flowers, their buds beginning to blossom, vines curling in the corner of the page. The moon sketched overhead was full and bright, bathing him in a divine silver light.

Was it possible that this could be the solution we needed? I didn't understand magic, not like Emmeline, but if you could make people fall in love, banish unwanted children, or draw wealth to yourself, couldn't you undo a mistake that had left somebody accidentally dead?

My heart thudded. It wasn't right—I shouldn't even consider it. There had to be something else. I flipped ahead, page after page of crackling paper, faded ink. My eyes snagged on another page towards the back of the book.

Commonly known as magic of Will rather than magic of Belief, blood (or other bodily fluids) is required to seal the Art of Bargains.

The debt. I gripped the page tighter.

This is the most dangerous magic of all. Its success rate may be higher, yet so is the payment. The Receiver is tied into a contract with the Giver, which must be paid in order to complete and stabilise the spell.

I stilled my trembling hands. What if the Receiver of the spell—
Arthur—died before the Giver could complete it? I read further,
skipping the details of blood drawn with an iron blade, runes carved
into the skin to mark intent.

*The blood debt is the strongest magical deficit. It is an imbalance:
power pulled from the earth without the appropriate level of recom-
pense. A blood sacrifice must be drawn willingly from both the
witch and the recipient, except in the direst of circumstances, when
a witch may use her own.*

I leaned forward, eyes scanning for an *if*, a *but*. An answer.

*In order to successfully form a Final Giving and seal a pact, there
must be an exchange of fresh flowing sacrificial blood. Without
this, the Giver may succumb to Witch's Noose.*

Here there was an illustration. Beneath an arc of nine perfect
silver moons there was a noose of crimson roses, crawling with sharp
thorns that dripped blood black and thick as tar. Far below, a skeletal hand reached from the wet earth, fingers clawing at the sky. I
fought back the wave of anger that misted my vision, blinking back
bitter, exhausted tears. I was furious, with Emmeline for being foolish enough to cast such a spell and with Bea for asking her do it, but
the anger seeped away as I pulled my eyes down.

*Worse, if the subject is compromised, the Noose will tighten within
the cycle of a moon.*

I stared at the bottom of the page, words swimming, horror
crawling up my spine. Instinctively I reached for the tether, which
lay dormant and indistinct.

*Death does not answer the call of this magic. It waits hungrily for
the witch who does not heed its warning.*

Chapter Five

Annie

E mmeline came down from the roof to meet me. Dread had driven me here, but a part of me thrilled at the sight of her long legs beneath her shirt, the small nod she gave me. The way she looked as if she was glad to see me. She beckoned me into the cool, dark house, and together we traipsed up several sets of stairs, up into the rafters.

"Nathan and Isobel are asleep," she said quietly, opening the door into a bedroom. "I don't think they'll be awake for hours yet. Isobel was brewing until nearing dawn and Nathan didn't stop pacing until well after that. I think he wants to go back out to look for Arthur later. I haven't got the heart to stop him."

Bea stood gazing out the window wearing nothing but an old shirt. The sight was so familiar it stole my breath. It reminded me of years of sleeping at each other's houses as children, mothers making hot tea and feeding us crusty, steaming bread fresh from the fire.

For a second tears prickled at my eyes, a longing so strong for the time before Sam and Eddie went to the front, before everything collapsed. Then Bea turned around and I saw the bruises on her face, and despite everything I was glad I had done it.

"We're still not telling them, then?" I asked. My father's spell book was heavy in my arms, but I didn't want to put it down.

"Darling, once Em makes up her mind you won't change it," Bea muttered. "The problem is Nathan. I suspect he knows more than he's letting on."

I shifted the heavy book to my hip, where its presence was like a faint buzzing in my limbs.

"You were meant to go home," Emmeline said tightly. The tether trembled.

"What is that old thing?"

Bea reached for the book, but I stepped back instinctively, pulling it away.

"It was my father's." It was surprisingly hard to choke out the words. Bea didn't react. She knew how I felt about him, yet her face remained impassive. Once I might have been upset, but all I felt was a distant pang at her selfishness. Emmeline frowned.

She gestured to the bed and I set the book down reverently on the rumpled sheets, which smelled faintly of blood and dirt.

"Your father." Emmeline stepped closer, although she didn't touch it. I steeled myself for her presence, but my body knew what to do and the tether remained steady, my mind clear. "He was—"

"A witch." I lifted my chin, daring her to challenge me. Daring her to throw me out again. She only blinked slowly, realisation dawning. "I was going to tell you. I was—afraid."

Bea peered at the bed. "And this book—"

"It has information about blood debts, bargains." I flipped it open. "I found it. I found *that*." I pointed at the page, my heart hammering loudly as Emmeline read the text, her eyes scanning hungrily.

I wanted to stop her, though she had to see it. Emmeline's lips thinned, her eyes growing dim. She folded her arms across her chest. "I…"

"What does it say?" Bea demanded. She didn't come near me or the book.

Emmeline said nothing. Shock was etched into every line of her, the way her spine curved as she hugged herself, her knees bowing as she sank into a crouch. Alarm swept across Bea's face. I held my hands up.

Bea ignored me. "*Em?*" she pushed.

"I have less time than I thought," she replied quietly. My stomach sank. I had wanted so badly to be wrong.

"How *much* time?" Bea spun from Emmeline to me.

"Em..." I said faintly.

"The next moon is my last." Emmeline blinked, slowly rising from her crouch. Coming back into herself achingly. "I thought—that is, I knew..." She swallowed.

"I thought you said you had months left?" Bea asked. She stared mistrustfully at the book.

"I thought I did."

"How do we even know it's telling the truth?"

"We don't." Emmeline turned to me. I glanced at the book, hoping she'd read on, hoping I wouldn't have to tell her. She didn't.

"It's not just that," I said. "Look at the last line."

Emmeline read it again. Her expression didn't change. But the tether trembled in my chest, squirming against her hold as she lost her grip. I reached for it, shoving it down although I longed for it to banish this fear that thrummed through every inch of me.

"Oh, for God's sake," Bea snapped. "What?" She stormed to the bed and planted her hands on either side of the book. She read the whole page. Read it again. "What?" she repeated quietly.

"'Death does not answer the call—'"

"It means I'm right to feel the way I do," Emmeline said. "It is worse since he died. And...it means we don't know how death will affect it." She skirted around it expertly, but I could *feel* her fear, feel the thread between us jangling with it as we both held it down.

I turned to Bea. "We don't know what will happen—to you—when Em is..."

"When I'm dead," Emmeline said bluntly.

Bea opened and closed her mouth. She slammed the book shut, recoiling when her hands hit the leather.

"That's not all," I said quietly. "I'm sorry—but I saw a newspaper. The police search for Bea is escalating because Arthur...He must not have been there to talk to them when he said he would be. And there was a man, he scared me. How long—"

"Shut up," Bea snapped. "This isn't helpful, Annie. None of this is helpful. Isn't there anything in this stupid book that can help us instead of just filling us with more dread? What is the goddamn point in you coming back here?"

Shock tied my tongue in knots. All the years we had been friends and Bea had never spoken to me like that. Maybe I deserved it.

"I don't know," I said hesitantly. "Maybe. I found something... Bea...I know we need to talk about this, talk about what I did. Please don't just yell at me. Let's take a minute—"

"Show me what you found," she said.

Gently, I let the book fall back open to the Awakening spell. Emmeline kept her distance while Bea looked, but I saw the way her back straightened.

"Is this real?"

She turned to Emmeline. Emmeline's face remained impassive.

"Em?" Bea pressed, tears forming at the corners of her eyes. "Can we bring him back? Why didn't you say anything before? Why didn't we *do this*?" She was nearly frantic, clutching her hands together, hope swelling in the new pink of her cheeks.

Emmeline's throat bobbed. "It's...I didn't know we could. It doesn't look safe—"

"I didn't ask whether it was safe," Bea hissed. "I said *can we do it*?"

"If we bring him back and he gives us the blood, it will break the debt," I said. "Won't it? I mean, all it says on the other page is the Receiver must be willing. Well, if we bring him back he'll be willing—"

"And what if he's not?"

The trembling was back in my chest. I tried to reach for the tether, grip that coiling thread that glowed brighter every second, but it danced away from me. Emmeline's body began to shake.

Bea's eyes sparkled with fresh tears. "Does it matter? If he's back, if he's mine again...I can convince him. It will be like it never happened. I want him back. Please."

"It's our only chance," I pushed, reaching for the tether again. "I've been through that whole book and we literally do not have any other choice, Emmeline. Without this you're dead within the month—and Bea too. Do you have a better suggestion? Because if you do then I am all ears."

"This isn't anything to do with you," Emmeline snarled. Her expression was feral and heat bloomed in my cheeks as my lungs constricted. I remembered my first impression of her—dangerous, seductive, raw. I truly felt that danger as she rounded on me, strength somehow in every part of her.

"Emmeline," I tried.

"You shouldn't be here. I told you to *leave*. I *told you*." Emmeline towered over me, her eyes dark, her hands claws at her sides. I shrank away just as she snatched at my arm, grabbing it hard. Her sharp nails dug in, my arm stinging as the skin broke like the flesh of a ripe peach.

"Emmeline," Bea cried. "Leave her alone. This isn't like you!"

Emmeline was vibrating, her pupils swallowing the irises. The tether swelled. She let go of my arm. Seconds later a gust of air rushed off her, hot as hell itself. Bea stumbled backwards and I did the same, knocked breathless by the force of the air as it slammed into me, just like the night of her Giving.

Only this time I was already cornered, my back pressed against the wall. The tether thrashed wildly. I needed to close my eyes but I was afraid to. I could taste it—Emmeline's magic—like blood on my tongue. Like metal chains. Like the earth from a freshly dug grave. My body recoiled, some primal part of me flinching away as I reached again and again for the tether; it snapped back and forth like a viper, fangs bared, whipped by Emmeline's strength.

"Get out," Emmeline growled. "Get out of here and take your book with you. Get out, get out. *Get out*." Her hands rose and I didn't know if she was going for my throat but I dropped into a crouch and closed my eyes, desperately trying to shut out the room so I could focus on her. On the tether between us, which was—*wrong*.

It wasn't Emmeline that I was afraid of. It wasn't her magic. It wasn't even the tether, truly, or the way she wielded it against me. It was the debt, a tar-like blackness that creeped up the connection between us like black mould; it was the debt that drove Emmeline wild, that thrashed through the tether, threatening to swallow me in its darkness once it was finished with her.

I reached out anyway, my mind curling around the bit of the tether that joined my heart to Emmeline's, yanking so hard that it jarred my bones, a grinding, juddering pull. It was like falling. It was like crashing. I cried out, eyes snapping open as Emmeline stumbled, as the magic coursing through her faltered.

Her knees buckled and she went down, hands hitting the floor hard. The wood trembled beneath my feet. The bed shuddered, wooden posts skidding.

Bea grappled for the wall to stop her from falling. I couldn't move, couldn't think, as I fought to hold the tether, to pull it back into submission, to help Emmeline subdue her magic by clamping down on it tight. My brain fogged, darkness crowding at the edge of my vision. A wetness trickled onto my lips from my nose. More on my arm.

Emmeline collapsed, landing in a heap on the floor, her face pressed to the wood, pale as death. Her nails were stained with my blood.

Bea was frozen, her hands cupped to her mouth in horror. The silence stretched. The tether stilled, succumbing to the pressure as I forced it down. Down so deep I could hardly feel it. My ears were ringing.

"We have to do it," I panted.

"What?"

"The Awakening. It's our only hope. Look at her." I could see the conflict on Bea's face, but I forged on. "I know we need to talk about this. I want to explain. I'm sorry for everything and it's eating me up. Right now, though, this is the only thing that might save her. Might save *us*."

Bea said nothing.

"I can do this alone," I said as forcefully as I dared. I hoped she understood what I meant: *I'd rather do it with your help.*

Bea's lips formed a thin line.

"It could bring him back," she whispered. "Right? There's hope that he could come back and be—himself?"

It was my turn for silence. In that instant I was sure of only two things: Whatever this cord was that glittered, that was so bright it burned in me, I had lost control of my own fate the moment I had tasted its power.

And if Emmeline died, it wasn't just Bea who would suffer.

Chapter Six

Annie

W hat are we doing?"
I glanced at Emmeline. Bea had disappeared into the endless halls of Cross House to get dressed. I had tried to talk to her again, to get her to look at me long enough that I could make sure she was okay, but it was no good. She needed time to herself. To think about what we were planning.

I wished she cared whether I needed time. Once she might have, but not anymore. It wasn't the island that had changed her, but I saw it more clearly than I had back home. Bea was so selfish she didn't realise the things I had done for her—the sacrifices I had made. But I gave her the space she needed. She would always be the girl I had grown with, played with; the sister I had never had. I loved her.

"If we're doing this, we need to go in prepared," Emmeline said. "We can't blunder." She walked stiffly, avoiding getting too close to me. We rounded the corner until we came to the greenhouse and the little vegetable plot again. The sun was baking but the shade here was so cool I shivered.

"The book didn't mention any preparation..."

Emmeline shook her head.

"It wouldn't. Those kinds of books—they're not for novices, Annie." We avoided the side of the greenhouse where Arthur's body lay, instead following a small path of cracked stones pressed into the grass that led to the door.

She didn't say what she meant: They weren't for *people like me*. What did that mean anymore? The book was mine, and I was the only one of us with a plan.

Emmeline paused by the greenhouse door. "We have to cleanse the space we're going to use, bring positive energy in to balance the magic we're going to call. It's a bit like—science, if you know anything about that." She pulled a set of keys from the pocket of her dark trousers. The door swung open and I was hit by the soft, damp scent.

"Show me," I demanded.

"Quickly. I don't want Nathan to see us in here." Emmeline grasped my arm and pulled me inside. My skin tingled at her touch, so different from earlier. It was a kiss instead of a bite. The half-moon shaped cuts on my wrist left by her nails stung in response.

The greenhouse was bigger than I'd thought. A good twelve feet long, the glass walls hidden from the world by a patina of moss, crawling ivy, trailing plants probably older than either of us. Work-benches ran against the walls, with a small gas stove at the back accompanied by a dirty cup and a wooden box next to it filled with filmy packets of dried herbs.

"Nathan would kill me if he knew we were in here."

"So why are we here?"

"Magic isn't all blood and desire. It's about balance, harmony, too. It's—it's complicated. There's what you feel inside, how you direct magic from in your body, your blood and your spirit, and there's...well, all of this."

I turned back and Emmeline was gesturing to the paradise of greenery around her.

"Nature is a tool, just like blood, just like will. And for the kind of magic you want to work with Arthur, we need the right tools. I've made the mistake of not using them before." She headed towards several of the plants at the back of the greenhouse, some of which I recognised as herbs.

Fresh lavender, real mint, maybe rosemary or basil—and those were only the ones I could name.

"This one's camphor," Emmeline explained when she caught my expression. "It stimulates your nerves. Wormwood—diluted, it makes great pain relief." She pointed at each one in turn, expert fingers selecting blooms and stems and reaching out to snick them with the round of her thumbnail, still stained with my blood. We noticed together and she drew her hand back self-consciously.

For a second I thought she might apologise. Instead she withdrew from me again, rounded her shoulders and shrank away, every line of her etched with horror.

"I know it wasn't you," I said. "In there. Your magic…"

"Don't, Annie." Emmeline shuddered. "I don't want your forgiveness."

"Maybe not, but I'm telling you that I understand. You didn't mean to hurt me. It's the debt, isn't it? Making your magic act like that."

Emmeline spun. We were so close that our breaths mingled as she asked, "Isn't that the point?" She pressed her lips together, sighed. "It doesn't matter if I wanted it to happen. It doesn't matter that I would rather die than hurt any of you. What matters is I can't control any of it—dead or not."

Perhaps I should have backed away, but I let her presence warm me, let it infuse my words with that same warmth, which was also truth.

"Does it matter that you scared me in there but I forgive you anyway? These aren't exactly normal circumstances, and we are not made whole by only the worst of our actions."

"And what if the worst is all I'm capable of?"

I didn't have an answer. It was a thought that preyed upon me too. Had done since I'd said goodbye to Sam—no, it had twisted my dreams long before that. It had tormented me from the moment I had let him believe I loved him the way Bea did; from the moment

I had let myself believe it too, even while knowing most women did not love their lovers like brothers. I had hated myself then, for the lie that had stolen that future from Bea.

I had no doubt that if I'd been brave, rebuffed Sam as I'd wanted to, he would have chosen her—and they would have been happy. Perhaps then none of this would have happened.

Emmeline turned away, breaking whatever softness had bloomed in the raw space between our bodies. "Here," she said gruffly, "grab that basket by the door and you can hold it while I gather. It'll be quicker that way."

Emmeline worked methodically, moving clockwise around Nathan's secret garden as I inhaled the scents and marvelled at her strength, surprised by it although I had seen firsthand how she might use it.

"If this doesn't work…" I said.

"If this doesn't work the world will move on without me and everything else will be fine," she lied. "You and Bea will go back to Whitby and live by the sea and you'll find a nice young man and get married and move on."

I let my eyes stay on Emmeline's. Let her see the truth in them. No matter what happened, whether this worked or not, that wasn't what I wanted.

"No men," I whispered thickly. It was the closest to an admission I'd ever come.

Emmeline's gaze softened.

"No men, then," she agreed.

The quiet inside the greenhouse was peaceful at first, but after long minutes sweat began to bead on my hairline, my lip, under my arms. I shifted uncomfortably and passed the basket from one arm to the other.

"I forget you're not used to the heat." Emmeline glanced up from where she was leaning across the workbench. Holding the tether was exhausting. I could feel Emmeline at the other end, but she was avoiding touching it—probably after earlier—and the burden to keep it subdued landed squarely on me.

I had started to ask about it once, twice, and given up both times, unable to formulate the question. I circled back to the same thought: How much of the way I felt about Emmeline was magic? Why else would I feel this way when it went against everything I'd been taught?

I wasn't sure I could bear to know the answer.

Emmeline rooted around near Nathan's tea station, coming up with a glass bottle filled to the brim with clear liquid.

"Is that water?" I asked.

Emmeline laughed.

"No, love."

My grasp must have slipped on the cord because that one word made my knees buckle. I went to push it down further, blinking slowly. It was already subdued. Emmeline watched me carefully as she offered me the bottle.

I uncapped it and lifted it to my nose. My nostrils were assaulted with a fruity aroma that I couldn't place.

"Just try it," she coaxed.

I only hesitated for a second before taking a small sip. The taste exploded on my tongue: it was bottled summer nights; campfire smoke laced with wild red berries and an undertow of rippling, freezing water. The taste was so bright and sharp that I laughed aloud.

"Stronger than the kyraz," I said.

"Isobel's speciality. She's been trying to imbue booze with memory since Cilla first taught her how to brew."

"Isobel made this?"

Emmeline smirked, taking the bottle and swallowing deep before she handed it back. "Oh, she makes all of our kazam. She's very talented. I only sell the stuff—which, predictably, she hates." She shrugged.

Emboldened, I took another swig, bigger this time. Another. This time I tasted bitter cocoa and a hint of sunlight. It was fire and gold; it was bright days on the pier drinking Mam's special hot chocolate. It was Bea and Sam and me sitting in the shop tasting Mam's chocolate on sweltering summer days and diving off the rocks into the freezing ocean while Bea and two soldier boys cheered on the sand. The taste of the memories was better than the memories themselves.

Emmeline took the basket from me, laying it to one side. She was taller than me, my head just about brushing her sharp jaw. I could smell her, iron and dirt, along with the fresh, spicy herbs by my hand, and I suppressed a shiver. She was so close to me I could see the flutter of her pulse in her throat, slower than it should be.

"Why are you showing me all of this?" I asked softly. I could hardly breathe. Emmeline's face was only inches from mine. She had a little mole on her neck, just above her open collar. *God help me*, I thought without sense. *I want to kiss it.* "Is it because of my father?"

"Not just because of that." Emmeline's voice was throaty. Her eyes searched my face, her lips slightly parted, the colour high on her cheeks. Her finger brushed my arm, electricity in my skin, and the silver cord between us flared bright as I lost concentration. Emmeline pulled back in alarm, like she hadn't intended to get so close. Like our proximity made her wild too.

I grappled for the tether again, suitably chastised. I shoved it down deep, deeper, until Emmeline stopped looking like a spooked horse. Until my pulse no longer thrummed at the sight of her.

"Sorry," I breathed.

"Have you told anybody else about him?"

She marched back to the bench and retrieved a cigarette out of a cloth bag there. Her tongue flicked out of her mouth, dark with blood, and she pressed it to the business end of the cigarette. It began to glow. The blood in the air was like a hum in my bones.

"What?" I asked.

"Your father."

Distantly my brain warned me to be afraid. We were locked in here and her behaviour was erratic. The magic she had cast between Bea and Arthur was clearly fraying her mind as well as her body. I had thought that maybe I should keep the book from her, just in case, but if I couldn't trust Emmeline, who else was there?

"No," I said. "Only you. I'm worried about his collection, though. How can I keep it safe? There was a man in the museum. I think he was looking for my father."

"He scared you." Emmeline's eyes shone.

"Yes," I said quietly. "But I don't know...I don't know if he meant any harm," I added quickly. "I'm just—I can't hide this. I can't lie. I don't know how. I want to get rid of all of it. My father—he had rare things, I think. A journal. Academic books. Mam always said those didn't exist. I never thought..."

Once the words were flowing I couldn't stop them until I clamped my hands over my mouth.

"Oh, they exist," Emmeline assured me, confident now, as if this was solid ground. "I've never seen anything like yours, but that just means it's old. Older than my aunt ever had. The sort of books witches have been fighting over for years. Cilla would have died if she'd known." Emmeline gave a mirthless laugh and I lost my grip on the tether again.

It built within me like a spark becomes a flame, fast and hot. The thread uncoiled, sliding out of my grasp. I caught it but didn't push it down all the way. I wanted her to notice me.

"Emmeline," I blurted, latching on to the courage that flooded me. "You feel it, don't you? This *thing*. I know you do. Do you know what it is?"

Emmeline snatched at the tether, wrenching it back, fast and hard enough to make me wince, before marching to the other side of the greenhouse.

I stood for a moment, gathering my fractured thoughts, trying to locate where my emotions ended and Emmeline's had begun. She kept her back to me, smoking in silence.

My cheeks grew hot with inexplicable embarrassment, as if I'd broken some kind of code. It dawned on me slowly that I had—twice—controlled the tether in order to get a reaction from her. The first had been to calm her, to shock her magic into submission. What about this time? I thought I hadn't let it go on purpose, but was that true? I had wanted her attention. And I had got it.

My stomach turned as a cold, familiar horror purged the last of the courage from my body.

"Emmeline, I'm sorry—"

"If we're going to do the Awakening, it needs to be in here," she said abruptly. "And we need to do it fast. Tonight, when the others go to bed. The quicker it's done, the quicker we can go our separate ways."

Chapter Seven

Annie

What will Nathan and Isobel say when you ask them not to go in the greenhouse?"

Several hours of dodging their glances, awkward chatter over a dinner of cold summer soup and fresh crusty bread Nathan made from scratch, and the moon was high in the sky as I finally asked the question. Bea and Emmeline and I sat on the beach at the back of Cross House, waiting for the others to go to bed.

The hours had felt like torture, each moment one closer to Emmeline's death, to Bea's doom.

Emmeline didn't answer at first, her gaze trained firmly on the house towering behind us as she watched for Isobel's bedroom light to finally be extinguished. Eventually she shook her head.

"I don't know. Nathan will sense the wards I've placed as soon as he comes near, but I had to soundproof it. The sooner we can get it over with, the better." She paused, inspecting her nails—which I noticed she had cut shorter after this morning. They were no longer ringed with my blood. "Are you sure—both of you—that you want to do this?"

Bea was silent, her face set in a mask of resolve. My heart tumbled. I wanted to say *no*, wanted to run, but what choice did we have?

We climbed to our feet without speaking and headed in single file towards the greenhouse, where Emmeline and I had finished our preparations earlier in frosty silence. Inside we had arranged a long wooden table and a lawn chair, cleansed with sage and sprinkled with lavender flowers and sprigs of verveine. Bundles of wild garlic and peppermint studded with star anise hung low from the glass roof, dangling just above our heads, and incense thickened the air.

Bea went inside to make a start lighting candles, consecrating the space further, and although this was because she did not want to help us dig Arthur from his grave, I was glad she was gone.

Emmeline and I grabbed our shovels and set about digging. She didn't look at me as we worked, first with the shovels and afterwards with our bare hands, hauling Arthur's body out into the silver moonlight. Panic and a roiling sickness made my stomach flip hard and I fought back the urge to vomit.

Emmeline laid her hand on my arm, her skin warm against my own.

"You don't have to do this," she said quietly. Her face was smooth in the moonlight, limned in silver and shades of grey, her dark eyes unreadable.

"This was my idea."

"I could make you forget."

"Is that what you think?" I asked. "That I'm such a coward I would want you to make me forget this? Forget you?" I filled my stare with as much steel as I could muster.

"No," she said slowly. "I suppose I just wish you were." She sighed, bone-deep. "People think magic is fun. I'm sure the fake stuff can be, squealing over party games, *guess the first letter of your true love's name*—those things aren't questioned here. The rich people, they grumble about the rules and then they go and find their kazam somewhere a little bit less legal and it's *still* fun for them. They don't understand the sacrifice."

The death.

She didn't speak the words but she didn't have to. The ghost of them hung between us anyway. I thought of my father's death again.

A heart attack—it seemed too easy. An answer for another life. I no longer believed it.

"Why do you do it?" I blurted, although I thought I knew the answer. It was the same irresistible pull that had drawn me to Emmeline after I had been warned away. "The spells you sell, the purple light. Why give people what they crave, knowing that it's no good for them?"

Emmeline's body was poised like marble as she gazed down at Arthur's body. I glimpsed the girl she must have once been—beautiful, powerful. Afraid of the world and what it might do to her if she didn't own it.

"I do it because...because this life chews people like us up and spits them right back out again. Because I have never asked for anything more than safety for my brother and sister, yet all we get is tolerance at best and downright hatred at worst. I've watched my family crumble and not been able to do anything about it. People don't think of us as being human. They don't care if we live and live well as long as their needs are fulfilled. I do it, Annie, because I'm good at it. It gives me power—a future—when I can see no other way forward." There was heartbreak on her face, not hidden behind her usual bluster or false amusement. "I do it," she added softly, "because magic is all I know."

———◦)●(◦———

Arthur's body was as long as the table. His dirty crown of blond hair spilled over the edge like threads of gold. While Emmeline cut the damaged clothes from Arthur's skin, Bea and I carried an old tin bathtub full of heated water from the kitchen. We soaped his blood-and-dirt-encrusted skin with a foaming liquid Emmeline called kashba—camphor, peppermint, and camomile mixed with salted water and charcoaled wood from the fire—until his naked skin was as fresh and clean as a newborn's. He looked almost peaceful, except for the spidered wound on his chest, dark and red around the edges.

I did that.

Emmeline dipped her finger into a mixture of sage ash and oil, swiping it at both of Arthur's temples. She sprinkled two pinches of salt on Arthur's forehead, just above his eyebrows. I did the same into his palms, and Bea massaged more salt into the soles of his feet. She did so with her eyes closed, breathing slowly through her nose.

My father's book was spread on the workbench behind Emmeline, and I consulted it before the next step. I passed a silver, glittering knife to Emmeline, who leant tiredly against the table as she pressed it into the soft, once-golden skin above Arthur's inner elbows, leaving behind two small crosses. Two more marks were etched into his upper thighs.

She paused, staring.

"Emmeline," I prompted.

She blinked once. Her dark eyes took on the swaying shadows of the flickering candle flames, green and black and gold. Her throat bobbed as she swallowed.

"I'm fine," she said.

"We have to keep going," Bea said. She had opened her eyes now.

The three of us stood around Arthur's body. Emmeline stood on his left side, and I stood on his right. Bea trembled at the crown of his head, the sage burning so she was obscured by a haze of greyish smoke.

Bea reached for my hand. I thought of all the years we had run and played together as children, the hours we had spent in her mother's tea shop. It was a lifetime ago.

"Em," Bea said. "Take my hand."

Emmeline didn't move.

"Emmeline, we have to," I pushed. "There's no other way."

Wordlessly I followed the tug of the silver cord between us, more tangible in this smoky green place than it had ever been before. Gently I eased up, letting the tether grow until I could feel Emmeline's fear and she mine, not letting it get far enough to obscure the emotion.

There was the warm brush of Emmeline's skin against mine, a singing in my blood. It was completeness; it was power. It was desire.

The air was thick with the scents of herbs and flowers, of sage and old cigarette smoke. Emmeline began to chant.

We lowered our hands until they pressed against the grain of the wooden table. The chanting was a low sound, rhythmic. Emmeline pulled away to lean over Arthur's body. In her hands she held a long needle, its end curved like a fishhook, and a length of black twine.

For the first time since she started I saw Emmeline pale at the task ahead, but she kept the chanting going as she reached over and began to stitch the wound over Arthur's heart. Bea closed her eyes again, but I watched every movement as skin met skin, puckered and lifeless beneath the needle.

I gathered three coins, warm from my pocket, one for each of Arthur's palms and one for just above his heart. An offering. An apology.

There was sweat on my brow, an insistent knocking on the inside of my skull. Everything was heavy. It didn't feel good. It didn't feel—*right*.

I pushed the thought back. It was what it was.

Emmeline nudged Bea, who reached for the bundle of colourful loose flowers Emmeline handed her and began to thread them into the gentle, damp wave of her husband's hair. Her breathing was unsteady as she tried not to look at the black twine in its grotesque star shape over his heart. I grabbed more salt to spread across Arthur's body, sprinkling the shimmering crystals across his forehead, neck, chest, groin, and legs.

We stopped. Emmeline sagged against the table.

My blood hummed with the magic that flowed between the three of us. My body was *alive*. I was aware of every inch of skin, every open and closed part of me.

I wanted to cry. I wanted to throw my head back and laugh. I could taste Emmeline's grave-dirt-and-blood smell at the back of my throat along with a hint of another scent—like ocean salt on a hot summer's breeze mingled with cut grass. It made my skin tingle and my legs weak, a power so familiar that it felt like my own name.

Emmeline swayed.

The summer-ocean scent was gone as fast as it arrived. The

candles guttered and darkness slipped into the hot, smoky green-house. The wind that flowed felt like it had come from the mouth of hell, and where it touched my skin it burned.

It reminded me of the wind Emmeline had summoned.

The debt.

"Maybe we should stop," I said.

A jolt of electricity flung through my limbs. I cried out and Emmeline grunted. The pain was white-hot, shocking.

Arthur's eyes were open. His heartbeat pulsed at his throat. Slow. Too slow. The full weight of what we were attempting crashed into me like a wave. This was why magic was outlawed, not because of silly kazam cocktails and party games. Not even because it was intoxicating, because it drew you in. It was because of *this*.

It was darkness. It was wrong. There was too much potential for—evil. We shouldn't have even considered it. How could magic create life where there was none?

It was too late.

Fear clawed at my throat as Arthur's body began to tremble. The coins dropped from his chest and his palms, jangling as they hit the ground. Bea backed away, one hand pressed to her mouth and the other to her stomach.

It was done.

Arthur blinked. And slowly, with the clumsiness of a new foal, he began to claw himself upright.

"Arthur," Emmeline said, voice low. "Are you with us?"

His head swivelled. His eyes, no longer blue but a tumbling twilight sort of grey, met hers. His mouth opened, wordlessly, as he glanced at each of us in turn.

Bea took a step closer to the table. "Art. Darling, can you hear me...?"

Nothing.

"He can't speak," I whispered.

Bea was almost close enough to touch him. Arthur's chest rose and fell. The gunshot wound had not closed. Sickness roiled in my belly. He wasn't normal. He wasn't—himself.

His mouth was still working, up and down, tongue over teeth, round and round.

Emmeline poured a glass of water from a small pitcher and passed it to Bea. She held the glass to her husband's lips patiently while he drank, greedy, water dribbling down his chest. I reached for the tether without thinking, hoping it might echo my questions. Hoping Emmeline might understand.

Why isn't he like us? Part of him is missing.

"Go," Bea said quietly. "Please. Give us a minute."

Emmeline didn't move.

"*Go,*" Bea repeated. Arthur's lip lifted, half a snarl, just a flutter, and his hands were on Bea's as she held the glass steady.

I reached for Emmeline, dragging her out of the greenhouse into the cool of the night where the sweat dried on our foreheads and we could *finally* breathe.

Except I could still feel the panic in my chest, binding my lungs, the incense inside my nose.

"Em," I whispered, so quiet that only she and the darkness heard me. "The shapes you carved in his skin. The wound. They aren't bleeding. How do we know he still can give the blood for the debt?"

Emmeline's eyes were dark.

"He isn't right," I said, panicked. "I thought this would fix him. Make him whole again. What if he stays like this?"

The thought in my mind was insistent, a banging drum of panic.

What have we done?

Setting Intentions

R. Crowther

Yule—Winter Solstice

Somebody has been in my house.

I'm only surprised it has taken this long for me to become a target. I have been collecting for years, after all. The local witches know me, or generally at least they know of me if they had any connection to the Council during the war. Perhaps I have succeeded at being invisible until now.

I could speak to the Council about what happened tonight, though I am not sure they would help. A basic bloodline charm kept the intruder out of my study, so they'll no doubt say there's nothing they can do. Their focus remains as it has increasingly since the war: on those witches drawing too much attention to themselves. Always the Council's priority is to protect itself.

These days I keep my distance, so I've lost a lot of my sway. It used to be about the people as much as it was the power. It was about those poor boys fighting for their freedom.

I suppose the fighting is here these days, a much different calibre. Rich men in their tailored suits and golden pins squabbling over scraps of extra power, everybody hungry for glory. The men quarrel amongst themselves, eager to prove that they deserve the Council's trust, and all the Council *care about is keeping our existence a secret. I should have done better to hide my collection. I never wanted it for myself.*

Though, if not mine, whose hands would these books be better in? At least I keep them safe. Their magic untapped. Could I say the same if they belonged to my fellow councilmen?

There is more about this that has been playing on my mind in the last hours. The moon is high and I can see her from up here, bright and sharp as hoarfrost. I'm reminded of the last time I felt the way I do tonight.

The first night I saw Priscilla's heir, all those years ago.

There are rumours—and I'm sure they are more than rumours—that she dresses in men's clothes and casts with abandon. That she sells her magic.

I wonder how long it will be before she is taken to task by the Council. How long they will let her playact like Cilla while offering none of the whispers or secrets.

Perhaps deep down they know the same thing I do. It's the reason I hoard my books and my spells, hide them behind wards and locked doors.

There are some things that should be left alone.

Chapter Eight

Annie

Bea stayed with Arthur all night. Emmeline and I took turns sitting outside the greenhouse on an old, broken lawn chair. We didn't know what we were waiting for, but we both knew it wasn't time yet. We couldn't interrupt them. Bea coaxing him back to himself was our only hope.

And we were both afraid of facing him.

"I bought these chairs before I understood that people really do want glamour, not comfort," Emmeline said wryly during our first trade of watch. I'd spent the first hour since Arthur's Awakening sitting by myself in the kitchen, banished from the garden to "rest" since I hadn't slept the night before either, but I didn't try.

I wanted to be in there with Bea. I was desperate to see if Arthur could speak, if there was any of his old self left. Mostly I couldn't shake the badness that clung to me like the incense; I didn't like leaving Bea alone with him.

When I turned up in the garden again an hour ahead of when Emmeline had told me to relieve her, she let me perch awkwardly on the wooden arm of the lawn chair, and she lit cigarettes—one for her, one for me.

I didn't like the taste, but I smoked it dutifully, letting the herby flavour sit on my tongue. Emmeline sat hunched, her elbows on her knees, the cigarette hanging between loose fingers.

"How many parties have you had?" I asked.

"Too many." Emmeline shrugged. "I hate them. All the excess. But needs must..." She drifted into silence.

We remained that way until I told Emmeline it was time for my watch. She didn't want to leave either, but I could see from her face that she was exhausted. She might actually stand a chance at sleep.

"Go," I said quietly. "The greenhouse is—what did you call it? Warded, right?" She nodded. "So you'll know if anything happens. Go, sleep. Make coffee. Eat. When did you last eat anything? I know you didn't eat at dinner."

Emmeline looked like she was about to argue, like maybe she wanted to stay as badly as I wanted her to. Her lips curved in a small smile when I frowned.

"Don't argue," I said firmly.

"I wasn't going to."

"Then why are you looking like that?" I wanted her to say it aloud, acknowledge that it wasn't only me who felt this spark.

Emmeline sobered. "I'll be back later," she said.

I sat in the darkness, relishing the stillness of the air, sensing another hot day ahead, and stared into the trees. Nothing moved. No birds, no foxes or scuttling hedgehogs. Nature had abandoned us.

I strained my ears, but I caught nothing beyond soft murmurs from inside the greenhouse, delicate, coaxing sounds that rose and fell, edged with gentle frustration.

Sometime later a sound shot out of the darkness. I jumped out of my chair, heartbeat slamming, eyes wide. The darkness blended into itself, smoky silhouettes of trees and bushes and the towering house in the distance. Then I noticed it.

A crow. Its shiny eyes caught the faint candlelight from inside the greenhouse and it flickered there. The creature had swooped down onto the lawn, not two feet away. It was huge, watchful.

"What is it?" Emmeline asked breathlessly, racing towards me. "I felt..."

"A crow," I said, clutching a hand to my chest, willing my heart-beat to slow as I nodded into the trees where the crow still sat, almost invisible in the dark. "One crow."

Emmeline rolled her eyes. "I woke up for that?"

"One for malice," I pointed out.

Emmeline followed my gaze. Her features softened, still smudged with sleep, as she said, "Don't believe everything you hear." She sighed, sinking down into the lawn chair I'd vacated.

"The poem—" I started.

Emmeline shrugged. "Magic is what we make it."

I thought of Arthur, of the magic we had performed on him, how even in the thick of the ritual I'd been thinking of bringing him back to life not because it was the right thing to do, but because it could save Bea and Emmeline.

A shiver wormed up my spine.

———( ) • ( )———

Arthur was like a child. Bea had wrapped him in an old tartan blan-ket, the green and red stark against the new pallor of his skin. He sat in another lawn chair, twin to the one outside, quiet and pliant, but his eyes darted back and forth like those of a newly caged animal.

For a long while I stood in the doorway and waited. Bea knelt at his knees, massaging her thumbs into his upturned palm.

"No change?" I asked finally. Arthur didn't acknowledge my voice.

Bea's shoulders hunched. My gaze went back to Arthur before flicking away again. It hurt to look for too long. There was a dark-ness around him, a haziness I didn't understand, like the waver of a shadow in the light of a sputtering candle. Perhaps Emmeline would know what it was, whether it was some kind of leftover magic from the ritual. It made my skin crawl.

"Bea, we're going to have to talk about this," I murmured as she continued to ignore me. "What I did to him. What that means for us. I want you to know I'm here for you."

"Really?" she asked, spinning to face me. "We're doing this now?"

"When else would you like to do it?" I asked. "I want to make sure you're okay. I didn't—"

"Okay?" Bea gave a laugh that sounded like broken glass, sharp and eager. "Of course I'm not okay."

"Bea..."

"I know, Ann," she said, quieter. "I know. You didn't mean to hurt me over Sam. I didn't mean to hurt you when I left Whitby. You didn't mean for any of this to happen. I get it. I'm not mad at you. I guess we started down this path a long time ago."

I stared down at my hands, still grubby with dirt and ash from the ritual. Was this what bravery had earned me? It was a disaster. The distant way Bea said Sam's name hurt as much as everything else combined.

"I just want to protect you," I said. "You're my best friend. You're the only one I have left."

"You can't live my life for me, Ann." Bea shook her head sadly. "I know you feel like you owe me because of—Sam. I'm not stupid. I let you feel guilty because I thought you deserved to, but that's ancient history. I did try, you know. To talk to you—before I left Whitby. I couldn't do it, though. You'd have judged me. You were always so disapproving, of the parties and the boys, of...everything."

Bea was right. I would have judged her. I always had. It was only because I wanted to help her, to keep her sensible and safe. It was only because I felt awful for keeping Sam for myself.

"I'm sorry," I said. Bea shrugged.

She glanced at Arthur, at the vacant slash of his mouth, his wandering eyes.

"You know what's ridiculous?" she said finally. "I was so excited when I found out I was pregnant. Pregnant—that's why I came to Emmeline last year." The colour was high in her cheeks and she glanced at her husband, but he didn't even blink. "The father was a dream. He told me his name was Ted, that he was an American—he had this lovely drawl. He said he'd come over during the war and decided to stay. We...I don't know. I thought we'd get married. I thought...

"It doesn't matter what I thought. I heard somebody at the Crown mention this place, once. It seemed like my only option. And—oh, I wanted Arthur as soon as I saw him." Her face softened as she took her husband's large hands in hers. "It was perfect—until the magic wore off. Now, look."

"I know." I didn't know what else to say. There was nothing I could find that might help. *I know*—that had always been our code. It meant *I understand. I forgive you. I love you. I'm sorry.*

"I've tried to explain things to him," Bea said, finally placing her husband's hands back in his lap carefully. "I don't know how much he understands yet. It isn't right, is it? It didn't work. I'm not sure he'll ever be . . . normal."

Arthur's fingers clenched at the word *normal*. Or perhaps, with the hazy film around him, I was mistaken and he only twitched.

"We can't just keep him in here like a dog," Bea said.

"No," I agreed. Arthur's eyes were trained on me, on my hands. On the hands that had fired the gun that killed him. The haziness still surrounded him. I shifted my hands behind my back. "We can't hide it for long, you're right. Nathan will figure it out when he can't track him down, I suspect. But I suppose we can manage a day or so? Just to . . . get him adjusted? Then we can ask him about the debt . . ."

Arthur's head cocked to the side, but his face didn't change. Had he understood me? That bad feeling, that sensation of *wrongness*, it was louder inside, without the calmness of the trees and the dirt and the sky. I took a breath and forced it down, but it was like a pebble, cold and hard and lodged right in my throat.

"Where is Em?" Bea asked.

"She went to make coffee. I'm meant to be keeping watch in case Isobel and Nathan wake up, though Em says it'll probably be ages yet."

"Isobel's rarely up before lunch," Bea agreed. "Nathan's the one you should be watching for."

"I should go, then."

Bea nodded, dismissing me. She resumed her massaging, this time at Arthur's feet, and eventually his eyes were on her again and not on me.

I stepped blinking into the sunlight. I was thinking of Emmeline again, of the way she had walked towards the kitchen, still graceful but her steps markedly uneven, her whole body drained to empty. If we didn't fix this soon...

A twinge of panic, momentary but all-consuming, made my limbs clench. My lungs were too tightly packed in my chest. My throat too narrow. I heard the whistle of my breath.

Which is why I didn't notice until it was too late.

The sound of a car engine still running in the distance. The jaunty whistle as somebody cut down the winding path between Emmeline's house and mine. Before I had a chance to process it, there was a man standing on Emmeline's lawn with his hat in his hands.

Chapter Nine

Annie

A h, Miss Mason, you're just the lady I was looking for."

I jolted at his voice.

"Mr. Anderson!" I exclaimed. "What are you doing here?"

I glanced down, intensely aware that I was still wearing the same dress I had for the last two days, its hem scuffed with black mud, though at least my hands were only grubby with ash. I clenched them.

Anderson inclined his head and stepped a little closer. Alarm rang through my body, but I tried to appear casual, just a young woman helping her neighbour to—to what? Plant vegetables?

"When you missed our appointment this morning I tried to telephone your home," Anderson said. His smile was warm, his red hair ruffling in the faint breeze. He took another step forward. My heart lurched into my throat. "You were going to come and sign those papers, yes?"

I jumped forward, away from the greenhouse, praying that Arthur didn't choose this moment to start talking, that Bea wouldn't call for my help. That Emmeline wouldn't come back. I wasn't sure why but I didn't want Anderson to see her.

"Forgive me," Anderson said, his eyes widening. "I didn't mean to startle you. I know it's rude of me to drop in, but I was worried about you. When you, ah, weren't home, I followed the path around. I thought I heard voices. Are you here alone?"

He cast his eyes across the dew-damp lawn. I had nearly reached him, where the lush grass met the tree line. I could see the path that led to my driveway, to my house and Anderson's car.

"Oh yes. At the moment," I said. "I've been helping to—party planning."

Anderson raised his eyebrows, surprise evident. He glanced behind me, up at Cross House, which loomed, casting a long shadow, before resting his gaze on the green-tinted greenhouse and its strangely placed lawn chair out front. I was thankful for the vines that grew up the walls, blocking the glass.

"I'm sorry," I went on, talking fast and quiet. "I know you're very busy. I completely lost track of time. The parties, you see—they're quite loud. I was hoping I might talk to my neighbour about moving her guests around to the back of the house..."

What if he could see some single thing we had missed? I was intensely aware of how close we were still to the greenhouse, to Arthur's grave, which we had not filled again after we dug him up. A shiver darted through me, a deep part of myself begging me to talk to Anderson. To ask him for help.

He'd told me to talk to him if I was concerned about Cross House. I was more concerned than ever, yet I could only shift awkwardly from one foot to the other, try to keep my face straight, my hands still, my heart beating steady and slow. What would he say if I told him? He didn't like magic. Didn't like Emmeline. I wondered if he would renounce his offer of warmth, of friendship, entirely if he knew about my father.

I was in too deep, and I couldn't see a way out.

"You are still enjoying the island, aren't you?" he asked gently, his forehead crinkling. "She's not giving you any trouble? I've heard such things. You ought not to get yourself involved, even for the sake of a night's peace."

"It's fine," I said faintly. "It was only—a conversation."

"She hasn't tried to make you do anything you don't want to?" he prompted. He stepped closer, rubbing his beard, his expression becoming intense. Discomfort squirmed in me as he added lower, "I can try to find you some more suitable accommodation, if you want. Somewhere less ... boisterous."

I wanted to say *Yes. Please. Take me away from this mess I've landed myself in, away from this horror that's curling inside me, this darkness. This desire.* Something in Anderson's manner held me back.

"No," I said, trying to smile. "No, that's okay. Thank you for the concern, but everything is fine. I'm only mortified I worried you."

Anderson's expression relaxed. "I'm glad. Very glad. I'm sorry, I must seem overbearing, meddling like this. Your father, ah ... He talked about you, sometimes. When he told me about his plans for you to come to the island, I wasn't sure it was a good idea. He asked me to keep an eye on you, to make sure you didn't allow yourself to fall in with the wrong crowd. He told me he did so once, let himself be beguiled by the island, and he regretted it deeply.

"I am glad that you're standing up for yourself." His lips narrowed to a thin line, his expression verging on disgusted. "My *only* advice, Miss Mason, would be caution. People like her ... Look, perhaps you would be better off up near me, closer to your father's place. If I were you, I'd think very carefully about whether you need to be here."

He smiled again and the moment passed. He straightened and gave one last glance towards the greenhouse before lifting his hand in a farewell. "My secretary will arrange another meeting, if that suits. Perhaps next week?"

I nodded, but distantly. It felt like my feet had grown roots, delving deep into the dark soil. I could sense Bea and Arthur at my back, the magic we had woven, and I thought again of my father's journal. The words I had read, the pages I had stuffed so carelessly under my mattress.

Anderson was gone.

She has a darkness in her.

"Annie?" It was Emmeline. Her hands were full, two cups and a croissant balanced on the rims where they joined. She passed one to me and placed the other on the lawn chair. "What's wrong?"

Was Anderson right? Should I, after everything, still be wary of Emmeline? For the first time I wondered a thought so insidious I wasn't sure where it had come from. What if this—all of this—was what Emmeline had intended all along? I recalled the way I had felt the night of the party. That balance of fear and hunger. How I had felt that I would do anything for her. And I had. I had killed for her.

Yet that was ridiculous. Why would Emmeline want to damn herself so entirely?

"Annie?" Emmeline pressed. "Who was he? Was he the man from the museum?"

I could see the tension running through her, in the slope of her shoulders, the cording of her neck. I sensed it in the silver tether that bound us together, alarm zinging back and forth.

"No. My father's lawyer," I admitted. "I missed my appointment with him this morning."

Emmeline's fear was so strong it might have been my own.

"He didn't see anything," I said quickly. "It's fine. I lied and said I was annoyed about your parties and I was here to talk to you. I think he believed me." Was it fine? Was Anderson merely a concerned friend of my father's? I thought of the man at the museum too. They were both harmless. I didn't know what was real anymore. "I—I think I convinced him."

Emmeline's jaw worked as she lit a cigarette, smoking it distractedly. I closed my eyes for a second, forcing down the fear.

"I didn't mean to scare you. I know you can feel it too." I sucked in a breath, pulling the fresh green air into my lungs. I needed to ask again. We couldn't dance around this forever. "What *is* it?"

Emmeline's gaze snapped to mine.

"What is what?"

"I don't know what to call it. The...tether. This cord that's between us. You can't keep pretending it doesn't exist. At first I thought I was imagining it, but I can *feel* you, your magic and your emotions. And I know you can feel me too. We're connected." I

reached out with my mind, searching for the silver thread and finding it, humming with anticipation between us. I gave it an experi-
mental nudge, just gently. Emmeline inhaled sharply.

"Don't do that."

"Why not?" I demanded. "What is it, Emmeline? Why is it
there? I think I deserve to know."

Emmeline smoked her cigarette in silence for a moment, her
frown deepening. When she looked at me next it was with an intensity that stole my breath.

"I don't know for certain," she said, her voice low. "I've never
known anybody who's experienced it before. I read about it when I
was younger. My aunt...She died before she could teach me more
about magic. I remember reading about this thing called a vinculum.
It's like a natural chemistry between two people. Not romantic, just
a sort of...magically aided connection. I didn't say anything before
because I was—scared." Emmeline gave one of her sloping shrugs
and lifted the cigarette to her lips again.

"Why?"

"You said yourself: We're connected. You can feel my magic. My
very unstable magic. How is that a good thing?" When I said nothing, only continued to stare, she continued. "I wasn't sure before. I
hoped it might be a fluke."

"And now you're sure?"

If it wasn't about love or desire, what did that mean for me? For
the feelings I had, the ones that couldn't just be pushed off on the
tether? I had felt it whenever we were close, the way I never had with
Sam. I had felt it even when that silver thread was coiled up tight,
shoved down into the recesses of myself. Just a glance from Emmeline and I wasn't myself.

Or maybe I was more myself than I'd ever been.

I had thought Emmeline felt the same about me. The way she
looked at me sometimes, the way the space between us seemed to
hum, to crackle with energy—but how much of that was Emmeline's magic? How much of our connection was because of *this*?

"I didn't want to believe it," she said. "It's a terrible, dangerous thing, Annie. It's powerful, yes, and I suppose it could be useful if we could control it—"

"Like when we were searching for Bea," I suggested. "You helped me."

"Yes." Emmeline looked disgusted—with herself, or with me, I couldn't tell. "I wasn't thinking clearly. I shouldn't have done that. I opened a door and I shouldn't have."

"It worked, though," I argued. "It helped me to focus, to help you find her. Isn't that a good thing?"

"No," Emmeline snapped, eyes flashing. "*No.* It isn't that simple. None of this is simple. Think of the other times, when you've been so close to me, when I've been so . . . out of control. I wish it had never happened."

I thought of the obsession that grew like wildfire, that consumed every waking thought. How at first any physical proximity I had to Emmeline had felt like a gift, and a curse, like a knife so sharp you didn't realise how badly you hurt. I thought of how I'd nearly lost every inch of myself to her presence.

It had never occurred to me that she might have struggled at first, that learning to hold the tether had been as much of a task for her as it was for me. I reached up and cupped my elbows.

"It's treacherous," she said. "Can you imagine how easy it would be to let it run wild? There'd be no stopping it if it got started. And my magic, the debt . . . I don't know what it could do. And holding it down—is exhausting. I'm not sure how long we can keep doing this."

"Why does it happen?" I demanded, ignoring the suggestion in Emmeline's words, ignoring the exhaustion she spoke of, the ache in my bones that went beyond lack of sleep—restraining the tether had been draining us both. "Why us? Why now?"

"I don't know," she said again. "I thought it normally happened between two people with magical blood. I suppose it's because of your father." She finished her cigarette and stubbed the butt on the tree trunk where she leaned.

"Does this mean I'm . . . a witch? Like him?"

"Do you want it to mean that?" Emmeline raised an eyebrow and my stomach tumbled. Her gaze felt hot, searching every inch of me.

"I...I don't know." *No*, I almost said. *Yes*. The truth was somewhere in between.

"Magic doesn't always run in the family," she suggested. "Sometimes there's a sensitivity; you might be in tune with magic without being able to cast. Or you might be able to conjure little things, practise small magic. Divination, for example. It doesn't mean your blood is—like mine."

"Will it last? How long will we feel like this?" I didn't say what I was thinking, that somehow I hoped it would never stop, because that thought alone terrified me so much I couldn't speak the words aloud.

"It seems proximity related, at least at the moment. From what I understand it's not about people; it doesn't matter how we feel about each other. It's a part of you calling to a part of me. An echo. I suppose because of the last few days, the stress, because of us testing it, it's become...stronger. The connection is like magnetism."

"Like soul m ”

"Not like that," Emmeline snapped, pushing away from the tree abruptly. I felt the alarm in my own body, just for a second, before it disappeared. And then...nothing. She had strangled the cord between us back into silence. "*Never* like that."

She began to walk away.

"Em, wait. I'm sorry, I didn't mean..."

I couldn't finish the lie.

"As soon as this is over, you can go back to Whitby," she said coldly. "It'll be gone there. Distance should fix it. I didn't want it to be like this, I never wanted you to *feel* like this."

She stood in the shadow of the trees, her chest heaving as my own lungs tightened painfully. My own pain was phantom, dissipating quickly. And when it was gone I saw only a careful blankness on Emmeline's face. Not disgust. Not *anything*.

My ears began to roar. I glanced around in confusion, shock

making me slow. It was wrong. This was wrong. My vision began to blur; I blinked it back, the world swimming.

"Emmeline, I'm—"

I didn't get the chance to finish, because a sudden, muted crash came from the greenhouse behind us, followed by Bea's muffled scream.

Chapter Ten

Annie

We raced for the building, tumbling over ourselves. I was dizzy, the roaring sound receding as we slammed the door open.

Inside the greenhouse the air was hot as hell, skin scorching and unnatural. Bea cowered on the other side of the scarred wooden table, her arms wrapped around her waist as Arthur loomed over her, about to lunge. The chair had crashed across Nathan's crop of kitchen herbs, debris of dirt and broken pottery scattered.

Arthur turned. He seemed bigger. Stronger. His newly grey eyes were stormy and dark. The runes we had carved into his arms stretched and flexed as he lifted his hands, and I saw two jagged shards of the water glass we had given him in his grip.

"Arthur..." Emmeline growled, raising to her full height.

"Bea, what happened?" I yelled, glancing left and right until I spotted the blade we had used to cast the spell, shining on one of the benches.

"I tried to ask him to help us," Bea cried. "I thought if he knew how important it was, that my life was in dan—"

Arthur's mouth yawned open.

"*Witch...*"

Arthur threw himself at me with startling speed. One of the

pieces of glass caught me, tearing a screaming line from my collar-bone to my shoulder. I let out a strangled cry as the collision knocked my feet from under me and we tumbled together, the glass gone, Arthur's hands at my throat.

"Annie!"

Stars burst in my vision. Black and gold. Then a spurt of something hot and rancid splattered across my face and neck. I rolled, coughing, fighting the nausea that surged in my stomach and scrambling backwards. Emmeline had hit him right in the head with a ceramic pot, but it hadn't stopped him.

He headed for Bea, climbing over the table easily. His skull had all but caved in at the back, brackish liquid streaming in rivulets down his back, pooling in the cracks of the floor and spraying up the glass walls.

He's bleeding, I thought. *Except it isn't blood.*

Bea didn't run. She shrank into herself, into the small pool of shadow beneath the table, both hands curled around herself protectively. Arthur came to a stop and sniffed, like a dog surveying a day-old carcass.

"*You...*"

Emmeline held me back with one hand, the pot still gripped in her other, ready to smash at his skull again.

Arthur's nostrils flared. Bea's whole body shook, and yet she didn't move. Arthur danced back, the movement so fluid, so *beyond* life that it was verging on demonic.

"Don't," whispered Bea. "Help us, Art. *Please.* That's all I'm asking. I want you to be yourself again."

"It's no use," I said. "Bea, there's nothing of him left—"

"No!" she cried angrily. "I won't believe it. I can't. It was working—we made a connection. Arthur..." She never took her eyes off him, black blood staining his flesh so that he resembled a hound from hell. Every instinct in me screamed to kill him. Whatever this creature was, it wasn't Bea's husband. How could we have believed this would save us?

"Arthur..." Bea's lip trembled. "Please. I can't lose you. I can't die. We need to fix this. I'm *pregnant*."

The words were like a spell. Emmeline and I froze. The world seemed to slow, blistering wind, surprise, panic—

Arthur lunged again.

The world tilted. I rushed to Bea as Emmeline did and we almost collided. Emmeline flung her ceramic flowerpot at Arthur, catching his shoulder blade with the sharp edge. He hardly flinched. He grappled with Bea's legs; she kicked him, hard, more black blood spurting from his face.

Helplessness constricted my heart with every breath. I stood for a moment, immobilised by my uselessness as Emmeline hit him again and Bea screamed. I had never felt so powerless.

Then I tasted it, the salt and summer scent at the back of my throat. My body began to tremble—not with fear but with *energy*—and I remembered the knife.

I knew what I had to do.

The knife, a blade that I was sure was made of some kind of bone, sang, drawing me towards it like my father's spell book had. Bea let out a plaintive yelp and Emmeline a muffled curse. I glanced over, caught Bea crawling away as Arthur roared again, dodging Emmeline's increasingly sloppy blows as she fought him with her bare hands.

The knife cut my skin. A thread of red blood blossomed along my finger and I jolted the knife backwards in shock, the blood already running down my hand. Yet the peeling of flesh made the salt scent bloom stronger on my tongue. It wasn't pure and fresh, not like real ocean air; it was tainted with a hint of rot, like an overripe plum, sticky and dusty.

It tasted like danger.

Like hope.

"Annie!" Emmeline's cry startled me back and I spun, finger cradled, intent in my mind and a single word on my tongue:

"*STOP!*"

The blood on my hands was hot. The ocean smell was everywhere. In my nose, my mouth, inside my body and my blood. And Arthur—he stumbled. One knee collided with the floor. It wasn't much but it was enough. Emmeline flung herself at him with renewed vigour, this time with one of the shards of glass Arthur had dropped. Her blow struck true.

A final spurt of brackish blood slashed the wall as Arthur fell, his hands at his neck as he gurgled, more sludge-like blood welling in his mouth. He was choking on it, on the life we had given him and taken away again.

My face was wet with tears. Anger and sadness and a bone-wrenching disgust fought inside me as Bea wailed. Arthur's body twitched once—twice. Emmeline and I both stood very still, watchful, until he stopped moving.

"Annie..." Emmeline said.

Bea sobbed harder, her face coated in her husband's blood, her skin underneath the colour of sour milk. She cradled her stomach with one hand, the other braced on the floor as she fought to calm herself.

"I...I think I did that," I whispered.

Chapter Eleven

Annie

Emmeline's expression was curiously closed as I fought the panic and the fear and the *longing* in my chest, my gaze jumping between her and Bea. Bea refused to look at me. Or at her husband. Her eyes stayed rooted firmly to the lawn chair, where everything had gone so wrong.

No, I thought. *It has been wrong for much longer.*

The air was still hollow, as if we had carved a piece from it. As if some darkness hovered overhead, waiting. I stared down at Arthur's body, my eyes searching for details of the haze I'd seen earlier, of the quiet childlike Arthur we'd raised. All I saw was death, the same as before, only—not. This was a restless kind of death.

"The blood," I muttered. "Arthur's blood. Is that even blood?"

"No. It won't work," Emmeline replied flatly. "We can't pay the debt."

The fresh, red blood at my finger pulsed vibrantly. Emmeline was right. The blood had to be fresh and it had to be willing—and Arthur's was neither.

"How...?" I asked, glancing between the knife in my bloody hands and Arthur's dead-again form on the floor. I recalled the way he had stumbled. That rush of ocean-air magic. "*Was* that me?"

"I certainly didn't do it." Emmeline made to fold her arms, then seemed to notice the blood that coated them and thought twice.

"How?" Bea blurted.

"Intent," Emmeline said simply. "Desire. That's the root of all worship, of all magic. And—I guess it is in your blood after all."

I nodded. It didn't explain why I had never been able to do it before, whether my ability to do what I had done had anything to do with Emmeline's blood magic, her debt, my father's book, the vinculum, or—and I pushed this thought away—how I felt about her. How badly I had wanted to protect us all.

"You...I can't believe you did that," Bea said.

"Well, I can't believe you didn't tell me you were pregnant, so I think we're even—"

Before Bea could retort the words I could see her chewing waspishly, there was a creak and a curse behind us, followed by a female voice.

"I knew you were in trouble, but *Jesus*."

We spun guiltily. Isobel stood in the doorway, a cup steaming in her hands. Her face was thunder—anger, disappointment. Beneath it all a curdled kind of horror.

"Is..."

"Hell's bells, Em..." Isobel slammed her cup down, sloshing dark coffee carelessly as she crossed to the bloody pool around Arthur's head.

It felt tight with her here, claustrophobic and jagged. I saw the room as she must see it, the streaks and spatters of black blood and Arthur's head cracked like a rotten piece of fruit. It looked like a murder site.

It *was* a murder site.

Emmeline didn't try to explain and Bea didn't speak at all. Isobel's judgement was sharp, and although I hadn't known her long, it cut deep. She helped people. She wanted to *heal*. And this...It was the opposite of healing.

"He tried to kill her," I explained weakly. "To kill us. So we had to stop him. To kill him. He's—dead."

"Well, quite." Isobel approached Arthur's corpse with a sort of detachment, her eyes scanning his wounds, cataloguing. She knelt down to inspect him, pressing a hand to his wrist, before lowering it again gently. A shadow of sadness passed over her face. "Why didn't you tell us?"

"Oh, Em..."

Nathan was in the doorway. He stood on the threshold, held there by some invisible barrier. While Isobel looked disappointed, Nathan looked truly ill. His face had gone waxen, his brown eyes glazed as he tried to find somewhere in his precious, private space without stains of Arthur's wine-dark ruin.

"Nathan, love," Emmeline said. "I'm so sorry. I promise—"

"Don't." His teeth flashed in pain. "Don't apologise if you don't mean it, Em. Don't make promises you can't keep."

He fled, Isobel loping after him. Emmeline hovered for a moment, indecision warring, but it didn't last long. She cast us a dark look, indecipherable—but I *felt* her heartbreak as if it was my own—and then she followed them.

With everybody else gone, there was just Bea—and Arthur—and me. Bea stood with her back to her husband's body, her jaw clenched and her arms folded tightly.

"Bea..."

"Frankly, Annie, I don't want to talk to you right now."

"I don't care if you want to talk to me, you've got to." I marched to her, reached for her arm to turn her towards me. She hissed, side-stepping with a shrug of her shoulder.

"Don't touch me," she snapped.

"Bea, stop this. We can't—we can't fall apart."

Bea spun at this. Her eyes were lit with fury, unrestrained and vicious. Gone was the Bea I had always known; only savageness remained as she drew herself to her full height, her lips a thin slash in her face.

"How dare you."

I bit back the responding anger inside me. She was hurt. Scared. But I was scared too, and I was tired of Bea making me feel like

I didn't matter. I stepped forward and Bea flinched—*flinched*. The anger flared hotter, and this time I did not subdue it.

"How dare *I*?" I laughed, a bitter, strained sound. "Bea, you're just as guilty in this as me. You wanted to try this just as much I did. It was our only hope."

"And look where that's left us. I should have known better than to trust you—"

"What is that supposed to mean?"

Bea's nostrils flared and she fixed her gaze over my shoulder. "What do you think it means?"

"I don't know, Bea. That's why I'm asking. I have always, *always* done my best by you."

"Oh, really?" It was Bea's turn to laugh. "You took him from me. You knew I wanted him—and you didn't—and you took him anyway." *Sam*. My heart thudded. Bea's husband lay dead at our feet and somehow we came back to this. "You watched me mourn him long before he left for France and you didn't care."

"This has nothing to do with him—"

Bea shook her head. "It has *everything* to do with him. Don't you understand? We would not be in this mess without you."

"He died!" I cried. "It doesn't matter who had his heart. It's not my fault you got fooled by some handsome soldier boy. All I've tried to do is help you."

"Did you ever stop to wonder why he signed up?" Bea's voice was cold, her face impassive, which betrayed more truth than anything else. My body began to tremble, whether from the magic or the fear or the words, I didn't know.

"Please," I said. "Don't."

"It's true. He told me himself. He wanted an adventure. You couldn't give him what he wanted, Ann, so he took it somewhere else."

"It wasn't my fault," I said weakly. "He wouldn't let me talk him out of it. He would have been conscripted anyway."

"Maybe. But maybe he wouldn't have been *there* in that fucking field. And maybe he wouldn't have died. Maybe I wouldn't have thrown my lot in with Ted and maybe I would never have needed to come here. None of this needed to happen. It happened because of you."

"You can't blame me for your mistakes."

"And you can't claim no part in them." Bea's eyes met mine, hooded and glassy and green.

"You wanted to do this," I whispered, sadness strangling my words. "You agreed. You said you *understood*."

"I lied." Bea tilted her chin and her bruises were visible through the streaks of black blood, peeling in flakes. The rancid smell was overpowering. "I never wanted any of this. And I don't know how we can ever move on from this. Arthur is dead—because of you. Emmeline is going to die because of you. And so am I."

"Emmeline was doomed to die long before I shot your husband." I filled my voice with all the conviction I could muster, but my anger had abandoned me. All that was left was a pervading sense of horror. Either way, Bea was right. It was over.

"I love you, Bea. I would never intentionally hurt you. I was trying to help."

"God, Ann, don't you think I know that? Just because you didn't intend this doesn't make it true. And it doesn't mean I'm not entitled to my feelings. It's not just me anymore. I have to consider—this baby was all I ever wanted . . ."

"You didn't tell me," I said. "Bea. I didn't know."

Bea shook her head sadly. "I love you, Annie, I do. But I need you to know that right now I hate you more."

The Magician

Emmeline

Five years ago

After the night of the winter party, Emmeline's anger was like a young tree in the pit of her stomach, its roots growing deep. Every day she felt it. Every day she was sure it was bigger.

She walked in a trance, her footsteps silent in satin slippers that felt like a betrayal of her true self. Her dress was constricting. Every day that went by that Emmeline wasn't brave enough to do what needed to be done was another nail in a coffin that had grown to imprison them all.

She spent her days thinking. Casting. A nibble of her tongue, a splash of blood, bright and hot. She was waiting, learning. Searching. She scoured the house, trying to find the root of Cilla's power over Nathan. There had to be *something*. Cilla had always taught her that their magic didn't come from nothing. There was always a price. The girls who came for their love potions would fall pregnant early, lose babies, and soon enough they'd be back on Cilla's doorstep with new secrets, more money, always wanting more.

Cilla's magic was the same, even if she used borrowed blood to mix in with her own. She'd cast too much, blood and herbs and kazam always flowing, every drip or sip pulling her deeper under the river of dark madness.

So Emmeline searched for Cilla's leverage. In Nathan's room she combed through his drawers, under his mattress. Hoping for evidence that Cilla had used—was still using—magic to bind him to her will.

She found no telltale cloth bag filled with herbs in his wardrobe or under his bed; she found no evidence of magic twisting his arm no matter how often she looked.

Emmeline wasn't sure what would be worse: knowing that Nathan was under Cilla's spell or discovering that she held enough power over him—over all of them—that he would do it simply because she asked him to. They were, all of them, caught in Cilla's web—but Nathan...He wasn't like Emmeline. He didn't deserve Cilla's control. His power was the soft whisper of summer rain, not like Emmeline's magic, dark and grasping. Nathan was good and gentle and kind. She should have protected him.

Emmeline wanted to talk to Isobel, but she couldn't bring herself to do it, to tell Nathan's secret. Not after Angelica. So instead she waited. And plotted.

In 1917 there was another party to celebrate Ostara, the spring equinox. The guests were the usual culprits, councilmen who paid Cilla to keep their sons out of the war, to keep themselves *unfit to serve*, because her magic was stronger than theirs. She would use the blood they were afraid to touch. She breathed politics and magic in the same breath, always reaching, always angling for more leverage.

Nathan was missing for the whole party. Not lurking in the shadows, not hiding in the greenhouse as he sometimes did. The hours passed and Emmeline felt the anger that was always inside her, the tree finally too big to ignore, its roots festering in the darkness around her heart. She tasted iron in her mouth. So she did what she always did when the anger hit: she went to Nathan's room to wait for him.

Except tonight, hiding did not help. Tonight it was not Cilla's cucumber sandwiches and piping hot tea, which had once saved her from the jaws of death, that she remembered. Instead it was Nathan's pale skin in the moonlight on that winter night, the way the stranger had been pressed against him, skin to skin. Nathan's blank stare. The way he had not talked about it since.

Nathan would never tell her how much her discovery of him hurt. He wanted her to forget everything she'd seen, but how could she? Cilla was supposed to help them. That hadn't been true for years, if it ever had. Cross House was safe from the outside. It had never been safe on the inside.

She drank Nathan's hidden stash of gin straight from the bottle. Guilt clawed at her. She drank until she thought she might vomit, and stumbled for the doorway.

A sharp pain in her leg stopped her. She winced, turning. It was a splinter, so long and jagged it cut the skin of her thigh through her soft, expensive dress. It ripped. The sound was as jagged as the splinter but more satisfying. In a wave of what felt like rebellion, she ripped the dress again, the screaming cloth the only evidence of how she felt inside.

She couldn't bear it. She scraped the dress from her skin, pulling and tearing until she stood almost naked in Nathan's room, panting. The shoes she flung to the floor, but the sound they made was not as satisfying as the ripping and shredding, and so anger drove her to the wardrobe, to the colourful shirts and long dark trousers that Cilla had bought Nathan in exchange for his silence and obedience. Emmeline laid her hands on them and felt their richness. She threw shirt after expensive shirt across the room, a bloom of colours in the darkness, and the loudness of the silence in the house below echoed inside her thundering pulse until finally, finally she was spent.

———)•(———

She didn't know how long it had been since she left the party. She took in the chaos that was Nathan's bedroom, the rainbow of silk and silver thread and smooth, shiny buttons. She was cold. She reached for the plainest shirt she could see, a white one with a high collar, and she felt her anger bloom again. She dressed quietly, Nathan's trousers too long on her but incredibly freeing, the shirt like cool water gliding against her skin.

After, she wandered in the bowels of the house. The party had long ended, the guests spilling out into the blossom-filled night. The girls who were still left at Cross House were sleeping. Isobel always made sure of that after a party.

They never had to drag Cilla to bed, undress her, and witness her scars and her blood. They never felt the sting of her hand or the burn of the fire pressed to their skin. That was saved for Emmeline. For Nathan. For Isobel. Her favourite pets.

Emmeline walked with a purpose, a thrumming in her blood guiding her deep, down into the dusty cellar where Cilla kept her kazam workshop. She wasn't sure what drove her, whether it was intuition or magic, but she let it lead.

Cilla and Nathan were in there together. The old witch had him sitting on one of the workbenches, each of her hands pressed on either side of his face. He tried not to cry. Emmeline didn't really understand how Nathan's magic worked, but it must be agony, for Cilla's mind was a jumble of blood and madness and Nathan could feel it all through her palms.

Cilla looked up, and there was not the remotest flicker of surprise on her face. She even smiled.

"Emmeline. I wondered when you might have the grace to join us."

Nathan did not meet her gaze. He kept his eyes closed and scrunched together, the bobbing of his Adam's apple making his tense throat look painful.

Emmeline stepped across the threshold, vibrating with anger.

"What are you doing to him?"

"Nothing he doesn't deserve," Cilla replied.

"I'm sorry," Nathan whispered. "He hit me. I was meant to—The Council need more information. I couldn't let him finish . . ."

He didn't open his eyes.

That's when Emmeline noticed the scissors glinting on the bench beside him. They looked viciously dull. Nathan had told her that unlike his skin, his hair was so sensitive he hardly liked to touch it himself; through it he could feel the world, shades of colour and emotion that were sometimes so strong they burned.

Cilla didn't move, still holding Nathan motionless with her palms pressed to his cheeks.

"I won't let you cut his hair." Emmeline sounded braver than she felt. Nathan trembled at her words; if Cilla's touch was this bad for him, Emmeline could only imagine what her grasping fingers would feel like in his hair.

"I'm not going to do anything of the sort." Finally—*finally*—Cilla freed his face. Nathan crumpled on the bench, folding in on himself as a whoosh of air left his lungs.

Cilla turned to Emmeline, picked up the scissors, and said, "You are."

For a second Emmeline thought she had heard wrong. But she hadn't.

"What makes you think I would do it?" Emmeline demanded. "I won't hurt him. I love him. He's my *brother*."

Cilla smiled a lazy, one-sided smile. She still wore her gown from the party, and it glittered gold and bronze when she moved. She reminded Emmeline of a serpent.

"Because if you don't do it, I will," Cilla said coldly, "and I won't be as gentle as you, my dear."

Emmeline's heart stuttered. She glanced to Nathan, who looked at her with brown eyes filled with regretful understanding. He wanted her to do it. Emmeline, who had been his first friend in this place, who had loved him fiercely and entirely. For all her faults, she was, and had been for as long as she had known him, his protector. His sister.

If it had to be anybody, it should be *her*.

Emmeline didn't know if she could. Her thoughts, sometimes they were so dark. She couldn't control them. Nathan would have to feel them all.

"I won't do it," Emmeline said.

She didn't sound entirely sure, and Cilla knew. Cilla always knew. She widened her eyes and lifted the scissors and took a step towards Nathan.

Cilla did not make idle threats. Emmeline wasn't quick enough to stop her, some part of her body rebelling against the idea that she might break this cardinal rule. The scissors were rasping open and the end of Nathan's plait was between them—and he let out a plaintive howl as Cilla started to close them, making sure to clamp her other hand down on the crown of his head while she did it.

"No!" Emmeline cried. She had thought hurting Nathan was the worst thing imaginable—but this was worse. She could feel Nathan's pain as if it was her own, and it scooped her out with its intensity. "I'll do it."

Nathan was crying, his whole body shaking. He didn't try to run. In another life maybe they would have, but Cilla had taken them when they were young and made them believe they could not do anything without her. Nathan hadn't been sent to war because of her. And Emmeline . . . she didn't know how she might control her magic without Cilla there to hold its terrifying focus. She had never tried to learn.

She had been a coward.

Emmeline took the scissors from the gleeful, mad old woman with hair the colour of midnight. Her heart raced, her palms slick with sweat. She rested one hand gently on Nathan's arm, where his shirt covered his skin, and she leaned in to him.

"I'm sorry, love," she whispered, willing him to feel how much she loved him, hoping it was enough to mask the anger, the pain.

She lifted the scissors to the braid. She held them just below the shoulder. Cilla slapped her hands away, barking a cry of "Higher than that!" and Emmeline took a breath that tasted like betrayal.

She held the silver scissors higher, just behind his ears where the braid was thickest. She closed her eyes and felt her strength ebb through her body and into the ground. With one swift movement she clamped down hard on her tongue so a spurt of hot, salty blood flooded her mouth, and she wished with the strongest thought in her mind that this pain would not touch him.

Please, please don't let it hurt him.

The scissors took three attempts to cut through the thick, dark hair. It was Emmeline, not Nathan, who felt every slice of the blade—like a knife in her mind, damning wave after wave of agony trembled through her like an eruption. Finally she truly understood Nathan's softness, his need for gentleness. When he experienced the world like this, when he understood the depth of emotion in each word, each thought, who could blame him?

Emmeline *felt* her own darkness, her own vicious anger like a thousand strangling roots coiling around her bones; she felt the cold, slimy knot of rottenness right at her core, a seed that had begun to sprout.

It took only minutes, but it felt like hours. When Emmeline was done they were both sweating. Tears and snot and blood. Nathan had seen her darkness, even if he hadn't felt the pain.

Cilla gathered every scrap of fallen hair. When she held it all in her hands, she gave them a curt nod.

"I hope this will teach you a lesson," she said coldly. "Now, Emmeline, for Goddess' sake, get out of those clothes. You look like a man."

Nathan wept. Emmeline didn't move. Despite the pain that had wrung her dry, she held Cilla's words in her mind with pride. This had taught her a lesson, although perhaps not the one Cilla had intended.

It was done; the worst thing Emmeline could imagine. What else was there to be afraid of? Cilla had, by forcing her hand, compelled her daughter to embrace the monster she had always feared was inside her. And although it did not feel good—it felt like freedom.

It felt like *power.*

Chapter Twelve

Emmeline

When I found Isobel she was already outside Nathan's bedroom, the door shut and her forehead pressed against it. Nathan must be inside; I could smell his cinnamon-and-coffee scent from here. Isobel whirled when I approached, barely concealed disappointment still etched in the downward turn of her mouth, the thick arch of her eyebrows.

"How could you?" Her voice was strangled as she cursed at me like she hadn't done in years. "What did you think you were doing? This kind of magic?"

"I thought we could sort it," I murmured, the quiet, dusty hallway muffling my failure. I was sure Isobel wanted to throttle me. I was surprised she didn't do it. "I thought if we could fix things— you'd never have to know."

"Don't you get it yet, Emmeline?" she barked. "You aren't the only one who hurts. You aren't the only one who feels guilty about what happened here. We are a bloody family. You can't keep shutting us out. Don't you owe us that? You're going to get us all killed."

"I didn't mean..." I pinched the bridge of my nose. This wasn't a time for tears. "I am sorry," I said earnestly. "I didn't tell you what had happened because...I told myself it was because I didn't want you to worry."

"It wasn't," Isobel said.

"No," I agreed. "It was because I was afraid."

She did not know what to say to that, so rarely did I agree with her, so we stood awkwardly in the hallway. A stalemate. Every time I started to speak the words shrivelled and died on my tongue. *I was trying to protect you both. I was trying to protect myself.*

"I did not want to be the monster she made me," I said finally, my throat thick. My heart beat in time with my thoughts. "And then it was too late, so I suppose...I suppose I didn't want you to *see* it. I thought if I kept this from you, maybe you...you wouldn't hate me."

Isobel's expression softened.

"You're not a monster," Isobel chided. "I could never hate you. Even if you are a damn fool." She turned towards the door, where I could hear a muted sniffling. "Isn't that right, Nate?" she called. "A damn *fool*."

"Go away, Em," came the response. His voice was quiet, reedy with panic and sadness. "You too, Is."

"We should leave him," Isobel said quietly. She reached for me, intending to guide me away, but I sidestepped her hand and pressed my palm against the doorknob. "Don't, dearest. He needs time."

"Time is the one thing we don't have." I took a deep breath. "Nathan," I said. "Please can I come in?"

"No, Em. I can't. I *can't*." His voice broke and my heart along with it. I cast Isobel a glance, a question. *Are you going to stop me?*

She held up both hands in surrender.

I opened the door. Nathan sat on the floor of his small room with his knees drawn to his chest. His skin was ashen, his sleeves pulled down over his hands, one covering his mouth as he fought back another sob.

I crossed to him. This was Nathan—my best friend; my brother; the boy who saw everything and said nothing. And I had broken him—just when he was becoming whole again.

I knelt at his knees, careful not to touch him.

"Nathan," I whispered. "Love, speak to me."

He said nothing.

I felt Isobel's presence at my back, a warmth in this chilly space. I wanted to flay myself, fall at his feet and beg for forgiveness, but instead I waited. Silence hung over us, punctuated only by his sniffles.

Finally he spoke.

"It made me think of her," he whispered. "*Cilla.*"

The way he said her name was like a curse, bringing memories of dark nights, glittering parties, men and women and Cilla's secrets. Nathan had been less a shadow than a ghost. He would disappear and sometimes he would stay gone for days.

When he returned he always smelled of cigar smoke and aftershave—and blood.

Nathan's eyes were warm pools in the dim daylight of his bedroom, tears spilling. His throat bobbed as he chewed and swallowed the words he wanted to say.

"It made me think of that night. The scissors. That unending darkness I saw—in you." He sucked in a breath. "It made me think about what I did. What Cilla made me do. How when those men were thinking of me I could feel their *other thoughts*, the ones they tried to hide. The way he was lying in—in my greenhouse... You know some of those men, the councilmen who Cilla flattered and coaxed for secrets during the war? The ones who now pretend magic doesn't exist so they can better steal it?

"Sometimes, when they were finished with me, they would lie there in the blood they asked me to draw from my skin, magic still zinging in the air, and they looked... They looked like the dead. And sometimes I wished that they were."

Nathan choked back another sob and buried his face in his hands.

A whisper of a sigh escaped Isobel's lips, and I felt it. She had known, then. This was the burden we shared. I wasn't the only one Cilla had ruined.

"I know I've said it before," I said, "but I mean it, Nathan. I am sorry. I didn't mean for any of this."

"No," Nathan said, wiping at his face and letting out a shuddering breath. "I know." He shifted, looping his arms around his knees. "It's only that this house—if we're not careful, it will belong to ghosts more than it does the living."

——◦❯●❮◦——

I helped Annie bury Arthur's corpse again, both of us terse and silent. I returned to Isobel's words over and over. *You're going to get us all killed.*

She was right.

There had been rumours about Cilla's house for years. It was true that I had been reckless. Trying to draw Bea back to the house had been my sole focus, and I hadn't cared what might happen if the Council thought we were causing too much trouble. If they encouraged the police to get rid of us. They had left us alone, content to let Cilla's heirs play, happy to buy our kazam and look the other way, but how long could we count on their secrecy? Especially if they discovered what we had done.

Bea and Annie—Cilla's memory could not protect them.

Annie...My chest hurt at the thought of her, her golden innocence and how quickly I'd dragged her down to my level. How quickly Cross House had seeped into her blood, twisted her and corrupted her just like it had us. We no longer had Cilla to blame. I should have never let the island get its claws in her.

The way I felt about Annie—it wasn't like the way I had felt about Bea. I had been foolish last year. I had been led by my desire to repay my debt to Cilla, to atone for my sins. Bea had beguiled me with her sadness, and then with the promise of her joy.

Annie's presence was a balm, soothing the parts of me that had felt jagged for so long, but it was more than that. There was a heat in her, a vow of strength, and I longed to connect, to know her and have her know me.

No, I told myself once she had headed back to the house, once she was safely out of reach and the cord between us grew quiet. *You cannot want her. You cannot have her.*

I had not told Annie that I'd read of witches who cemented their vinculum through blood to make their magic permanently powerful.

They were priests and priestesses who would *celebrate* the bond and their newfound lives as One Being. It was a blessing.

To me it seemed more like a curse.

I was no priestess—and my magic was already stronger, wilder, than I could control. The debt sucked the strength from the beat of my heart; I could feel it inside my veins, inside my blood, the pulsing, roaring desire for *more*. More magic, more casting. More destruction.

What would happen if I had unfettered access to Annie's strength too?

Still, it was her golden smile I saw when I closed my eyes. It shouldn't be. I couldn't stand it.

———)●(———

The sensation of Arthur's sticky blood clung to me long after my hands were clean. The foreboding persisted as I changed my shirt, choosing a dark satin one this time in the hopes I might be able to keep it clean.

In the mirror my face was haggard, the cheekbones sharp like knives. The house felt heavy all around me. The debt thundered behind my eyelids, stronger than my own pulse. I fell to my knees, prying my konjure set from its safe spot under the loose floorboard, needing the comfort of the old cards in my hands.

The set seemed to vibrate as I slid the cards out and sprinkled the remaining grave dirt across them to ground them. They were as familiar as my own skin, and more welcome as I shuffled them and drew a selection with my eyes closed.

I refused to think of Annie—and instead my mind turned to Bea, a clawing unease growing in me. She was pregnant. She hadn't told me. Did it change anything? No, I supposed, but resentment boiled in me all the same. She had let me believe I had ended this future for her.

Bea might have Arthur's blood growing inside her, but I would never live long enough to ask the child to help me. It felt like a taunt, a solution just out of reach. Though perhaps the debt would take Bea too, and this was only a reminder of our sacrifice.

I opened my eyes. I had drawn a circle of five cards around a sixth in the centre. The first was the Magician. This had always been mine—a young witch, gender indeterminate, hair oiled, dressed in a smart suit, hands slim and pale and holding a deck of cards. The second card wasn't a surprise. It was the Tombs, a crooked alignment of headstones etched with faded insignia, freshly churned dirt at their base. Uncertainty. *Death*. I'd been seeing nothing but that card since I took on the blood debt.

I hissed as I drew the next. The Bone Queen. She sat on her throne of yellowing bones, a crown of ivory claws on her head and her dark locks flowing. This wasn't good. The Bone Queen meant unsettled scores, a dangerous road ahead—a trial. If I had been seeking reassurance, the cards had not obliged.

Cards four and five were the Storm and the Beast. For the first time I found myself wishing Cilla was still here. She would know what this meant. She would know what to do.

An energy around the final card made my fingers still just millimetres above its worn surface. My skin stiffened in goose bumps and a faint hum of worry started in my veins. What could be worse than this?

I turned it over.

The Drowning Boy.

He sat, half-submerged beneath the murky grey of his lake, one hand clawing the surface and his face contorted in panic. My blood ran cold. I had always thought of the boy, in grey pyjamas with a bloody nose, as Nathan's card. Vulnerable, manipulated. I had never drawn it in a reading.

The card looked different than I remembered. The boy was older. His hair was golden, a halo in the murky water, and his second hand pawed desperately at his neck. Suddenly I saw a flash of Arthur, blood spurting from the wound at his throat, panic-stricken face and mouth open in a futile scream.

The Drowning Boy. Arthur—or Nathan?

The room seemed to spin around me, cobwebs gathering at the corners of my vision. The air was freezing. For a second—just a second—I thought I felt hands on the back of my neck, nails digging into my flesh. I jerked away, picturing Cilla's ghost, grey and wicked, teeth stained red and eyes black as coal.

I jumped up, spinning. The shadows pooled despite the daylight. The whole house felt like it was waiting. There was nobody but me. And the cards, with their warning.

I abandoned them on the floor, scattering grave dirt as I hurried back to Nathan's room. My thoughts were a jumble, Cilla's ghost chasing me through the halls. I didn't want to stop, to consider— that what we had done to Arthur would come back and haunt all of us in ways I couldn't comprehend.

Could I save any of us? Perhaps if I offered myself up to the police, if I got far away from this house, from all of them—maybe this curse wouldn't take them all. Except Bea, tied to me by the debt. I could run to the ends of the earth and still this magic I'd wrought would kill us both.

"Em, you're like a bad penny," Nathan said, putting on a brave smile when I flew into his room. When he saw my face he dropped the bravado. "What's wrong?"

"I—"

We heard the sound together. A car engine. Footsteps on the path followed by the distant clang of the doorbell. Nathan rushed to the window, peering down, his whole body rigid. Nobody used the front door without an invitation.

"What?" I whispered. "Who is it?"

He turned to me, his eyes full of fresh fear.

"Police."

Chapter Thirteen

Annie

Inside, I searched for something to wear. Emmeline's clothes were all I could find—tailored trousers and smooth shirts that smelled like her. I did not wish to return to my cottage, to the emptiness, or to the hints of normality I would find tucked in its little kitchen, a cup left on the side, dresses half-folded on my bed. I considered the memory of the man in the museum, the way he had grabbed my shoulders. *Had* I imagined the threat? I was less sure than I had been only hours ago. I tried to force my mind to blankness, but it twisted back again and again to the dreadful memory of Arthur's skull caved in.

I stood for a moment, mesmerised by the fine materials of Emmeline's clothes, and I wondered, not for the first time, who she really was. Whether the hints I had seen, of her vulnerability, a softness beneath her sharp edges, was a truth—or a lie, built by the magic that drew me to her. Was she the woman who had laughed with me at the dinner table, exposing her throat, a girl who wanted connection and safety, or was she the one who hated her own vulnerability so much she had banished me from her home? Were they the same woman, or was one simply an act? I wasn't sure I would ever know.

I borrowed a shirt that was too big and trousers that were too long, finishing the outfit with a belt. I wandered back downstairs, on the lookout for Nathan or Isobel, for Emmeline or Bea. Bea…My heart ached, her words a knife that scored my soul. She hated me. She loved me. Wasn't that exactly how I felt about her too?

I sighed. There was nobody around.

The clanging sound of the doorbell echoed through the dim hallways. Immediately my ears began to buzz, skin prickling in fear. It was likely nothing—just a client, somebody looking for Isobel or Em. Yet the humming in my head said otherwise—and I was learning to trust it.

The doorbell rang again and I forced my body into motion. At the threshold I came face-to-face with a severe-looking man, old enough to be my father, with a stiffness in his gait that immediately set my teeth on edge.

Police.

"Hello, Miss Delacroix?"

Anderson's image popped into my head, the way he'd peered behind me as we stood on the lawn earlier. His expression was curious. Had he seen what we had done? Panic seized me but somehow I made my limbs work, stepping out of the house and into the golden light, letting the heavy front door close behind me.

I tried to smile. Tried to wick away the layer of dread that had accumulated on every inch of me, as if he might smell it.

"No," I said. I tried to picture how Emmeline would handle him. She would be tall; she would be firm. I tried to square my shoulders, to shoo him away by sheer reputation alone—but he merely raised an eyebrow.

"No?" asked the man.

I wasn't like Emmeline, could never be like Emmeline.

"I'm sorry," I said as warmly as I could. I reached out to shake his hand, although the motion made me feel seasick. My ears were still humming, only faintly, in a way I'd come to associate with danger. "I mean to say I'm not Miss Delacroix. My name is Annie—I live just next door."

The man eyed me curiously, taking in my borrowed clothes, my wild hair. Whatever he saw must not have impressed him. I hoped, at least, I was nonthreatening enough.

"And you are . . . ?" I prompted, ignoring the thunder of my heart. If I could get him away from the house—then what? I acted fast, without time to think, biting down on the inside of my cheek so hard I tasted the salty tang of my blood. A strange lightness filled me, like the sun shining through clear, still water.

"Constable Marches," he said, his tone curt. "I'm here to speak to Miss Delacroix. Is she home?"

"No," I lied cheerfully. "I'm so sorry. She's headed up-island to drop a friend off home. We had a little soiree yesterday evening and it ran rather long. Why do you need to speak to her? There hasn't been a complaint or anything, has there? I'm very sorry if we made a little noise. We have the most darling gazebo and I'm afraid we got a bit carried away. The weather has been so lovely we thought we ought to make the most of it. It's wonderful, would you like to see?"

I had no idea what I was doing, but as I spoke the lies flowed thick and fast. In the back of my mind I thought I could taste that salty-ocean magic threaded with my blood, feel its power thrumming inside me. I made to walk, pushing the police constable down the front stairs, infusing each step with a bounce I had never employed before. I channelled Bea's old enthusiasm, thought of the women at her gathering, of Joey in the bathroom—and let out a laugh.

"And the clothes!" I cried. "I can't believe you've caught me like this. Clean forgot I was wearing them. We played a fancy-dress game. Emmeline is *ah-may-zing* at those—what do you call them? Ouija boards?"

The constable shook his head, apparently baffled by my outburst.

I went on, "It isn't urgent, is it? I'm sure she'll be horrified."

"Urgent? Ah, well, yes it is. We need to ask her some questions regarding a gathering that occurred here. There might be a lead to a pair of missing persons—"

"Oh that *poor* couple!" I exclaimed. "I read about them in the paper. What an absolute tragedy. You think Emmeline knows anything about them?"

"We think they might have been here, yes. Perhaps she remembers them."

"Oh, I doubt it," I said earnestly. I stepped closer to the constable, leaning in. "She hardly speaks to anyone at her parties, just hides in the kitchen." I made my eyes wide, thankful for what Mam used to call my "angelic" face. "In fact, sometimes she's not here at all!"

"Oh, well..." The constable didn't know what to make of me. He glanced up at Cross House, looming behind us. The windows, thankfully, were all dark, most of the curtains closed up tight against the sun.

"I love big parties," I carried on, pushing him farther away from the house until we were on the lawn. The panic was growing again, but I tamped it down, thinking instead of the house. Of the salt magic. Of how badly I wanted to protect that space, to refresh the wards Emmeline had laid before Arthur's death. "They're so much fun, don't you think? You can really get to know people at a big party..."

"Yes, I— Listen, can you let Miss Delacroix know I stopped by? I'll head back again to try to speak to her. It's just an inquiry, but it could be very helpful."

I beamed and simpered until the man fled for his car. I stood on the drive once he had gone, shaking. My mouth throbbed. My heart *ached*. Beneath the still water I had imagined during that first spurt of blood there were hidden depths, and the closeness of them scared me.

I was still lost in my whirling panic when I heard the door close.

"'I love big parties,'" Emmeline mimicked, her voice husky. She rewarded me with a smile. "Where did that come from?"

Not for the first time I marvelled at the way my stomach flipped whenever she was near. This couldn't just be the tether between us, could it?

"I don't know. I've never been so scared in my life," I breathed. "What if he comes back?"

"Well, then we may have a problem." She grimaced. "I don't like it. We should have had warning. The police sergeant is a witch, a councilman. A...well-paid colleague. I suspect this visit was off the cuff, which is lucky for us."

"What if he *does* come back?"

"I'll come up with a plan. In any case, I don't think it will be tonight. You look exhausted."

"I am." I could feel the toll of whatever I had called with my blood; it was like I'd run two lengths of the island's Spine on zero sleep. I was embarrassed by it, both by my eager carelessness and by the fact that it had worked. That it had felt so natural, like breathing. "I'm not going home, though."

"I suspected you might say that."

"I don't want to be alone."

Instantly my cheeks grew hot. I couldn't bear to see her look at me the way she had before, outside the greenhouse, when I'd dared to ask if the vinculum was like finding a soul mate. I shouldn't have said anything.

"You should stay here," she volunteered. I snapped my gaze to hers. "It makes sense. If the police come back—if you're afr—"

"I'm not afraid," I lied. "I just..."

Emmeline shrugged. "Unfortunately, I think afraid is exactly what we both should be."

Chapter Fourteen

Annie

I lay in Emmeline's bed, staring wide-eyed into the darkness. My borrowed nightdress was too long, tangling around my legs. Emmeline's shadowy presence in the armchair beside the bed was like an itch I couldn't reach.

I thought of Arthur, of the way he had crumpled at my command, the way his black blood had soaked into the packed dirt, sank into the foundations of the greenhouse like roots. I thought of Bea, of the secrets she had kept, of what I had taken from her by killing her husband. She had refused to eat tonight and would not take the food I carried to her door. She would not talk to me or look at me. Grief was like an ocean, threatening to drown me. Magic clawed at my ankles.

My thoughts looped back to Emmeline. With Arthur gone, what hope did she have? Would it hurt when she died? How badly would I feel it through the vinculum?

Would it kill me too?

I heard her breathing in the dark, steady but shallow, caught in her own web of waking nightmares. She hardly moved in the armchair, but when she did I saw the ghost of her outline at the edge of my vision and my skin sparked with longing. I wanted, desperately, to press my hands into hers, to be sure she was there.

Finally I could take it no more. My voice escaped, impossibly loud in the darkness.

"Did you..."

For a moment, silence.

"Did I what?"

"Did you do it—the bargain, the debt—only because you loved her?"

Silence, again. Emmeline's breathing shifted and I heard the gentle *swuff* of fabric as she got up and came to rest at the end of my bed, elbows on her knees. A sliver of moonlight caught her jawline.

"I didn't think..."

She stopped.

"You didn't think?" I couldn't help the hurt in my voice, the silver vinculum between us winding and writhing: *If only you had.*

"I intended..." She swallowed. "It doesn't matter what I intended."

"It matters to me."

Emmeline shifted. "I thought I loved her. It wasn't love—not really. I wanted her to stay on the island. I didn't think beyond it. My selfishness cursed us both. I'm just like—*her.*"

"Who? Your aunt?"

"No." Emmeline seemed surprised that I remembered her. "No, Rachel was a witch too, but she was clever. She was a midwife. She helped women, delivered their babies. And sometimes she made them go away too..."

"It's okay," I said. Emmeline's voice was so raw with the memory that I wanted, suddenly, to spare her. "You don't have to tell me if—"

"I want to," Emmeline said sharply. Then, softer: "I've never told anybody, not even Nathan, and I don't want to die without somebody knowing about her. I wanted to keep her to myself, but...I don't want her to be forgotten. She saved so many women, so many lives. She was so *good.*"

The starkness of her words was so crushing it took my breath. I reached out in the darkness, my hand groping the bedsheets until I found Emmeline's.

"What happened to her?"

"They killed her. People where I grew up didn't like what my aunt did. Once the rumour starts that you help women, that you value them—that you *love* them—that's it. The men came for us. My aunt told me to run, so I did. And then I ended up here. It's like the crows call to us, orphans of magic. And—orphans need a home. Cilla...she collected us and gave us that home."

I could tell from the way Emmeline said Cilla's name that this was a story she *didn't* want to tell.

"I..."

"It was a long time ago," Emmeline murmured. "Anyway, you should sleep."

Her weight lifted from the end of the bed and it was like my heart was being ripped from my chest. The vinculum tensed, the cord snapping tight. I wasn't sure whether it was me or her.

Her.

"No," I blurted. "Don't go. I want to hear about your life. I want to know you—anything you want to share." *I want to know every part.* The words hummed in my mind. The tether was strong, so strong, and I was tired of holding on tight. *I want to know you beyond this glowing coil.*

I want you to know me too.

Emmeline stopped.

"Please come back," I whispered. "I can't bear it."

She stood for a second, indecision warring on her face in the dark. I wanted to nudge the vinculum, to give her the courage, but this was a decision she needed to make on her own.

I knew I'd won whatever battle raged inside her when she reached up, her dexterous fingers beginning to unknot her braid. Her hair curled, catching the moonlight so it rippled like a dark river.

"Roll onto your side," she commanded.

I did as she asked almost without thinking, my limbs obeying the power in her tone and the longing surging within me so forcefully it was painful. For long, silent seconds I lay as rigid as stone, until I heard the gentle sound of Emmeline's shoes dropping onto the wooden floor.

She climbed onto the bed and her body folded around mine, the presence of her sending a delicious warmth right through to my very core. The shining silver cord that connected us clenched again, neither of us burying it all the way as Emmeline's arm wrapped along the length of mine, cradled just beneath my breast. I suppressed the shudder that started somewhere near the top of my thighs.

"Is this okay?" she whispered. Her voice was in my ear, tickling the hair that curled there. I nodded.

It was more than okay. The sigh of her voice crystallised what I had known since the moment I had seen her standing outside on the porch smoking that cigarette. It was the reason that a future with Sam had always filled me with dread; the reason it felt like I had spent my whole life waiting for the permission to be who I really was. Our fates had been tied together since the first moment we met—because, magic or not, I had never wanted anyone or anything other than *her*.

The sound of my swallow was audible. I could feel the slow, steady beat of her heart at my back, feel the pressure of her palm curved so perfectly under my breast. A humming brightness filled me, a wild and wicked thing. I could taste that saltwater magic on my tongue again and I couldn't just lie here and pretend that I didn't want more.

Emmeline pulled back in alarm as I wriggled onto my other side, but I held fast, pleading. She stopped. We were inches apart, her face so close the soft rush of breath tickled my cheeks, shallow and rapid. Her long hair tangled in mine, brightness and darkness together. Heat pooled in my stomach.

I waited. For Emmeline to get out of bed. To leave. I waited for the disinterest, or the anger, or perhaps disgust. Instead she did not move, and her chest rose and fell and rose and fell to the flutter of my own pulse.

I lifted my hand, slowly, to trace the outline of her cheekbone, sharp and shining with silver moonlight. Her breath hitched. Her eyes were oceans of darkness. Her lips, that perfect Cupid's bow.

Her hand was on my hip. A wild spike of adrenaline raced through me as she gripped the folds of my nightgown, her skin hot.

Our lips a breath apart. They met in a spark, flying colour flashing behind my eyelids, softness and sharpness and everything in between.

She tasted like magic. I grasped her face between my hands, drawing her closer. Her hand tugged at the hem of my nightgown, lifting it away from the tangle of our legs. Her fingers tensed on my bare thigh and I let out a *hiss* of pleasure and impatience.

She kissed me again, harder. Fireworks in my chest. The vinculum pulsed, glowing brighter as we both lost our grip. I didn't care. All I wanted was Emmeline's mouth on mine, her hands searching, her breath hot and lips moving to my neck, our bodies pressed together as her fingers—

A jagged scream in the distance tore us apart.

Chapter Fifteen

Annie

Emmeline was out of bed before I had a chance to process what I had heard or where it had come from. She set off at a run, her bare feet pounding the floorboards as I battled with my nightdress, tugging the tether back to its dark corner of my chest.

I tumbled off the bed seconds later, skidding on the worn floorboards and banging into the dresser with a yelp. Outside the bedroom the temperature swooped immediately.

We ran towards Bea's room on the floor below. It took what felt like an eternity. The door was open but at first there was no sign of anyone, the bedroom as still and dark as Emmeline's had been—darker, in fact, with no silver crackles of moonlight around the edges of the curtains. I spun, eyes searching the dark.

Bea emerged out of the shadows, her expression contorted with terror.

She stood frozen, her white nightdress and pale skin seeming to glow. I ran to her, did not hesitate to wonder if she wanted me. I grasped her hands in mine and they were like ice.

"Bea, what's wrong?"

"Annie..." Bea's face crumpled. "He was here. He was *here*."

"Who was here?" I demanded. "Who?"

"Arthur."

My thoughts stuttered.

"No, you were dreaming," I said, pulling her to my chest and holding her tight. She resisted, but only for a second before melting against me. Her head came to rest on my shoulder and she clung on to my nightgown tight, like a child. "You had a nightmare. It's over now."

A dark shape shifted. My heart slammed—but no, that was only Emmeline. I prised myself away from Bea and flicked on one of the low electric lamps, making the shadows snap to brightness.

"He's dead," Emmeline said.

"I saw him," Bea insisted. "I wouldn't make that up. He was right *here.*"

"No." Emmeline was firm. "He wasn't."

"Bea, would it make you feel better if we checked?" I asked hesitantly. I didn't know if it was the right thing to say, the right thing to do—but it was what the old Bea would have wanted.

"Yes," she said gratefully. "*Yes.*"

Together we made our way down the stairs, Bea holding one hand to her stomach unconsciously. I remembered the baby growing in Bea's belly, felt a different kind of concern wriggle inside me. All Bea had wanted since Sam died was a new life, a new family. An adventure that would take her far away from the sadness. All the boys and the booze, they had been nothing more than a tourniquet for the wound I had caused.

I squeezed Bea's hand, hoping it felt like reassurance. She smiled at me sadly, gratefully, all the hatred she had warned me of melting away.

"Please don't let go," she said softly. Her fingers tightened in mine. "Thank you."

Emmeline grew bolder with every step we went unhindered. There was no sign of anything out of the ordinary. The lights had been extinguished down here hours ago, and the whole house felt empty, abandoned, except in the kitchen, where an urgent patter of conversation guided us towards Nathan and Isobel. Their cups were abandoned on the table and they blinked at the three of us, alert and alarmed, as if they had been about to come to us.

"Are you all right?" asked Nathan.

"Nightmare," Emmeline said tersely.

Isobel hurried forward, reaching for Bea. She fussed for a moment, hands flapping, and I wondered then if Emmeline had told her about the baby. "You poor hen. Do you want a cup of tea? I said we should come and see. Sometimes it feels like this house is . . ."

She stopped, but we all knew what she had been planning to say. *Haunted.*

"No, no," Bea said. "I'm—fine. A little shaken. I just need some air."

Isobel hovered uncertainly, her gaze flicking to each of us until Emmeline gave her a small nod.

"It's fine, Is," she assured her. "You settle. We're just taking a walk."

I heard the press of the ocean against the shore, and it grew louder as we stepped out into the rattling, empty darkness and hurried around to the greenhouse. Emmeline lit a candle, the flame dancing green as it reflected off the mossy glass walls. All was as we had left it hours ago, though Bea moaned again, pressing her hand to her mouth.

"I think I'm going to be sick," she winced. "It just— Oh God."

Arthur's grave, freshly filled, was as it had been before. Bea sank down to her knees in the churned earth, hands clasped together in prayer, breathing slow through her nose.

I turned back to the house, taking in the hulking shape of it, Bea's window the only bright box. I squinted. There was a shape—fluid and hard to define, like a shadow.

"I don't understand . . ." Bea whispered. "How is it possible? It seemed so real."

My limbs tensed.

"He's not here," Emmeline said again firmly. "He's dead. Bea—*please.* Just try to stay calm. We can't do this if you lose it."

"Em . . ." I said warily.

"What?" She spun to me.

I opened my mouth to speak—but the shadow was gone.

———⟩●⟨———

Emmeline did not come back to bed. I tossed and turned, staring into the crawling darkness of the room. It felt so empty with her gone. I wondered where she was, if she had regretted what we had done—what we *hadn't* done.

I thought of my father. How could he have thought hiding his heritage from me would keep me from this life? It wouldn't have mattered if he'd died in five years, or ten, I would have ended up here all the same. Would I have ever been able to resist the call of his magic in my blood? The thoughts turned bitter fast. Thinking of Bea and Arthur wasn't much better. My mind kept turning to Bea's baby.

Could it be the answer to Emmeline's problem? Could its blood, shared with Arthur, fulfil the blood debt? The thought soothed me for a moment, my mind whirring, until I understood that it was no good. Emmeline didn't have that long left—and if she somehow survived long enough, her sanity would soon be in shreds.

I rolled to my side, hands pressed to my face. The cool night air chased my spine. Hours seemed to stretch. Every sound set my pulse thundering, thoughts of the shadow I had seen in Bea's bedroom twisting in my mind. Every sway of branches outside the window, every *clink* of pipes through the old house sending me closer to a panic.

I sat bolt upright.

There.

That hadn't been the house, or a branch. It was a human sound—like the whistle of a breath. I peered into the darkness, eyes roving, mouth dry. I waited, listening for it again. There was nothing but the solitary shiver of moonlight like a crack down the wall.

Or was there? For a second I thought I saw a shape in the darkness, lines shifting and swaying with the faint breeze. I inhaled sharply, drawing my knees to my chest. The air tasted rank, like decaying leaves.

"Who's there?" I hissed. "Emmeline?"

It wasn't Emmeline. Couldn't be. The whistling happened again, and this time it reminded me of laughter. A faint wheezing chuckle, dark and humourless.

I threw off the bedclothes, tumbling over myself to reach the electric lamp. The shadows disappeared with a snap, the room swaying into lightness. I spun, taking in every inch. Nothing. There was nobody here but me.

I sank back onto the bed, hands trembling. It was my imagination. I was anxious about Bea, that was all. Still, I did not turn the light back off, only waited until I saw the faint prickle of dawn before dressing in another shirt of Emmeline's and the same trousers, longing for the armour they provided. I headed for the kitchen, sure that I would find Emmeline there, but the room was empty.

I traced the loop of a careless circle left by a cup in the velvet material of the tablecloth. A few days ago I would have been saddened to notice it marring such a beautiful item; now I only wondered who had left it.

I wondered if Mam would recognise me. It had been hours since I had thought of her, and home—and Sam. I was relieved, even if it tasted sour.

There was a noise behind me, a clearing of a throat. I spun, jumping as Isobel appeared. Her hair was glossy but mussed from its braid by sleep and covered in a plain red kerchief. Her face looked bare without its usual smudges of kohl around her eyes.

"I didn't mean to startle you," she said.

"Sorry," I murmured sheepishly. "I didn't sleep well."

Isobel set the kettle to boil on the stove, reaching for three cups and watching me carefully out of the corner of her eye.

"I'm not surprised. It mustn't have been very comfortable, both of you in that single bed. All those nightmares."

My cheeks flamed and I fought the flip-flopping of my stomach.

"She didn't stay in there with me," I blurted. "She was going to sleep in the chair but..." *Bea interrupted us when she thought she saw her dead husband's ghost in her dreams.* I refrained from saying that part aloud. I didn't want to think about it.

"Right," Isobel said, sipping her tea.

I didn't know what to say. Part of me wanted to beg Isobel not to judge, that old, primitive part of my brain screaming that how I felt about Emmeline was *wrong*. Unnatural. But that wasn't how I felt anymore. Perhaps hadn't ever felt, deep down. And the truth was I did not want to share this Emmeline: the Emmeline who had looked, when my lips met hers, as if the whole world might burn and she could be content; the Emmeline whose breath had whispered promises on my skin, whose hands had tangled in my hair, who had driven me to wildness. This was *my* Emmeline.

"It's okay, Annie," she said. It wasn't warm, but it wasn't hostile. "What you and Emmeline do together is nothing to do with me, but—"

"But what?" Isobel's tone made me wish I had claws. "Am I not good enough for her?"

"It's not like that." Isobel put her cup aside. "There are things you don't understand about Emmeline. The things that Nathan and Emmeline and I have experienced... They change you.

"When I came to this house I was almost feral. Magic took my parents. My friends, sisters—girls I loved, girls I tried to help—I watched them fall to *schemes*. For money, for power, for love." Isobel scoffed at the last one, but the expression on her face was so raw I wanted to look away. I made myself hold fast, desperate to tell her that I was sorry, knowing that was no good. "Some of them didn't make it," Isobel said. "The life we lived was cruel.

"Emmeline and Nathan are my family, Annie, and I will protect them at all costs. If that means protecting them from themselves by removing you from the equation, I'll do it."

I couldn't imagine how hard it must have been for them; Isobel was right about that. I would never know that pain up close, and the coward in me was grateful for it. I could only try to help in my own small way, and what use was that?

"I want to protect Emmeline too," I said.

"Well, you can't," Isobel snapped. "It isn't that simple," she added, softer. "Emmeline doesn't want to be helped. She won't ask—and frankly, I'm getting tired of trying."

"Let me help her," I pushed back.

"You *can't*," Isobel repeated emphatically. "I've been trying for years. Emmeline is on her own path. Look, I'm not going to argue with you this morning, dearest." She sighed through her nose. "Magic is a *monster*. It takes and it takes—and if you're not careful there won't be any of you left. The whispers in these walls are proof enough of that."

I shook my head. It was far too late for saying that now—and pointless, since I had never listened anyway. I couldn't leave, not seeing the things I'd seen—doing the things I'd done. I'd turned to magic so easily with the constable, and I'd done that without thinking. Truly, this was the risk people spoke of when they said magic was dangerous. How easy it was to slip, to fall, and find yourself buried.

I had seen Emmeline practise her darkest magic, felt that tether snap into place and alternately hated and longed for it. Worst of all, I had experienced that satisfying salt-whipped power for myself—and a deep, feral part of me craved to do it again.

"You're wrong," I said coolly. "This isn't the time to give up. Emmeline needs our help more than ever."

"You're careless, Annie," Isobel returned. She looked broken, resignation etched in every pore. "All of you are careless. I just hope it doesn't get us hanged."

Chapter Sixteen

Annie

B ea, are you awake?"

I peered into the dim room, making out the closed curtains and the shape of Bea sitting hunched upright in her bed, one arm looped around her knees. She waved me over.

I perched on the end of her bed with my legs crossed, as I so often had when we were growing up. Her bruises had started to fade a little, a sickly green colour against the pallor of her skin.

"Do you need anything?" I asked softly. "Have you eaten?"

She rubbed a hand over her face tiredly. "Nathan made me breakfast. I think I kept some of it down."

We sat in silence for long minutes. The house creaked and settled, the gentle rush of the waves audible through Bea's open window. Outside it was another glorious, dirt-baking day.

"I'm so sorry, Bea," I said eventually. "I know that doesn't make any of it better, but I want you to know that if I could change it I would."

"I know." Bea shrugged. "I'm sorry I said those things about Sam. It's not all your fault." She picked at one of her nails, no longer neat and perfectly painted. Another reminder of what she had lost.

"I truly didn't mean to hurt Arthur—"

Bea let out a long breath. "Annie, can we not? We've been over and over this. And let's face it," she said, her shoulders hunched, her eyes staring distantly ahead, "if you hadn't killed him somebody else probably would have." Her expression softened, just a fraction, as she looked up. "And there's every chance it would have been me. At the end I wasn't—neither of us were ourselves."

I leaned forward and laid a hand on her knee.

"What was it like?" I asked hesitantly.

"The debt?" Bea paled. She still had the wound on her palm from the broken glass the night of the party. It was long and jagged, and although Isobel had done a good job patching it up, the skin was still raw. "It was like a dream at first. I wish you could have been at my wedding, Ann— Don't give me that look. I know I didn't invite you. How could I?"

"I would have supported you," I offered.

"No." She shook her head sadly. "And I don't think you should have. It's all right, I've made my peace with that. I don't regret it. Maybe I regret everything else, but Arthur made me happy and I wanted it so badly. God, the wedding was beautiful, though. Really intimate. Arthur was so nervous all day he cracked joke after joke. I've never laughed so hard." Bea smiled, her eyes lighting up at the memory. A pang cut through my chest for her loss. "We had a honeymoon on the island. Arthur has a yacht."

I squeezed her knee.

"*Had*," she corrected. A shadow flashed across her face and she looked like she was going to be sick again. She lifted a hand to her forehead, her eyes tracing some invisible spot above my head. "I'm sorry, I'm really not feeling well. I keep going—dizzy. I keep seeing these dark shapes whenever I close my eyes."

"Is it...the baby?" I asked gently.

Bea pulled her knees away from me. "I don't want to talk about it. It's early days yet. Let's not get ahead of ourselves. I'm not sure if I'm going to keep it."

An emptiness settled in my chest. I couldn't help her, not really, but that would be the final loss of the dream she had once had. It hurt so badly, the pain so large, that I could hardly speak.

I left Bea to her thoughts with a renewed sense of determination. We couldn't let this be the end of things. I had to speak to Emmeline.

I bumped into Nathan downstairs, after I'd searched several dark and empty hallways to no avail. The house felt strange to me today, a sensation I couldn't pin down exactly but which felt like being just cold enough to need a jacket. Shadows pooled in corners, the bright sun barely illuminating the dust motes.

"Have you seen Emmeline?" I asked. Nathan stood in the kitchen with a basketful of eggs. "I get the distinct impression she's ignoring me."

"Don't take it personally, darling," he said. "When she's sad, angry, scared—any emotion at all, really—she shuts herself away."

I hovered in the doorway. I wanted to find her, to talk about last night and the new fears that swarmed me. To ask her about my father's book, about what we were going to do now.

"Come on," Nathan said, noticing my frustration. "Give her some time to think. I'll make breakfast and you can try again after."

He encouraged me into the warmth of the kitchen, making coffee and cooking the eggs and toast while I sat at the table cradling my head in my hands.

"Here," Nathan said. He placed a steaming cup of coffee before me, white and sugared, along with a plate of eggs and toast.

"Scrambled eggs are my favourite kind," I said. Eggs always made me think of my mother, who for a few years when I was very small kept chickens in the shared garden.

"I'm very good at guessing," Nathan said.

"Is that how it works?" I asked, my mouth already full. I hadn't noticed how hungry I was, how little I'd eaten. The eggs were good, fluffy and yellow. "Your magic?"

"Not exactly," Nathan said, his lips quirking in a half smile. "Close. Most magic is—it starts as a feeling. A premonition or a sense of what feels right. Like instinct. It's different for everybody. I can't read people's minds, but the closer I am to them, the stronger the intuition. I knew you would probably be hungry, and when I looked for it, the information was there. Not fact, but like a reasonable assumption. That's how I know you want to get something off your chest."

I swallowed two mouthfuls of piping-hot coffee and sighed, newly sick. There was a strange taste in my mouth that hadn't been there before, a little bitter. I pushed the rest of my breakfast away.

"What are we going to do?" I asked.

Nathan's face clouded, a storm brewing, and he turned away. I recalled the way he had run from the greenhouse yesterday and recoiled at how insensitive I was being. There was so much I didn't know about them, about this place.

"This thing—between you and Emmeline..." he said instead.

"Oh, don't you start too," I snapped, unable to help myself. "I've already had an earful from Isobel about that."

Nathan turned. "No," he said. "Isobel is trying to protect Emmeline. I love Em, but I don't want you to get hurt."

"Doesn't it matter what I want?" I thought of the vinculum, how it made everything so impossibly complicated. "Emmeline can teach me things about myself, about my family. My father... It's not just about *this*." I pressed my hand to my heart.

"She'll never be entirely yours," Nathan said quietly. "She has too much anger inside her. Too much pain."

I pushed back from the table, toppling the wooden chair to the ground.

"You're wrong," I said, my voice threaded with surprising steel. "I—"

We were both startled by a fluttering of wings as a crow swooped down from a tree. I glanced out and looked again harder. There wasn't just one crow out there, or a few. There were *dozens*. They flocked on the lawn, in the trees, their eyes and beaks impossibly shiny.

A murder, I thought.

I turned to Nathan, horror crawling under my skin. The bitter taste was back in my mouth, stronger than before.

"That many crows can't be a good omen," I said.

Nathan stalked to the window and peered out, counting under his breath. When he stepped back he'd grown pale.

"No, it can't."

———)•(———

"I thought I could hear you slamming around in here."

The room had been so quiet that I jumped, dropping the heavy book I was holding onto the desk. Emmeline peered around at the mess I'd made of her library, books in piles all over, some open to pages I was marking with bits of paper or pencils or, in one case, an overturned empty vase. The books weren't the same calibre as my father's collection but I'd also hardly scratched the surface.

"Oh, you've finally decided I exist," I said, ignoring the spike of adrenaline at the sight of her dressed in a clean tweed suit, her hair freshly washed and swept back—ignoring the bite in my own words.

Emmeline let out a bark of surprised laughter, stepping farther into the room. "I wondered where you were. I was worried."

"I'm trying to solve this. Have you read all of these?"

Emmeline shrugged. "Most of them. Nathan and Is have read the rest between them. They were—Cilla's."

"The witch who adopted you," I said. Emmeline's expression darkened. I noticed how she didn't come any closer, hovering on the other side of the room like I might bite her. I did a mental check of the vinculum—still slumbering in place where I held it—and turned back to the books.

I wanted to talk about last night, but not if Emmeline wished it had never happened.

"Yes," Emmeline said. "She raised us all. Took in children from all over the mainland—magical children."

"And she never taught you any of this?" I pressed, waving my hands. "About bargains and debts? What was the point?"

Emmeline folded her arms, leaning against a free patch of wall.

"It wasn't... She taught us small things, charms. She taught Isobel how to brew the kazam. The bigger things she did herself."

I could see there was more to it than that, but I didn't press. I was full of too many thoughts, my brain ricocheting amongst them.

"Bea's not well," I said instead. "She said she felt very dizzy."

"Perhaps it's the baby. I'll get Is to check on her."

"Maybe." I wasn't convinced. "You saw how badly shaken up she was last night. I don't think that was just a dream. This morning there were crows on the lawn—a lot of them. An abnormal amount, even for here. Nathan agrees with me. And Arthur, before we... There was a haze around him—like a shroud."

"The energy is normal after a death," Emmeline said calmly. "And Arthur's was a bad death..." She trailed off. "Perhaps that's why the crows are here when they weren't before. They can probably sense it."

"And who are the Council?" I rushed on, unsatisfied. I pointed to the book I'd been holding before. "A few books mention them. Are they some sort of... witch elders? Could they help us?"

Panic flashed as Emmeline stood upright, no longer lazy but alert. "No," she said firmly.

"Well, who are they?"

"They... They were elders, I suppose, to start with. It became— about money. During the war a faction of them worked to help the British men. Cilla... knew a lot about them. Secrets. She kept them in line. Since the war there's nothing to unite them. And Cilla's death left a—hole."

"Might they be able to help, though?" I asked desperately. "Might they know a solution we don't?"

"No," Emmeline snapped. I could see her growing frustration but I couldn't stop myself. "We must never allow them in. Half their purpose since the war is keeping an eye on—people like us. Making sure we don't get everybody in trouble. If they knew..."

She didn't need to finish. I slammed the next book in my list shut.

"Annie, listen—"

"No, *you* listen." I spun around, taking three steps towards Emmeline before she flinched away. My stomach bottomed. "You are all just giving up and I can't bear it. This can't be over. Not when we..." My eyes burned with unshed tears and I blinked them away furiously.

To make it worse, Emmeline's face was so sad.

"We can't do this, Annie," she whispered. "Look what happened last night."

"Emmeline..."

"It shouldn't have happened." Emmeline's anger was on the surface. I should stop—I shouldn't provoke her—but I couldn't.

"Don't lie," I said hotly. "Don't lie and say that you didn't want it to happen as much as I did."

"That's the point!" Emmeline shouted. Her voice thundered in the tight space. The air changed like it had before, a ringing in my ears, the iron tang of blood on my tongue. "I can't control myself when I'm around you. You make me want to be reckless!"

Emmeline's hold on the tether faltered and it slithered free. Her nostrils flared, her eyes growing wide, and I could taste the magic on the air—as if, unrestrained, the vinculum gave her power permission to multiply, to fracture.

I leapt to grab it, my mind snapping to attention and my whole body humming. I pulled it back, glorious and silver, yanking it so hard it made both of us wince.

We stood panting. Emmeline's face was a mask of horror.

You make me want to be reckless.

That was it. That was how Emmeline made me feel too.

"We can't carry on like this," I said. "We need a plan."

"What exactly would you propose we do?" Emmeline's gaze was hot. Her chest rose and fell rapidly but she hadn't fled. I took that as a good sign.

"There's only one thing we can do."

The Tombs

Emmeline

Four years ago

She couldn't do it immediately. For months—years—she had let Cilla's treatment of Nathan continue out of fear, but now it was out of necessity. While the war was waged, while the men still came to Cilla out of desperation, out of some perceived loyalty, it couldn't happen.

So Emmeline waited. She hid Nathan when she could, cloaking him in magic that she practised endlessly, until she had nearly bled herself dry.

Isobel stayed with him often. She had been there, to help soothe the raging fever he developed after what Cilla had made Emmeline do. His body purging Emmeline's thoughts, her anger, the dark intentions that he had seen.

Isobel knew what needed to be done. What Emmeline was planning. They didn't discuss it, but they didn't need to.

When the end finally came, Emmeline had to be ready.

There would be no turning back. She knew that. Perhaps she had known that for a long time. This path had been hers since before she had accepted the food that had stopped her from starving that day in the harbour. Perhaps since the very moment the men knocked at the door and her aunt ushered her out into the cold with nothing more than a few coins and her old konjure cards, saying, "Don't let them take all of you."

Of course, she couldn't plan for everything. Cross House was the only home most of the girls had known. Perhaps the few who remained living here would hate her. It was worth being a villain. In the end, it came down to what it always came down to.

Blood.

Two nights after the armistice, Cilla called Emmeline to her side. She wasn't herself. The air smelled strongly of rotten fruit. Platters were laden, dotted around the room where flies could hum and crawl their way to bliss. Emmeline held her hands to her nose as she followed the woman into the mess.

"Undress me," Cilla demanded. "It's time to Give."

Emmeline didn't speak, couldn't force the words out. Instead she helped Cilla out of her dress. Cilla's skin was like alabaster, but marred with thousands of tiny scratches. One for every day she refused to end her curse.

Cilla picked at a spot of flesh on the inside of her left elbow, drawing it into the faint light from the candles. She gathered one of the bone knives that she kept in her bedroom; this one was covered in sticky, sweet plum juices, but she didn't seem to care. She made Emmeline watch as she nicked the soft skin at her elbow, squeezing out a single drop of blood. She whispered some words—it sounded like a prayer—and when she opened her eyes her expression was one of release.

"I'm tired."

"Do you want the water tonight?" Emmeline asked. It was laced with laudanum and sometimes it was the only thing that made the old witch sleep. Perhaps, Emmeline thought, it was guilt that kept her awake. More likely it was a lifetime of blood magic. Cilla was the only other witch Emmeline had ever known who had preferred blood—hot, sticky, honest blood—to formal spells and incantations. She wondered if there were other witches on the island who knew what Cilla had done for her throne.

"Yes, the water," Cilla muttered. "Stupid girl." She reached out and grabbed Emmeline by the arm, yanking her towards the fire and drawing her magic around her like a cloak of smoke.

Emmeline struggled. Cilla was weaker after she Gave, but she could hurt them just as badly. Cilla won the scuffle, drawing enough of her fire magic to her fingertips that the skin on Emmeline's arm began to bubble.

"The water, girl," she snapped.

All Emmeline's planning had come down to this.

Blood and water.

Clutching her arm, agony making her movements slow, she crossed to Cilla's pitcher of water. It was stale—like the whole room—and smelled of Cilla's signature blood-and-fire scent.

The laudanum came in a little bottle. Emmeline poured a glass of the water, inhaling slowly so that her body didn't crash with the fear that pressed down from above. She'd pay for what she was about to do, but it would be worth it.

Into the glass of water went two drops of Cilla's special sleeping draught. Her shoulders hunched, next Emmeline slid one of Cilla's knives close to her. She did it quickly so she couldn't change her mind, the sharp bite of the bone into the skin of her finger and the tug of her magic as the blood welled to the surface.

She closed her eyes. *You won't hurt anybody ever again.*

She opened them again and watched the single scarlet droplet fall into the water. Then a second one, and a third. She stirred it before handing the glass to Cilla, who was already sitting in her grand four-poster bed, furs and blankets pulled up to her chin. She took the glass and drank from it greedily, belching when she was done.

"Sit with me, child," she demanded, though Emmeline was a child no longer. "Tell me a story."

Emmeline forced her liquid limbs to respond. She climbed onto the edge of the bed as she had done so many nights since she came to Cross House. She let Cilla pick up one of her hands in her own, ignoring the throb of pain from her scalded skin.

"There once was a little girl with hair like midnight," Emmeline started, repeating the story Cilla had told her. Her mouth was as dry as rocks. "She lived in a grand old house that was built in the shape of a cross. The house was big and empty."

Cilla was nodding, her black eyes and black hair standing stark against the whiteness of her skin as she slumped against the pillows.

"She didn't like the house when it was empty. Her grandfather had always had parties, and there were always plum tarts and crisp apple fancies and the sweetest wine. There were always witches, a coven of them a hundred deep, who danced naked under the moon and wove charms of the most intricate beauty.

"The girl remembered the parties. How good it felt to be wanted. So when the little girl grew up, when her grandfather and father were dead and the house was hers and hers alone, she decided to make it full again."

Cilla continued to nod. It was like her head wasn't attached to her body anymore. She looked glazed, more than the usual distance behind her eyes. Emmeline tried to focus, tried to tell the story Cilla had told her a hundred times before.

"And the children..." Cilla prompted.

"The girl grew up. She didn't have any children but she wanted them more than anything. She tried magic, but she could never get it right. The Goddess did not smile on her. And the world...The world didn't like her, or her kind. Not anymore. So she decided to make orphans her children."

"Tell her about the crow girl," Cilla slurred. Emmeline's heart lurched. The old woman was slumped in the sheets, her skin waxen. The blood had not been much, but it was acting fast, burning Cilla up just like Emmeline knew it would. Emmeline would have the same symptoms in the hours to come—and she, too, would have to fight. To pay.

But she was young and strong, and Cilla was not. It would be worth it to wake up tomorrow *free*.

"The crow girl?" Emmeline whispered.

"The girl. The girl with magic black as crows. Three for a death."

Cilla smiled and the movement unnerved Emmeline. She recoiled as Cilla's beautiful, sharp white teeth became stained with blood. She scrambled backwards.

"Tell her about the heir," Cilla pressed, her smile growing wider. Her eyes were dark, and when she blinked a redness began to seep from their corners. Emmeline panicked, her whole body going rigid as Cilla started to bleed.

"The heir, the heir," Cilla repeated. "The crow girl who gets it all. Tell her she loves her. Tell her she hates her. Tell her *she's afraid of her.* Tell her it's a curse. Tell her she'll die. Tell her…"

Cilla began to convulse. Blood seeped from her eyes and the corner of her mouth. Emmeline let out a low cry of panic and horror, clamping one bloody hand over her mouth, unable to breathe, unable to truly comprehend what she had just done.

——)●(——

They gathered around the churned earth. The rain that fell was cold and it lashed the ground, sending dirt spitting up their clothes. All Cilla's children had been there to bury her, but the money she had left behind had been shared out equally, and most of them had gone.

There was just Nathan, Isobel, and Emmeline left. Nathan and Isobel could have left, could have taken their share of Cilla's fortune and gone too. Isobel talked sometimes of heading to America and starting a new life in New York. Yet both of them stayed.

Emmeline could not leave.

The morning they put Cilla in the ground, Emmeline found a letter amongst her things, the paper crisp and the ink still dark.

Emmeline Delacroix,

Cross House will be yours. It has always belonged to a Delacroix, and before long you may be the only one left. This is your price.

You will not let them forget my legacy.

Priscilla

The letter was sealed with a thumbprint in dried black blood. A spell, woven into her words. Emmeline was numb. Cilla had cursed her.

The love she had felt for the old woman, even at the end, mingled with anger, with hate, was her cross to bear. In death Cilla had bound Emmeline to the house, to the island, and damned her to a name—a legacy—she had never wanted.

Chapter Seventeen

Annie

W e need to have another party," Emmeline said.

The kitchen at the back of the house was hot and cramped, too small for the five of us. Emmeline lounged against the stove as the rest of us sat.

"Are you out of your fucking mind?" Bea swore. She had been silent for long minutes, her focus somewhere on the wall behind Emmeline's head.

"Are you sure that's wise, darling?" Nathan echoed. "We did just bury a man in the garden." He nursed a fresh coffee and the air was thick with the scent of cinnamon.

"We have to," Emmeline replied calmly. "We host most weeks. As far as the rest of the island is concerned it's business as usual, and to act otherwise would be foolish." Her lips when she stopped speaking were a thin line. I remembered the way they had felt against mine and felt instantly ashamed. This wasn't the time.

But then, when was?

"Fuck the rest of the island," Bea retorted. "What are you planning to do, post signs everywhere saying 'Don't go near the greenhouse, there's a corpse in the vegetable patch'?"

The only indication of Emmeline's anger was the small spots

of colour high on her cheeks. She glared at Bea and then looked at Nathan and Isobel. She didn't let her gaze linger on me, sitting between the two of them.

"I actually agree with Bea for once." Isobel shrugged, half apology. "If we invite people into the house we risk them finding out what happened. We've already had the police—and God bloody knows who else—snooping about." I wondered if Emmeline had told her about Anderson. "We've cleaned up but I'm not sure it's safe to bring a bunch of nosy, kazamed Bright Young Things into the house, even if the garden's warded."

"That's exactly what we're going to do," Emmeline said firmly. "It would be more suspicious if we turn off the lights and pretend we're not home. We haven't had any clients all week. Right now it's our job to convince the island that we are the most innocent bootlegging bastards out here."

"It makes sense," I added. "What's the least likely thing a guilty person would do? Throw a party."

Isobel rolled her eyes at me. "Of course you think she's right."

"It was my idea actually," I snapped.

"That's enough." Emmeline's voice was tired but firm. "This isn't up for negotiation. We're going to have a goddamn party, same as always. And Bea is going to the police to officially report her husband missing."

"What?" whispered Bea.

"You can't hide forever. If the police dig about they're going to find you eventually. And if they find you here they might find things that will incriminate *all* of us. There's too much history buried here. Better to beat them to the punch."

Emmeline looked at her brother and sister in turn, her gaze penetrating. Nathan flinched. I thought back to our conversation earlier. This—whatever secret communication passed between the three of them—was why he and Isobel were so keen to get rid of me. Whatever had happened here had ruined them all.

What could possibly be worse than this?

Something made Bea jump. She wasn't really paying attention to us, her eyes glassy and darting between the two back corners of the kitchen, where the shadows gathered.

"We're going to have to confine the guests to the house," Nathan said.

I wasn't listening anymore either. Bea's gaze had shifted. She sat, unmoving, staring out into the hallway. Then she started to whimper. I swallowed, that foul, bitter taste in my mouth again, the same as over breakfast.

"Dearest," Isobel said, noticing. "Are you feeling all right?"

Bea's mouth opened in a silent wail—I felt the promise of it in my bones. Isobel jumped up from the table and Nathan leapt in front of her, his body a shield. Emmeline rushed for Bea, grabbing her arms as she fell from her chair.

Bea's body twitched, her eyes rolling back. Emmeline grunted, lowering her onto the tiled floor, while Isobel nudged Nathan out of the way and hurried to her side.

I couldn't move. The others were all so focused on Bea that they didn't see it. They didn't see what I saw—what Bea had seen.

Incorporeal, a shadow against the dimness in the hall, barely there except for a smudge where his face should be . . .

Bea was right. It hadn't been a nightmare.

It was Arthur.

———()●()———

"I'm telling you that I saw him," I said emphatically once Isobel and Nathan had carried Bea back upstairs to bed.

"I know you think you saw him," Emmeline said. "I told you, though. There's energy when people die. Sometimes bad energy."

"You're acting like this is normal!" I let out an incredulous laugh. "Emmeline, come on. Energy? That's nonsense."

"Is it?" She turned on me. "What makes you an expert all of a sudden?"

Her face was flushed. This close I could smell the magic on her, the vinculum taut between us. Couldn't she sense it? The badness in the air?

"You're not exactly an expert on this sort of thing either," I said sharply. "Isn't it possible that he's...trapped?"

Emmeline shook her head. "I don't know," she admitted. "You said yourself Bea's not well. Being exposed to all of that magic..."

"It can't just be in Bea's head. I saw it. I felt it. I can *still* feel it. And it's—bad. Dark."

"It might not mean anything," Emmeline said stubbornly. "Magic feels different to every witch—and every witch has their own relationship to casting. Like...I know that Nathan's magic is warm and soft, but insistent," Emmeline went on. "And Isobel's is like fresh water, rain and thunder and wind, unpredictable but— natural. And mine—"

"Blood," I said without thinking. "And dirt."

Emmeline met my gaze, unflinching. "Exactly," she said, step- ping away from me again. "It's possible that when we Awakened Arthur it changed some part of him, and that's what's left behind. I'm sure it'll pass."

It didn't sit right with me. This wasn't just *energy*. There was noth- ing harmless about it. Some visceral, deep-rooted part of me tolled like a bell, a warning. Whatever we had seen—Arthur or not—it felt wretched; it felt spiteful. It felt like maggots feasting on living flesh. And the part of me that tolled rebelled against it like a rearing horse. Perhaps Emmeline was too blinkered by her debt and she couldn't see it. Perhaps she was right and it would pass.

But I didn't believe her.

———)●(———

The taste in the air made me long for my little cottage, for its peace and solitude. I needed to be away from Emmeline. At Cross House thoughts of her crowded my brain, nudging into every inch of me.

Emmeline had fetched my father's spell book from where she had locked it away, and I carried it next door, kicking off my shoes and padding barefoot through to the kitchen, which felt strangely unfa- miliar. I had slid so easily into Emmeline's life that the one I'd left behind felt like a phantom.

My father's book fell open at my touch. I flicked back and forth, scanning the pages for anything that might be useful, resolutely avoiding the page with the Awakening spell.

I stopped when one of the pages became dislodged—no, not a page. Tucked between two of the back pages was a photograph.

A man, tall and dark, and a young woman holding a child with pale curls. Instantly I recognised the curve of the woman's protective smile as she cradled the child.

A wave of sadness crashed over me, leaving me breathless. I grasped the photograph, lifting it up to the afternoon sunlight streaming through the window. The woman was my mother, her mousy hair long and braided away from her face.

The man was my father.

They looked so normal, posing in their Sunday best, my father's tiepin glinting and my mother's necklace curled in my chubby fist. It was wrong. Mam had told me more times than I could count that I had not met my father until that day he took me to the art gallery when I was five years old.

This photograph proved differently.

I thought of my mother's reaction when the letter about his death had arrived. We had calmly continued our dinner, oxtail soup and bread that she had baked, and afterwards she had gone straight to bed.

When a second letter came, Mam had asked me not to go. Was it sadness for his death that had haunted her eyes? I hadn't thought so at the time. Perhaps she suspected that she was about to lose me too.

I stared at the photograph in my hands. I noticed things that I hadn't seen when I was fifteen: that my father and I had the same eyes, pale and clear; that we had the same hairline, the same firm jaw. That I looked like him.

The man in the museum—it seemed increasingly likely that it *had* been my father he was looking for. The resemblance between us was stronger than I had ever considered. The question was whether he was a friend. Whether he knew of my father's magic, whether he shared his predilections. I rubbed my finger over the photograph, focusing on my father's tiepin. The picture was grainy, colourless, but if I squinted it looked almost like a crow—perhaps even the same crow pin the man had worn. Was he a friend, or was their connection more sinister?

I had become so entangled in Emmeline's world I had had no chance to consider what I might have missed, what instinctual fears I had dismissed as silly. I had so little information about my father—and his death. Was it possible his magic was responsible? How would I know? I couldn't ask Anderson. It felt a little like being trapped, questions on all sides and never any answers.

I tucked the photograph back between the pages.

I returned to my search, poring through the book until my eyes grew dry. It didn't matter what Emmeline thought—Bea hadn't imagined what she'd seen. *I* hadn't. I recalled the shadows I'd glimpsed, last night on the lawn, this morning in the kitchen, and I shivered.

And it wasn't just that.

The way Bea had passed out earlier—the timing of it—felt like unfinished business.

I finally gave up my search long after the sun had set. My little cottage felt empty. Every corner was dark and shadows seemed to loom whenever I turned my head. The fear of seeing him again, Arthur here in my own house, drove me to light as many lamps as I could.

But the light was little better. It only made the humming in my ears feel louder. It was like a panic, only fractured, foreboding creeping so gently it was hard to tell what was reality. I sat with my hands pressed firmly against the table, as though that might ground me. Felt the push and pull of my pulse. I focused on it, a cool, prickling sensation unfurling inside my skin. The sound of the surf outside was like a metronome.

I blinked. A flash of *something* cut across my vision. Like a drop of blood drifting through water. Blink. A dark room, ruby-red walls. A four-poster bed. Blink. Rotting fruit. Flies. Blink—

A skittering sound made me snap to attention. It had come from the back door. I held my breath, wondering if it would happen again.

It did.

I shoved my father's book under the table, pulling the cloth down just as a quiet knock made my heart thump. I pictured the constable come to arrest me. One of Emmeline's Council members, the man from the museum, sent to round us all up.

"Annie," came Nathan's voice. "Are you there?"

I hissed a sigh, opening the door to find him standing in the dark, hardly visible against the night.

"Have you got a minute for a new friend?"

I heaved another breath against my pounding heart and nodded.

Out on the beach the wind had whipped up and the sand bit into the skin of my ankles like a thousand tiny insects. Nathan strode ahead, away from Emmeline's house and mine, along the stretch of narrow beach that led eventually to the house of another neighbour, another rich family with a private boat and hired staff. I had forgotten that there was a world out there, a whole island of people who looked up at the same stars as these, stared into the same roiling ocean waves.

"Nathan, can you wait?"

I fought to keep up with him as he strode through the dense sand. I stumbled. My leg complained as I landed hard on my knees. It didn't hurt badly, but I couldn't stop the tears of frustration that stung.

When Nathan turned, his face was a pale oval in the night, his mouth downturned, his warm eyes hooded. He handed me a handkerchief from his pocket, well-worn but clean and smelling of cinnamon.

"I'm sorry," he said simply.

I dried my eyes, then brushed the sand off my knees. As I tucked the handkerchief into the pocket of the trousers, a small spike of pleasure flared in that one defiant, unfeminine act.

"It's all right," I said. "I didn't mean to cry. Are you okay?"

Nathan scrubbed a hand over his face. "Do you ever just wish you could escape?"

Yes. That was why I'd ended up here in the first place—and look what had happened.

"I used to think that's what I wanted. Now I know I could never leave," he said. "Not while Emmeline is here."

He bent to pick up a stone, turning it over in his fingers.

"She's your sister," I said simply. It was the same reason I returned to Bea over and over, although we had treated each other so badly. She was, blood or not, family.

"Em never told me she was in trouble." His expression crumpled. "She'd rather Give herself away than lose herself by accident. And I was too wrapped up in this blind relief, you know, this *gladness* that we were all here, all together. I didn't see it."

Nathan switched his gaze to the dark ocean. A few spots of rain fell, but the clouds overhead were only small, the rest of the sky clear like black crystal. I didn't know what to say. It was clear that Nathan felt he owed Emmeline a part of himself, his loyalty and his love.

"You could sense it too, today," Nathan said abruptly. "Couldn't you?"

"The darkness—"

"Nate. Annie."

We both spun. We had been so locked in our ocean-roaring world that we hadn't heard Isobel approach. She held her dress off the sand with one hand and her wild hair blew around her head, whipped this way and that.

"What happened?" I blurted, terror right through my heart.

"You were right. It's Bea. *Hurry.*"

SINNERS

AND

SAVIOURS

Chapter One

Annie

The second we stepped into the old house I could feel it. On my tongue like poison, my vision clouding dark, a dreadful rattling in my bones. It felt like magic—and not the good kind.

Isobel led the way, taking the stairs at the back of the house two at a time, the worn servants' carpet muffling our footsteps. The hallways were dark and they smelled faintly of the salt air, of incense. Of blood. Isobel and Nathan raced ahead and I followed on almost-silent feet that were bare and covered in sand.

When we reached Bea's bedroom Isobel didn't stop. She ploughed in through the open door and immediately began to peel off her cardigan. She threw it aside and rushed to the far side of the room, where Bea was slumped in an oversize armchair, Emmeline leant over her.

"I found them," Isobel said in a rush.

"She's not changed." Emmeline glanced up at me, took in my bare feet and my windswept hair, and her eyes softened for a second before the look was replaced with one of stark panic. "She started to convulse again about half an hour ago," she explained, "and then she stopped and I thought it was over. We couldn't get her onto the bed. She..."

Bea's arms were scored with red lines, thin and ragged and

uneven. Five at a time. She'd done it to herself, as if she'd been try-ing to dig under her own skin.

"What..." I breathed.

"I don't know," Emmeline said. "I don't know. One second she was fine and then she was—"

We all stopped as Bea let out a moan, low and gravelly in her throat. Emmeline leaned back down over her, shushing her with surprising gentleness.

"I need a cool cloth," she said. "I didn't want to leave her."

Nathan didn't need to be asked twice. Isobel clutched at a strand of beads that hung from her dress. I hadn't noticed them before. They looked almost like a rosary, except made of jade-green stones that were freckled with mossy brown. She saw my gaze and stilled her fingers.

"I told you I could taste it," I said. "I saw him. Is this the kind of thing energy can do?"

Emmeline's lips thinned.

"I don't know."

"You don't know. You never know. What good is having power if you don't know how to use it? Move out of the way."

I made to shove Emmeline to the side, the vinculum trembling as Emmeline reacted to my presence. She sidestepped me before I could touch her, and I stumbled towards Bea.

"It's no good," Emmeline warned. "It's like—"

I reached for Bea, aiming for her wrist to check her pulse. I didn't get within an inch before I met some kind of force, a barrier that felt like a barricade of darkness, hard and moist like the wall of a deep well. I recoiled immediately.

"—I'm being blocked," Emmeline finished.

"What do we do?" I looked between Emmeline and Isobel. "We can't keep her fever down like this."

Bea moaned again, her head back, pale throat exposed. Nathan came bearing a bowl of cool water and a clean white cloth. He pushed it towards Emmeline, but she didn't move to take it. Instead it was Isobel who gathered the material in both hands, dunked it into the bowl, and held it over Bea's forehead, releasing a stream of water.

The water hissed as it touched her skin, faint steam rising.

"It's Arthur," I said.

The room was dark, darker than it should have been with three lamps glaring. Shadows pooled and danced. On the wall by the window I recognised a pattern of black mould, creeping around the edges. It hadn't been there this morning.

"He's still here. Energy or not—he's haunting her. She looks the same as he did, all fuzzy. Like I'm looking through warped glass."

Isobel blanched, pulling back. We all turned to Emmeline, who stood with her arms crossed, her eyes distant as she gazed at Bea.

"We've got to *do something*," I pushed. "Do you have any ideas?"

"We don't want to hurt her," Isobel warned. "The baby."

Nathan shook his head. "Whatever it is, Annie's right. We can't do nothing."

"A cleansing?" Isobel suggested.

"We're getting low on supplies—"

"We can get more," Emmeline snapped.

"If you two go get what we need, we can set up in here," I said quickly.

Isobel didn't so much as even look at me, but she and Nathan left the room together. As the door swung inwards I saw Nathan's arm snake towards Isobel's shoulder, hovering hesitantly before settling on the soft material of her dress.

"What do I have to do?" I turned to Emmeline.

Her gaze was tortured. "We can't lose her," she whispered.

"We won't lose her. What do we need?"

"This is my fault. It reminds me so much of—*her*. She burned up. Burned…"

"Just tell me what I need to do—"

"Cilla said I was cursed…" Emmeline's nostrils flared and her chest heaved.

"Emmeline, you have to calm down. You're no good to anybody like this."

I fought my own panic. Bea looked so unwell, her skin slick and pale and waxy. I reached for Emmeline, for comfort—for her or for me I wasn't sure—but she reared back from me.

"Em—"

Somehow there was fresh blood on her lips, unnaturally dark, seeming to glitter. She must have bitten herself by accident. The air thrummed. She looked wild. The china on the sideboard began to rattle, a glass half-filled with water tumbling to the floor with a smash. The tiny jagged pieces rumbled together, ready to attack.

Without thinking I thrust myself at Emmeline, pulling her close as I searched for the tether, still buried deep. *Good.* I wrapped one arm around her, my free hand going to her lips. I used my sleeve to wipe the blood away.

Emmeline recoiled but I held on tight.

"It's going to be all right," I lied, breath coming fast. "Get it under control."

I stared into her eyes, willing her to see me. Panic eclipsed her, but slowly, slowly, she stilled. Her tongue flicked over the invisible wound and she swallowed, throat bobbing hard.

"Okay?" I asked hoarsely.

She said nothing, only pulled me closer, a crushing embrace so surprising that it sucked the breath from my lungs.

Bea let out another ungodly moan, driving us apart again. Emmeline rushed towards the chair. Before I could blink she was propelled backwards, clear across the room. The bowl of water on the nightstand crashed to the floor. Emmeline landed in a crumpled heap against the wall, the vinculum blaring with her pain—real pain that was too much like my own.

I must have screamed. All I could see was Bea, her eyes rolling back and bloody froth at her mouth. Agony—she must be in agony. She was going to die.

Footsteps. Isobel and Nathan skidded back into the room, panic etched on their features. Isobel looked at Bea, then Emmeline.

"Quick." Isobel thrust a bundle of fragrant dried sage at me.

Nathan held a pillar candle, the white wax scarred with runes and symbols.

"*Annie.*"

Isobel had begun to create a circle around the armchair, drawing a line of salt around all of us—except Emmeline, who was still unconscious. My heart lurched again at the sight of her, but she didn't look like she was in any real danger, unlike Bea.

I grabbed the box of matches that Isobel had pointed at and lit the sage, letting its grey smoke cloud the room and my vision. Silently I bit down on the inside of my cheek, flooding my mouth with salty blood.

I could feel the call of magic, the vinculum writhing. I held it fast.

Isobel took the candle from Nathan and put it at a point in her circle of salt next to a fresh dish of water. She had scattered herbs at another point and some dried flowers.

I followed her to the final unadorned length of circle, jumping at the tug in my fingers and the responding tingle under my skin. I laid the sage, still smoking, along this stretch and turned to Isobel.

"Bless this circle," she intoned, "so that we may be free and protected. Fill it with light and healing."

Nathan repeated Isobel's words, his face grey. Bea's eyes were open, wide and filled with panic. I repeated the words.

"Bless this circle..."

"Cast out those who wish us harm."

"Cast out those who wish us harm..."

Isobel's voice was melodious, filled with intent. I focused, willing my blood to follow Isobel's wish.

Slowly, so slowly, Bea's pain seemed to subside. Her eyes fluttered, her breathing growing steadier. Eventually we fell to incense-scented silence, the vicious tingling in my skin dulled to a gentle throb.

I glanced over to Em, who was still out cold. "Is she going to be all right?"

Isobel swept a doorway out of the ring of salt and headed to

Emmeline. She laid a hand on the older witch's forehead, and when Emmeline moaned and rolled onto her side, Isobel nodded.

My cheek throbbed where I'd bitten it, blood still on my tongue. It was like ocean salt, crisp and clean. Isobel frowned.

"Blood," she said. "Annie, you mustn't use it—"

"You used it on Emmeline after her Giving," I retorted. "Emmeline uses it all the time."

Isobel stared. "—until you know *how* to use it…I know it's tempting but you don't know enough about it."

"Well, teach me," I argued. "Please. I can't just stand by and watch these things happen!" Tears formed in my eyes again, the anxiety and fear of the last days welling up. I'd rather be angry, lit by the incandescence that provided. "I don't understand any of this! Why can I do it now and I couldn't before? What is happening to me?"

Isobel's face softened, but she didn't comfort me. Instead she pursed her lips.

"Is this always what it's like?" I begged.

"What?"

"Magic. Is it always so…bloody and awful?"

Nathan and Isobel exchanged a glance.

"You're coming into yourself later than most…" Isobel hedged. "The island—"

"And Emmeline," Nathan added. I wondered if he had sensed the vinculum, this tether—if he knew what it meant.

Isobel frowned. "And Emmeline, yes. All of this…it's woken a magic in you that was lying deep for some time. Emmeline told me about your father. I suspect it was always in you but you lacked the will. Magic can do great good, but…"

Nathan shook his head. Isobel didn't finish her sentence. The answer was clear. Was magic always so bloody and awful?

Yes.

"I need to get some things to make a tonic for Bea." Isobel shook herself. "Nate, can you get Em to bed, dearest? She'll have a royal headache tomorrow."

Nathan reached down with surprising strength and lifted

Emmeline to her feet. She was mostly conscious, but her eyes had a glazed look to them. She was getting weaker—her magic more out of control. How long would we be able to trust her power?

"Can you stay here with Bea?" Isobel asked.

When the room was empty of everybody but Bea and me, I knelt down beside her chair. I could smell that same bitterness on the air, but fainter. Less like death.

"Oh, Bea..." I murmured.

She opened her eyes. They were bright green and shiny like cut glass.

"Annie," she whispered urgently. "Please help me."

"It's okay. We cleansed you." I blinked. My eyes were so tired that Bea's shape was strange in the chair. Almost hazy.

"No." Bea let out a wail, small and pitiful and terrified. "Annie, he's still trying to get *inside me*."

Chapter Two

Annie

B ea?" I asked with a trembling voice. "What do you mean? Bea?"

She didn't respond. She scrunched her eyes against me, a fresh wave of pain contorting her body as another pitiful sob broke my heart. Without thinking I grabbed hold of her wrist, and this time there was no force stopping me. She was hot to the touch, beyond feverish, and when I inhaled I could make out the telltale scent of rot. Of decay.

I glanced about, desperately casting my eyes around the room in search of anything useful. Bea grabbed for my hand, fingers grappling for mine.

"Bea, what's happening?"

Bea roared the next word, so close to my ear I was momentarily stunned. *"ARTHUR."*

Panic flooded me. I was torn between staying and running to find Isobel or Nathan or Emmeline, but if I left her...I couldn't leave her.

Bea thrashed like a dying bird, back arching into the chair, her head bouncing against the wings. Her grip on me was solid, too strong. The bones in my hand ground against one another as I tried to pull away.

"No," Bea moaned. "No, no, don't let him in. Annie, *please*."

Bea's nails dug into my flesh, right where Emmeline had cut me, the wounds opening up eagerly.

"Bea!" I cried, pulling harder. "Let me go!"

I could taste my blood on the air, that eerily familiar deep-ocean tang. Was this how Emmeline felt when her magic rose snarling without her permission? I couldn't stop it. I couldn't get the blood to stem. I didn't know what to do.

"Leave her alone!"

The room had grown dim; it was like peering through twilight, shadows spilling from impossible places. The mould around the window had spread, spidering across the wall. The blood ran from my hand, a steady claret drip of it down towards Bea's skin, pale as marble.

She moaned again. The sound was like the flap of wings, hoarse and soft at once. I pulled harder but the blood only slid between our palms. I scrambled back, my free hand reaching for something—anything—I could use to prise Bea away from me.

There was nothing.

I braced myself against the arm of the chair but it was no good. Bea was easily as strong as two men, ten men. The chair skidded across the floorboards. A deep, mocking sound cut through my panic. Laughter. I searched the ceiling, the corners of the room, but could see nothing.

My chest flooded with untamed rage, a riot of heat. I refused to give up.

I recalled the way I'd been able to visualise the fog around Bea earlier, like a dark wall. I sucked in a deep breath and closed my eyes, the darkness there too black, too full of monsters. I focused on the blood dripping from the wounds on my arm, the taste of it in my mouth, the humming in my veins.

"Arthur," I said. The darkness behind my eyelids seemed to ripple. "Arthur Croft, is that you?"

The chuckling grew, a malevolent sound that turned my muscles to water. It echoed inside my ears, left and then right. I shook my head, resisting the urge to open my eyes.

"Will you show yourself?" The words echoed in my mind.

The laughter drifted further towards Bea. I peered into the darkness, just making out the shape of her. She seemed impossibly far away, separated from me by a wall of ash the colour of moonlight instead of linked by our hands.

"What do you want?"

There was no answer, only Bea yanking my arm again, fending off monsters I could not see.

"Arthur, *what do you want?*"

I focused on the blood again, the growing sensation of a gale brewing inside my chest. I longed to unleash it, but fear stayed me. *Intent*, I thought. Emmeline had said blood magic needed intent.

"Show me," I ordered.

My ears roared, ocean waves inside my brain. I leaned into the sound, willing my mind to follow the dark path they created. Bea's hand tugged away, so hard I almost let go. This time it was me who held on as I forced the darkness in my mind to stretch, to shift, until it felt like I was walking through a wall of coal clouds and out into light.

The view shifted. It was no longer Bea's body wracked with pain. Instead it was a street, one I thought I recognised from my walks, perhaps my trip to the museum, but it was hard to tell, the world distorted like looking through a glass bottle. A narrow street stretched, a blue house, and then moving on again.

The day was bright and hot, but it was not *today*. The girls had long hair, their skirts kissing their ankles. I recognised the harbour, the same one where I had disembarked on my first day here. I walked without moving, following the figure who had appeared in front of me.

Arthur.

He whistled a jaunty tune and I caught the eerie echoes of it like wisps of smoke inside my ears. The water beyond the sea of expensive yachts bobbed and glittered. Arthur cut towards the water.

My vision bobbed in time with the boats. The coal-dust around the edges of my vision obscured my view of two bodies embracing, a longing surging between them so strong that I could trace the fractures in Emmeline's love spell, Arthur's true emotions shining in the places where it had begun to unravel.

They shifted into my view, the blackness separating to reveal the two of them sitting on a bench, a hand's width apart, their bodies straining to be closer to each other. The woman was young and pretty, shiny mahogany hair in a soft chignon, and an open, rosy expression.

"How's Georgie? How's my boy?"

Arthur's voice was different. Warmer. It was a tone I hadn't heard him use with Bea. There was an echo of menace in my ears, but it didn't come from this.

"He's fine. Feeding well, still. You should come see him."

The woman's eyes were tired.

Arthur's smile was that beaming brightness I had only caught glimpses of, liquid charm, his posture relaxed. So, this was the man before the magic scoured away his truth, his future.

"Good. That's good," Arthur said distractedly. He ran a hand through his golden hair.

"Why did you do it, Art?" she asked. "The parties, the drinking... I understood all of that. I knew you didn't want to settle. Not with me..."

She stopped and started awkwardly, her hands dancing in her lap. "You've hardly seen Georgie since he was born. It wasn't conventional, but I thought he—*we*—were precious to you."

Arthur looked right at this woman, and it felt like he was looking at me. My stomach contracted, a kick to the gut as it hit me. Arthur and this woman, they had loved each other—real love. This was the life he had chosen—and I'd made sure he would never be able to choose it again, never watch his child grow. I clenched my teeth against the sickness in my belly.

"I need her, Vi," Arthur said. The words were simple, but they contained multitudes. Magic hummed inside the phrase.

"You promised me when I got pregnant with Georgie that things would be different."

"I *need* her," Arthur said again. This time his voice was darker, a guttural vibration. My bones trembled with it. Slowly, I became aware of where I was, not watching from the safety of a dusty, warm street but from the floor in Bea's room as she writhed in the chair, stitched with pain. The darkness had spread, tinging the edges of my vision, tendrils like roots that crept inwards.

I couldn't open my eyes. The blackness was so complete, so devouring, and I could see only Arthur, his golden crown of hair shining.

He turned to me. His skin was the colour of death, his eyes the silver of starlight.

Ruby blood welled at the corners of his lips. He clawed at his throat, spitting black mucus that spilled into rotten soil at our feet. The roots around my vision grew, tangling, grasping for my legs, my arms. Blood welled between Bea's palm and mine, and I knew, irrevocably, that I had lost too much.

I tried to scramble away, heart slamming, my hand still held tight. The magic wavered, but the coiling heat of it was inside me. I felt it. I felt him.

"Help!" I screamed. But my voice was muffled, as if underwater. Somehow his presence was like a blanket, his energy smothering us. "Emmeline, help!"

They couldn't hear us.

I did the only thing left, reaching down deep into the recess of myself and hoisting the vinculum from its slumber. The silver thread began to glow, sparking eagerly as I wrapped it in my hand and pulled. Hard.

The roots were thicker, more like vines. Black vines with vicious spikes. The air was heavy, filled with the taste of grave dirt, moist and thick. I tried again to open my eyes, but I could see only darkness, feel only the vines as they slithered around my arms, their thorns pricking at my skin.

I cried out.

A flash of light winked across my eyes like sunspots. Beyond the pulse of my heart in my ears, the lashing of waves, I heard the slamming of feet against wooden boards. The tether inside me grew stronger, more tangible. I tried to grasp it, to pull it back, but I couldn't. Some dark, treacherous part of me didn't want to and I couldn't force it.

"Emmeline," I cried.

Bea screamed.

There was a *bang* that sounded like a gong against metal, reverberating through every inch of me, rattling my bones.

"Get away from her," Emmeline growled. The tether surged and I spun, the darkness disappearing from the edges of my vision like smoke.

Emmeline looked every inch of her power as she stood in the centre of Bea's room. Her teeth were bared and her expression feral. Isobel and Nathan weren't far behind, one carrying a copper gong and the other burning sage in both hands. The smoke was white and pure and I sucked it in, drew it deep into my lungs.

A rumbling inside my ears was the only evidence of Arthur's displeasure. My blood pulsed and I saw how slick my skin was, Bea's clothes coated in my blood, the wounds on my arm much larger than they'd ever been before.

Instead of rot and dirt I finally tasted my own magic again, salt fresh and eager, my limbs filling with golden relief when it crowded inside me. It felt like near drowning, hauling myself to the surface with arms screaming. Choking. *Breathing.*

Finally, finally, Bea released my hand. I withdrew it, wrapping it in the cloth that Isobel thrust at me, stemming the blood. The darkness in the room had receded, the sage clearing the air.

Isobel dropped the gong and headed for Bea, who panted hard, sweat beading on her face, in her hair.

I opened my mouth to thank Emmeline, but she whirled on me, her eyes glittering and dark as onyx.

"Did he see you?" she demanded. "Did he see it?"

Horror filled me. Emmeline strode towards me, grabbing hold of my good arm and hauling me to my feet. We were inches from each other and I could feel her urgency—her fear.

"I—"

"Did he *see it*?" she pushed.

I knew without having to ask that she didn't mean *me*, didn't mean my magic or the vision.

She meant the vinculum.

"Yes," I said.

Chapter Three

Annie

Y ou have to leave."

"What? Emmeline, no—"

Isobel spun around with her finger on her lips.

"Outside," she said. "Both of you."

She herded both of us towards the door, and I was so exhausted that my bones felt hollow; I didn't argue. Nathan stayed beside Bea, ever faithful.

"*Emmeline*," I said.

Emmeline's eyes flashed and I could see it again, whatever darkness lived inside her clawing to get out.

An excruciating pain washed through me, starting deep inside my chest but flowing out to my fingers, my toes, like water. The tether was too tight, not tidily tucked away but suffocated. I went limp, my body biddable as I tried to prevent collapse. I was still losing blood, but slower now. The cloth I'd wrapped around my arm was already damp, and I could taste the magic but it was bitter, like the ashes blowing off a smouldering fire. Spent.

We stumbled away and down the stairs, out into the brittle dark before Emmeline let go of me. I flinched away from her, drawing myself upright as the pain slowly subsided. Emmeline was panting.

"You…" I wheezed. "You said we should never use it—"

"You broke that rule the second you used the vinculum in front of him," Emmeline hissed. This wasn't the woman I'd grown to know, with her wolf's smile and her capable hands. This Emmeline was every inch the witch I'd been afraid of, sharp and mean.

"I didn't know what to do! I couldn't stop it. Bea was so strong, she grabbed me—the scabs on my arm, *which you made*, broke open. Arthur… I was trying to figure out what he wanted."

"And you used your blood?" Emmeline demanded. She towered over me. I shrank back. Regret passed over her features and she pulled away, correcting herself, pulling the tether back so fast it left me breathless.

I thought of the way she had held me not long ago, that crush of relief, of gratitude, as her raging magic waned. I needed *that* Emmeline.

"I had to!" I explained. "It was already flowing. I didn't know what to do. It triggered a—vision. Why does this keep happening to me?" I sank into the dirt outside Cross House, pulling my knees to my chest.

Emmeline was silent. Eventually a hand landed on my shoulder, barely there, just a whisper. I looked up. Her concerned face hovered over me, soft and limned with moonlight.

"I hate this," I whispered. "I thought I could do it but I'm not brave without the tether."

"Yes, you are. Annie, you're stronger than you think—and that's the problem," Emmeline said, much gentler now. "I think you're a water witch. That's why you have the visions. You have a natural affinity for divination, premonitions. Do you—see things before they happen? I don't mean actually see them… but do you get a sense? Like an intuition?"

I thought for a moment. All the years I'd thought my panics were a symptom of bad things happening—Sam signing up and not coming back, Mam nearly losing the shop, Bea leaving—but no. The panics had always happened *before*.

"When Sam went to war," I said. "I told him not to go. I thought

I was just worried the same as everybody else. He seemed different that day, though. It was like there was this layer of glass around him, warped. Like a bell jar. It scared me."

Emmeline held out a hand and I grasped it, climbing to my feet.

"It was the same when we brought Arthur back. Only...darker. Hazy. And Bea just now."

"We can't let him near you again," Emmeline said. A fierce protective fire smouldered in her gaze. "Not without a plan. If he figures out how to access the vinculum...It's energy, same as he is."

Same as the debt, I thought, remembering the black mould on the tether I'd felt when Emmeline had lost control and hurt my arm. Perhaps she was thinking of the same thing, because she pulled me closer, just enough that I could feel the heat of her body.

"What are we going to do?"

"I'll think of something," she said softly, her breath ruffling the top of my hair. She stood back then, and the space between us thrummed. She reached up, hesitant at first and then bolder, to brush my hair back off my face. "Go home," she said gently. "You've lost a lot of blood and you need proper rest. I'll watch Bea."

———()●()———

I let myself into my cottage, feeling like a guest. Padding around silently, I stripped off my borrowed clothes. I ran the bath and stayed submerged until the water was cool.

Two weeks ago, I hadn't thought that any of this might happen. All I had been worried about was escaping Sam's ghost. Here it was my own magic I could not ignore. I had been drawn in, tempted; I had allowed myself to taste a future brimming with power. With viciousness, yes, but possibility too. It was in my body—in my blood. The ocean-polished stones I had always collected, the roar of the waves in my ears, those were parts of myself I had shunned, parts that glittered with frightening potential. And—perhaps this scared me the most—these things no longer felt unnatural.

What Emmeline had said about my magic made sense, and I barked with laughter in the silence of the bathroom. I'd spent more than twenty years running from the only thing that might make me feel powerful. I had fallen prey to the very dangers I had been warned about; I had done dreadful, *wicked* things, things I was certain would haunt me forever. But the salt-and-wild magic that bloomed inside me, the hint of liquid moonlight in the tether... Somehow these felt as if I had been born to them. They felt *right*.

Emmeline's magic was another matter. That scared me more than I'd admit even in the silence of my cottage. It had woven a net around Cross House, this town, this whole *island*. We had raised a man from the dead and been driven to kill him twice; if Emmeline's power continued to grow—if I helped it—what might she be capable of? And if Arthur's energy latched on like she'd suggested it might, what then?

I was thoroughly chilled before I managed to climb out of the bath. I bandaged the wounds on my arm and my shoulder, already crusted with thick scabs, and drank two cups of strong black tea heaped with sugar to help the shakiness in my limbs.

I hardly slept. When I did, in brief snatches during the darkest hours, I dreamed I could see Arthur by the side of my bed, his presence a black hole, an ominous pressure against my skin. I dreamed of my father's attic, his dusty books and dried herbs. I dreamed of the ocean. I dreamed—

It was the same room I had seen before. Snatches of a bedroom with ruby-red walls, dominated by a four-poster bed. In my dream I felt the hairs on my arms rise, the taste of rot and smoky red wine blending on my tongue. I tried to creep closer, saw only shifting shadows, furs on the bed, the wavering of a candle flame.

A figure stood before a table, a blade in their hands. The air trembled with magic. Blood in the water, a pain blooming in my chest. It felt like I was burning from the inside, skin alight with wicked fire.

I awoke with a start, my skin drenched with sweat and that black taste in my mouth. The sky outside my window was still purple velvet. The dreams had left me weak, as if I had run for miles. It was a new exhaustion, bone-deep.

I dressed quickly in an old grey dress and my worn, supple boots and got into my car. I couldn't go back to Cross House, but the thought of sitting patiently waiting for news about Bea made my skin crawl. Besides, the dreams of my father had given me an idea.

For the first time I noticed that my father's house was nicer than Emmeline's. Cleaner, despite his death and its subsequent neglect. The white walls were crisp and fresh, the gardens carefully cultivated. I thought of Emmeline's house, which was bigger, bolder— yet held about it an air of neglect, of sadness. It was almost garish.

What I'd once seen as grand, beautiful, wilted under a second glance, a dark rot seeping in through its foundations. Was it Emmeline's darkness? Or had it always been there? Cross House wasn't like magic: Emmeline hadn't been born to it; she had inherited it like a curse.

Somehow this made me think of my dreams. The figure in them had reminded me of Emmeline, but not the Emmeline I recognised. It had been another Emmeline, conjured by the darkest parts of my heart, by the fear that thrummed beneath the desire. The images of a knife splitting flesh, of blood seeping from pores, were vivid even in daylight.

I crossed my father's cropped front lawn. Inside the house I was struck again by how quiet it was. My footsteps echoed on the polished wooden floors. I wasn't sure why I was here except that I couldn't bear the solitude of my cottage and I couldn't simply sit and do nothing. Perhaps my father's books might help.

It wasn't until I reached the attic that a slimy horror unfurled in my belly. The door was wide open.

I pushed into the attic with my heart hammering, eyes reluctantly taking in the disarray. Books and crystals lay scattered on the floor, herbs crushed to dust underneath a heavy tread. My father's precious rugs and cushions were ruined, scorched and smudged with ash.

And the books…

Gone. Pages had been torn from the tomes seemingly at random, burned to nothing but piles of ash in my father's copper cauldron. Those that had survived the fire were mutilated, strewn aside, whole volumes reduced to cracked leather covers housing nothing but bindings and air. I stood stock-still and catalogued the destruction. It was calculated, focused mainly on the books and his desk, where the papers I had seen when I found the journal had been obliterated.

The smell was different too. Gone was the gentle dusty aroma of drying herbs and ocean salt. Now, alongside the bitterness and smoke, I caught an acrid whiff of a manufactured scent, hair cream or aftershave—a clean, masculine scent.

It was ruined. All of it, *ruined*. Any hope I had of finding a fresh solution hidden amongst these pages was gone.

Chapter Four

Emmeline

We kept the sage burning all night. Isobel made poultice after poultice: one smelled like ripe blackberries and was pasted onto Bea's dry and cracked lips; another made the whole room reek of fungi, damp and earthy. We'd managed to get her into the bed and she dozed fitfully.

Nathan paced back and forth and back and forth until Isobel snapped, "Hell's bells, Nate, I love you to pieces but please can you just go away? You're giving me a headache."

He sat on Bea's empty armchair for a minute, his hands clasped between his knees. "It's bad, isn't it."

I refused to look up from the examination of my hands, counting the blood-scars as I'd done a thousand times before.

"This one seems to be helping," Isobel murmured, smearing a jelly-like infusion containing peppermint and lemon down Bea's inner arms for the second time, focusing on her palms before dabbing it at the pulse points of her neck.

"That's not what I meant, darling."

Isobel stood back to admire her handiwork, always the most herself, the most in control, when she was in charge of a patient. My heart swelled and I bit back the retort that rose as an antidote.

"I know," she said. "We can do this. We always do."

Nathan yawned, rubbing a hand over his face, fingers scratching at his chin, perpetually hairless thanks to Isobel's concoctions. He looked exhausted. I searched his face for a hint of my Drowning Boy, fresh worry seizing me. But no, he was only tired. We were all so tired.

They were both waiting—for me. I always had a plan, a solution. With Cilla it had taken me longer, but I was the one who always came through. And now...I had nothing.

Bea and Annie were in danger. We had the police—and potentially the Council—breathing down our necks; this situation with Arthur; and the debt, growing larger each minute, its fingers prying at my magic, my body, my *mind*. I had to think. I had to.

"Both of you should go," I said brusquely. "We've got a party to prepare for tomorrow, so we can't be in bed 'til noon, and somebody is going to have to sit here with her tonight."

Nathan cast me an infuriatingly warm look. I scowled. Isobel only shrugged, her usual capable self. She gathered up the bowls, a flicker of disappointment in her eyes that I might have imagined, as if she'd been waiting for me to say something different.

"Go," I muttered. "Rest. I can handle it."

The words reminded me of those I'd said to Annie. *Go home. You need proper rest.* It was empty without her here. I regretted sending her away, though it was for her own good. How had we spent so many months just the three of us, lonely orphans thinking we could change the world? We had been naïve. Stupid.

I perched on the edge of Bea's bed. She twisted when she felt my weight and groggily reached out to push away a lock of hair, slick with sweat. The way she lay reminded me of a statue. Her hair, fire bright, fanned on the pillow around her, and her skin, so pale, was dusted with freckles that looked, in the dim light, like a patina of moss.

One of her hands curled unconsciously to press against her belly, her palm moulded to the child that grew there, invisible to everybody but her.

"Bea," I whispered. "How are you feeling?"

Her green eyes were open, less glassy than earlier. I prayed that Isobel's medicines would work, that the energy in the room would vanish. I breathed a lungful of sage-scented air.

"Better," she said hoarsely. "A lot better. I might even have the energy to kill you."

I fought a laugh.

"Kill me? Go ahead. It'll speed up this whole bastard thing."

Bea blinked. "How can you be so..."

"So what?"

"So calm. You seem totally unfazed by all of this."

"Is that what you think?" I asked. "That none of this bothers me? I'm trying to hold myself together. For Nathan and Isobel—for you. And I don't know how much longer I can. I'm not well, Bea."

"You can fight it," Bea urged. "You're strong."

I thought of the way my magic had released itself earlier, the remains of the smashed glass still glittering on the floorboards. I hadn't meant to make myself bleed. As the debt grew, so did my own magic—no longer a slave to my whims. It was as if it had a mind of its own. Only Annie's quick thinking had stopped it from going wild, from lashing out in fear that would have hurt just like malice.

"Not strong enough," I said sharply. Anger at my impotence rose. This was easier to swallow than the other thoughts that swarmed me, of Annie's lips in the dark, of the way when I was with her everything was brighter—warmer. Of the vinculum, how it was completely unfair that we had met in this life and how I could never have her. Of how badly I didn't want this bargain to devour her too.

"It's getting close, Bea," I said. "Every day that goes by—every hour. I'm dying. I need to make sure that if—*when*—you and Annie make it through this, you don't hang at the end of it. Do you understand? You must do what it takes."

"We won't make it," she said. "*I* won't. You saw Annie's book. I'm tied up with you."

"We don't know that," I argued. The next words clawed at my throat, words I'd been considering more and more often lately. I locked my gaze on Bea's. "The only thing I do know is that it'll be over soon one way or the other. And if it comes to it, it's better if I do it willingly."

Bea's eyes widened, understanding dawning.

"Em, don't..."

"I could do it," I said fiercely. "One big Giving. All I have left to pay the debt. I could finish this. And maybe that would be enough to banish him too."

I pulled a crumpled cigarette from my pocket and tried to light it from the scab on my lip. The blood twisted, magic guttering and then dying. Nothing. I shifted so that my hands were pressed tightly between my knees, so I wouldn't see how badly they shook.

This—my death—was the only plan that would sever my bonds to both Bea and Annie without hurting them. It was the only thing that might keep everybody else safe from this curse. In truth, giving up was fast becoming my only option.

My only worry was whether my magic would let me.

Chapter Five

Annie

Crow Trap was already humming to life when I left my father's house, the sun shining, girls whispering outside a café that I had visited not long ago. The streets were teeming with families taking advantage of the warm weather. A few café patrons had spilled out into the road, the tables they sat at laid with bright white cloths, and half a dozen people queued beneath a sign for *Madame Leroux's Faux Palmistry*.

I drove directly to the office at the address Jonas Anderson had given me before we had met, finding a squat, ugly-looking building at the end of a street not far from the museum. My heart was in my mouth the whole way, my palms sweating. I wasn't sure what my plan was, but fear swallowed any reasonable logic.

I parked the car outside the office and rushed inside before I could change my mind. There was a dim, sparse entryway with a small lounge and a receptionist in drab uniform who told me to wait.

Moments later Mr. Anderson appeared, bounding down the stairs in his usual cheerful manner, another perfectly cut suit with ridiculous, glittering cuff links. He stopped, however, when he saw my face.

"Miss Mason, what a sur—"

"Who else has keys to my father's house?" I demanded.

Anderson looked over his shoulder at the receptionist, who hovered, and she quickly ducked out of sight. He made to lay a hand on my arm, to guide me into the offices ahead, but I pulled back. I could hear a general hum of chatter, male voices and the *click-clack* of typewriter keys.

"Who else?" I repeated.

"There is a spare key for the front door, which I've kept with your papers," he said. His face shifted in concern. "Why, what's happened?"

"Who has access to the key?"

"Well, my secretary for starters. My colleagues too. We all knew your father, though, and wouldn't do anything untoward."

"Somebody has broken in. They've ruined everything!" My voice was so high and loud that Anderson's face grew ruddy with embarrassment.

He made for my arm again. "My dear, what are you saying?"

I dodged out of reach. It was hot in this building despite its dimness, and sweat beaded on my forehead. I refused to let the panic have me.

"Do you know who might have been in his house? Any of your colleagues?" I asked. "My father had some things. *Private* things. They've been disturbed."

Anderson straightened. "Not here," he said abruptly, his whole posture shifting as he glanced over his shoulder again. "Outside."

This time he didn't try to touch me but opened the door and gestured that I should follow him out onto the street. I took a moment to draw in a lungful of fresh air before I rounded on him.

"Do you know who did this?"

Anderson ran a hand through his greying hair nervously, glancing both ways down the street before asking, "Your father's private things—were they of, ah, a *sensitive* nature? Not strictly legal?"

He was so close I could smell his aftershave. His pale grey suit reflected the sunlight, so I had to shield my eyes.

I didn't know what to say. Admit the nature of my father's

collection and Anderson could turn on me, renounce me like he had Emmeline. *People like her*—that's what he'd said. On the other hand, if he knew who had been in the house, who had discovered the study...I wanted to know.

"Yes," I admitted quietly.

"What kind?"

"Books mostly. Some, uh, artefacts."

"Was there anything important? Anything rare or valuable?" Anderson's hazel eyes were alert and he watched me carefully as I fumbled.

"I—I'm not sure. I don't think—"

"You must think," he said gravely, his voice deepening. "Think hard, Miss Mason."

His urgency scared me. What was it to him the exact nature of the things my father kept in his private study?

"I really don't know," I said warily. "I'm not familiar with these things."

"You didn't catalogue them, then?" Anderson demanded. "When you were packing up his house?"

"I've hardly started packing," I hedged. A coldness crept into my voice as I stepped back. A beam of sunlight caught Anderson's face, and his eyes shone with more than just alarm.

"And you haven't been approached by anybody about your father? Anybody asking questions? You haven't let anybody in or given anything away?"

"There was a man at the museum," I said, fresh fear whipping through me. "He asked about my father. He frightened me—I ran. Do you think he—"

"You haven't seen him again since?" The lawyer's features morphed into a scowl. "You didn't let him into house?"

"No!"

"Well, what proof do you have of a break-in if you have nothing catalogued?" he pressed.

"I told you, my father's things were disturbed. Damaged."

"I always warned him." Anderson's voice was a hiss as he

continued. "I warned your father this would happen. Miss Mason, you must be very careful. The people here would have you believe that magic lives and breathes in these trees and rocks, but it is not that straightforward. As much distaste as I have for lawbreakers, there are others who have *more*. For as long as magic has lived on this island, so have those who have coveted its power for their own, those who would use it for ill or hoard these treasures for themselves. It's not worth the risk to get wrapped up in all of that.

"If your father had things of this nature, books and artefacts as you say, they are not safe in that house. Not any longer. It puts you in danger."

"How did they know about my father?" I blurted. "Whoever was in the house—how did they know? Was it the—" I almost said *Council* but held back. How much did Anderson know?

"I couldn't say. Your father was a brilliant man. People knew him while he did not know them. If this goes public, *you* will be the one to feel their wrath, my dear. I suggest you get rid of what's left of his things. Bring them to me and I'll do it for you. Do not let anybody see these items again, and keep no record."

The warning was sharp, but it sat strangely in the air, tinged with another nameless thing. It felt like pressure, like Anderson was waiting for me to be grateful. Waiting for me to let my helplessness cow me. All I felt was fire.

"No," I said, squaring up. "I can get rid of them myself. Just— give me my father's key. The spare. I want it."

"Miss Mason," Anderson tried.

"No," I pushed. "Now, Mr. Anderson. Please. I'm not leaving without it."

For a second, just a second, I thought I saw a flicker of anger in his eyes, but it was gone so fast I was sure I'd imagined it.

Chapter Six

Annie

I drove the short distance to the museum, unable to consider going home. To be so close to Emmeline and Bea and yet unable to do anything. My thoughts turned to Arthur, to the vision I had seen.

The vision he had wanted me to see.

He had held my magic pinned and said, *Look, look what happened. Look what magic took from me.* There had to be a reason why.

As I drove I was half-alert, my eyes searching the street corners for one I recognised. Crows flocked above the museum as I drove past it.

One part of me, the old part that still thought magic was for other people, warned it was futile. I'd be better off climbing the walls at home in case Bea or Emmeline needed me. Another more eager part of me, a part with fangs and claws and a bloody bandage around her arm, remembered the vision of Bea by the water, how Emmeline and I had saved her because of it.

So I slowed. I breathed, focusing on the details. I pushed aside thoughts of my father, of Bea, and tried to recall the vision, matching trees and street signs against what I could remember. I considered crooked shingles and lush green lawns bordered by stubby fences.

The street came into sight as I rounded a bend, and my stomach dipped in anticipation. It was the one from the beginning of the vision. I slammed the car to a halt and clambered out.

Here was a narrow crook of houses that leaned together like friendly neighbours, painted in various shades of white and grey and dusty rose. This was the first real sign of the islanders I'd heard about—the people who ran the shops, who cleaned the houses of the rich people and manned the beach tents. The real people, not led by money or false magic—the ones who reminded me of Mam and home.

There were a handful of people out enjoying the sunshine, mothers with prams and young children in tow. I searched each one for a flash of brown hair, warm cheeks, but my memory was hazy.

I walked until the street began to narrow. My legs ached and exhaustion threaded through me. I hadn't slept properly in days, couldn't remember the last full meal I had eaten. I had just turned to head back towards my car when my attention snagged.

The house at the end of the row was small, nice but badly in need of a fresh coat of paint. It was the same eggshell blue I'd seen in my vision.

My heart slammed in my chest.

I stood in the street for what felt like an age. I couldn't walk away. It felt like the world had shifted and left me, only me, standing there, out of place and out of time.

I was far enough away that I didn't hear the footsteps right away, and when I did I half turned to see. Back the way I'd walked there was a child toddling down the street at full tilt. He was young, perhaps only two years old, with a crop of golden curls. His mother panted after him, her arms laden with bags and a hatbox that framed her incredibly pregnant belly.

"Georgie-boy, you are such a handful! Come now, we have to get some food in us both before your appointment."

The world roared as realisation swept me backwards, out of sight behind a crooked elm tree housing four big, silent crows.

It was *her*.

She was shorter than I expected. She swiped sweat from her

WILD AND WICKED THINGS 353

brow with the back of her forearm as the sun beat down. The little boy wriggled as she grabbed his wrist, and he let out a plaintive cry.

The boy was the spit of the painting I'd seen of Arthur in Bea's house. Same glorious golden curls, same round face and wide blue eyes. A wave of sadness hit me. This was the life I had stolen from Arthur as surely as magic had. This was his son, his blood. This boy might have been his future.

I watched as the woman fished her door keys out, lifted the bundle of bags and boxes up the short front steps of the little blue house and in through the door. She hefted the boy up onto her hip in a practised swing.

I didn't know how long I stood under the shade of the elm tree. Too long. The sun had moved directly overhead, the heat dripping through the leaves, sweat slicking my skin under my dress.

I didn't move.

Thoughts began to swim. They were dark thoughts, soured by desperation. Emmeline had said that the debt could be broken by blood—close blood. I'd thought Bea's child a possibility, but Emmeline was too weak to wait.

Here, though, was a child carrying Arthur's blood. Could the child help to release Emmeline from the debt's clutches? Is that what Arthur had wanted me to see? Perhaps there was some human part still inside whatever energy devoured Bea. Perhaps whatever was left of the old Arthur had only wanted an end.

I didn't know enough to guess how much blood Emmeline would need. I didn't know if it would work, if the boy's mother would agree, if a child could consent to such a thing. And all the while I was sick to my stomach, angry with myself for thinking such things and yet knowing I couldn't ignore them. Not while this was our only glimmer of hope.

I reluctantly left the row of painted houses, heading back towards my car. I wanted to run straight to Emmeline, to tell her what I'd found. To insist she tell me that I was wrong, or that I was right, and take the burden off my shoulders. It was what I would have done only weeks ago.

Instead I walked far enough down the street that I could only just see the blue house. There was a low wall on the opposite side of the road that ran between two houses, and I perched uncomfortably, waiting.

I sat with alarming patience, a plan forming somewhere in the recesses of my thoughts. Rather than an absence of fear or disbelief, instead I found a reserve of what felt remarkably like courage, a shimmering, twisting black thing inside me that urged me to wait, wait, *wait* until the door of the blue house finally opened once again, and the woman and her young son stepped squinting back into the sunlight.

I watched, panic thrumming under my skin, as mother and son walked down the road hand in hand. I waited, gaze averted, as they passed me, heading back towards town. Farther down the road the boy stopped to pick up a ribbon that blew down the street.

Neither of them noticed me. Or if they did, the woman did not find me strange. They did not realise what I meant to do.

Once they were gone, I hurried back to the blue house at the end of the terraced street. There was a small gap at the end of the row, between these houses and the next. It was narrow, perhaps only just wide enough to squeeze through, but I suspected it might lead to the back gardens like the ones back home.

I was right. I shoved and scraped my way through, my elbows complaining after the second and third times that I skinned them. Finally I came out on the other side in a dense patch of greenery. It was a garden—if you could call it that. A lush, wildly overgrown patch of grass and shrubbery. I worked my way back to the right house, approaching it as though it was a cat I might startle.

The door was locked. Through the window I spied a small kitchen with a round table. The window frame creaked when I leaned against it.

With a sharp exhale I slid a fingernail underneath the corner and lifted. It started to give. I stopped for a moment, my breath coming thick and fast and my thoughts roaring ahead. What was I doing?

Before I could give myself a reason not to, I'd pulled the window open. It was low enough that I could hoist myself through and into the woman's kitchen, elbows and knees barking again as I slid gracelessly to the floor.

It was tidy enough, dimly lit, with evidence of two lives scattered throughout. Clothes were drying neatly on a wooden airer, dresses and gloves and little brown socks. There was a half-drunk glass of water on the side, reminding me that she could be back any minute.

I walked hesitantly through into a hallway, noting a staircase and a lounge. I had no idea what I was looking for. Signs of a husband, perhaps. Or signs of a lack of one. I saw no men's slippers, no smoking jacket—or clothes of any kind except for her own and the boy's.

In the lounge there were toys scattered from a small woven basket, expensive-looking dolls and wooden trucks spilling far into the room. A few books sat next to a pile of knitting and mending. The whole place had a zigzag air about it. Expensive things were scattered sparingly through the small space. A pretty gold filigree picture frame with a painting of the young boy, a beautiful glass vase filled with wilting peonies and violets that had once been vibrant and lush.

The clothes I'd seen in the kitchen were the same. The dresses and gloves were old and worn, but the boy's clothes were new. I trailed through the house, finding no sign of a man.

I paused at the bottom of the stairs. I should leave. Instead I crept upwards, not daring to use the bannister to steady myself. My breath came in little panicked puffs, but I was surprisingly calm, my whole life leading me to this moment. This gentle, intrusive crime.

Upstairs I found a bathroom. No shaving set, no hair pomade, only a few beauty oils and an old boar-bristle brush with a tarnished handle. I found the boy's room next. It was as big as the lounge, decorated in white and blue, little wooden ships lining the window and a mobile hanging above his bed. I didn't step inside.

I stood outside the main bedroom, frustration arcing up and down my arms and making my hands tingle. I should come back with Emmeline, or at least learn how to cast one of those wards. Absurdly, I wished for my father, for the guidance I had never known I needed.

But he wasn't here, and I was. I nudged the door open with my foot. This was a smaller room than the boy's, with a double bed cramped between a dresser and the wall. It was spotlessly clean, every surface washed or polished, the bed pristinely made but welcoming. Expectant.

I peered around, drinking in detail after detail. How different this room was from the one at Bea's house. How homely it felt, how warm. I crossed the thin carpet and found myself staring at a block of notepaper beside the bed, a leather-strapped wristwatch sitting next to it. The notepaper was expensive, creamy and thick, headed with a bouquet of violets. Another gift? The word *Violet*—the woman's name, I realised with a shiver—embossed on each page in gold.

The sheet on top was dark with messy scrawl. I leaned in and saw a list, words leaping out at me like fireworks, my brain unable to keep up.

> *Buy hat for dinner—white and rose pink?*
> *Georgie at doctor's!!*
> *Dinner tomorrow. Salad?*
> *Ask about dog again?*
> *Give Arthur his watch back.*

Waxing Light

R. Crowther

Imbolc—February Quickening

*T*hings have only grown worse since the solstice. Before, I thought my whole collection was putting me in danger. I was wrong. The grimoire is the culprit. It has taken me many years to understand the breadth of its power. With my study complete, it only fills me with unspeakable dread.

It is too powerful, and too tempting. For all of us, but especially for him. He thinks I cannot see his renewed interest in the book, that I haven't noticed the way he speaks about nothing but glory and power. At first I thought it was the war, the good that we did then—and now—filling his head with delusions of grandeur. Not anymore.

The book belongs somewhere else, somewhere safer than here. Where? Outside of Crow Island it would be burned—and as much as I know this would be for the best, I can't bring myself to let that happen.

I have faith that the Goddess will guide me. Just as she did all those years ago, when I left my family. I am increasingly glad that I did not stay. The vision I had, a grey death shroud over A——'s beautiful golden head, my sins putting her in mortal danger—I still sometimes see it in my mind. The wicked curve of a knife, burning blood inside her, the call of the ocean in her veins.

I wondered for many years if my escape made me a coward. In fact it was the bravest thing I have ever done.

At least she will never know the weight of her magic. I hope that I will live long enough that the binding I placed on her will remain for a good many years. Enough years, I hope, that she will never know magic's pull. That she will be grown before she senses the twinge, and puts it down to nothing more than... longing.

My only hope is that I have done enough to keep her safe after I am gone.

Chapter Seven

Emmeline

I slept on the floor beside Bea's bed. I craved my own bedroom, the bed that would smell like her—like Annie—but I couldn't bear to leave Bea. Instead I dozed, cocooned myself in the wind blowing warm, salt-scented air through the window, right into my nightmares.

I dreamed of Cross House, of the crow maidens come to life. Their hands were turned to claws to avenge Cilla, their mother. They had always hated me because I could never be strong enough to rule this house like she had.

The maidens' luscious wings spread dark as night as they moved like shadows through the empty rooms. The house rejoiced. It was not built to be empty; it drank the blue swing of jazz like water, the gold and dazzle of party frocks like wine. These cavernous rooms were empty coffins, three orphans' bones not enough to sate them.

The crow girls plagued me through the glittering ballroom, through the twisting attic corridors and down into the cellar, where we stored our kazam in vials and jars, sealed crates of rich, dark wine whose scents spilled into the air. I felt the scrape of their claws on the back of my neck, the cold weight of their birdlike stares—a reminder that there was always time to fall.

I stood in the garden, our old vegetable patch turned to ashes the colour of storm clouds. The fountain was empty. The crow maidens were nowhere and somehow everywhere. The ground teemed with little black worms, and I shook with the knowledge that it could just as easily be Nathan or Isobel buried beneath the dirt.

Death had followed me here—from the crooked, happy house I'd shared with my aunt—to this bedevilled place. It would follow me wherever I went.

It would be the kindest thing for me to go before the debt took me. Yet, even in my dreams, that growing, glittering silver core pulsated deep in my lungs, my heart. I had tried to fight it. I fought it still. It was everything that scared me, a lack of independence that felt like a cage.

It was everything I needed.

When I woke, head pounding and body aching, it was still early, the morning air cool with the promising kiss of a pleasant summer day despite the curling dread inside Cross House. Cotton clouds already dotted the sky, six beautiful crows scattered on the roof outside the window.

Bea was not in her bed.

The sage was long burned out and the room smelled stale with sleep. Bea's sheets were still warm, though. She couldn't have been gone long. I called for Nathan and Isobel as I tumbled into the hallway, our footsteps thundering as we ran from room to room calling Bea's name.

Nathan hadn't heard her as he set up the ballroom for tonight's party, hauled brew after brew of Isobel's new collection upstairs to fill the shining glass decanters and crystal goblets. Isobel hadn't heard her as she parcelled up yet another salve for Hilda's daughter, her fingertips dyed red with beetroot that was as dark as blood.

Bea must have been silent as a ghost, for my dreams had been fractured by sleeplessness. I left Nathan and Isobel searching inside and raced out into the garden. The sun was warm on my shoulders. As I ran I thought over and over: the party was a bad idea. If I couldn't keep a handle on Bea in her own bedroom, how would I do it with a house full of people tonight?

I paused for a moment and listened for anything beyond the telltale surf sounds. The beach outside my house had always been quiet, far enough away from the back of the crescent where the families holidayed in grand hotels with red-and-white-striped awnings. I thought of all the days and long nights after Bea left that I had found myself sitting on the little dock between my house and the small empty cottage next door, my eyes scanning the horizon, waiting to see if she would see my purple light and come back.

I wished Annie was here. She would know where Bea might go; they surely had enough history between them. She couldn't be here, but selfishly I wanted her anyway.

I inhaled and told myself to stop. Annie wasn't *for me*. She could never be mine.

I had to stop the vinculum from growing more than it had in my panic. I had to forget the press of her body against mine, the steady lull of her heartbeat, the sweet scent of her hair on my pillow.

Then I heard it. A scuffling, burrowing sound. I followed the sound around the edge of the greenhouse to where the vegetable patch extended into our own private graveyard.

The dirt was churned. Two fresh mounds of it sat on either side of the grave, the earth brown and fragrant. And in the middle sat Bea. She wore only her nightdress, which had been mouldered to a dense grey-red by the muck.

"Bea? What are you doing?"

She looked up, her face slack. Her mouth rounded into a little O and she squinted up at me, blinking, colour leaking back into her cheeks. Mud was streaked up her arms, embedded in the scratches she had given herself yesterday, clumps in her hair and caked around her bare knees.

"I have no idea." She blinked, the last remaining confusion dropping away like a mirage. "What time is it?"

"Still early," I said.

She let me help her to her feet. I kicked the dirt back into the holes she had dug and took her firmly by the hand, guiding her back to the house.

"What's the last thing you remember?" I asked.

"The pain," she said quietly. One of her hands wandered absently to her stomach, and she left a grubby handprint behind. "Then the dirt in my hands. The sun." She frowned. "I don't know. It's all such a mess, isn't it, darling?"

"I know." I helped her inside through the back door. The staff for the party would be arriving soon, and they couldn't see Bea looking like this. They had probably better not see her at all.

"I'll make this better," I swore. "I promise you, Bea. After the party I'll finish it."

———◦•◦———

The house glittered. The staff moved seamlessly through the rooms carrying trays of canapés and kyraz. We had opted for the extra-strong stuff and it was going down a treat. People forgot that the purple light had been extinguished this week, or they at least forgot to be mad about it, lost themselves in the foxtrot, in the arms of strangers, in the heady scent of Nathan's white roses. The richest people from all over Crow Trap milled in my foyer, dusted my reception rooms with their false praise and approval. They drank the concoctions, tasting the glamour, the sweetness of relinquishing control.

You could spot the holidayers a mile off. They wore last summer's fashion—because to be entirely up-to-date was uncouth—and they swanned through my house like they owned it. They greeted old friends, threw shiny gold coins into my fountain, draped their shawls over the crow maidens, and cried on the beach when they felt the magic leak from their veins, normality too painful to endure.

I surveyed it all from the mezzanine in the ballroom, Nathan not far away. I could not shake the warning of my Drowning Boy, and Nathan sensed enough of my concern to stay close. He pointed out several visiting mainlanders, one of whom we hadn't seen for years. We had always suspected him to be involved with the Council, and seeing him amongst the guests tonight ratcheted up the tension in my bones, Isobel's reminder about them in my ear.

Nathan hung back, cloaked in shadows, unwilling to be seen by the men who had broken him once before, whom Cilla had pumped for money, for praise, for supply chains and legal know-how. These men had once ruled this town, and now they fought for scraps, every single one of them hungry for a glory that made them feel as good as avoiding European bloodshed had.

I muttered one of my oldest spells and nibbled the edge of my tongue until I drew the tiniest amount of blood. Nathan's outline shimmered faintly. I didn't let him see the way I cringed when my veins constricted, when my body ached for another Giving. *Another, another, another...*

I searched the crowded ballroom. I was looking for Sergeant Perry, who was usually here in his subtle Council regalia with two young women on his arm and a full bottle of kazam in his blood. Nathan's eyes circled the room, scanning for him from afar.

Perry had been a member of the Council for longer than I had been alive and a member of the police force for almost as long. He should have warned us about the constable who'd questioned Annie, alerted us that he was coming, as had been our agreement since Cilla. I remembered what Annie had said, about a man at the museum asking about her father, and wondered if this might have even been him—or another councilman sniffing around. My head felt full of Cilla's old politics, plan after plan forming and dissolving in my mind.

I forced my lips to curve around this highball glass filled with liquor I couldn't taste. We needed to get through tonight, and after that... I would figure it out.

Tonight's party had taken on a kind of frenetic air, magic and alcohol mingling. I pushed down the clenching in every inch of me and the strange emptiness in my chest where the vinculum slumbered. Its absence consumed me.

Nathan appeared at my shoulder, following my gaze into the crowd.

"I haven't seen her," Nathan said, "if that's what you're going to ask."

I swivelled and raised an eyebrow at him. "Who? Bea's still upstairs, isn't she?"

"Annie. *Obviously.*"

I turned away, afraid of what Nathan might see. "She can't be here, but I'd rather she was here than out there." I gestured to the sea of dancers below, hot jazz spinning in their blood, kazam in their veins.

"Bea's got Isobel to check on her. Annie can take care of herself," Nathan said. "She's strong."

He said these last words carefully, each one measured. This was him warning me. He knew about the vinculum. I'd told him about Annie's magic, but he must have sensed the bond blossoming, becoming brighter and stronger and sharper—more dangerous. I couldn't hide it anymore.

Nathan always knew me better than anybody.

"I know," I said, hoping he understood what I meant.

I let my eyes rove over the sea of jewel-toned dresses, the small jazz band we'd hired playing in the corner of the ballroom. How many of these people had I ever met? How many had been invited and how many had come anyway?

I felt ill watching them, although I kept my face a mask of casual arrogance. These people didn't know me, but all of them knew *of* me. Emmeline Delacroix, the great-niece of the famed Cilla Delacroix.

We were the witches of Cross House. The unspoken rulers of Crow Island. We sold desires, traded in dreams; we gave people what they wanted, regardless of what they needed. Nathan, Isobel, and I were royalty—untouched by the law.

It was all a lie.

I rolled my shoulders back. I was thinking about the konjure cards again. The Drowning Boy. Arthur. Bea. The same sensation of *wrongness* pooled in my gut as it had then. I forced myself back into this old familiar role, face schooled to neutrality, my intricately embroidered waistcoat and tailored lavender suit the armour I wore like Nathan wore his butler's garb.

"I'm going to go and see about clients," I said. "There will be a queue, and we don't want it to go on all night. Tell Isobel that I'll do time-sensitive ones only and then take over to watch Bea. And get Ruth and a couple of the other waiters to do another circuit and make sure none of our revellers have strayed near the greenhouse."

Nathan wasn't watching me anymore.

The ballroom was awash with colour and at first I didn't see her, but her presence bloomed in the cord inside the cavity of my chest, miraculous and wild. I let it grow before I snatched it back.

Her curled hair was like freshly burnished gold and her skin fresh as cream. She wore a dress made of silver spangles that danced when she moved like moonbeams through swaying pines.

"Annie."

Nathan and I moved at the same time, driven by Annie's expression. I left the mezzanine balcony and crossed the ballroom, dodging and weaving between the dancers in their kitten heels and shiny wingtips. Annie was breathless. I had almost reached her, my chest swelling, an admonishment on my tongue that she was here, one that would be insincere.

Her gaze flicked behind me, towards the mezzanine.

She froze.

Chapter Eight

Annie

I drove home as fast as I dared. I was in a sweat, my dress soaked under the arms and my hands clammy on the steering wheel. Arthur's watch—I had stolen it—burned against my thigh with imaginary heat. I could think of little else.

It was getting dark already. The world had shifted again. The fear that had been surging in my body on and off for more than a week felt like a caged beast prowling in my skin.

When I got home I could already hear the sounds of Emmeline's party beginning. I was too exhausted to acknowledge the fresh wave of fear that shot through me. I let myself into my house and ran for the kitchen, where the book I had taken from my father's attic was still hidden. I let out a sigh of relief, gathering it to my chest and carrying it into the bedroom—where my father's journal was still, untouched, under the mattress.

I pulled it out, the front cover bent and moulded, lightly, to the shape of my body from the few hours I had actually spent sleeping on it. My heartbeat slowed, little by little, as I held the notebook in my hands. I pictured my father holding it like this, caressing the embossed letters on the front. *R. Crowther.*

I turned through the pages of the notebook with cold fingers, my father's sloping hand on every page. I had not read it properly before. Only that section about the party, about Emmeline, about Cross House, a few other sparse entries that made no sense. I should have read more.

Perhaps it would have helped me to stay away.

I flicked farther ahead, though it was too late. There were recipes, spells. Crossings out and pages that held pressed flowers and elegant watercolour paintings. A journal of his life, and his craft.

A twisting emotion caught in my throat. It all felt so heavy. All that he had done to protect me, and I had simply thrown it away. Why had he brought me here? He must have known the magic in my blood would call to the island like a homecoming.

What would he have thought about Emmeline, about her bargain and the debt—about that little boy and his mother, a solution that made my heart ache. Was it so awful to feel a bubble of hope inside me? Even if the hope was mingled with a bone-deep grief over what I had done?

How much of my desire to help Bea and Emmeline came from my own selfish desire to feel needed? To make amends? With startling clarity I understood: it didn't matter. This was the only option we had.

I rubbed at my eyes angrily, until they felt bruised, before turning back to the journal.

There was a ritual here, written in black ink next to an image of a figure standing solid and pale beneath the blackness of the sky. At the top he had written in thick, curling letters: *Drawing Down the Moon*.

Beneath the picture were instructions followed by another small block of text.

The High Priestess (or in this case Priest) invokes the spirit of the Goddess in this precious ritual. Somewhat like the Witch Bond, it is a combining of power. Through the trance one enters, the coven may hear the words of the Goddess herself, her wisdom and her warmth. I have been contemplating such a ritual. Now is the time more than ever to bring faith to our circle, but I suspect some members of the coven will be unwilling given its unpredictability and the murmurings of a change in the law. The war has hit us all hard. M——lost her son last week, another boy claimed by the battlefield.

Perhaps I shall wait, and J——and I can try this on our own first.

The entry was dated October five years ago. I flicked ahead, but there was no more mention of the ritual. I folded the pages closed and held the journal to my chest, breathing in its leathery scent.

I couldn't sit here forever. I had to go to the party. I had to talk to Bea, to Emmeline, to tell them about the boy. It was the only solution that didn't rely on Emmeline, on her magic.

I allowed myself one moment more to dwell on how angry and awful and tired I felt, and then I got to my feet.

I chose a dress to change into, bundling the journal and the other book in the outfit I took off and hiding them back under my mattress. I wrapped a headband around my curls to tame their wildness and splashed water on my face as an afterthought, washing away the grime of the day. I would go to Emmeline, and I would tell her what I had learned, and she would have a plan.

And then the doorbell rang.

———◦●◦———

I froze in place, seconds ticking by. What if it was the police again? What if they'd figured out about my friendship with Bea? I could leave through the back door, I considered. I could run to the party and find Emmeline—and what if I led them directly to her?

I swallowed my fear and made an attempt at casualness as I pulled the door open.

"Hello, Miss Mason."

It was Mr. Anderson.

He still wore his grey suit from earlier, those same ridiculous cuff links glimmering, only he looked so out of place here, so much bigger than I remembered, that it stole my breath. "Still ignoring my advice about mingling with *them*, I see."

I glanced towards Emmeline's house, bright like a beacon. The sound of laughter spilled out onto the lawn, jazz music and the raucous thunder of feet as a fast tune played. When I looked back, Anderson's expression had shifted. It was colder. Not cruel, but calculating. I gripped the doorframe nervously.

"What are you doing here?" I said. It wasn't polite. Neither was this, though. No respectable man would call on a single young woman at night. This wasn't a missed appointment. This wasn't fatherly advice.

I wanted to shut the door in his face, but I didn't. Some sliver of self-preservation, some tiny part of me that wasn't thinking about Bea and Emmeline and their problems, stopped me. My gaze drifted to his chest, to the tiny gold tiepin that had not been visible before, tucked underneath his jacket. The man at the museum...Anderson...The way Anderson had acted when I told him of the break-in at my father's house. A cold chill snaked through me.

It was him. *He* had destroyed my father's things.

I had to find out what he wanted.

"I think you'd better invite me inside so we can talk privately," Anderson said.

"No, thank you. I'm about to go out and the house isn't fit for visitors." I wondered, if I screamed, whether anybody at Cross House would hear me.

"I think you'd better," Anderson repeated.

"Why?"

"Because I don't want to discuss matters regarding your father—and his *interests*—out here on your doorstep."

I was right, then.

"No." I swallowed hard. "Whatever you have to say you can say right here."

Anderson's double blink was the only sign of his surprise. He recovered quickly and I tried to keep my back straight despite my watery bowels. I searched for the tenuous bubble of magic inside me, but it was hidden, whether by fear or common sense I didn't know, and I didn't dare close my eyes to try to call it when I didn't know what I'd do with it if I found it. I couldn't take the risk.

"I'll be frank with you, Miss Mason. Your father wasn't just my client or my friend. He was a partner of sorts. A mentor, ah, many years ago. That's why he left me to sort out his affairs. That's why I encouraged you to come here, because I thought it was what he would have wanted. It's what *I* would have wanted. That's why I gave you the advance for the cottage. I thought you needed to be here." Anderson paused as though this should be of interest, but I stared back blankly, ignoring the discomfort that wriggled inside me. Anderson had brought me here—not my father.

"Your father was a great man," Anderson went on. "Very clever. He did all sorts of studies, you know. Wrote for papers and the like. Very well respected in our community. Of course, you wouldn't actually know that, would you? Since you've hardly cared about learning who he was."

I fought the hot feeling in my belly, kept my gaze level.

"I reached out to you again and again, offered both help and advice. You haven't taken me up on the offer. I've been thinking about today. How rude you were. Just what kind of daughter are you?"

This time I definitely didn't imagine the shift in Anderson's expression.

"Not yours," I retorted as hotly as I dared.

"Well, I'm grateful for that truth. You're just like him, you know. Selfish. Careless. He stole an item from me before he died. I was hoping you'd come across it before somebody else did, that I wouldn't have to do this. I thought you might ask me about it."

"I don't know what you want me to do about any of this," I snapped. I tried to hide my trembling legs, but I still probably looked exactly like what I was: scared and alone. "As you so carefully reminded me, I know nothing about him—and he knew nothing about me."

"I wanted to wait until you were ready. I warned you about your *neighbour.*" He pulled a face. "I can see that her influence is as corruptive as I thought it might be."

"I—"

"I want to be reasonable with you, Miss Mason," he said. "All I want is what your father took. It was a book. I think you know the kind I mean—you've seen the sorts of things your father was up to. I cannot have you sharing its secrets with the rest of them—or with *her*. It's bad enough that they're already on you like vultures."

"I don't know what you're talking about."

"Oh, I'm sure you do. I think you know exactly what I'm talking about. The book he stole from me is an heirloom, an antique. There are others who want it—yes, like the man you told me about, I'm sure. But it is mine. Your father and I were working on a thesis together, and he never gave it back. I was hoping I might be mistaken, that it might be safe still, but your father's study... Well, I'm almost certain it's not in there."

I thought of the book I had brought home, the one that contained the Awakening spell. That sat bundled under my bed. A spark of recognition lit inside me, and for a second—just one second—the meek Annie, the mouse, wanted to run and grab it and hand it over. Share the burden of its dark potential with somebody else.

I didn't move.

I had seen firsthand the damage this book could do in the wrong hands. What if my father had kept it from Anderson and those others who sought it on purpose? As little as I knew of him, the thought that he would steal this book for academic research didn't sit well with me.

"I said I've got no idea what you're talking about," I repeated firmly. I raised my chin and kept my voice as level as I could. "There were hundreds of books in my father's study, which I assume you well know since you have seen it. They're gone, burned to a crisp. Perhaps you set the wrong ones alight, Mr. Anderson."

"Maybe you have it here. I can just come and take it." Anderson moved forward again. This time the cold gleam in his eyes was beyond aggressive. It was like calling to like, a recognition sparking somewhere in my blood. Perhaps these men—Anderson, the man at the museum, my *father*—were the councilmen Emmeline had warned me away from. Men desperate for power, for magic, for money, lost without a war to focus them.

"Mr. Anderson, I think you're drunk," I said. "You need to go home and stop bothering me before I call the police. I'm not afraid to do it. My father's study can be empty in mere hours and you'll have no proof. I, on the other hand, am not afraid to tell them that you came here at night looking for some kind of—of *spell book*. How do you think they'll feel about that?"

Anderson faltered. If he had seen us, seen Bea, Arthur, the empty grave that day beside the greenhouse, he did not mention it. Instead I could see his face change. It grew calm. Still.

Cunning.

I wasn't about to wait around to find out what he would do next. I shut the door in his face. I walked, slowly, into my bedroom, slid my father's journal and the book from their hiding place under the bed, and shoved them into a satchel, which I tossed over my shoulder.

And then I ran.

Out the back door, the sand cold and spilling into my shoes. Up the stone stairs, past the silent gardens where people did not, perhaps *could* not tread, their feet bewitched by some invisible force. I ran into the glittering darkness of Emmeline's familiar house.

The ballroom was alive, thronging with a hundred people in sparkling gowns, their faces flushed with Isobel's bootleg kazam. A tower of champagne flutes flowed with purple-white kyraz, its sweet summer scent alluring with the promise of a good time; a piano tinkled, the jazz band swinging as a crowd of women danced a shimmy on Emmeline's dining table. The walls were crowded with white blooms. Their floral scent overpowered me as I threaded deeper, losing myself in the chaos.

There was only one thought in my mind.

Emmeline.

And—there she was. I lost myself for a moment at the sight of her as the tether in my chest came unstuck. Her hair was slick, her dark eyes roving the room, and her expression full of the raw, feral beauty I had come to expect. She wore a lavender summer suit with the sleeves of her jacket rolled up, and the way she stood, with her thumbs hooked in her pockets, made my knees tremble with a different emotion altogether. Whether it was the adrenaline or not, I only wanted to kiss her, to forget everything else.

She saw me, and she and Nathan were rushing into the crush of bodies to meet me. I lost my words for a moment, and when I found them I couldn't get the right ones.

Before I had chance to explain, the world fell to silence, another tilt that threatened to send me crashing to my knees as I caught sight of the figure on the mezzanine.

It was Bea.

She stood on the balcony alone, surveying the party as if it was a circle of hell and she was the devil herself. She was Bea and yet she was *not* Bea, glowing from the inside with a golden darkness. Her gaze slid across the room to us. To me.

No matter what Emmeline had said, this wasn't just energy. It was Arthur, every arrogant, monstrous inch of him.

He had found a way in.

I'd thought, all along, that it was Bea he wanted to hurt. Bea, who had taken his children from him, who had stolen the woman he had loved and condemned him to a marriage driven by vicious, unwavering *need*.

But I was wrong. It wasn't that simple. It wasn't only Bea he wanted to hurt—because Bea hadn't killed him. I had.

Chapter Nine

Emmeline

The room hummed with collective excitement. Bea was ethereal in a gown of gold silk, the full skirts pooling around her elegantly and the pearls dotted along the bodice shining brightly. A gown I had seen before, once, on Cilla—at the end—left to moulder in a wardrobe because none of us had the heart to throw it away.

Bea's red hair was wild, untamed, her cheeks flushed. I could hardly see the bruises that had marred her beautiful face only this morning. When she moved, taking a confident step out onto the mezzanine balcony, there was a collective inhale from the crowd.

The slow glug-glug of the blood in my veins punctuated the moment as the poison of the debt recognised Arthur's spirit inside Bea and surged for it. I set off through the crowd.

Nathan was already ahead of me, not slowed by magic and exhaustion. Annie wasn't far behind him, dodging and weaving as noise began to swell again, chatter and curiosity.

"Do you think it's a show?"

"Just like the music hall!"

The musicians on the platform seemed unable to decide what to do. Some of them looked to me and Nathan, but others were talking amongst themselves, half their attention on Bea, who still stood on the balcony with her body glowing like she was lit from within.

Nobody was sober enough to realise that the way she commanded their attention wasn't normal. They saw only a red-haired angel, ethereal. Beautiful. Her copper curls nearly aflame with Arthur's light.

Nathan reached Bea, his pace slowing as he approached the stairs, his hands up in surrender like he was coaxing a wild dog.

"Look, Meredith, she's like that Hetty King. I bet they're doing a show!"

I tried to signal to the musicians, but they were no longer looking at me. The guests grew restless, their eyes lifting to watch Nathan expectantly. This wasn't supposed to happen.

"What are we going to do?" Annie was white-faced with panic. We were close to the stairs now. A lone musician had, mercifully, seen my frantic hand signals and begun to play again, a mournful, empty sound. "People will see."

"They're too drunk to remember it," Nathan said. He gestured to the guests on the dance floor, many of whom were still drinking, still dancing. "They'll think it's a fever dream."

"They will if she goes berserk again," Annie said earnestly.

I wanted to laugh. It built up inside my chest like an explosion. I fought it down, watching Nathan as he inched closer to Bea, who had not moved. She stood at the balcony, her stare fixed on the ball-room below, as if—

"Nathan, I think she's going to jump!" Annie screeched.

Nathan launched into a run, faster than me. He'd just about reached her when everything went to hell.

With one short, sharp movement that startled us all, Bea whipped around and twisted Nathan into her grip. She laid a hand on the back of his neck—her bare hand, his bare neck—and Nathan let out a cry of pain.

"Nathan!"

I jumped forward to haul him back—and that's when I noticed Bea's other hand, and the bone blade that sparkled under the chandelier.

"I wouldn't do that," she said.

Distantly, I heard the band swing into a fresh jazz number, and somebody squealed in delight. I could do nothing but watch as Bea grasped Nathan's neck in one pale hand with such strength that her nails cut into his skin, and I smelled as much as saw the blood beading there.

"Bea..." Annie pleaded.

Bea tilted her head. It was animalistic and hungry, her eyes roving Annie's face.

"Try again."

The voice was Bea's. The words were not. They were scooped out, filled with grave dirt and wriggling, biting worms.

"What do you want?" I asked.

Bea didn't break Annie's gaze as she answered my question. "You know what I want."

"I'm sorry," Annie said, and the words were everything. She trembled but her voice was steady, steadier than my heart.

Neither of us dared move for fear that Bea might slit Nathan's throat. My brother met my gaze, his eyes pleading.

"Sorry?" Bea scoffed, bitterness coating her words like tar. "You're *sorry?*"

"Please don't hurt him," Annie begged. "I didn't mean to—we didn't want to..."

"I didn't know there'd be magic tricks!" came a shout from below, not quite drowned by the music. I started to bite my lip, to call my blood—but I couldn't. It was too unpredictable. I couldn't risk Nathan's life.

"Bea—Arthur. *Please*," Annie begged. "We can talk about this."

"I don't want to talk," Bea snapped. She pressed the bone knife into Nathan's skin just beneath his jaw. A trickle of fresh red blood ran down to meet the pristine collar of his shirt. His face was ashen, the contact with Bea's skin enough already to make him sweat—Bea's consciousness and Arthur's together...It must hurt like hell. Like Cilla. Like me.

"Arthur, we can't do anything here. You must realise that."

"I want goddamn witnesses!" Bea yelled. She gave Nathan a little shove and he was forced to stumble closer to the edge of the balcony, where my guests were gathered beneath. There was a collective gasp as a few more dancers turned back to the "performance."

"Don't!" screamed Annie.

"You've got your audience," I hissed. "What do you want *right now?*"

"I want you to bring me back again. I can feel the thread. It's inside my head and it's eating me up. That thread—that goddamn thread. Just pull, pull…It's in my *brain*, the wanting and the aching—"

"What thread?" Annie asked.

"*LIFE!*"

Nathan grunted as Bea's grip tightened on his neck. His hands clenched at his sides, but otherwise he did not move.

A light flashed through the room. Nathan's eyes snapped open the same second that a clap of thunder rumbled around us. The sound was so loud that Bea stumbled, the sharp bone blade sliding against Nathan's neck. He yelled and I lunged at them, throwing myself with full force so that my elbow knocked the dagger away.

The thunder was inside. The chandelier disappeared inside a roiling, bruise-edged cloud. Another flash illuminated the room as the people downstairs began to scream—some with terror and some with delight, as the music stopped.

Annie shouted my name. I'd knocked Nathan clear of Bea's grasp, but I couldn't see yet whether he'd been hurt. Bea was trying to climb to her feet, unsteady in that haunted old gown of Cilla's.

Isobel.

She climbed the last of the stairs, her hair like a dark halo that sparked with electricity. Strands tensed like snakes, nipping and snapping at the magic in the air. Seconds later the clouds split like that day so many years ago in the yard when she had last found the magic deepest inside her and called forth the rain. The floor was instantly soaking, rivulets of water streaming towards the bannister. Bea slid from my grasp.

Isobel climbed with eyes that were clouded by the storm she had created, a maelstrom of purple rage. She didn't run, but she caught up with Bea in no time, the flood she had created diverging around her ankles to rush towards the rest of us. It pushed Bea towards the balcony, a wave of Isobel's rainwater gushing and driving at her.

Bea skidded away, her legs going straight through the bannister. All around us people were screaming. Those who had thought it was fun only moments ago were panicking as the rain fell in torrents and they were knocked to their knees, their clothes ruined, their fun extinguished. I heard the crashing of glasses and shouts of panic as another rolling clap of thunder echoed so loudly it rattled my bones.

"Isobel," I yelled, dragging myself off the floor.

Bea was hanging on for dear life, and for a second I saw a true flash of *her*—truly her—as fear made her scream. Isobel stood on the sleeve of her dress and Bea's other hand clung to the bannister, white with the effort.

"Help her!" Annie screamed.

I forced my body to move against the water. Isobel helped nobody but herself.

"Isobel, Nathan needs you. I need you. Please." The pleading tone was strange on my tongue, and I realised, with a sharp jolt, that I had never *asked* for their help. I had demanded it. Expected it. Shunned it.

Never asked.

"Please, Isobel, please," Bea begged. And it *was* Bea's voice, spoken through gritted teeth. "Help me. I know you are tired of helping everybody, but please, I'm begging you. Get him *out of my head*."

Isobel's chin lifted, barely. The rain slowed. The thunder rumbled, once, but distant. Her eyes fogged back to their normal colour, though not before both she and I had flung ourselves at Bea, hauling her back onto the balcony. Isobel grabbed Bea's wrists. The dagger had been lost somewhere in the deluge of water below.

I glanced downstairs. My guests were gone, driven out by the ungodly flood. My ballroom was ruined, almost half a foot deep in water already, debris floating, broken glasses and rose stems torn asunder. If there was a Goddess, she had deemed us unworthy and sent the mighty waters of her wrath to rinse us from the earth.

Annie reached for me and I held her to my chest. She was sopping wet, her golden hair stuck to the thin headband she wore across her forehead, her dress hanging off her and an old satchel banging against her legs from a battered strap. I could smell her, fresh and bright like midday on the ocean. Salt and lemon sharp. My stomach tumbled, the vinculum snapping between us taut as a wire.

"Are you all right?" she asked.

Bea let out a low laugh. Mirthless. I could see in her face, the set of her jaw, that Bea was gone again, eclipsed by Arthur's darkness.

"Look at you," came Arthur's words, each one thick, as though spoken through a glut of grave dirt. "You make me sick." Bea's head spun slowly, her nostrils flared and eyes alert, like a predator tracking each of us. She did not struggle against Isobel, merely opened her mouth in a grin so wide it looked painful. "Dear, sweet little Annie. I bet you wouldn't cling to her if you knew..."

"If I knew what?" Annie pulled back.

Dread made my body like lead.

"These walls whisper..." Arthur hissed. The words seemed to come from nowhere and everywhere all at once. Isobel shrank away, her grip going slack. Nathan looked faint. "There are spirits here... one in particular. She speaks to me, you know. Whispering, always whispering. Tales of agony. Of injustice."

Annie looked at me, a question in her gaze.

"No," I said.

"*Yes.*" Bea laughed again, though her mouth hardly moved. The sound was like the crackle of a flame. It reminded me—of Cilla. I swore I could smell her, ashes and red wine and blood. Nathan began to tremble, his shirt stained crimson. "I have seen things," Arthur went on. "I bet you've seen things too, haven't you, Annie. A perceptive little witch like you."

"Annie, don't listen—"

"The tales I've heard..." Arthur went on. "Red walls. Blood in the water." Bea stared right at me as he said, "Of a crow girl. A *murder.*"

Annie's face paled. She saw as Arthur's words hit me. There was a sudden flash of understanding in her eyes as she tightened her grip on the vinculum. A dreadful *knowing* that filled me with horror.

"Annie—"

She had to understand. This, as much as the vinculum, was why I had pushed her away. She was too good, too bright for me.

"Is it true?" Annie asked. "I thought I saw—I didn't know that's what it was. God, Emmeline, I didn't think for a second it was *real*. I thought I was having dreams, or . . . I don't know. When you didn't want to talk about her—I should have known. All this time you let me believe it was about Bea and Arthur, and it wasn't, was it? It was never just about them."

My throat was too tight for words. Isobel's eyes were soft and she gripped Bea tight as she began to cackle again. Nathan stared above our heads, his face troubled. If Annie was looking for reassurance, she wouldn't find it.

"I said *is it true?*"

Bea laughed harder.

"It's true," I whispered. "I killed Cilla."

Chapter Ten

They don't see him. He's been here the whole time; he watched the scene on the balcony—he alone seeing it for what it was. Not parlour tricks or a burst pipe. Not a nightmare or a kazam dream. Magic.

His body tightens at the thought of these uninitiated witches playing with power they do not understand. Power that should belong to him.

He had trusted Richard. His leader. His High Priest. Together, Richard said, they would help other witches who wanted to study the Craft. They would teach. Richard vowed he would build a collection so complete that no witch would ever become lost at the hands of their magic again.

Jonas had wanted to keep the book. When Richard explained, though, it all made sense. It was all for a greater good. They were moving forward, creating opportunity for those who had not had the chance to learn. Witches like Jonas, whose mother had abandoned him when he was just a boy, with only his weakness and the book—they would benefit from Richard's library. It was a noble cause.

After the war, a noble cause felt good. Less bloody than those battlefield boys whom they had tried to help, shell-shocked by the darkness levelled against them. The laws had changed, but magic had always existed on this moneyed isle and it would exist regardless. Richard only said they had to be careful, keep it a secret. Jonas understood.

Richard had a way with words, made it easy to part with his birthright. Richard explained that the grimoire was special. He said they could study it together.

If Jonas had known how rare it was, how others would crave its power... If he had known what the book could do in the right hands, he would never have parted with it. He had not understood the way his blood sang when he opened the book, when he tried to cast from it. He saw only his failures and thought that he was not ready for it.

He did not realise that all he was missing was desire. *Intent. Direction.*

Richard said he would teach him.

Richard had lied.

He kept it from Jonas, hidden away behind locked doors and wards. Like it was just another title in his growing collection. When he taught, Richard always chose lesser texts, children's spells, but never the grimoire.

It is Jonas's birthright, and he will be stalled no more.

He watches as Richard's daughter and the others leave the destruction of the ballroom behind. He follows them like a shadow, his magic guiding him gently through the shallow water still pooled in the grand room. Blending in is his speciality. Kindness as a weapon. He had hoped it would win her over, or that burning those useless texts might scare her, but he has a few more tricks up his sleeve.

He does not know exactly what happened here tonight, but he does not care. It is the perfect distraction. Because he knows *the book is here. He can sense it.*

Finally, after years of searching, the tug of it is once again under his skin, like a crooked finger calling him home. The magic of his mother, dark and wild and mad and brilliant. *They have it.*

He had wanted to bide his time, but if they—those other men who have so long claimed to be his friends, his brothers—are starting to sniff around the girl, then he has to act fast.

He will do what it takes to get it back. Richard should have known that. But he never understood what it felt like to hunger for power, to yearn for more. He had always borne his magic like a cross.

Well, Jonas knows. Hunger licks his soul like flames.

He will *have the book. And Goddess help anybody who tries to stop him.*

Chapter Eleven

Annie

We hurried Bea through the halls. My soaked dress clung to me and the old house groaned. Perhaps it would be justice if the walls collapsed around us. I followed Emmeline, who held Bea tightly as we trailed up to drier ground. She did not look at me. Did not acknowledge the magnitude of what Arthur had revealed.

"Are you all right, dearest?" Isobel whispered.

Nathan leaned into her, his body sagging with the weight of the water and of the contact with Bea's skin and the knife. I didn't need to look twice to know he wasn't all right, but he nodded anyway.

"I'm sure I'll live," he joked. "Who else will tend the garden and keep you two from each other's throats?"

Emmeline said nothing.

I tried to remember what I had seen before, those brief spells of darkness. Visions—for that's what they were—of death. Of white satin drenched in blood, of shovels and a grave. Of fire burning a curse into unknowing flesh, of retribution. Of rebirth.

I had seen what Emmeline had done. My magic had stirred, had warned me again. She was a murderer. I ignored the small voice in the back of my mind that reminded me that I was a murderer too.

The scorched smell didn't leave my nose as we dragged Bea away from the flooded ballroom and squelched up to a room I recognised. This was Cilla's room—the very same from my visions. Still Emmeline did not meet my gaze. Nathan inhaled sharply and Isobel consoled him, hovering her hand just above his elbow.

There was an oversweetness in my mouth, like the aftertaste of rotting fruit.

Emmeline gave Bea a shove inside, and although the spirit inside her fought, claws and fangs, Emmeline was prepared. When she grunted I noticed the stain of black blood on her teeth. Bea staggered forwards, her movements wooden. A second later a faint shimmer of silver followed her—almost like her spirit was fighting to keep up with her body.

Emmeline nodded to the four-poster bed, which dominated the room, its wooden frame conjuring images of raven hair and red blood, water. Emmeline's salvation—her curse.

Isobel gazed at the bed and Nathan's face had paled, but Emmeline raised her chin and looked at me defiantly. A defiance edged with worry. It was a question; it was an openness, her darkness laid bare just the same as mine.

The vinculum trembled. Emmeline released it slightly—gently. I felt the nudge as her emotions slipped into my consciousness: relief that her secret was out; guilt for what she had done; shame that she had hidden it from me. The hope on her face was nearly too much.

"Why here?" Nathan winced. Isobel's lips were a thin line. Disgust. Sadness. This place was haunted for them both in ways I would never understand.

Emmeline gestured. "The bed's made of mahogany."

"We need to tie her up," I said thickly.

It took all four of us to get Bea strapped down. Arthur's spirit exploded with rage. She flung out her arms, legs, fingers clawing, head swinging. I caught her elbow on the side of my head. For a second I saw fireworks.

"For Christ's sake don't hurt her," Emmeline growled, her own body contorted to pin Bea's right arm to the bedpost.

"Easier said than done," I growled.

Isobel swore as Bea bucked off the bed. She was still wet from the storm, her skin slick with it. I threw myself on top of her, pinning her knees. She was hot to the touch, a new fever burning her up from the inside.

"Can't you do your rain spell again, darling?" Nathan bit out.

Once Bea was secure, Emmeline stalked out into the hall. Nathan and Isobel were finishing a second knot around Bea's left wrist with the curtain ties. I hesitated.

The vinculum trilled, sharp and bright in my chest. With a shiver of surprise I understood that Emmeline had flicked it. I wiped my palms on my dress and trailed after her out into the dim hallway.

"I had to do it." Emmeline stood with one foot hooked against the wall and crossed her arms defensively. "I know it's hard to understand—but I did what I did to protect my family."

"You didn't tell me," I said. Emmeline started to speak, but I held up my hand. "You let me think that Arthur—that what I'd done was..." I let out a breath, unable to unpick my thoughts. "How could you?"

"How could I?" She raised an eyebrow. "That's rich, coming from you."

My cheeks heated. "I didn't mean to hurt anybody—that was different."

"Was it?"

Our gazes locked.

"Did you plan it?" I asked.

Surprise flickered across her face. "Yes," she said honestly. "I—waited. Until the time was right."

"Would you ever have told me?"

"Yes. No—I don't know."

"Did it...hurt her?"

"Yes," Emmeline said again. "Not that it makes it better, but it hurt me too."

"*She* hurt you," I realised. The knowledge flooded me, understanding tempering the fire of my anger like cool water.

"She hurt Nathan and Isobel," Emmeline corrected. "It felt

like— It *was* the only way. I think she knew it would come down to me or her. That's why she left me this house and twisted it so I'd stay. There isn't a day that goes by that I don't feel bad about what I did. But I won't say I regret it, Annie. Not even for you."

The vinculum writhed and twisted, hovering higher than normal, with neither of us capturing it. I could still pinpoint the soft hum of her emotions, feel where they lined up with my own—but I did not feel capsized by her presence. We had used the tether and it had only grown stronger.

Emmeline watched my face cautiously, waiting for me to run. It was what I would have done, once.

In the bedroom I could hear echoes of Isobel and Nathan trying to pretend they were all right. The way they spoke to each other had the kind of comfort I'd missed since Sam died, the warmth of genuine affection forged in shared history.

If they were my family, I would have wanted to protect them too.

Emmeline must have seen the change in my eyes, because she sagged against the wall, hands dropping to her sides.

"Everything is falling apart," she said.

"It's not just Bea," I said roughly. "My father's lawyer came to my house—"

"The man who was here before?" Emmeline leaned forward, her expression sharpening. I nodded.

"He was very… He had this pin on his tie, like the man from the museum. The same one. Is it a Council pin? I didn't… I thought I was imagining things, but… not anymore." I shivered. "He knows about my father, Em. He knows about the book. I think he broke into my father's house looking for it. He tried to take it from me."

"Is it safe?" Her eyebrows stitched with fresh concern. "Do you have it?"

"I have it, but…" I fished it out of my satchel, placing it on a crooked side table. The pages were wet and beginning to stick together. "What do we do about Anderson?"

"One thing at a time. We need to get Arthur out of Bea first. His energy, his spirit—if it stays inside her we've got a problem. She's not got any magic of her own, so he'll drain her body dry. She's burning up already, and I don't know how long she'll last. There's also the baby to consider."

Emmeline looked at the book but made no move to take it.

"You *do* have a plan, don't you?" The look on Emmeline's face said it all. Fear balled in my chest. "What about breaking the debt? That would get rid of him, wouldn't it?"

"Annie, we've been over this. There isn't a way to break it without—"

"Arthur has a child!" I blurted. I explained about the vision, about Violet and the boy. Her face remained passive. "You said we needed blood," I said desperately. "This boy is Arthur's son. Wouldn't he be able to—"

"It's no good, Annie," she said softly. "If he's small—there wouldn't be enough. I owe a lot. In trying to avoid being like Cilla, I Gave too much. If it had been six months ago, things might have been different. But... it's too late."

The last shred of hope fled and my legs went weak. Nothing. We had nothing. Just two witches who rarely used their magic, and Emmeline, whose magic was drained like a dried-up well. And me.

"So, what?" I demanded. "If you don't have a plan, what the hell are we going to do?"

"There's only one solution. We give Arthur a better alternative," she said. "A conduit."

"A conduit?" I'd read a little about the concept in my father's books before they burned. It was a way of conducting energy through an object—or a person. My blood chilled. "And who, exactly, are you going to force his spirit into?" I demanded fiercely.

Emmeline tugged at the vinculum again. Like she was testing it. Weighing up whether she was strong enough—whether *I* was strong enough.

"Me."

Chapter Twelve

Annie

E mmeline, you can't be serious."

"I'm completely serious," she said. And she was. She was so serious she reached out and took me by the shoulders. Her palms were warm and I focused on them, how strong they felt. "I'm more serious than I've ever been in my life. I will not be responsible for another death, especially not hers. Do you understand?"

I did. Bea was my best friend, had been the other half of me for so many years. We had to try.

"You can't," I whispered weakly. "If he gets inside you, with your power—"

"I'm dying, Annie. I haven't got any power left. It's been coming in fits and starts for months. We'll need the collective pull of all of our magic, and mine is . . ." She let out a huff. "I can't control it. Better to have him inside me, where the debt should slow him down."

"What about the vinculum?" I argued.

"Annie, we literally have no other choice!" Emmeline's voice broke and she rubbed her hands over her face, her knuckles pressing against her eyes. "You're strong. You know how the tether works. He doesn't yet. If I can hold him, you and Nathan and Isobel might be able to exorcise him. Whatever happens, we can't leave him inside

Bea." She paused, a pained look flashing across her face. "Please," she added. "I'm asking you to help me do this."

"You can't ask this of me," I whispered. I was embarrassed by the tears that sprang to my eyes. "I need more time. It's not fair."

"Life isn't fair. This is the way it has to be. I'm so tired of making mistakes. There's no other way."

"How can you act like this?" I exploded. Anger was a white-hot spike through my skull. I got closer still, raising my finger. "You're acting like you don't care if you die!"

To my surprise, Emmeline only smiled. A half smile, where only one side of her lips quirked upwards.

"There she is."

"What?" I asked, furious.

"You. The real you. Not the soft, kind, gentle Annie. Not the light that people think of when they picture sunshine. This is *you*. Sunlight that burns, blinding. Real, vital—strong. You seem so mild, but I know you're secretly angry all the time. Nobody wants to escape if they already have everything they need."

Emmeline was so close I could feel the heat from her body, feel her breath on my face. I remembered the pressure of her hand on my thigh, her arms around my waist, the way they'd belonged there. My heart swelled and broke at the same time.

"I asked you once what your greatest desire was," Emmeline challenged. "And you couldn't answer me properly. I'm asking you to do a great thing, Annie. It could save her. So really, love, what is it you want?"

Emmeline's face was centimetres from mine. My blood rushed and the words tumbled from my lips before I could stop them.

"You," I blurted. "I want you."

I reached for her, my lips pressing against hers with fierce urgency. She responded with a hunger that made my heart race, lips locking, tongue searching. Her arms wrapped around my back and I held her body to mine. I felt her heartbeat. Felt the heat of her skin. She tasted warm and dark and rich, kazam on my tongue.

I lifted a hand to her hair, the other to the nape of her neck. Our breath mingled as our bodies intertwined. It was fire, it was blood, it was magic like no other, and the silver cord was hot and bright, and there she was, shining at the other end.

In that second I wanted nothing else. No debt to keep us apart, nothing to hurt her. I wanted to take Emmeline's burden and I prayed that we could find a way. *Nothing but you and me together*, I thought, *that's all I want.*

We emerged breathless. Emmeline's lips were red from the crush, and she panted with glazed eyes. It was not surprise in them, though. Instead there was a flash of pain.

She pushed away and left my head spinning with the scent of her, my lips throbbing with her kiss. My heart cracking in two.

—)●(—

My hands gravitated towards the spell book, although I was desperate for a reason to stop them. Emmeline was right. It didn't matter what I wanted, because there was Bea, still tied to the bed like a prisoner.

When I entered the room, Emmeline didn't look at me. The energy in here had changed, and there was an urgency to her movements that I hadn't seen before.

She was busy arranging candles, and somebody had lit incense so that the room had a smudged, smoky taste to it. The hairs rose on my arms and the magic inside me coiled with tension. Now I knew what to look out for, the sensation was so familiar—I'd felt it for most of my life and just never had a name for it. It was a stirring, insistent and alive.

"Did *you* know what she's planning to do?" Isobel rounded on me the second she saw me. She was wild, her long nails like talons as she grabbed my arm tightly, but her voice was barely above a whisper. "You can't think this is a good idea."

"No," I said, wrenching my arm away and hugging my father's book like a life float. "It's the stupidest thing I've ever heard."

"Then we stop her."

"And do what?" I asked. "What other choice do we have? She's right. We can't trust her magic to help us, but maybe the debt will drain him."

We spoke in hushed tones, unsure whether Arthur was listening, whether it mattered if he knew what we were up to. Bea wasn't going anywhere, but none of us liked that *he* might get ideas.

"She's not strong enough," Isobel hissed. "He could kill her."

"Who else is going to do it?" I asked. "You? Me?"

Isobel's face blanched.

"I'll do it," Nathan said uncertainly, wiping his hands of the salt he'd used to create a protective circle around the bed. "I could."

"No. You couldn't," Isobel said softly.

This was all too real. It was happening too fast.

"Do we have to do it now?" I said more loudly. Emmeline turned and met my gaze for the first time. I saw the hunger there, the burning need to make things right.

"You saw the mess they made downstairs," Emmeline said.

"That was Isobel," I murmured, but the retort was empty.

"We'll have police here before dawn. Best if Bea's not possessed by a spirit when it happens." She said this as a joke, but all four of us turned to look at Bea, and we knew what she actually meant.

Best if Bea was alive.

And that was looking less and less likely. Where the golden aura had given her that uncarthly glow, now her pallor was marked, her skin waxy. Her eyes were so pale, an incandescence within them like she was being devoured from the inside by firelight. She let out a groan, which was coarse and deep.

"Let's get it over with, then," I said.

Emmeline gave me a rare, genuine smile. Not wry, not quirked, just sad and soft, like the girl I wondered if she had once been. Then it was gone. She took the book from my hands and laid it aside.

"I think it'll work best if we call the Corners and cast a proper circle," Emmeline said. "It'll help reduce the risk of him crawling back inside her if this goes pear-shaped."

Nathan and Isobel set about gathering what we would need. I ventured as close to Bea as I dared, wishing I could hold her hand.

None of them spared me a glance as they gathered objects that would mark the four elements into the circle: earth, air, fire, water. In place of a candle Isobel held on to a chunk of red jasper that glowed like a flame in the dim light.

Nathan had wrapped a white ribbon around his right hand, the material shining. He handed me a silver goblet, a relic from years gone by, that was filled with water. I instinctively knew it was salt water, the taste on my tongue and a warm readiness in my belly.

Isobel led the way into the circle, cleansing it and asking that it welcome her despite the way her body visibly tensed at being so close to Bea. Nathan followed. I went next.

Finally came Emmeline holding the length of a vicious-looking bone blade. It was one I hadn't seen before, but glancing around this room, I was almost certain it had belonged to Cilla. It was long and thin, with a point like a needle.

We stood roughly evenly spaced around the bed. Bea lay very still, her groaning temporarily abated. The room was eerily quiet and my limbs filled with leaden dread.

Emmeline started to speak, her words indistinct but some-how strong. The magic in my chest surged. Bea began to twitch. Emmeline lifted the bone dagger higher, angling the tip towards the ground, then up towards her chest to guide him in.

"Emmeline," I warned. "Be careful—"

Before she could respond, there was an almighty crash as the bedroom door slammed open.

Emmeline lowered the blade, momentarily stunned.

My eyes were slow to focus through the incense-smudged world, but when they did it felt like drowning.

It was Anderson, panting with exertion and an anger that hardly seemed natural. He took in the scene, the circle of salt and Bea tied to the bed. Realisation morphed his face, curving his features into a knowing smile.

We had to stop.

But it was too late, the ritual already begun, the Corners called, our intentions laid bare.

Bea gave a triumphant roar, but it was Arthur's voice that raised the hairs on my arms. And Anderson, unprotected outside the protective circle we had drawn, not fortified by earth, air, fire, or water, only understood how foolish he had been as Bea let out an earsplitting scream and a surge of dark energy knocked him to his knees.

Chapter Thirteen

Annie

There was a blinding flash, the light white and burning. I fought to keep my eyes open, watching as a secondary force slammed into Anderson, knocking him onto his back. I started to move towards Bea, to make sure she was okay, and Emmeline yelled.

"Don't break the circle!"

I tried to stop, but my feet were seconds behind my brain and I skidded through the line of salt. My skin prickled immediately, painfully, like being stabbed by a thousand tiny needles. Anderson began to climb to his feet, the movement strangely fluid, limbs no longer ruled by muscle and bone.

He wasn't Anderson anymore. Unlike with Bea, there was no softness in him, no vulnerability that could lull us into thinking he was anything other than lethal.

His eyes were black like coal from corner to corner, his skin the bleached white of fresh-born maggots. His whole body moved with a kind of grace that Bea's had never possessed, that Anderson himself had never shown.

He stood to his full height and rolled his shoulders, testing the muscles there. I wanted to run at him, to run away from him, but

I was rooted in place. And from the stunned silence in the room, Emmeline and the others felt the same.

The hatred that rolled off Anderson was not just Arthur's—it was that of the man who had threatened me at my house too, the man who had claimed to be my friend, the man who hated my father.

Arthur wasn't fighting against his host anymore. They were joined by their common rage, their desire to annihilate.

"Annie..." Emmeline's warning was as distant as a church bell.

Anderson's head turned smoothly towards Emmeline. He faltered when he saw my father's book, propped at the edge of the decimated circle of salt. His black eyes shone with hunger.

He was quick, darting across the room with the deadly grace of a demon.

"The book!" I yelled.

Emmeline flung herself towards it as Anderson raised his hand into a fist and opened it, a kind of heat blasting forth from him and knocking into us like a solid wall. It threw Isobel clear across the room, where she landed with a sickening thud, her eyes rolling back. Nathan stumbled to his knees, screaming. The heat punched me in the gut, knocking the wind out of me with searing accuracy.

Emmeline stumbled but she did not stop. She forced herself towards Anderson, reaching him just as his hands connected with my father's book.

"Don't let him have it!" Nathan shouted, too late.

Emmeline was a creature possessed, black hair flying, fingers clawed as she tried to pry it from his hands. Anderson and Arthur together were too strong, and with a crunch Anderson's hand connected with her face. She stumbled, blood pouring from her nose.

The magic in the room shifted and surged. Even her unwilling blood knew that this was fight or die. She swiped a hand through the blood on her face in a practised move, then flung her arm at Anderson in a shooing gesture.

Nothing happened.

Anderson let out a ruthless chuckle, giving a sharp flick of his wrist. Emmeline's eyes widened as another wall of heat smashed into her with the power of a hurricane.

She went down hard, crumpling under the weight of Anderson's magic. Months of Givings had drained her of more than just her blood. She didn't have the energy to fight him. He started to advance on her, a mirthless anticipation on his face.

"You don't have to do this, Arthur," I tried to reason with him. Anderson stopped, cradling the book like a child as he caressed the cover. "We can set you free—"

"Oh?" Anderson's auburn eyebrow raised and it was so like what I'd seen when Arthur was alive that sickness crowded my throat. "And how exactly are you going to do that? I know what you were planning."

"We weren't—"

"You were going to banish me." His words echoed in my skull.

"You were killing her," I gasped through the pain. "Killing Bea. And your child..."

"I already have a child," Arthur snapped, Anderson's nostrils flaring. "She thought she could trap me. *Keep* me. Silly girl."

"Don't you care at all?" I begged. Emmeline stirred, visibly trying to rally. "She's your wife!"

"She's a pretty, careless, goddamn *fool*," he spat. "And now I'm free of her I don't have to bear it any longer. That simpering, pathetic longing. My *God*."

"Please."

"Please what? Don't hurt you?" His laugh was dry, like the rasping of dead leaves. "Why shouldn't I? You deserve it. So does the other witch, but I'll have to save her for last."

I could see Emmeline out of the corner of my eye. She scrambled for the bone dagger she had dropped, grasping the hilt with both hands and lifting it high as she had done before, right above her heart. My pulse stuttered.

Suddenly her resignation made sense, her anger, the way she had pushed me away again and again. Emmeline was going to sacrifice herself, to Give the last of herself to pay the debt.

"No!" I screamed.

There had to be another way.

There *was* another way. With startling clarity I remembered the ritual my father had been planning to try. I was filled with a cold, dark certainty, a sense beyond my others, akin to the silver-skinned magic coiling deep in my chest.

I knew what would happen. I had witnessed the beginnings of it, felt Emmeline's pain like my own, her sadness too. She had been afraid of what would happen if the vinculum grew to fruit, what it would do to her magic. To me and mine.

I was more afraid of what would happen if it didn't.

I skidded across the floor, catching Anderson off guard and feinting back to hurl my full weight towards Emmeline. I wrestled the dagger from her, the hilt already slick from where she'd cut herself. I could taste the magic of her blood on my tongue, mingled with the salt of mine as I bit down hard.

Emmeline grunted in surprise.

I didn't stop to think.

Anderson dove for me again as I danced away, the dagger in my hand. I dodged left, another wave of his magic going wide as Nathan tackled him, his own spilled blood making the floor slick. I darted back to Emmeline, who was still dragging herself upright. She looked at me with bright anger in her eyes.

I took a single breath and swiped the bone dagger in a clean line right across my right palm.

Blood bloomed.

Emmeline hissed, feeling my pain as I felt hers. I thrust the dagger towards her, willing her to understand what I wanted. Imploring her to trust me. *Do it*, I begged silently. *Make this sacrifice instead.*

She hesitated.

Anderson roared as Nathan elbowed him hard, the two of them a blur of motion on the floor. A fresh wave of magic slammed into me. My skin burned, flayed by the winds of hell, but I held my ground, screaming against the pain of it. I closed my eyes, picturing Emmeline as I unlatched the vinculum from its prison, launching it into the air between us. The taste of salt and grave dirt was thick in my throat, the roar of crashing waves in my ears.

I opened my eyes. Emmeline lowered the knife.

"Emmeline." *Trust me.*

The vinculum tightened. Nathan scrabbled away, grabbing a vase from the nearby sideboard and hurling it at Anderson. He dropped the book and it skidded away. Nathan dove after it and Anderson followed.

"Quickly," I pushed.

We locked eyes. The tether began to unfurl again as Emmeline let go. The thread—no, it was a *vine*—began to flower, glorious moonbeam blooms that I could see when I blinked, like sunspots.

She made the same cut, wincing as the bone bit into her flesh. Blood glittered across her palm. I reached with my ruby-stained hand and grabbed Emmeline's, our eyes meeting as the vinculum blossomed.

There was no ritual. No flame or earth or air. Not the roaring of ocean waves in my ears or the taste of grave dirt. There was only my desire to keep Emmeline safe, her desire to live, to accept my help, and two types of willing blood as I Tied myself to her.

A debt for a debt.

Chapter Fourteen

Annie

It happened so fast the world spun. Light and heat blasted forth, knocking Nathan and Anderson to their knees.

Some integral part of me shifted—not changed so much as *grown*. There was myself, my pain, the salt and water of my magic, but there was another thing too. The vinculum was no longer just a blossoming vine connecting me to Emmeline at the edges.

It vibrated in every inch of me, silver filigree in my skin, incandescence in my bones. It was no longer like a tunnel through which all emotion passed; it was everything, everywhere. I felt Emmeline, felt her pain. She was me, and I was her.

Instantly I was heavier, dread and sickness wearing on me. Also lighter.

Anderson recovered first. He crawled with alarming speed, rushing to the knife Emmeline had dropped. And then he was on both of us like a rabid dog. He slashed forwards without ceremony, and it was only the spurting of hot blood from my forehead, a wild shock of agony, that drove my body into action.

I jerked away, pain and blood blinding me. Emmeline grunted as though the wound was her own, scrambling in the other direction.

The promise I had made after our kiss was now the tie that bound us together. *Nothing but you and me together.*

Anderson was closing in on Emmeline, swinging the blade again and again. The first time he missed. The second he caught his target, and if not for a surge of fresh ocean-and-iron magic on her part, just fast enough to dull the blow, he would have slashed her throat.

I tried to call on the magic the way Emmeline had, pushing both hands out as though I might shove him away. He stumbled, but barely, a coarse laugh echoing. His movements weren't fluid any longer, but there was an inhuman speed in him that made me cold.

This power, this new strength in both of us, wasn't enough. We weren't strong enough.

Anderson lifted the blade over Emmeline again, Arthur's vicious hatred seeping into every jerky movement.

"No!"

Nathan.

There was a brief second where our eyes met before he threw himself in front of the knife. The blade caught his shirt, but Nathan twisted and jabbed his elbow into Anderson's crotch. They fell together, the floorboards vibrating in a tussle of arms and legs, the knife disappearing for a long second. I clenched my hand tight, blood dripping hot and heavy as agony wracked me.

My brain was a scramble of fear, words slipping amongst my salt-and-dirt magic so all I could manage was a single plea: *Stop. Stop. STOP.*

Anderson's body was Arthur's shield, my magic rebounding off them uselessly. Anderson swiped again, but he missed.

Nathan had the blade.

An arc of blood slashed across the wooden floor. Nathan dropped the bone dagger and staggered backwards. Anderson clutched at his neck, fingers scrambling, his hazel eyes wide and shiny with fear, the expression all his own.

It was Anderson, not Arthur, who felt the caress of death, his ruddy face growing steadily grey, rinsed of colour as he fell. A gurgling sound echoed in the shocked silence.

The ghostly light that flowed upwards like a silver mist was all Arthur, the final hints of pink fading from Anderson's face. The air was taut with the tension, but instead of drawing back to Bea, the energy began to tremble.

Go, I urged silently. *Move on.*

I could feel the magic in the blood, the wild ocean waves and bright summer sunlight. And Emmeline's magic was there too, the old thick blackness in her veins lightening as my own darkened in response. Her debt to Arthur was weakened. Replaced by the newly bound vinculum. We had, together, Given enough to fulfil this bargain.

Our gazes locked. Her eyes dark and mine bright. Desire and intent.

"Arthur Croft, I banish you!" I shouted.

"Leave this place," Emmeline growled.

Without the debt there to hold Arthur's spirit, without Anderson's body to house him, with the remains of the circle still surrounding Bea, and with the firm push of our combined strength, the light around us only grew brighter and brighter, until there was a flash. So bright it burned, knocking me down again, my knees barking against the wooden boards. It ricocheted inside me, cutting my magic right down to the quick, razing the vinculum to its roots.

I scrambled upright, ears ringing and body aching, blood still dripping.

Arthur's spirit was gone.

———— ◦ ● ◦ ————

"Jesus Christ."

Emmeline let out a whoosh of breath, which quickly turned to laughter. It was a sound I wasn't sure I ever wanted to hear again, brittle and imbued with horror, but it was somehow contagious.

I glanced across. Isobel still lay where she'd fallen, but I could see the steady rise and fall of her chest. Bea was breathing too, quiet but alive.

Nathan wasn't laughing.

His whole body had gone rigid.

"Nathan?" Emmeline noticed first. His face was ashen. "*Nathan?*"

She hauled herself towards him. Together we scrambled around Anderson's body. There was so much blood. Fresh blood, not from the ballroom, not from Anderson. Nathan was hot and sticky, and I pressed my hands to his chest, where a gaping wound appeared through a slash in his shirt. He swayed.

Emmeline caught him. Together we lowered him to the ground as he blinked and blinked.

"Hold down on it," Emmeline barked. "Pressure. Don't touch his skin!"

I pressed down, but the blood was flowing fast and Emmeline's terror swept through us both, the new presence of her inside my mind sending me into hyperventilation.

"Oh Christ. Isobel, I don't know what to do. Please, help me!" Emmeline begged, veins in her neck bulging as she struggled out of her shirt, trying to make a compress from the damp material. "Nathan, Nate—can you hear me?"

He swallowed hard, his throat bobbing.

"Nathan, you can't. Why did you do it? You *idiot*."

"Had to . . ." Nathan managed, his bloody smile a red slash against his pale face. He reached for Emmeline, latching onto her wrist, forcing her to stillness. "Couldn't let him have you *both*, darling. *Isobel*. I want Is. Please." He groped blindly with his other hand, but Isobel was still out cold and I didn't dare let go of his chest. I tried to find the thread of my magic, that taste of salt, but it was gone; all that was left was blood and pain. How could it abandon me now?

I trembled with rage. Emmeline scrambled, trying to get Nathan's shirt up, to see the damage. She swiped her bloody fingers across his lips, but it was red blood, ordinary and *weak*. The combined well of our magic was no longer deep enough because of the power we had expended.

"Hang on, love," she repeated. "I just need time. Just time. It will come back, and when it does I can help you. Just hang on." *Hang on. Hang on.* But nothing happened. Only more blood from his skin and more greyness in his face. "Nathan, let me have a look. Come on, my love, *move*."

Nathan wasn't moving anymore.

———( ) ● (———

Bea woke as though from a long sleep. Her skin was the colour of bone, but her fever had broken, sweat cooling on her forehead. Emmeline looked like she had aged a hundred years in one minute, guiding Isobel to wakefulness slowly and watching with dry eyes as her sister lost control.

Isobel threw herself on Nathan's lifeless body and howled, anger and grief pouring out in a ragged crescendo.

"I could have saved him!" she wailed, pelting Emmeline's chest and arms with blows. "I could have fucking saved him! This is your fault! All your fucking fault. I hate you!"

Emmeline weathered the blows as a welcome punishment—and I felt every single one.

Only when thunder and lightning rolled in like before, the dam broken and the atmosphere in the room growing thick and wet, did Emmeline put up her hands. She guided Isobel away.

"Outside," she said softly. "Don't—don't drown him."

They made it to the backyard before the sky split open and summer rain pelted down, tooth-rattling thunder booming. Hail threatened to shatter the glass in the windows, the sky as dark as pitch, as she screamed and screamed.

Bea groped for my hand as I sat beside her on the bed, sorrow and new, bone-deep exhaustion in every inch of me. We huddled until the screaming stopped.

"I wanted to leave the island," Bea whispered. She hadn't moved, and likely hadn't understood what had happened. I'd released her arms and legs and she lay like the dead. "After we got married I said we should go. He wouldn't. It didn't make any sense, but he wouldn't explain. So I chose the house across the bay, where I could always see Emmeline's light. I knew I'd have to come back one day."

"Bea," I said. These words weren't for me.

She continued regardless. "I wanted him so badly, Ann. It consumed me. I thought I *deserved* him, after Sam. I didn't think you'd be hurt by any of this—please believe me. I'm not sure he ever loved me, anyway."

"He had somebody else," I said as softly as I could manage. I groped for the wristwatch that I had brought to the house in my satchel, forgotten. The watch was waterlogged, the glass face spiderwebbed. Bea's eyes focused on it sadly, but she didn't seem surprised. "I saw her," I said. I told her about the vision, the woman and her son. Bea said nothing at first. She took the watch from me slowly, her fingers clenching around the leather strap and holding tight.

"I bought him this when we got married," she whispered eventually, rubbing a finger over the fractured face. "I used everything I had left. He was never very fond of it, always leaving it lying around..."

Bea cried then. Great, body-clenching sobs as she wrapped her arms around her stomach, rolling onto her side and weeping into the pillows. And there, with Nathan dead at our feet and Anderson's body cooling on the other side of the room, I held her tight.

Chapter Fifteen

Emmeline

The night was barren.

I waited in the doorway, watching as the thunder boomed and the lightning rolled across the sky, until finally the weather abated and there was only Isobel left, hunkered down in the dirt like the first time I had seen her.

"I didn't get to say goodbye." Isobel's face was smudged with mud. She looked up in the half-light from the silver moon, clouds scudding away, and she was like a ghost.

"I know."

I didn't know what to tell her—that I hadn't had a chance either? That somehow I should have seen the Drowning Boy card and *known* and instead I had watched the light fade from his eyes? That I couldn't make myself cry for him, the man whom I had loved as a brother? And my traitorous blood flowed more easily than it had in more than a year, and my heartbeat was strong, and I could feel Annie—stupid, beautiful Annie—upstairs with Bea like a warm hand at the bottom of my back.

"Who was he?" Isobel asked. "The man who..."

"A lawyer. A witch. Council. I think he wanted the—book." I knew I would see the look on his face in my dreams as he came at me with the knife, half Arthur and half himself.

"Wrong place, wrong time?"

"The Delacroix curse."

Isobel settled on the porch steps and I sat beside her, and together we watched the rain pool in the dirt between the lush green strands of grass. Isobel was stooped like an old woman, her arms resting on her knees.

"Annie Tied herself to me," I said. "She paid the debt. The vinculum... Christ, I tried so hard. I didn't want this for her."

Isobel didn't say anything right away, but I knew she was thinking about what I'd told her. Weighing it up like she always did, ever practical. I couldn't figure out how she felt. And without Nathan I'd probably never know what she was thinking ever again. The pain that cut through me was like a hot knife through butter. The first prickle of tears started behind my eyelids.

"Do you love her?" Isobel asked.

This wasn't the question I had expected. "I..."

Yes, my heart trilled, but my brain held tight to its fear.

I wanted her. I had wanted her since the first time I saw her, golden hair shining, that lightness inside her, the vinculum only just germinating. I had wanted her to want me too, wanted to let her in. I wanted to lean on her—but I couldn't do that to her.

"It doesn't matter, I suppose," Isobel said when I didn't answer. "She loves you."

"She doesn't know me. All we have is this connection. It can be toxic, make you believe things so that the magic gets its way. What if she doesn't really feel anything towards me?"

"I don't think that's true." Isobel turned to me. Her face was puffy from crying, but she was calm. "Not anymore. She's seen the worst of you, dearest. And she loves you anyway."

"Without Nathan I'm not sure there is a me."

Isobel scoffed. "Of course there bloody is, Em. You were the first of us. You protected us when nobody else would. It doesn't matter how we got here. What's done is done."

I thought of the mess upstairs; I thought of the blood and the bodies. I looked up and blinked the tears from my eyes, and there it was—in the trees, a crow. The biggest of the crows, on her own again. *One for malice.*

"We can't bury Nathan with Cilla and Arthur," I said quietly. "No matter how much he loved that greenhouse."

"Maybe that's exactly what we need to do," Isobel said. "And once you and Annie are stronger again, we cleanse it together. And that's the end."

———⊷•⊷———

Bea was asleep when I made it back upstairs, her fist curled against her damp copper curls, a leather strap between her fingers. Annie looked exhausted, her blond hair streaked with blood, but when she saw me her face brightened just for a second.

"We need to bury them," I said brusquely.

Annie stood in the middle of the room and nodded, but she was distracted. Her gaze was fixed on her father's book. She stared at it for a moment before looking down at the long line she'd cut into her palm, the blood already crusting over as the Tie between us settled. It would scar.

"Do you regret it?" I asked.

"No."

"You know this means that we're . . . linked."

"Yes."

"Our magic—my magic—"

"It all comes from the same place now," Annie said assuredly. "I know. I can feel that. The well is . . . shallow, but the power burns brighter, hotter. I don't regret it, Em. I was just wondering about my father. I don't think he ever wanted me to come here after all . . ."

She went silent, staring at the body of the other man on the floor. Then her gaze flicked to my brother.

"I'm sorry about Nathan."

"Nathan made a choice," I said. "Just like I did and you did."

"I think Mr. Anderson killed my father," Annie blurted before she flung herself at me. I staggered back in surprise as her warm body pressed against mine and her arms snaked around my waist. I held my hands up awkwardly before letting them rest on her back. She cried gently, with her cheek resting on my chest. "I'm sure Anderson killed him—for that damned book."

"I thought you didn't care about your father," I said uncertainly. I could feel her heartbeat in my chest, the weightlessness of the blood in my veins. Effortless.

"I didn't! I don't. Oh God. I don't know. He was still my father, wasn't he? I think he thought he was protecting me. If he didn't know me, if he didn't encourage me, maybe I would live a safe life. Would never feel the magic. He didn't want me to *want this*."

"You can't help what you want."

"It's not about that. It's about responsibility. People are dead because of us, Em. Magic eats everything up, doesn't it?"

Annie was right—but she was wrong too.

"People die all the time because of decisions other people make," I said. "That's not magic's fault. It's ours. We have to learn. We have to do better. We *can* do better."

Annie pulled back, and she was no longer crying. I saw realisation settle on her face, and it hurt me to see the pain I'd caused. The way she had changed because of me.

Magic or not, we were both the same now.

———) ● (———

We buried Anderson with little ceremony, but I spent longer digging Nathan the perfect grave. We laid him to rest facing the north, where the wind off the sea could ease him into infinity. The sun was just rising as we finished, filthy and bone tired, and trudged back to the house to bathe.

Bea lay in her bedroom, dressed in a clean dress and with her hair freshly washed and braided. She looked almost like her old self, except drawn and tired, the bruises still marring her white skin.

"Do you want me to...?" I asked.

She rolled onto her back, not quite meeting my gaze but not looking away either. I crossed to her, pulling a stool over to the side of her bed and taking a seat. I'd washed my hands, but I still swore

I could see the crescents of blood around my nails. I wondered if I would ever feel clean again.

Bea exhaled slowly, giving me silent permission to lay my hands on her. I did so gently, reluctantly. We were not the same people who had played these roles before.

I pressed my hands against the soft fabric of her dress where it covered the very gentle swell of her belly. I closed my eyes and remembered the days I had spent practicing this exact thing on Aunt Rachel's pregnant dogs until I could feel the difference between new life and the body's early stages of growth and change.

There was not yet much to sense inside Bea. A quickening that was only just starting as the child inside her belly began to have its own blood. I *could* feel it, though. It was still growing, still progressing.

I must have nodded or smiled or in some way acknowledged it, because Bea began to cry.

"Are you...okay?"

Bea sniffled, nodding. "I didn't think it would ever happen again," she whispered.

She struggled up in bed, taking one of my hands in hers and making sure that it was my uninjured one. She held it gently until she was ready to speak again.

"I keep thinking about the woman—Arthur's woman. God, I can't call her that. His lover? His love? I keep thinking about her. About what Annie told me. She has a child too. Not born out of spite or that selfish kind of need. Not like with me." She sniffled. "I think I'm going to find a way to get her to forgive me."

"Bea," I warned.

"I know," she said quickly. "I'll be careful. I just know there's got to be a way to do it. She's going to be heartbroken when she finds out he's gone. When she thinks he's left her. I hate that I did that to her—but I would make the same decisions a hundred times over despite hating myself for them."

"He hurt you. That doesn't just happen once. I'm sure she's more than capable of understanding what sort of man he was."

"He wasn't always hurtful. Not in the beginning..." She sighed softly. "I'll go to the police in the morning. While the bruises are still visible. Not that I should need them, but...you know." She let go of my hand and gave me a small, brave smile. "I can probably tell them about—*her*. People leave the island all the time. Why should he be any different?"

We sat in silence for a time before Bea spoke again.

"Annie will be good for you, you know. You must treat her kindly. She's so gentle."

"She's strong too." A painful emotion stirred and I did my best to suppress it so Annie wouldn't feel it. I had been thinking about this all day. I knew what I needed to do—I just wasn't sure if I was brave enough.

"She's not indestructible, though."

"I don't know if I can stay with her, Bea." The truth of this squirmed in my stomach uncomfortably. "I can't keep her here, tied to this house because of her Ties to me. It's not fair. This is my curse, not hers. I can't cage her and watch her shrivel up like Cilla— like me."

Bea watched my face carefully, searching for any hint that I didn't believe what I was saying. I kept my expression fixed.

"Don't you dare hurt her," Bea said finally, steel in her eyes. "Whatever you do, make a decision and stick with it. Don't tell her you love her if you don't. Don't mess her around like I did with you. If you can't give her what she needs, then you have to let her go."

"I know," I said. "That's what I'm afraid of."

Chapter Sixteen

Annie

The wind that whips off the sea is fresh and scented with fish and coffee from the boat that heads for the harbour. I watch as a fisherman hauls a thick rope across the small deck while his wife offers him a steaming drink in a tin cup. There is an easy companionship between them that I admire, although I don't dare to stand and stare for too long.

There is some new strangeness to being back in Whitby after months on Crow Island. It is like I have grown two shoe sizes over the summer and am still trying to force my feet into boots that are too small.

The sky is threatening rain. I promised myself I wouldn't come here yet. I don't have time to spend hours staring at the ocean today, but I couldn't stop myself. A new café had opened and I had spent half an hour needlessly trying two different kinds of cake and sipping hot tea out of a pristine new cup while the scents of frying bacon and fish lulled me into comfort. Sam would have liked it.

Mam was thrilled to see me, though she could see my discomfort at being back. She asked about my father's house, about the island. About Bea. I kept it brief. I told her that Arthur had left her, that she was pregnant, and that the last time I saw her she was leaving for Europe.

Mam didn't seem surprised, nor when I told her I wasn't home to stay. She simply wrapped me in one of her gentle hugs and nodded like she had been expecting it. She had already done her grieving.

I didn't tell her that I plan to leave immediately. I didn't tell her that it isn't a job or a man who has swayed my decision. That it is a *woman*. Emmeline might not be ready for it, this thing that has bloomed between us, but I am. I have enough money from the sale of my father's house, from my share of the inheritance, that I know I can keep the cottage until I find somewhere cheaper. I'll clean houses; I'll work in a tea shop. I'll get a license and peddle faux magic. It doesn't matter what.

I don't have to be *with* Emmeline—I just want to be near her. To be able to sense her the way I did right after the Tie snapped into place. This far apart I can feel nothing but a faint hum at the back of my mind, and it is *wrong*, knowing that she is out there and I'm not with her.

The first spat of rain on my forehead makes me lift my gaze to the grey clouds. My stomach drops, the coiling of my magic there swooping. My heart jumps in response.

I spin.

She walks like she owns the world, dressed in a dark suit that looks so good on her I might cry. Her jacket has a high collar, which she has turned up against the wind, and her hair is slicked in a fresh boyish bob, so short it only just grazes the back of her neck.

I am stunned. I didn't feel her coming. I was so afraid she wouldn't come at all.

"Hello, love," she says.

"You're early," I reply breathlessly. "I didn't feel you get close."

"I've been practising. So I can teach you."

I can't stop the grin that spreads across my face as she reaches me and pulls me towards her. She doesn't care whether the now-distant fisherman and his wife see us. She probably hasn't noticed them. I can't stop the breathless swell of joy that says, *She noticed you.* It makes me want to kiss her, but I won't do it yet.

"I thought you were packing up your things today," she says. "Aren't we driving back for the ferry tonight?"

"Turns out there isn't anything I want to bring home. I already have everything I need."

It's bolder than I have been before, but Emmeline doesn't seem to mind. She wraps her long arms around me and holds me as the rain starts to fall. I can smell the fresh water on the wooden pier, the sea and the fish, and I inhale deeply, a gentle magic stirring inside me.

"Have you thought any more about your father's things?" Emmeline murmurs. "About what you want to do with them?"

What's left of his books, his crystals, currently hidden in Emmeline's basement now that his house is gone. I've done nothing but think about them.

"We'd better keep them. We can't get rid of them without attracting a lot of attention. I expect more councilmen will be sniffing around before long. Maybe one day we won't have to hide them. In the meantime I'd like to learn more about magic."

"Are you sure you want to do this, love?"

"Yes." *I can live in the cottage*, I repeat to myself. I don't have to be *with her*, if she doesn't want me. I could still have a life on the island.

"The house is cold in the winter," Emmeline warns. "It will be empty without Nathan. Isobel is talking about going abroad for a while..."

"I don't care."

Emmeline holds my face in her hands. They are cold and they send a shiver of excitement through me. This is an adventure, I think. Not the kind I had pictured, but an adventure all the same.

"My clients come at all hours. It might be boring sometimes. It might be dangerous too, if the situation with the law changes again. We don't know about the long-term effects of the Tie, what that means for us..."

She's watching my lips like she wants to kiss them, but she doesn't. Anticipation zings through me and I hold on to her tighter. The couple on the boat have gone and the seafront is empty. It is as if we own the world.

"I don't care," I repeat. I mean it. Whatever there is to come, it won't be easy. But I can learn. We can teach each other.

Emmeline smiles and her eyes crinkle at the corners. The gesture is new. I love it. There is a lightness in her that wasn't there before, an ocean breeze stirring all that blood and earth.

I get sick of waiting. I stand on tiptoes so I can press my lips to hers, a kiss so effortless it is like magic—no, better.

Regardless of the rain, of the harbour winds, of the discomfort of the streets of my childhood closing in around me, I finally feel like I'm home.

Drawing Down the Dark—A Ritual

R. Crowther

If I command the dark, it will come down; and if I wish to withhold the day, night will linger over my head; and again, if I wish to embark on the sea, I need no ship, and if I wish to fly through the air, I am free from my weight.

—The New Witches of Thessaly

Drawing down the dark is similar to the ritual known as "drawing down the moon," yet the end goal speaks less to guidance from the Goddess than it does to bringing equilibrium and fresh perspective. The bond formed will settle over time, forming an exchange of magic that is mutually restorative and balancing for both witches. Only those witches who wish to have their magic bound for life should consider this beautiful experience, hence why it is often performed by married couples / lovers with a long history of working magic together. The physical effects can be intense and long-lasting. It should not be considered without strong evidence of the existence of a magical connection already in place, but romantic/sexual affection is not required.

The ritual is typically performed under the dark of a new-moon sky. It is often, but not always, carried out in a cast circle by a coven's High

Priestess as she joins herself with a worthy witch of her blood's choice, but may also be performed by a solitary pair of witches with the presence of a strong vinculum.

For witches who prefer incantations to baser blood magic, the following may be used once the circle is cast and the Four Corners called:

> *Oh Mother, darksome and divine,*
> *Mine deep,*
> *And mind the empty kiss;*
> *The five-point star of bonded bliss—*
> *Witness we as one emerge.*
> *Here I draw you, with this blooded sign.*

The witches should now wrap a ribbon around their joined left hands to signify the blood bond and may wish to repeat the following:

> *Bringer of fruitfulness by seed and by root,*
> *I invoke thee and call upon thee,*
> *Mighty Mother of us all.*
> *Ye who are inclined to sorcery,*
> *I bring ye secrets yet unknown.*
> *Touch with her hands, kiss with her lips,*
> *Draw down lightness and darkness into harmony.*

> *So mote it be.*

And if she did wild or wicked things it was because she could not help them.

—Ernest Hemingway, *The Old Man and the Sea*

Acknowledgments

I have seen other writers use the phrase "this is the book of my heart," but until I wrote *Wild and Wicked Things* I didn't understand what they meant. This novel is the book of *my* heart. I wrote it first and foremost for myself, and I have loved every second.

But I couldn't have done it alone. I owe gratitude beyond words to some very special people. Firstly to my agent, Diana Beaumont, for your unwavering dedication and trust. Secondly to my amazing editor, Nivia Evans. This could not have happened without you. Thank you so, so much for seeing something in this book, for taking a chance on it, and for your insight and keen eye. I will be forever grateful for your very early feedback and for the journey it has taken me on.

Thanks to others at Orbit/Redhook US, especially to Ellen Wright, Rachel Goldstein, Paola Crespo, and Stephanie Hess. I am so grateful to Lisa Marie Pompilio for creating a cover that is beyond my wildest dreams! The first moment I saw it I cried. Huge thanks to my UK editor Emily Byron for your enthusiasm and additional insight, and to Maddy Hall and Nazia Khatun and the whole team at Orbit UK.

A big thanks to all the booksellers who have shown such excitement, and especially to those who are so close to my heart. Thanks to everybody at Waterstones Derby. Jo, you are the best advocate I could ask for. Michelle, I'm not sure what I'd do without you! I'm honoured to call you my friend. To David and Laura, there is nobody I'd rather play card games in a pub with. Su, Catherine, Greg, and Helen, thank you.

A huge thanks to the Doomsbury Crime Writers, to the Crime Kissers, and my #SauvLife crew, especially Lizzie—thank you for your amazing feedback. It saved me more than once!

I will always be grateful for my early readers but never more than for this book. Thanks to Molly, Kapri, Hannah Whitten, Liv Wright, Rowan Detmers, Paul Cockburn, Michelle Robins, and everybody else who has been so supportive.

Callie! Where would I be without you? You are the reason this book exists at all. Thank you for encouraging me to write it and for reading it when I did, for letting me cry on your virtual shoulder at all hours of the night, for listening and for telling me off at all the right intervals. I wrote parts of this book (*cough* Nathan *cough*) as much for you as I did for me, so it's kind of your fault—and I love you for it. Thank you for being my best friend.

Tom, you deserve a whole book, not just a paragraph. I know you've always got my back. Thank you for being there for me, for replying in GIFs so I know I'm not alone, and for always being super chill when I cancel our plans because I have to write.

Thank you to Sian for being this book's champion right from the start, for reading the first draft and not telling me it sucked. Thank you for all your cheerleading and for putting up with me when I cried on your actual shoulder. Sorry about that.

I'm lucky enough to have the best friends in the world. Ginny, Allison, I love you and I miss you. Natalie, Vanessa, Isabel, you guys deserve medals. Alex, Becky, Freddi, thank you!

To my family I owe a debt, for your patience and your support. Mum, Dad, Steve, Alisha, you've all been so kind and given me so much. I love you all. Kat, Luke, Isaac, you guys rock. And to the pet gang: Zeus, Xena, Juno, Jet, Atlas, and Athena, this has been fun but spending time with you is obviously funner. Shadow—you might be gone from my side but you'll never be gone from my heart, and I owe you everything.

Finally, thank you to anybody who has taken a chance on this melancholy, witchy sapphic book. I am so honoured to have such wonderful readers.